THE RIVER IS INDIGO

THE RIVER IS INDIGO

A Novel

SULEIMAN MANAN

PARTRIDGE

To order additional copies of this book, contact
Toll Free 800 101 2657 (Singapore)
Toll Free 1 800 81 7340 (Malaysia)
orders.singapore@partridgepublishing.com

www.partridgepublishing.com/singapore

For Ramona

Acknowledgements

I am most grateful to my wife Ramona for urging me to fulfil my dream to write a novel knowing my passion for books. I wouldn't have been able to complete *The River Is Indigo,* which took some time to conceive and put into words, without her constant encouragement and whole-hearted support.

My deep gratitude also goes to my longtime and dedicated secretary Lina Cheng, who has been tireless and extremely patient in typing the drafts, which I have the awful habit of altering, changing and redrafting innumerable number of times.

My thanks to my son Mussadique, for acting as my agent, in liaising with the publisher and editors; and to Yasmin my daughter, and her Studio Voxel for the wonderful artwork on the cover. I must also not forget the contributions of the editors and consultants for their professional advice and suggestions, and my thanks to them as well.

Contents

Part 1

Mataram House

JAVA, 1940

Chapter 1

That night before going to bed, I sat by the verandah, admiring the village down the hill over the Great Gate with its shy display of oil lamps dancing joyfully in the quiet night. My thoughts went back to the time when I was six, when I heard a lonely dog from the belly of the village crying sorrowfully into the night sky, longing for the moon. I wished very much to be his friend so that I could comfort him. But that was not to be. The world beyond the Great Gate was not mine to step into, and so it might as well have been at the end of the world.

I shifted my mind to Buyong, my new-found friend from that village. He would be fast asleep by now with his siblings in their small house, a place of homeliness and happy simplicity – in stark contrast to my Mataram House of great pomp, with its overly demonstrative design and symbolism, icons, art, and artefacts. I thought of Buyong's simple world, free from form and ceremony, unfettered luxury, and stifling attention. How different our worlds were. How different we were. I envied him.

The night was unusually quiet, so quiet that it seemed aimlessly afloat in the surreal air. Even the voices and sounds of the kitchen had disappeared before their time, as though someone had silenced them. The odour of cloves had free rein, and sure enough, Pak Ali came into view. He appeared strangely excitable, his short-cropped head and pugilistic bulk bopping about in the dusty light, a cigarette hanging precariously from his mouth like a part of his face. It was odd that the usual guards were not at their post by the Great Gate. Pak Ali strutted with his customary swagger to the Great Gate, slid open the spy window, and peeped outside, his eyes staying there for a few long moments. He retreated and then nervously retraced his steps to the house.

Suddenly, a strange, unearthly scent pervaded the air. It was as if a curious spirit had invaded my nose. It was not Pak Ali's cloves but something alien I had never encountered before. I felt drowsy, like I would faint. I stepped back into my room, fearing I would fall over, and went to my bed.

As I lay my head on my pillow, my head spun like a top. The strange air pulled me into a salubrious peace, placing me into a baby's cradle. I sensed someone rocking the cradle. My head was light and my body too, as if lifted by the air. It was a great feeling that I didn't want to end. I passed out – for how long, I don't know.

I fell into a dream in which I was lost in a forest of stunted trees no taller than I was. Though lost, I wasn't afraid, because a bright light in the far distance was beckoning me to come and follow it. There was no sense of time. Then a voice rang out from a distant light. It came closer and closer, and it got louder. "Hamzah! Hamzah!" the voice called out.

I struggled, but my feet were like lead, as if anchored to the ground.

"Hamzah! Hamzah!" the voice called again, now louder.

I struggled to my feet, and my eyes opened slowly. In the next moment, I was confronted with the face of my father, so close it startled me.

"Father?" I said in bewilderment, sleep weighing on me.

"Wake up, Son!" he hollered, his tone firm but gentle. I was surprised to find him sitting by my bed and leaning towards me. He had never before come into my room. Our relationship, though affectionate, had always been formal.

"What's the matter, Father?" I asked. He noticed the frown on my face as I narrowed my eyes against the glare of the light. "Why are you here? Why are you waking me? Is anything the matter with Grandma? Is she sick? Is she dead?"

"No, no such thing. Your beloved grandma is perfectly all right; she's well and worshipping in Mecca. Don't you worry about that."

"What's the matter, then?"

"We're going on a journey."

"Journey? Now? Isn't it night?"

"Yes, it's night. We're going away. All your things have been packed. A carriage is waiting below – you know, a horse-driven carriage. You've always wanted to ride in one of those, remember? I arranged that especially for you."

"But why? Are we going on holiday?"

"Something like that, yes, we are. Now hurry."

"Is Mother coming too?"

"No."

"But why not?"

"Because she doesn't want to." With my barrage of questions, the glinting white light could not hide the momentary shadow that cast over the brown, piercing eyes of my father as they dropped on me. He appeared about to raise his voice, but he refrained. "Look, Son, we're going on a journey. We have to arrive in Batavia before the sun rises, so we must leave now. Mother is not coming with us because I planned it to be a men's affair – you and me. She agreed, thinking that it was an excellent idea for father and son to spend time together now that Grandma is not here."

"Would she approve?"

"Who?"

"Grandma."

"Why shouldn't she?"

"Because I've made a promise to her not to leave Mataram House."

"Look, Son, your grandma is crazy."

"No, she is not!"

"I am your father. There are certain things a father knows that a grandmother doesn't. She loves you very much, no doubt, but I love you too. I want to be honest with you. I think it's time I take you away from this madhouse – for your own good. Trust me. I am your father."

I must have subconsciously craved those words from Father, for my heart instantly opened up to him. In that split second, my promise to Grandma vanished into thin air.

"Let Mother stay in Mataram House, at least for now. We can't all go at the same time. You understand, Hamzah?"

"Can I see Mother before we leave?"

"She's asleep. We don't want to wake her."

"Father, I want to see her!"

He gently touched my shoulders with both his hands and then lowered his tone. A shade of sparkle returned to his eyes. "All right – promise me you won't wake her up."

Mother's room was next to mine. As I opened the door, I noticed stray beams of moonlight stealing through the blinds and falling on my mother's reposing body, revealing the whiteness of her cheek. Her eyes were closed. The gentle elegance of her frame moved me. I rushed forward to embrace her, but Father held me back.

"Hamzah." He placed his finger to his mouth. "Don't disturb her."

Remaining at the door, he released me. Mother was facing away from the door, lying sideways. I kissed her cheek long and affectionately. My heart quickened, my mind grappling with trepidation and confusion. She moved. In those brief moments, as brief as the twinkling of my eyes, my mind took a sudden turn to nowhere. The surprising motion made me feel like falling.

Father pulled me away and closed the bedroom door. We tiptoed like thieves into the corridor, moving down the stairway into the hall and then out to the courtyard.

Father must have noticed how sad I was. He patted me on the back. "We'll come back for her later."

"Promise?"

"I promise." I sensed the lack of will in those words.

"And Grandma?"

"That's enough, Son."

A carriage, one of those made in Europe, with two horses, was waiting at the Great Gate. The luggage had been secured at the back. The driver, a dark, sinewy young man, was posted on the high driver's seat, looking haughtily down at me.

I approached the carriage. As I was passing the guardhouse, my eyes caught something in the half-open door at the Great Gate. I swung towards it and found one of the guards lying on a chair, his legs splayed apart like planks. With his head hanging to one side, he seemed dead. The other guard was curled like a cat in one corner, his saliva dropping from his mouth.

"What happened to the guards?" I exclaimed.

Father yanked me out of the guardhouse. "Nothing's the matter with them, Hamzah. They're just sleeping very soundly," he said.

"Sleeping? Shouldn't they be guarding? And why do they look as though they are dead?"

Father refused to answer.

Just then, Pak Ali appeared on the scene. He was smiling, his round, fleshy face flushed with mischievous pride. "All my handiwork," he boasted to me.

"That's enough, Pak Ali," Father blared at him.

I quickly recollected the events of the night just before I had gone to bed: Pak Ali at the Great Gate, peering at the spy window; the odd premature silence of the kitchen; that strange psychotic scent that pervaded the air; my drowsiness; my salubrious dream. I had witnessed strange things in Mataram House, so it wasn't hard for me to accept this abnormal scene. I hadn't the desire to ask; no answers would have come anyway. It was almost 3 a.m. The quietness was unnerving, and distress crept into me.

All of a sudden, Pak Ali burst into tears. I had never seen him in that state before – not Pak Ali, the Malay martial arts master, my mentor, the epitome of strength and confidence. He took Father's hand and kissed it as one would in homage and affection.

Father was moved; his eyes began to shine with tears as well. I knew that, to him, the man was not just a manservant but also a friend, and a loyal one at that – a loyalty measured in life, for Pak Ali would die for Father. He would not have engaged himself in this outrageous scheme, one that presented him with grave consequences, if not for his love of Father. I wondered at that moment what would happen to him if Grandma were to discover what he had done. As if to allay Father's concern, Pak Ali said, "If one does not fear death, what else is there to fear?"

Father placed a brass box into Pak Ali's hands. Pak Ali must have suspected what it was and what was in it, as he refused to accept it, gently pushing it away.

"In the name of God, Mr Norredin, I did this for you, not for anything in the world – and certainly not for this. You are like my own son."

"I know, Pak Ali, but this is to take care of you should anything happen to you. I had begged you to come with me, but you declined. Your responsibility was with Mataram House, you had said. No one had ever been so willing to sacrifice like this for me, so if you treat me like a son, then accept this as a father. Please, I beg of you."

Father was very much a private person. Never would he exhibit his feelings publicly. But this time, he let them go. He clasped the older man with both his arms and, with trembling emotion, embraced him. Pak Ali again broke into tears. This unusual display of emotion by Father for Pak Ali, his manservant, evoked in me a feeling of anger towards my father, as I had seen not the slightest of sentiment in his leaving Mother sleeping as we departed from her room.

Seeing how earnest Father was, Pak Ali relented. He took the box, looking at it with dolorous eyes. He dropped the same eyes on me. "Hamzah, my child," he said. "What is happening may be incomprehensible to you now, but you will know and understand by and by. Trust your father: all this is for you. Go. I pray for you both. May Allah's blessings be with you."

It was little comfort to me then, for at thirteen years of age I was not yet ready for God. Oddly, I felt nothing and was unaffected by the flood of emotions. After years of growing in the structured and orderly world of Mataram House, where I had lived since my birth – a world Grandma had created for me – this sudden upheaval sent me into an incomprehensible shock. I tried to cope with that incomprehensibility. I had known nothing of what lay outside Mataram House before this. The world outside the Great Gate had been out of bounds to me. Then Father's sudden appearance into my life, like a new character in a play – not delicately but in a burst, as with a man in a terrible hurry – added to my confusion.

As we mounted the carriage, drops of rain pelted me, the moon hid behind clumps of clouds, and claps of thunder were heard from afar. After succumbing to the urge to look back at Mataram House, I saw a figure on the balcony of Mother's bedroom. It was Mother standing and gazing while we departed. Or was that just my befuddled mind playing tricks on me? Now I could not be sure. It was too momentary. Hadn't she been sleeping soundly when I kissed her? What game were they all playing? I was a ball of portentous feelings that rolled in every direction, feelings that were hard to express in plain words, for they couldn't do justice to how I actually felt. The world beyond the Great Gate, the real world that I craved to know, was now thrown on my lap in one fell swoop.

Father had been a father of the traditional kind, distant and formal. Only his existence gave me the assurance that I had a father. His aloofness was strange and mysterious. He spoke to me only when it was necessary. He never played with me except for the rare forays in his study to watch the stars, which were his companions in his lonely moments. Never did he demonstrate his affection physically. Never was I embraced or even patted on the head. But I had no doubt he loved me. I had come to this conclusion after hearing something that he had once said to me. It was on my sixth birthday. He called me over and asked me to sit opposite him. He looked into my eyes and held me by the shoulders, as if about to deliver something of momentous proportion. My eyes met his in a curious and unsure sort of way. Like a cat unused to close proximity, I wanted to wriggle out and flee.

"I love you, Hamzah, and I shall give my life for you. Remember that, Son." Father's voice was not grave at all, as I had anticipated. It was gentle and had a kind of pain, which ran through him like fear. Why he chose that moment to say what he said to me, I have no idea. Later in my life, when I became a man, I would look back at that precious moment and hold it close to me as if I were holding him.

"Yes, Father," I had replied meekly.

It was a big concept to me then, this giving of your life to someone. I had no idea what it really implied. One thing I was sure about, though: Father was giving me a big present, bigger than all the other presents I had received on that day.

"Now go away and do whatever you were doing," he had said.

"Yes, Father," I had replied

It was such a brief encounter, and yet it had made me very happy.

*　　*　　*

The night had fallen into a pall of gloom, making the trees lose their form. They looked now like wandering ghosts. In the distance, the thunder persisted. The horses trotted steadily, the coach yawed and rolled, the ghosts followed, and in the glow of the carriage lamps I saw my life passing through the night to nowhere.

My heart was like the fuzzy night. Not a word came from Father or me. How should I begin to talk to him? Should I ask him why he was doing all this? He did not seem to know how to begin either. To console me would be to admit guilt; to cheer me would imply that something cheery was happening.

The heavy silence ghosted with the night, drowning the crunching of the horses, the rumbling of the wheels, the heavy breaths of the horses. The image of Mother by the balcony again flashed before me. I sank deeper into the boring doldrums of the journey – a journey in a European horse-drawn carriage hired specially to cheer me up. But I wasn't cheered. The horses bounded on without breaking the silence. Everything went by without regard. The earth below groaned. Distant flashes forewarned of a storm. The moon finally retreated and the night capitulated. I was about to meet my secret melancholy – wind and rain.

When I was a child, the rain made me sad and the wind gave me a feeling of longing. Since everything around me was happiness, I could find no reasons for the sadness and longing. Those emotions came and went by without ceremony, until the next cycle of rain and wind. I told this to no one, not to Grandma Tutik or to Mother or to Father or even to Pak Ali, the only people who actually existed, or were allowed to exist, in my childhood, each one of them engaging a specific part of me. In the sum total of all their roles, Grandma Tutik took the plump part, almost to the exclusion of the rest. Norredin, my father, observing from a safe distance, was a sentinel without a role. Dewi, my mother, took me as a possession of love, no more than that. She would cry if she saw me hurt even by a scratch, and she often hugged me passionately to show her love. Yet she seemed unable to play the mother, although I knew she wanted to do so very much. At every opportunity when I wasn't with my governess or Grandma, Mother would take me for a walk in the garden. We sat under the bough of the willow tree and talked. She would tell me about her childhood and how cloistered she was. There was always a certain sadness in her telling me that. She once said she had never been outside Java except on two occasions: a three-month stint in Bali to learn the Balinese version of the Ramayana, and a trip to Ujung Pandang in Sulawesi with her father, as he had wanted to show her the unusual burial ritual of the Toraja people. She then told me, somewhat in a low tone as if afraid of being eavesdropped on, that when I grew up I must travel the world and not be cloistered like she had been. Just then, Grandma appeared out of nowhere, so Mother quickly changed the subject.

Grandma asked, "What are you talking about, you two?"

My mother replied, "Nothing of importance, Mother."

On another occasion, when I had fallen and injured my knee, Mother took me into the kitchen to dress my wound. When Grandma heard, she quickly came rushing down from her room and took over the task. I so wanted Dewi to be mother, and she wanted the same, but there was always the omnipresent figure of Grandma, who felt that she must play the grandmother and mother all at once.

The courageous Pak Ali was an extraordinary kind of manservant with a silent defiance of Grandma. He became my only friend in Mataram House. During my early childhood, the concept of friends of my age was totally non-existent, since Mataram House, where I had been born and where I lived, was my only world.

In the months of July and August, the monsoon was always visibly felt, and with it came unending rains, which could sometimes turn pitiless, accompanied by winds. At night it was like a troubled soul, this wind, restless and wandering, making enemies of everything, flogging windows, scraping roofs, and causing the trees to have sleepless nights. It was during this period that Mataram House took leave from its exuberance, a kind of respite from its otherwise boisterously bizarre life. Grandma Tutik would catch up on her painting, which was more self-indulgence than art, or would breathe on the servants to clean and polish the rich horde of historical collections of doubtful provenance: arts, antiques, furniture, artefacts, the family of statues and icons. Father would be in his study with his books and telescope, although there was nothing he could see then in the heavily smudged sky. Mother would be in her room, which had become her personal world. When she was not catching up on her embroidery, she would stand on the balcony and stare into the night as if in search of a companion. I would surreptitiously creep up from behind and give her a hug, startling her. And each time I did this, my garment would become wet with her tears. My presence in her room was enough reward for both of us. I would join her, neither of us saying anything, to survey the vast, dark heavens. Her sheer presence, her touch, her beating heart, her breathing, became my companions of the moment. No words needed to be spoken.

* * *

The coach continued its rumbling. I could hear the snorting of the horses as Ardi, the young, plucky driver, drove them as if in a chariot race.

Then in one terrible fury, the rain, like glittering shards of a piercing black deluge, obliterated our path, throwing the horses into frenzy. Ardi lashed the whip hard. He seemed sure of himself. Pools of water came from nowhere, and the horses fought against them. Again Ardi whipped the horses. The ground squealed. The carriage swayed madly like a pendulum, throwing us against the sides and into each other. This madness went on like eternity. In the next moment, we heard the cries of the horses when the earth swallowed a part of the carriage. Father and I hit our heads against the roof and then were thrown forward. Next, everything went dead. Like a defeated beast, the carriage lay hopelessly on its flank. The horses breathed out steams of fatigue. I counted my breaths. Father was visibly shaken. Ardi jumped from the driver's seat and landed ankle-deep in a pool of sludge.

"What happened?" Father yelled, craning his head out of the window. I peeped out too. The rain kept pouring down defiantly. "Hope the wheel is not broken," he said. There was fear in his voice. He went down. I wanted to follow him. "No, you stay there," he ordered.

A mud-filled gaping hole had swallowed nearly half of the left wheel. Ardi, after examining the damage, said with bravado to Father, "Mr Norredin, you push the wheel and I'll drive the horses. I think I can get it out."

Father rested all his weight against the wheel, and Ardi pulled the pugnacious horses hard. They bellowed and steamed. The wheel advanced a little before it fell back. This was done again and again. The horses puffed, wheezed, and panted, yet the wheel stubbornly refused to budge, not even an inch.

I leaped out of the carriage.

"Let me handle the horses. You and Ardi can work on the wheel. Then we can have the strength of two men," I said to Father.

He looked at me. "That's an excellent idea," he said.

"Can you drive?" Ardi asked me.

"Just tell me what to do."

Ardi broke into a smile, swung open his oilskin raincoat, and wrapped it around me, even though I was already soaked to the bone.

"Come over to the driver's seat. I'll make a driver out of you in a jiffy. It's easy." I jumped onto the driver's bench. "Here, hold the reins like this, relax, and don't pull, or else the horses might think you're asking them to stop. Shout *whoa* at the top of your voice and whip the hell out of them. Tell them you're the master. Can you do that? By the way, the brake is here," he said, pointing to the long lever to my right. "Use it only when I say so." He went down and stood by the distressed wheel with Father.

"When the carriage begins to move forward, I'll shout for you to stop. You must pull the reins hard or else the horses will gallop away and you'll be on your way to Batavia alone."

"Ready, everyone?" I called out nervously. The driver's seat was so high that I felt on top of the world.

"Yes," they cried.

"Whoa!" I crashed the whip with my right hand, the harnesses tightened, the horses cried furiously, Father and Ardi pushed and pushed, and in one huge movement the horses and carriage lunged forward and into freedom.

"Pull!" Ardi cried out. I reined in the horses and pulled the brake, and the carriage came to a complete stop. Just then the rain subsided. Father and Ardi were profuse in their praise. When I descended to the ground, Father came to me and rapped my back like a friend.

We recommenced our journey. The mood in the coach completely changed. Father and I broke into small talk. The silent tension of the earlier moments went down with the rain, as if having been washed away.

It was midday when we reached Wonosobo. The sun torched down upon us from a furiously bright blue sky. Our clothes were in shambles, our bones were battered, and the horses looked worn down. To add to our failing nerves, we ran into a farmers' fair. The only liveable hotel in Wonosobo, the Singasari, was fully booked out. The Chinese proprietor expressed his profound regrets with a broad smile. "It's always full when the fair is on, but you can get rooms in Dieng. It's not far from here," he said. Seeing that we had come in a horse carriage, he added, "You'll take an hour or two. The air is very good there. You'll like it. It is where the Dutch go for vacation."

13

Before he could ramble on, Father took his offer.

The route to Dieng was a climb along a serpentine road that twisted like a corkscrew. The air had cooled considerably, but still an invasive air crunched our chests. Volcanic craters and hot springs came into view. Gunung Perahu sprouted in the distance. On its shoulders, the broad, green cultivated fields sprouted like carpets. Farmers were seen hiking unperturbed next to the volcano's awesome presence. Our breathing began to become a deliberate undertaking in the rusty air.

I saw Father suddenly slumping against the coach bench, the high-altitude air seeming to cause a tremulous wheezing in his chest. As I moved close to him, I discovered that he was like a burning stove.

"Are you all right, Father?" I asked.

"I'm all right. Why? Do I look sick?" His brow curled in displeasure.

I saw a fever in the making, and he was denying it.

*   *   *

We arrived at the Hotel Indes, a small recuperating resort with a low sloping roof, long windows, and stone walls that had become mossy and weathered by time, but the place was rendered charming by its wide terraces and flowered trellis overlooking a neat garden and an awesome valley beyond. The sun was a giant orange slipping behind the mountain. A well-attired young European couple were seen curiously taken by the profane beauty of the coppery dome. Judging by their animated exchange and the seriousness with which they had set their huge long-range camera on a tripod, they were obviously trying to capture the magnificent sunset. I wondered who they were. *Could they be on their honeymoon?* I asked myself. At the far end, on the wide verandah, a middle-aged, swarthy, moustached man sat by a table alone. He was also gazing at the mountain, as if hypnotised by the unnatural world. A pot of coffee was his company. Otherwise the place looked empty. A glimpse of the inside showed an elderly European couple having dinner. I didn't see any locals, except for the staff. Gunung Perahu stood by menacingly close, so close that one could touch it. The mountain terrified me. The air was overpowering. It had the feel of death. Strange, I thought, for a recuperating place. Maybe it was the health-giving thermal springs that normally sprouted in such a place that made people go there.

We washed, changed, and ate a meal of lamb chops, mashed potatoes, and beans. Father ended the meal with a pot of thick Java coffee, which irritated his throat. He coughed, cursing the terrible brew. I noticed an advancing bleariness in his eyes. His body was burning; I could feel the heat from where I was sitting. Father checked into his room. He wanted an early night, he said. I saw a slight sway to his walk.

I sat with Ardi by the terrace and took an interest in the bearded European, who was still glued to his table. He seemed transfixed by the mountain. The valley had changed colour from smouldering primeval yellow to funereal pale white. The unwelcome air hid behind the grey cloak of the night. Somehow the image of the bearded European irked me. Upon my enquiry, the hotel manager said, "His name is Ottovenger. A Dutchman, he has been a permanent resident of the hotel for the last year. He thinks Gunung Perahu is going to erupt anytime now. We guess he is some sort of expert on volcanoes."

When I returned to our room, Father was not in his bed. I panicked. I rushed to the bathroom, and there I found him sprawled on his stomach, his faced pressed to the floor.

"Father!" I cried, fear running up my head.

"Yes," he said in a hardly audible voice.

I tried to lift him, but he was barely conscious. His dead weight was too much for me.

"I'll get help."

I rushed out of the room and went out onto the terrace. I was relieved to find Ardi still there.

"Ardi, come, I need your help." I was shaking.

"You look pale. What has happened?"

"It's my father."

We rushed back to the room.

Ardi was agape upon seeing father's undignified body on the floor. He closed his mouth with his palm. Turning to me, he stretched his hand out consolingly. "Don't be afraid. Let's lift him up first."

With great difficulty, we lifted Father onto the bed. His body was indeed burning, his breathing was heavy and frighteningly guttural, his forehead was swollen by the fall, and he moaned deliriously. We could not make out a word he said. He was without life but was still living.

"What shall we do, Ardi?" I pleaded, lost because of this totally new experience.

"You guard him closely. I'll alert the manager, and then I'll go and get help. I'll be back as soon as possible. I doubt if there's a hospital around here. The nearest one is in Wonosobo." He looked at me with a frown and then said, "Don't worry."

From the immobile body, I heard groans intermingled with purring like a cat in pain. When Father opened his eyes, I could see that they were bloodshot. He moved his hand in a desperate bid to hold me. When I gave him my hand, I felt a pull. "Yes, Father, I am here." His breathing turned heavier. Again I felt the tug of his hand as he became agitated. I realised he wanted me to be close enough for me to hear him. I put my ear close to his mouth, but all I could hear were incoherent mumblings which sounded like "Tutik," repeatedly. But why was he calling Grandma's name in his present predicament? There was hardly any love between them. He closed his eyes, and his grip loosened. I shouted, "Ardi!" There was no response, as Ardi hadn't yet returned. Father moved. I was relieved. He was falling in and out of consciousness.

Alone, hemmed by four unfamiliar walls, and with Father lying sick, I felt terribly impotent. This sudden proximity with a father I hardly knew brought with it unease. I had never touched him before, and now I had to touch him like a nurse, propping him up in bed. It felt strange and unnatural. It was a painful task.

"How do you feel?" I asked. There was silence. "Ardi has gone to seek help. A doctor will be here soon. Is there anything you want? I heard you calling for Grandma?"

At the mention of Grandma, Father moved his head from side to side as if in protest. A guttural sound ensued; foam trickled down from his lips. Just as thoughts waded in my mind, I heard knocking at the door. I thought that Ardi had returned. When I pulled out the door leaf, there stood a man of medium build. It was the swarthy European with the beard, the volcanologist, addressing me in a most proper fashion, his deportment reminding me of Governor General Vervoort, the kind of deportment displayed by accomplished men.

"I heard someone is sick. I may be of help," the bearded European said in very good Malay.

"Yes, it's my father."

"My name is Ottovenger. I am a doctor, retired. May I come in?" He had a black leather bag with him. He pulled up a chair, unclasped the black bag on the side table, and sat next to Father. Removing the blanket, he unbuttoned Father's shirt and placed a stethoscope on his chest, reading his pulse against his watch. When Ottovenger examined the whites of Father's eyes, Father mumbled something like, "Humph." Ottovenger proceeded to open Father's mouth to see his tongue, and then he touched the bruise on his forehead. "It's only a slight bruising of the skin, not serious. I'll get a cold compress for the swelling. But I fear that your father has contracted pneumonia."

I stared at Ottovenger speechlessly, my mouth open.

"I believe your father has a history of a chest ailment, bronchitis, maybe, and this dampness and the air have triggered a relapse."

"We were caught in heavy rain last night," I added.

"Ah, that explains it. Now this certainly is not a good place for him to be. Not to worry. A jab of the needle will do the trick. We'll see what happens after that."

He rolled up Father's sleeve and administered an injection. I felt ashamed to have prejudged this swarthy, bearded man, thinking he was somewhat of a crank staring at emptiness. He turned out to be a gentleman of breeding – a doctor. When I thanked him, I made it a point to have a good look at him. He was not dark at all; instead, he was tanned. The play of the sunset on his face, and that reddish tint of his brushed hair and beard, had made me think he was dark-skinned. There was a smudge of the East in his heart, which accounted for his polite disposition with the locals and his command of their language.

*　　*　　*

When Ardi returned two hours later, he brought a man with him. "This is the pawang Haji Agus," he said.

That took me by surprise, as I had been expecting a doctor, not a village pawang, a shaman. I had forgotten to warn Ardi about Father's aversion to village shamans and faith healers. "Hocus-pocus spiritualists," he called them. The fact that these people were Grandma's first port of call in times of calamity added to his contempt for them. Everything Grandma loved automatically became Father's secret peeve. Few opposites could possibly be more defined.

He was diminutive, this shaman, with a pinched face and with the trademark *songkok* that a shaman wears resting neatly on his head. When I took his hand, I could feel his bones.

I welcomed the pawang in. Father was in no position to protest, as he was already in a deep sleep from Ottovenger's medication. An ill-fated encounter was averted. The pawang pulled up a chair and sat close to Father by the bed. He began his examination, putting himself into deep concentration while his lips moved as though talking to himself. He traced every part of Father's body from head to toe with his eyes, without touching. He closed his eyes, but his lips continued to quiver, mouthing unintelligible words. He remained in that state for a good ten minutes, reciting under his breath some incantations.

Suddenly he jumped out of his chair and smashed the air with his palms, jolting Ardi and me from our seats. I thought Father would have been jolted too if he had not been sleeping.

He cried out, "In the name of God, Most Gracious, Most Merciful, depart, you recalcitrant spirit, from this body. This is not your place. Depart this instant! Descend to where you came from, or I shall summon the wrath of God upon you. Depart! Depart! Depart" Then with both his hands, he conjured the act of expelling the evil spirit, beginning at Father's head and moving down the length of his body to his toes in a manner of sweeping. Three times he repeated the motion. Then, taking a glass, he filled it with water from the jug and spit verses into it. From his mouth, he sprayed the water into the air in three circular motions, some if it dropping onto Ardi's face and mine. I dared not wipe it off. Then he made another potion, again spitting verses into it. "Ask your father to drink this when he wakes up. God willing, your father will be well in three days. Three days!" He was pretty definitive about the three days, as he repeated it to me with divine certainty. Ardi and I were speechless.

When that was over, I whispered to Ardi, asking what kind of recompense I should make to the pawang for his work. He in turn whispered to the pawang. The pawang smiled. "You are merely a boy, yet you are compassionate. I see that in your face. I shall not take money from you. It is my gift."

I bowed and kissed his hand. Before he departed, he turned around and remarked, "Let me look at you close." He asked me to sit in the chair, since I was much taller than he. He stood before me and examined my face, tracing its features with his eyes. He smiled. "You are on a journey, yes?"

I said nothing, perplexed by his question.

"I know. It is an unsanctioned journey, yes?"

Still I said nothing.

"This journey will be long, and you will never return from where you came."

I was glued to his curiously intense eyes – eyes that seemed to know what they saw. I didn't think much of what he had said to me. Prophecies didn't count for much in a mind of a thirteen-year-old. But his ability to read my present state of predicament with such accuracy perplexed me.

The following Sunday morning, three days later, Father was out and about before I was. When I opened my eyes, I found a bright, cheery smile greeting me. Father was clean-shaven and wearing fresh clothes, as if about to go somewhere. The change made me jump out of bed. Three days, just as the pawang pronounced – or was it the medicine that Dr Ottovenger had administered? I couldn't decide, but whichever way I looked at it, I couldn't help but think that the pawang was indeed uncanny.

"Father, you have recovered?"

"Yes."

I didn't tell him of the pawang's visit, and had asked Ardi to keep his mouth shut about it. Fortunately, Father had no recollection of the event. I told him about Dr Ottovenger and his regular morning visits.

"Who's this Dr Ottovenger?" he asked.

I introduced the good doctor to him, and we all became friends, having breakfast every morning together after that.

Ottovenger was no volcanologist at all. When I asked why he spent his time watching the mountain, and whether he was predicting an eruption, he laughed. He said the hotel manager had this notion that he was a volcanologist, an idea which the manager had spread to every guest. Ottovenger condoned it, amused to be thought of as eccentric. Actually the mountain was a piece of memory – a memory of his wife. She had died two years ago in Dieng of the same illness that had afflicted Father. That accounted for the doctor's ability to detect pneumonia in Father so easily. Ottovenger was head of the sanatorium in Brastagi, Sumatra. He and his wife had come to Dieng Plateau to seek the curative properties of the hot springs for arthritis, which his wife suffered from. Out of his own foolishness – more concerned about his wife's arthritis than about her asthma – he exposed her to the bloody fumes. Yes, "bloody" – he had used the English word. So badly exposed was she that she died from a severe asthmatic seizure. This was the second anniversary of her death. He wanted to replay that memory of their visit to this place before he returned to Holland for good.

We were taking a walk in the garden as evening set in.

"My wife, whose name was Ingrid, was buried here in Dieng at a Christian cemetery in the valley. There wasn't any facility available here for me to embalm her remains and transfer her to Holland for burial," he said.

Feeling a tinge of sadness for him to have his wife buried so far away from home, I wanted to say a word of kindness but didn't know how. So I said, "I'm sorry, Mr Ottovenger."

He smiled. "Don't be. She had lived in this country a long time and loved it. Maybe she wouldn't have mind being buried here. By the way, I'm visiting her grave tomorrow. Would you like to come along?"

"I'd love to."

"Good. We'll set off after breakfast."

"Let's go in now. Your father must be waiting for you."

* * *

It had been a week since we left Mataram House. Father's recovery had been remarkable, the blood returning to his face. I felt much obliged to the good doctor, who oversaw Father's recovery diligently as though Ottovenger were his personal physician.

20

Ottovenger took me to where Ingrid was buried in the outskirts of Wonosobo, an hour's drive from the hotel. It was a small and well-kept cemetery shaded by trees on its perimeter at the edge of the valley, with a caretaker. I brought a bunch of flowers, which I had plucked from the hotel garden. When I placed the flowers on the gravestone, the epitaph immediately caught my attention:

> To see a world in a grain of sand,
> And heaven in a wild flower,
> To hold infinity in the palm of your hand,
> And eternity in an hour.

"It's a beautiful epitaph," I said to Ottovenger.

"It's Ingrid's favourite poem by William Blake."

Though the meaning eluded me, the epitaph gave me goosebumps, a message striking deep into my heart.

"What does it mean?"

"It's what life is, in Blake's eyes."

"Too deep for me."

"Just think of how each of us sees the world in our own way. How do you see the world, Hamzah?" Ottovenger lifted his brown eyes enquiringly, while I found myself at a loss. It took me a while, an eternity perhaps, like in the poem, to answer, yet he waited as if my response would be a revelation.

"I see life being as confusing as the poem," I said.

"Whatever you are looking for in this world, you'll find it in that verse." He gently tapped my shoulder with a comforting gesture as if he had seen what was in my eyes. On our way back to the hotel, the sun threw a final burst of life before reposing. I heard a distant howl of a dog – maybe I thought I heard it. An old dog I used to know had returned. Ottovenger observed me with keen eyes as I drifted away like a boat drawn by the tide.

"Still thinking about the poem?" he asked with a smile.

"Well—" My thoughts stumbled.

"It's too early for you to think of life in a sort of profound and philosophical way. That time will come."

"Perhaps not as early as you might think, Mr Ottovenger. In the last few days, my life has seemed to accelerate beyond my expectation—"

"Really? I shan't venture to ask why. Personal, I believe?" he asked.

"Yes." I tossed my gaze at the fading horizon.

Silence ensued as the dusk came upon us. I felt a longing for home. The epitaph found its way into me. How vainglorious and unreal Grandma had made my world; how sadly insane it had been. On the other hand, maybe it wasn't all madness after all, not the way Blake had delightfully put it, I thought. My heaven in a wild flower. Isn't that what Grandma wanted Mataram House to be for me?

To break the silence, the doctor asked me a rather personal question.

"You seem quite mature for your age. I'm curious about your coming here in that lovely carriage. The last time I saw something like that in this part of the world was in Batavia – a carriage owned by the governor general. Why are you here, anyway?"

I smiled sheepishly. "That carriage is my father's idea of a treat for me, as I admire horses and carriages. The carriage could possibly once have belonged to a governor general. I don't know. You have to ask my father about that. We were on our way to Batavia and were diverted here because there wasn't any accommodation in Wonosobo due to the farmers' fair."

"Tell me something about yourself? You don't mind me asking, do you?"

"Not at all, sir."

"Come on, cut that 'sir' bit. Just call me Otto."

"Yes, mister – I mean Otto."

He laughed. I did too.

I felt very at ease with him, and was taken up by his keen interest in me. The moment I mentioned the name of Mataram House, it jolted him to have a greater curiosity about me, as he had heard that name before in high circles. So in the next hour during our journey home, I told him about Mataram House and the environment in which I had been brought up, without, of course, revealing things that were not supposed to be spoken.

I spoke to him in English, sometimes throwing in some Dutch. He was amazed at my command of languages and thought I was a prodigy. I told him I had my grandmother to thank for my abilities. He made the comment that I talked a great deal about her. When we parted, he said to me that I should start a diary and jot down every detail of my life. "Start young when the memory is still fresh," he suggested. He regretted not having done so himself. It was late evening when we returned to the hotel.

That night at dinner, Father asked me about my day with the doctor. I told him that we had gotten along marvellously and that I was very pleased and flattered that he had treated me like an adult.

"That's good. Now you are meeting real people from the real world, not those demons created by your grandmother for you. Soon you will understand why I'm taking you away."

This taking a swipe at Grandma was nothing new. At every opportunity he would do it.

Talking to the doctor that day about Mataram House, and hearing Father's terse remarks about Grandma, made me suddenly homesick. I was overcome by a sense of guilt. Father's harsh words about her particularly weighed on me. He might have had issues with her to which I wasn't privy. If such were the case, then I was not told what those issues were. But what grouses did I have with her? No matter how crazy Father thought she was and how weird her ways, Grandma had done a great deal for me. Shouldn't I be beholden to her?

In the hotel room, once father had gone to sleep, my mind floated in the darkness while my guilt began to form images of the past.

I began to reminisce about the world Grandma Tutik had created for me – as Father had said over dinner that evening. Were there demons? No, there were none. They were memories I sometimes loved to recall, such as what I thought of the valley down the road, beyond the Great Gate, those carpets of small houses of planks and bamboos, the cultivated fields, and how I thought they starkly contrasted against the grandeur and pomposity of my own Mataram House, a mansion like no other in the whole of Jogjakarta. It was Grandma's idea of a nebulous past relived, a realm of make-believe, with me at the centre of it all.

In the light of day, the tiny dwellings, the fields of rice and peppers, and the strange odours carried by the wind always pricked my curiosity. At night, the timid lights twinkled shyly under the empty sky. When my eyes feasted on them from my balcony with Grandma by my side, I could sense her pride when she lifted her head high, as if she were the mistress who lorded over them.

As the past flooded in, once again the memory of that solitary dog returned. I remembered his cries, so mournful that they once drove me to imagine that those cries were meant for me. I was a six-year-old then, and I recall trudging across the corridor and knocking on the door to Grandma's room. When she unhinged the door, her first words were, "Why aren't you asleep? It's the wind again, is it?"

How did she know the wind had always affected me? I didn't remember telling her about it. *She's uncanny, this grandma of mine,* I had thought.

"No, not the wind, Grandma."

"What is it then?"

"It's a dog. It's crying. I think it's looking for me. I want to go there to the village and see what's wrong with it."

"Dog? I didn't hear any dog. If it was barking, I would've heard it."

"Maybe your window is closed."

"It's wide open. Look at it yourself."

I ambled behind her. She was in a long night garment. Her long black hair was loose but neatly gathered at her nape. She towered over me as she walked with the grace of a queen. Even in my presence, her perfume floated about her. Fragrance never left her.

"Come. Sit with me by the window. We'll listen together."

As if by her influence, the dog was silent. I peeked out over the balcony and strained my neck, searching for a sound. Except for the oozing wind, there was not even a squeak from the poor dog.

"I am sure it is there, Grandma. I am sure. I wasn't lying."

She sighed deeply. Through my watery eyes, I noticed she was visibly upset. Her eyebrows arched and her forehead rippled, the night sky painting shadows of concern in her face.

The next moment, she went to say something she had never said before. "That world over there in the valley across the Great Gate will eventually be at your feet. The time has not come, but it shall. Be patient. Though you're only a child now, you are more than any other child of your age. You are special. Trust Grandma. You do, don't you?"

"Yes, Grandma."

Grandma always had a hypnotic effect on me. All those questions I wanted to ask again retreated somewhere in my mind, as they had done since I was born. I never made mention again about the village or the dog. Strangely, the dog never called me again. That episode never left my memory. Why is that? Someone or something out there was calling me.

Now I was with father in Dieng, a godforsaken place, on this strange journey he had conceived for me. Grandma had planned my world for me. Now it was Father's turn. What it was – this plan of Father – and where it was going to lead me, I had no idea. Could this be an answer to that call from that lonely dog? *That would be strange,* I thought. But strange things did happen in Mataram House.

Time passed. I noticed a trace of light from the approaching dawn across the hotel window. Father was still slumbering. I became tired as my reminiscences drifted me into my own, much needed sleep.

Chapter 2

I t was our eighth day in Dieng. My recent past had yet to blur from my mind, but Father's illness began to draw me closer to him. Strange, my life was, surreptitiously changing in an extraordinary way without my being aware of it. I had to do a lot of things on my own, like make the bed without the aid of servants. And in a twist of irony, I had become guardian to Father rather than he to me, a prospect beyond anything Grandma Tutik would imagine possible. A new-found world had entered me.

Father had returned to his normal self – his brooding, divergent, elusive self. He had become bored of being holed up in this fuming volcanic crucible, and so had I. We had no news of the outside world – papers did not come this way. People here were too preoccupied with their own toil, their own impending calamity, their own resignation with a precocious mountain, to care for the outside world. Then one afternoon, a very excited Ardi came rushing into the dining hall with a newspaper in his hand. "You should see this, Mr Norredin," he said, pointing to the newspaper without regard for the other guests.

"Calm down. Don't raise your voice," Father cautioned him.

"There's a picture of you. You're in the news, sir." He handed the paper to Father.

"Where did you get this?"

"In Wonosobo."

Father took the paper and began to walk towards the garden, away from the rest of us in the restaurant. I wanted to follow him, but he turned and gesticulated with his hand for me to stay put. When he was far enough, he leafed through the paper page by page and then stopped. His eyes were transfixed. Even from that distance I could see his face taking an ominous turn. The gravity of his countenance spread across the lawn to reach me like a biblical sign of the end of the world. I rushed towards him in panic.

"What is it, Father?"

Ardi wanted to say something, but Father flashed his hand, making a gesture to shut him up. I sensed a rising anger building in Father.

"What is it, Father?" I asked again. I tried to get the newspaper from him. He pulled it away abruptly, obviously not wanting me to see it.

"Come, let's pack. We have to leave Java immediately."

Chapter 3

Now I was leaving Java. Our journey had never been about Batavia. That had been merely a ploy by Father to take me away. There always existed hidden warnings from Grandma that I should never leave Mataram House. Did she know something that no one else did? Was that why she erected the Great Gate and the grandiose palace – just to keep me in? Was there any truth about my birth? These questions ran about wildly in my mind as we left Dieng in the evening.

We, Father and I, continued the journey in a hired car. We travelled under the shadow of darkness, to where I wasn't told. In the quiet of the night, little conversation ensued between us, as he seemed quite occupied.

I had never seen Father acting with such determination and ferocity, judging by the length he was prepared to go to extract me from Mataram House.

I took to reminiscing about the past again, as I had a deep suspicion I might not see Mataram House again. Recalling every detail of my extraordinary childhood, I might find some answers, especially as to why Father was so contemptuous of Grandma.

According to Pak Ali, I had been received with a flourish of celebration when I first came into this world. He remembered that event very clearly in his mind as if it were yesterday, he told me. The whole sky was lighted on that twenty-eighth day of March in 1927. Every inch of ground in Mataram House was ignited with decorative flames. Hundreds of cows and goats were slaughtered, and people from the village lined up for miles to the Great Gate for the slaughtered meats. I was wrapped in gold cloth, cradled in Grandma Tutik's arms, as she proudly announced, "The sultan is born," to resounding applause of those present. There were dances and music and a great feast.

As I grew up, it came to me that I was not really a sultan. In Jogjakarta, there was already a living sultan residing in Kraton Palace, although he was no longer reigning. The sultan I was supposed to be was of Mataram. The real Mataram kingdom had disappeared centuries ago. But to Grandma Tutik, I was the descendent of Sultan Agung, the greatest of the Mataram kings. How it came about that I had in my veins the royal blood, no one – not Grandma Tutik, not Mother or Father, and not even Pak Ali – could explain.

The most curious thing about all this was that no one ever questioned the validity of Grandma's statement. Everyone, from the Dutch governor general of Java to Father, Mother, Pak Ali, and all those who had passed through the Great Gate and walked the corridors of Mataram House, meeting with its icons and figurines and relics, accepted it. Such was the aura of Tutik, my grandmother. No matter how preposterous her ideas were, she lived up to them with great conviction and aplomb.

She was in every way exceptional. Not least was her own beauty. But, except for those who had entered the doors of Mataram House, few people had viewed her in person. There were no paintings or photographs of her. She had refused to sit for even the most well-known of Dutch painters. She believed that the spirits of paintings and photographs would steal her beauty. Some said she had gold needles inserted in her face, an ancient art of holding back the ravages of time. It seemed to be true, because when standing side by side with Dewi, my mother, Grandma Tutik did not appear to look a day older than she.

When it came to appearance, Mother was everything that Grandma was, filling the mould to perfection. But that was all. In every other way, Mother was not Grandma Tutik. She lacked her mother's passion about everything and had none of her faddish imagination, her idiosyncratic ways, or her inexplicable power over people. Yet Mother secretly held steadfastly to her own sense of reality, acquiescing in her own doleful way to the contradictions that surrounded Mataram House only because of her profound love for her mother.

Throughout my childhood it was Grandma Tutik who filled my life. She was mother, guardian, mentor, and mistress, moulding me with great alacrity into the living image of her dreams.

She said I was an exceptional child. I had three governesses to instruct me: one for the English language, one for Dutch, and another for Javanese. At the age of ten, when most children were just beginning their first lessons at school, I was already able to converse and read proficiently in the three languages. My recreational activities – and the idea of fun – were not of my choice. Fun meant music, dances, theatre, archery, and martial arts. Of all these, I enjoyed martial arts the most. It wasn't for the art itself, but for the company of Pak Ali, my instructor. The deprivation I suffered in Mataram House with regard to friends was more than compensated for by Pak Ali.

Pak Ali was much older than Father, but he was a bit younger than Grandma Tutik. He was short, was thick-set, and had a melon face and an onion nose. He wore his hair short-cropped, which lent toughness to his appearance. Unhandsome but utterly amiable and comical, and cunningly defiant of authority, Pak Ali turned his trespasses into acts of jocundity. Even Grandma had to suppress her amusement under a severe countenance. When Pak Ali smiled, one could see that he had a full set of teeth, but they seemed roasted by smoke. He waddled when he walked, like a chimp, and all the other servants laughed behind his back. So did I. I loved him a great deal. I also admired him.

In the entire Mataram household, Pak Ali seemed to be the only person who was not in mortal fear of Tutik. Servants in Mataram House lowered themselves to their knees when speaking to Grandma, and when withdrawing they walked backwards, only to turn at a distance. I had never seen Pak Ali do that. Pak Ali was a tobacco addict. A stick dangled permanently from his lips. Tutik abhorred tobacco. "An uncultured and plebeian habit," she had said to him. Tutik and Pak Ali were like the proverbial chalk and cheese.

Mataram House had all the trimmings of a royal court, down to every detail. A strict protocol to that was maintained. Everyone, including the chief butler, housekeeper, servers, cooks, washers, and drivers, had some kind of attire, Javanese in fashion, except for Pak Ali. His normal dress was a loose-fitting top, a sarong, and a songkok of black velvet, reflecting his homeland, Sumatra. His apparel made a kind of statement that he was Sumatran, not Javanese. This gave him standing in the eyes of all the servants, without exception, and earned him an unwritten right to exercise command over them.

My birthdays were always celebrated with some kind of event. As far as I can remember, they were all-adult affairs. Children of my age were nowhere to be seen. The occasions were always meant to display my skill in something, indicating a kind of progress on my path to become sultan. My thirteenth birthday was particularly momentous. Little did I know then that it would be the last of any birthday celebrations for me. No one, including me, had known then that my life at Mataram House was about to end.

Guests were ushered into the hall and sat in a semicircle. I, dressed in regal attire, was placed before them on the floor with my legs folded, dressed in regal attire. Before me, laid on a yellow cloth, were krises that had come from every corner of the Malay Archipelago. In the front row of people was Vervoort. His eyes glowed at the magnificent array of exotically decorated weapons. I not only named every kris but also described each, naming its origin and then explicating every detail of its character and the meaning it contained – the mystical, the physical, and the spiritual. A particular kris may often contain as many as twenty aspects and characteristics.

"Look at this kris. The hilt is a demon's head with eyes of ruby. The damascene is of powerful symbols, and the blade is of seventeen waves. This is the kris of Majapahit, to be worn only by a nobleman. And this is a Malaccan kris. Observe the flowering form of the hilt. This is a typical Malay kris, which disallows the depiction of deities and human forms," I proclaimed, to the delight of my audience.

When it was all over, it was Vervoort, the governor general of Java, who came to congratulate me. He appeared genuinely possessed. "What an accomplished young man," he said, shaking my hand firmly. The other guests, seeing Vervoort's enthrallment, followed suit, although some of their praises seemed perfunctory. The most elated person was Grandma Tutik.

When night fell, a greater event awaited the guests. The Ramayana was to be staged.

Mataram House became an enchanted forest. The night was torrid gold, and the air was redolent of frankincense, drowned in music. I was Prince Rama. My theatrical hair dropped to my shoulders, my face was painted, my lips were adorned with whiskers, and I walked like a warrior. Mother, as Sita, was youthful – not a trace of the gap in age between us. The night, the forest, the play, the music, and the air deceived the senses as reality withdrew into the shadows. Even Father could not recognise me.

Governor General Vervoort's eyes were transfixed upon Mother as though he had been struck by a spirit. He was conspicuous in his colonial regalia. But the man was scholarly, sincerely loving the Indonesian theatre. Still, his interest in Mataram House was more than just about the art. I wondered whether it was Mother who had provoked his senses, motivated his interest. Father, too, who was sitting next to Grandma, could not take his gaze off Mother. His habitually sedate self was coming alive. I noticed how transfixed he was upon Mother as she transformed into Sita, as if this were the first time he had set eyes on her.

For the first time in my life, the Great Gate was opened. The villagers came like drones, young and old, men and women, wearing their best clothes. Mats were laid. The villagers sat with legs folded, their eyes flirting with the wonder that struck them. Babies dozed in mothers' laps. Even old ladies with bent torsos, and old men with canes, were in attendance. I had never set eyes on such a myriad of faces and forms, such worn-out eyes, laboured hands, clothes that had lost their will to exist. It was an invasion of my senses – a welcome invasion. On the far side of the garden, the villagers feasted on roasted lamb, beef, and chicken; fragrant rice; and sweets. It was like the end of a famine. After the performance, I mingled with the people. They treated me as if I were their real sultan. To me, the air seemed heavy with unfamiliarity. The villagers' voices rang with strange humble crudeness, but it was real, unrehearsed, unhindered by formalities. I tried to acclimatise myself to their scent – a scent I had never known existed. Suddenly everything was so unlike Mataram House. Real people walked the garden, not like the stone gods and deities of Mataram House. Father observed me with a mixture of puzzlement and gratification. Mother coiled into lovingness. Grandma Tutik? Well, her eyes never left me. At one point, she came close to me and whispered, "These are your *subjects*. A royal must keep his distance. Familiarity breeds irreverence. Remember that, Hamzah." I said nothing, allowing her to live out her dreams.

When the evening ended, I hugged and kissed Grandma, noticing a wetness in her eyes, faint but unmistakable. I was happy, not about the performance – which to me was more for Grandma – but about finally having met the people of the valley beyond the Great Gate. "Thank you, Grandma, for the greatest birthday," I said to her, revealing not my inner secret. She searched my eyes as if looking for something. She smiled after a moment and then kissed my forehead. A shadow of sadness in her eyes betrayed her anxiety. She must have found in them what she had feared all those years.

In the days that followed, as if assured of me, Grandma loosened her hold and let me fly short distances away from the nest. In one particular instance, at my behest, she allowed me to visit a young boy of my age in the village whom I had befriended during the celebration. He was the only boy who had come to me with innocent bravado, pulling my hand, asking me to sit by his side with his friends. When he rose and approached me, I noticed a limp in his gait. His left leg was a little shorter than his right. His self-assuredness impressed me. That raw confidence and brazen honesty, his never thinking he was below me in any way, endeared him to me with ease and naturalness as if he were a brother. "I am Buyong. What is your name?" he had asked, grinning to show a set of broad teeth, his chocolaty complexion shimmering in the ochre light. Shorter and stouter than I, he brought out a pair of strong hands to hold mine. He had eyes with an oriental slant, a nose that rose gently, and a handsomeness one sees in Javanese paintings.

"I am Hamzah," I had replied.

Feeling my embroidered garment with his fingers, he said, "You have very beautiful clothes. My mother has promised to make new clothes for me too for the coming Aidilfitri celebration. Their colour is green. It's her favourite colour, but I would have preferred gold like yours." Again he touched the richness of my costume with admiration. "Are you going to have new clothes too?"

"I think so."

"We will go to the mosque together in our new clothes, shall we?" He dropped his eyes to my gleaming, European-made leather shoes. "You have pretty shoes," he said, but he mentioned nothing about having a pair himself. I instinctively gazed at his feet: he had no shoes on, and his feet were very broad at the toes, not having met any footwear in their lifetime.

For my first visit to the village, I was accompanied by Pak Ali, who was too eager to chaperone me, as he had said he wanted to be away from the stifling air of Mataram House. Buyong's house was made of bamboo and palms, with a floor of raw cement. It was tiny by my reckoning of a house. He had three siblings, younger than he, and all of them girls. The youngest had a nose that seemed to be perpetually leaking. Buyong's duty was to take care of his sisters while his parents worked in the pepper fields a kilometre away. He said that he was twelve years old. When I showed him the book I had brought to give to him, he gleaned the pictures with bewildered eyes, caressing every page lovingly. After having savoured all the pictures from cover to cover, he raised the book to his face and smelled its scent as if it were a precious thing. I knew that this was the first time he had ever encountered a book. He had never been to school, he said. "This will be my very precious possession. Thank you." He hugged me and thanked me again. I was taken aback by this profuse gratitude over such a simple gift.

Buyong kept the house spotlessly clean. It was lunchtime, and he insisted on cooking us a meal of rice and vegetables with chicken – yet to be slaughtered. But first we had to get the chicken, he said. He gave me the honour of slaughtering it. I was horrified even to think about it. Pak Ali laughed. Capturing the poor creature took the combined efforts of the three of us. The pesky chicken gave us the runaround, which lasted a good half hour. Once the chicken was finally caught, Pak Ali held it with its neck stretched out. Buyong cut the jugular vein, said "bismillah," and let the blood flow. I couldn't even watch. For a few excruciating moments, the chicken performed an extraordinary ballet, its neck half severed. The body was in spasms as the breaths slowed. The chicken finally fell dead. I promised myself not to be anywhere near animal slaughtering anymore.

It was one of the loveliest meals I have ever had. Buyong was a good cook, or perhaps the scenery, the air, and the homeliness of everything made the food tastier. We ate under the cherry tree, its berries sweetening the air. A couple of birds sang to each other, a stray breeze brushed my face, the sun stole through the breaks in the canopy, and Buyong's world drew me into its heart. I wanted to stay there forever.

When the sun went down, it was time for me to depart. Sadness struck me. I gazed into Buyong's eyes. An enquiring admiration swarmed me when I saw no despair, no envy, no grudge about what he did not have compared to what I had. He was naively contented, perhaps believing that the world was equal and fair for all. I wondered if he knew that the real world was neither equal nor fair, as I myself had just discovered.

"When will you come again?" he asked me. "I'll take you fishing."

"Really?" I exclaimed. My heart raced with excitement.

In the months that followed, my friendship with Buyong grew. In that brief space of time, I encountered more life than I had in the previous thirteen years, or so it seemed to me. Without Grandma Tutik knowing, and keeping the excursion secret between Pak Ali and me, I had gone fishing three times, swam in the river, climbed a rambutan tree, played tops and marbles, and even bathed by the well with Buyong and his siblings, with sarongs tied around our waists.

Three months after that thirteenth birthday celebration, something unexpected happened, and the person who had least expected it was Father. And unbeknown to me, my own mettle was about to be tested.

Grandma called me to her room late one night. We sat at the balcony. The sky was totally clean of smudges, the stars from their heavens were enjoying an uncluttered view of the earth, and a much-welcome coolness swept across the garden after the late afternoon showers. With the cosmos in such a glorious mood, Father would be at his study with his telescope, a God-given opportunity he wouldn't miss. The inhabitants of the kitchen were having their sumptuous dinner and engaging in lively chatter. But Pak Ali was out of sight, out of earshot, and out of Grandma's reach, as there wasn't a whiff of cloves. Grandma commented, "What a wonderful night, fresh and festive, without a trace of smoke to mar it." She patted my hand.

"Your eyes tell me you are in a very happy mood," I said.

"Hamzah, my child, I am going on a pilgrimage to Mecca. You're the first to know. Even your mother has not been told. And your father – well."

"When are you leaving?"

"I am leaving next week."

"When will you be back?"

"In two months." She paused and scoured the stars with her thoughts as though searching for something in the night sky. "What a display of splendour in the heavens on the eve of my departure. A propitious sign from the Holy Land. Don't you agree, Hamzah? I shall leave with a happy heart. I feel it in my bones." She turned her contemplative face back to me without moving her eyes from the stars. "You know, Hamzah, our destiny is written in the stars. Could we change it?" Again she paused. I didn't realise the question was specially meant for me. She turned towards me. "Can we change our destiny, Hamzah?" she repeated.

"I don't know, Grandma. I've never given any thought to my destiny."

"On the other hand, I have, Hamzah. Very serious thought."

"Of your destiny, Grandma?"

"Not mine, yours. Since you were born I have dedicated my entire life to see that your destiny will be as written in the stars. Do you understand what I am getting at?"

"I think so."

"Do you know what is your destiny?"

"I guess not. As I said, I never gave it a thought."

"Your destiny is intertwined with Mataram House. Do you know what that means, Hamzah?"

I shook my head.

She pointed to the sky. "It's in the stars, your destiny. The finest astrologers in Java have confirmed this. Of course, your father has pooh-poohed this. But then again, your father does not believe in anything. Your having royal blood in your veins – that too had been confirmed by an astrologer. Why do you think I built this Mataram House to be a reflection of the old kingdom? It is something for which your father has nothing but disdain – a figment of my fantasy, he had said. He chided me for having gods and icons in Mataram House – a Muslim house. He forgot or perhaps chose to forget that Hinduism and Buddhism preceded the Muslim Mataram Empire. Having images and statues in this house in no way affects my faith as a Muslim. I am performing my haj in Mecca. Doesn't that show I am a good Muslim? Has your father done his pilgrimage?"

Again a long pause.

"Hamzah, I have watched over you since your eyes first opened. I held you in my arms before your mother did, and already I could see in those little eyes the sparkles of nobleness. I watched you grow, and I could see in you the characteristics of a man destined to command over men. As the stars have preordained, yours is a destiny linked inexorably to Mataram House. So, for that to happen, you must not leave Mataram House. I fear that if you do, something grave will happen to you. Your entire destiny will take a different path – an unpredictable path beyond your control. Do you comprehend the gravity of my exhortation?" She held both my hands in her palms and was almost pleading with me, her eyes misting with tears.

"Are you crying, Grandma?"

"Yes, my child. Your father is irresponsible. He has no inkling of the gravity of the prophecy. I fear for you if he were to act against my wishes. So I want you to make a solemn promise to me not to leave Mataram House when I am away."

"Yes, I promise, Grandma."

"That's not enough. Say it in God's name."

I raised my voice and pronounced aloud, "Yes. I swear in God's name not to leave Mataram House."

"Much, much better. I am proud of you. It's getting late and time to say goodnight." She held my face in her palms and kissed me on my forehead.

The following night at dinner, when we were all seated as usual, with Grandma at the head of the table, Father to her right, Mother to her left, and I beside Mother, Grandma tapped the crystalware as a prelude to an announcement, a practice she had acquired from the Dutch governor general. I saw Father give a sly smile and shake his head as if in disdain.

"I am going on the pilgrimage to Mecca to perform the haj," Grandma said, lifting her head in her characteristic peremptory air.

Father pulled himself back against his chair in undisguised shock and swerved his head towards Grandma. In a rare display of fake exaltation, he exclaimed, "Alhamdulillah. God be praised," raising his hands to the ceiling, his palms open in a gesture of gratitude to the Almighty.

Mother rose from her chair, walked towards Grandma, embraced her, and kissed her hand. "That is the most wonderful news, Mother. When are you leaving, and how long will you be away?" she enquired.

Fortunately, neither Father nor Mother noticed my lack of surprise. Mother turned to me and said, "Hamzah, go and give your grandma a hug and kiss her hand. Do you know how glorious it is to make the pilgrimage in our lifetime?" Turning back to Grandma, she exclaimed, "Oh, Mother, how I wish I could come with you."

Tutik tapped her daughter's hand affectionately, "Your time will come, my daughter. It shall come. I shall pray before the Kaaba that you will perform the haj with your husband." Then, lifting her head, she took a swipe at Father. "That is, if you, Norredin, are ready and willing. The pilgrimage is a call from Allah. One will feel it in one's heart when He calls."

Father looked straight at the table and smiled.

"Did you find that amusing, Norredin?"

"No Mother, not at all. I agree with you completely." He whispered to himself, "What would the gods and deities of the house say about this?"

"I heard that, Norredin."

"Sorry, Mother. No offence intended."

"The pilgrimage is not something anyone should take lightly." Addressing Father and Mother, Grandma proclaimed, "Now about the oath—"

All of a sudden, Father swung his head towards Grandma. As a matter of habit, Father rarely looked into Grandma's eyes. If he did, it was a precursor to an altercation. "What about it, Mother?" Father retorted, stopping Grandma in her tracks.

"I must remind you of it."

"Do you have to raise it here, Mother, in the presence of the child? Haven't I kept faith with you all these years?"

"You have, rather grudgingly."

"Does it matter? So long I have kept faith."

"But this is the first time I am going away for a long time and to a far, distant land. I may not return."

"I pray for your long life, Mother, and that you shall return in good health."

"Let's end this night happily, Norredin. In a week's time I shall depart. All I want from you is your word."

"You have it, Mother."

"Good."

All throughout this exchange, Mother sat in silence and I listened with great interest. It was the first time I heard about an oath. *What is it?* I asked myself. There was not a chance in the world I would ask Father or Mother, and neither would I expect them to tell me. But one thing I was sure of: it was about me.

Chapter 4

Far out in the open sea, Semarang Harbour was a blue spectre of moribund light in the oncoming dusk. Junks, sampans, skiffs, and all manner of crafts moved about their business like ants. A running breeze swept the watery expanse of the receding tide. Boisterous seabirds hovered low to make their final flight before the approaching darkness finally descended. I was alone with Captain Samuel O'Keeffe, master of the *Shanghai Star*, waiting for Father to arrive. He was nowhere to be seen. The captain became agitated, as Father was more than two hours late for his scheduled rendezvous with the ship. The last forty-eight hours had been a journey of stealth. We had hired a car and had slithered through villages, avoiding towns, police posts, and people. The old-fashioned horse carriage had been nothing more than a short romance. Ardi had been discharged along with the horses. Father had paid him handsomely, buying his silence. Nothing had been said to Ardi about where we were heading.

Father could no longer hide the fact that he was taking me away from Mataram House. I wasn't totally surprised, as suspicion had already built up in me. He showed me the newspaper. Tutik's influence with Governor General Vervoort was enormous, something that Father had grossly underestimated. Our pictures blazed the local Dutch and Indonesian newspapers. The accompanying text indicated the offer of a reward – a princely sum – to the person who provided reliable information about our whereabouts.

We kept close to routes that no one cared about. With the help of an old friend of Father, a Chinese merchant in the gold trade, we chartered the schooner *Shanghai Star*. This sailing ship of the Old World, a dying mode of sea travel, was the least expected mode of escape. It was Father's clever way of making Vervoort's running dogs lose our scent. And this was an accurate instinct, as the captain was himself a dying breed, unaccounted in the present seafarer world, I happily discovered.

When Father first introduced me to Captain Samuel, the latter came like a storm, startling me. "My name is Samuel O'Keeffe, Irish. Call me Captain Sam, or Sea Dog Sam, but don't ever call me O'Keeffe, you hear? *Keeffe* sounds like *kafir*, and *kafir* in these parts means 'infidel', so I shall resent being called a kafir." His voice sounded as if he were addressing an assembly of people. When I recoiled, he caught my shoulder with such gentle force that I almost toppled over. Then he laughed. "Don't you mind me, my boy. I tend to speak out. Got to, what with the sea and wind, eh, and the pesky crew. I am not too bad, really, when you get to know me." He winked at me. After that I felt at ease.

There I was with Captain Samuel O'Keeffe on the rail, with the wind and the putrefied fumes of pipe tobacco assaulting my face, listening to a lecture on the virtues of sails against steam. Meanwhile, my mind was walking the streets and alleys of Semarang, searching for Father. We had separated company to avoid detection. Father went about to make some plans – what plans, I couldn't guess, as he hadn't revealed them to me. I could only hold on to the idea of a kind of journey he had offered me when we departed from Mataram House, and I had placed my wholehearted faith in what he had said because he was a father I had just found. Now the idea of a journey had become just an idea, no more than that. The captain went on giving me a lesson on sailing ships to lift my spirits, but my spirits were as dim as the dying light – and reluctant.

"You haven't sailed in one these before, have you?" Captain Samuel tapped the polished railing of the ship with his pipe and shifted his eyes from the sea towards me.

I shook my head.

"She's a charm, this grand old lady. Really delightful, you'll see." He sucked his pipe. Stacks of smoke lifted by the breeze blew into my face and made me cough. "You'd better get used to that, my dear fellow, if you're sailing with me, eh. Can't do without it. It's part of me, just like this old lady."

"I don't think I can get used to it, sir," I said bravely.

"Which one? The pipe or the old lady?"

"Both"

"You will, I promise you. The sea will cure you of your aversion. The sea cures anything, even your sorrow. Trust me on that." Captain Samuel let out a merry laugh and then knocked my head with his pipe.

Everything about this captain was red: his skin, his beard, and his long tousled hair, which looked as if it had been burnt by the ocean. Seemingly determined to make it clear to everyone who he was, he wore a seafarer beard and donned a sea cap in addition to smoking the trademark pipe. I noticed something else distinctive about him: he could not stop talking. It was all about the sea, as if nothing else mattered to him. This added to my distress of the moment.

When the fire in O'Keeffe's pipe suddenly died, he knocked the contents over the bulwark, spilling the spent tobacco into the sea, which produced a rancid odour, not unlike leftover garden humus. He went on again. "I must tell you about this ship. You must know of her if you are to sail with her." I saw the pride in his eyes. "The *Shanghai Star*, my dear boy, was built in Plymouth for Lord Winslow, a wealthy aristocrat. Work of art, really. I mean this ship, not Winslow, of course." He chuckled. "He died, this Winslow, poor soul, before the *Shanghai Star* was launched. Bless him. The ship has changed hands many times since then. After more than fifty years at sea, she was bought by Ramsay Tong, a friend of your father, a man of impeccable taste, lover of wines and antiques. Not a sea person, this Ramsy Tong. Pity, really. Bought this schooner as a collector's item. Sailed in it only once, just after he first bought it. Now he just charters it out. Old as she is, I am proud to be her master. 'Grand Old Lady' I call her, yes indeed. And when she goes, I'll go with her."

Captain Sam filled me in on the polyglot crew. There were twelve in all: a Burmese first mate, an Indian boatswain, a Chinese cook, a Malay cabin boy, four Bugis, and four Makassarese seamen. The Malay cabin boy was just his title; he wasn't a boy at all, but a man, I noticed. When I asked the captain what his job was, he said, "Assist the cook in the galley, lay the table, and clean the cabins." The Bugis and Makassarese were experienced sailors who knew every part of the ship, he added. Their duties included setting the sails and trimming them, helming the wheel, and anchoring. "And you know what, Hamzah?" Then he looked at me. "The most dangerous task is to climb up the mast right up to the masthead when a sail or a sheet gets entangled, even when the ship is under way. In the old days a sailor would be sent to the masthead as a form of punishment. Are you afraid of heights, Hamzah?"

"Yes," I replied shyly.

"Not to worry. I will not send you up there." He laughed.

The *Shanghai Star* was anchored two miles out into the sea under the silver sky, out of sight of the pilots, marine patrols, and everyone else. As darkness approached, Semarang was now just an orange glow in the distance.

Father still had not arrived on board as planned. He was now four hours late. The tide had begun to ebb, and the breeze was picking up. Captain Sam paced about the deck. His frown was visible even in the faint light. As the breeze heightened, so did his anxiety. A couple of the crewmen stood by the bulwark, silhouetted against the faint black gleam of the harbour, waiting for their orders. My heart was slowly sinking. To my surprise, Captain Sam's arm was around my shoulder, lending me the emotional support I much needed.

"What has happened to Father, Captain Sam?" I asked nervously.

"We'll wait a while longer," he said in an unexpectedly low tone.

The tide had receded far out, so the *Shanghai Star* had to be re-anchored farther out in the open sea. I could hardly see Semarang Harbour now. At times it disappeared behind a passing steamer. Captain Sam paced about restlessly on the quarterdeck, his eyes peering into the cheerless void as he hoped that a little boat would emerge from the blackness. His hope became mine and twice over. Soon enough, I learned that he actually knew more than he wanted to reveal to me. He had been looking at the time more frequently, and all of a sudden he said, "It's midnight. It's time."

"What is it, Captain Sam?" I was afraid, really afraid, to know what was on his mind.

"Come, my boy. We need to talk. Come into my cabin."

Captain Sam's cabin was just below the quarterdeck. The stateroom was fairly spacious, with twin beds, an en suite toilet and cupboards, a large chart table, a dining set for ten, bookshelves, and portholes the size of large balls. It was well appointed, with polished teak woodwork and furniture giving it the Old World charm of the sea.

Befitting the sombre situation, Captain Sam became a totally different person. A solemness took over his earlier cheeriness.

"Sit down, son," he said to me in a fatherly tone, pulling up a chair for me. His expression was serious and caring. "Your father gave me precise instructions for what steps should be taken in the event that he was caught or detained and unable to join us on the boat. I am to convey this to you. I am to sail out and head for Penang, and there in George Town I am to place you in the care of your paternal aunt, Maimunah, who lives in Kelawei Road. She has been informed and is expecting you. But I am to ask for your consent. Should you decide otherwise, I am to return you to Mataram House. I know not the background to all this, but your father and I, we go a long way back to the gold-trading days. I knew your father's father, Said Alhabshee, too. So there you are, young man, a big decision for someone so young." He looked straight into my eyes enquiringly and gave a faint smile.

I hardly knew him – we met only a few hours ago – and yet he drew me into his complete confidence by that little speech, as though some power had asked me to trust him without hesitation. I said, "Yes."

The captain was stunned, obviously not expecting me to answer yes.

"Yes what?" he exclaimed.

"Yes, I shall go with you."

"That's it?"

"Yes. I will go with you."

He was dumbfounded.

"I didn't expect that at all. Don't you want to go home with all this uncertainty? I am a total stranger after all."

"I don't know. I had made up my mind even before you spoke to me. I think this is what my father would want me to do."

"I am a bit baffled here. Tell me, don't you love your mother and your grandmother? Aren't you afraid of leaving home and not knowing what's in store for you?"

"Sure I do, very much so, but I believe in my father. I think he is doing this for me."

For a few seconds, he stared at me, and then he said, "Right, then I shall question you no more."

"Captain, what has happened to Father?"

"My best guess is the police must have got him. There's no other explanation for his non-appearance. He's a smart man, your father, so he could've gotten away if he found an opportunity to do so. I am sorry to be plain and honest." He put his broad hands on my shoulders.

"Thank you, Captain."

"You're one brave lad, I must say. We're going to get along just fine. Come along, back on deck. We've to set sail. Everyone is on deck. I'll make a sailor of you in no time at all. What do you say, eh?"

Crowned by the dark luminous sky, I thought of Father, contemplating the rare moments when he invited me to his study, showing me the sky and its celestial patterns, the incredible vastness, and the infinity that so enthralled him. How lonely were the stars in that infinite space, each assigned to its own place, all of them seemingly near to the others but separated by millions of miles. "What a lonely existence," he had said. Those words came back to me. I believed that the stars were reflecting Father's own feelings just then.

A glimpse of the captain in the metallic light reminded me of Father. Maybe I was dreaming, or perhaps my mind was playing tricks on me in my worst moments. Father was a Sumatran, yet he didn't look like one, except for his whitened-coffee skin and the black swirls of his hair. His eyes, nose, and facial features were well defined and distinct, courtesy of his father's Arab origins. With a full beard, he could pass as O'Keeffe in a glimpse, although Father was a little shorter than Captain Sam. Father's good looks were the only reason Mother married him. My family often said that I inherited much of Father's features, although I had the benefit of Mother's fair complexion.

We weighed anchor. The crew went about setting the sails up. As the sails caught the wind, the *Shanghai Star* cut through the water on a north-westerly course. Sam brought me to the steering station, standing me immediately behind it. If it had been happier times I would have jumped to the challenge. But it was not the best of times. Helming a sailing vessel, especially one like this schooner, needed deep concentration. I just didn't have it. With my wandering mind, the boat's heading began to wander too. The captain's idea for having me steer was to take my mind off Father, but it wasn't working. I was vexed, and my thoughts were irrepressible. It was the not knowing what had actually happened to Father that afflicted me, turning my thoughts into wild bats in a cave. The *Shanghai Star* moved through the water majestically, its long bow rolling gently in a see-saw pattern. Pride shone in the captain's face as he held the Grand Old Lady steady on her course.

"If the wind stays like this, she will make good time, clocking twelve knots – and in five days or less we'll be in Singapore," he said.

The wind in my face, and the Old Lady majestically punching through the water, evoked in me a feeling I had never experienced before. My troubles disappeared momentarily. "It's really exhilarating, Captain Sam. I love it," I said.

"What did I tell you, eh! Now let's learn some basics. She's a hundred and fifty feet from bowsprit to stern, and she is a schooner, with a main mast and two smaller ones – fore and aft. You'll get to know her well before we reach our destination. But first let's agree on the matter of protocol."

I turned my head, and replied nervously, "Yes, sir."

He laughed so loud that a crew member swung his head towards us in curiosity. "Nothing of the sort, my boy. From this moment on, you are to call me Sam, not Captain Sam or Sea Dog or any other name. Just plain Sam. Agreed?"

"Yes, Cap – I mean Sam."

"Jolly good, my boy"

My cabin, next to Sam's on the starboard side, was an exact replica of his but smaller. I wasn't seasick, so I went to sleep as soon as I put my head on the pillow. So slumberous was the rocking of the boat, I had to be wakened the next morning by the cabin boy when the sun was already up.

On the afternoon of the fourth day, the wind died and the *Shanghai Star* drifted aimlessly under a blazing sun, the clouds high and wispy – a condition hated by sailors. A violent storm has its element of challenge and surprise, but being holed up in a dead wind for long periods is sheer torture, Sam told me. It was an ironic statement given what was to come. We drifted and waited. The crew looked at the clouds for winds and wet their fingers and held them up, hoping to detect a zephyr. Time became an eternity. Acute boredom set in.

A few of the crewmen asked the captain's permission to jump into the water for a swim.

Nightfall finally came, giving respite from the heat. We had been with a dead wind for over fifteen hours.

Close to midnight, the sails began to flap and slowly fill. All of sudden the *Shanghai Star* picked up speed, and a violent gust crashed into the sails, yawing the boat precariously. The wind freshened, causing the sea to build up into bigger and bigger waves. In no time, the waves swelled into little mountains. The captain looked at the navigational instruments and told me that the barometer was plunging. I had no idea what that signified. One thing I was sure of, though: it wasn't a good sign, judging by the frown on Sam's face. Mark, the Burmese first mate, ordered all hands on deck, including the Chinese cook. As the *Shanghai Star* sliced violently through the sea, the waves responded with equal force, pouring mountains of white water further and further midship.

"A nasty gale coming," the captain warned me. Suddenly he cried out to the boatswain, saying, "Reduce sails." But even after the crew had done as ordered, the *Shanghai Star* continued to plough through the deepening valleys and mountains. Ribbons of lightning flashes came nearer and nearer with greater frequency.

Worried that the confused sea might frighten me, the captain ordered me to get below deck. I obeyed. The moment my feet got below, the dinner I had just eaten spilled out from my guts, spraying the cabin floor. The boatswain, who also acted as ship doctor, pulled me back on deck. Now that the contents of my stomach had been expelled, I felt much better (I had been feeling quite sick). We were sailing fast into breaking waves. The *Shanghai Star* rolled like a roller coaster as the waves pounded. Then suddenly a giant black wall of water came smacking into us. A reefed jib came undone. One of the Makassarese seamen on the foredeck scrambled forward to secure the line, which was snaking furiously as if possessed by the Devil. The captain cried out to the seaman to let the sail be, but the roar of the wind drowned his voice, making his words incomprehensible. The bedevilled line caught the seaman by the ankle and carried his body over the bulwark, straight into the jaw of the raging sea. The other crew members rushed to the railing, but they could find no sign of him. The dark, frothing, screaming sea had swallowed him whole, leaving no trace of him behind. I watched in horror. I asked the captain why we were not stopping the boat.

He looked at me. "Stop this boat? How the hell do we do that? I am afraid he's gone, my boy." His voice rang in the wind indelicately. I was aghast. Sensing how upset I was, he turned to me and said, "To go about under these conditions is bloody mad. I'd be risking the lives of every member of the crew, including you, not to mention this old lady. In any case, there isn't a hope in the world we can find him. Mishaps like this are the law of the sea, my boy."

I thought he was callous and uncaring. I had never seen death in any form. When I did see a death, it had to be a violent one, leaving a terrible stain in my mind for a long time to come. I was quite angry with the captain.

I found out later that the drowned sailor was Rustam from Makassar. The death of a mate had a deleterious effect on the morale of the other crew members, making the already perverse night more insufferable. The other three sailors from Makassar on the foredeck abandoned their stations and sat by the lifeboat in protest. The effect was contagious. Others joined in. The captain would soon have a mutiny on his hands, and he knew it. He raised his six-foot frame upright and cried into the wind that he would throw everyone overboard if they did not return to their stations. The effect was electric. The crewmen quietly returned to their posts. Seeing that I, too, had been affected by his outburst, the captain said, "Life is sometime lost. It's the law of the sea. Every seaman knows that. They are just being bloody emotional. I am not heartless. I'll see to it that Rustam's family is taken care—" Just then something in the darkness caught his eyes. "What the hell is that?" he exclaimed.

A flash of lighting burnt a ghostlike image onto the near horizon.

"I hope that is not what I think it is," he said.

He passed the helm to Mark, the first mate, and then went below deck. I went down with him. He spread the chart on the table and began moving the glass and compass, applying the instruments to confirm our position. "Gasper Straits! Damn it! We've been blown off course," he said to himself, ignoring my presence.

"What does that mean, Sam?"

"What?" He looked at me, but his mind was not with me.

"What does Gasper Straits mean?"

"We've been pushed away from our set course by the wind and the current. Bad, really bad. It's shoals and rocks – poorly charted." I was silent, not comprehending the significance of it all. "That dark object ahead on our starboard bow? It shouldn't be there at all. What the bloody hell is it doing there! That's a rocky outcrop. I don't like it a bit. Come along."

We rushed up onto deck. The captain took over from Mark at the helm. "The freaking storm!" he cursed. "You'd better get the lead line and start swinging," he told Mark. "We're entering shallow uncharted waters." Turning to me, he said, "You'd better stay close to me, my lad."

The sky threw another flash, and again the ghostlike image appeared.

Slamad swung the heavy lead attached to a line into the depth of the sea. "Thirty feet," he cried out in Malay.

After a pause of several minutes, he swung it again. "Twenty-seven feet," he cried out.

The black image seemed to pull the *Shanghai Star* towards it. The bow rose and fell as the sea slammed, the wind howled, and mountains of white water boiled into gigantic masses of froth. My fears grew ever so silently. I stayed close to the captain as he had ordered. Despite his strong physique, he seemed to struggle against the helm. The Grand Old Lady, overwhelmed by the elements, seemed unable to obey her master.

"Twenty-feet," Slamad called out.

He paused before making another cast of the lead, dropping it into the ocean. "Eighteen feet."

I knew one thing – the sea was getting shallower. The mystifying black ghost now on our beam was growing larger by the second. The captain commanded me to climb onto one of the lifeboats lashed midship, instructing me that whatever happened, I should hang tightly onto that craft.

Another cast of the lead. "Fifteen feet," Slamad howled.

At that very moment, an uncanny voice whispered behind my ear: "Didn't I warn you, my child?"

I instinctively turned my head. "Grandma?" I cried. There wasn't anyone there.

A few seconds later, a demonic crunching sound bellowed through the underbelly of the boat. The *Shanghai Star* lifted herself up like a giant whale into the blackness and then came crashing down. In the next unbelievable moment, the forward section of the ship began to split apart. Slowly and frighteningly, it began falling away to be swallowed by the raging sea, taking with it a number of crewmen. Foam sprouted from everywhere. I heard cries mingling with the sound of wind and sea, and then the loud cracking groans of the ship in the throes of death. The next moment, there was no longer one *Shanghai Star*, but two. I held tightly to the lifeboat, and all of a sudden I found the captain close by me. With a machete, he slammed the ropes that shackled the longboat to the cradle, setting it free. I saw two other men jumping onto the longboat. I could not see their faces in the black rain and white water. I watched with horror as the *Shanghai Star* slowly diminished around me and then disappeared. Later, I could not remember my feelings. Fear is like pain: additional pain makes no difference anymore. Death no longer existed, as I had thought I was already dead. After all, the pawang at Father's sickbed had said to me, "You are going on a long journey, never to return."

I was jolted when a head popped out from the tarpaulin. It was Ah Fook's. I took a count of everyone: Mat, the cabin boy; Ah Fook, the Chinese cook; and Slamad and Irwan, the two remaining Bugis. At first I could not figure out how Ah Fook had gotten into the boat, as I hadn't seen him on deck before that. Then I recalled: when I boarded the longboat, there was already someone in it. It was Ah Fook, hiding under the tarpaulin. There was no sign of the other lifeboat or the remaining crew.

The *Shanghai Star* had sunk within minutes of our lifeboat's being afloat. We watched with dour faces as the stern sank slowly into its watery grave. Sam looked on, his expression one I cannot describe in words. Suffice it to say that his spirit died with the *Shanghai Star*, although his body had not, as he had promised. He had broken his own honour as a ship captain by electing to be with me.

In the aftermath of the horror, our lifeboat floated in silence over a glassy sea. We, the survivors, were at the end of our exhaustion and had only the funereal blanket of the night to comfort us.

BANKA ISLAND, EAST SUMATRA 1941

Chapter 5

The little house on the beach was devoid of dreams, unlike Mataram House. It was built only of palms, bamboo, planks, and earth, just like Buyong's house. There was no bedroom and no dining area, only plain living space, which was raised. The kitchen on the lower ground was a platform of planks with walls of plaited bamboo. The bathhouse was a well, also with bamboo walls. The house was not very different from the other rustic, poor abodes in Tobali, but it was neater and more charming, courtesy of the garden of luxuriant red and white bougainvillea, which the captain had passionately planted and tended, surrounded by a picket fence. A small raised verandah overlooking the ocean became the captain's coveted space – a place of solace for him, with the sea as a reminder of hope. I shared that hope with him. Together we would sit at sunset, staring at the horizon to forget the recent past that had gone on without us and to search for a future that couldn't be found. Tobali, a village at the southern tip of the island of Banka in East Sumatra, had become our home. At high tide and on a clear day, we could see the faint shadow of the craggy atoll that had smashed the *Shanghai Star*, bringing her to her tragic end. It was that grey ghostlike apparition on the ship's starboard bow that beckoned the *Shanghai Star* moments before she was sent to a watery grave. The harbinger of death, I called it. I refused to know its name, this atoll. Every time it came into my view, I felt nothing about it but an intense sickness, thinking of *Shanghai Star*'s last gasping moments.

It was Tok Rejab, the elderly headman of the village, who found us when our lifeboat finally beached on the shores of Tobali after being at sea for twelve days. The strong currents had taken us into the open sea. We had drifted aimlessly with one paddle, without food and with only rain for water. One paddle could hardly move the boat against the strong current, which was pushing our boat away from the coast. Slamad, the strongest among us, was sturdy and young, but he too finally succumbed to fatigue. Mat, the cabin boy, had a broken arm after a piece of the masthead crashed on him. Ah Fook was a good cook, but he was also a coward – and no sailor at all. The other Bugis, Irwan, was a good sailor but had no strength. The open boat and fierce sun had made Ah Fook delirious, leading him to hang his head over the stern. The captain had to pull him away before he could drink the seawater. It was left to the rest of us to paddle, taking turns.

One night, from extreme fatigue, Slamad lost his grip on that single paddle, causing it to drop in the ocean. Our lifeboat then floated like a dead log. Mat was all the time praying, burying his head in his knees and rocking. The Bugis held onto him, not for safety but because he hoped to benefit from his prayers.

One early morning, as if by a miracle, the current took us back to shore. We beached on a bay. Mat raised his hands to the sky, thanking Allah for answering his prayers. The captain said that the spring tide, which occurred once every fortnight, must have brought us to shore.

We settled ourselves in Tobali and made the best of our temporary home. We planted our own vegetables and fruits on the bit of land next to our little house. Sam was already an adept fisherman. He joined the local fleet, and they loved him. He could have easily gotten a job at any of the European tin mines, but he chose not to be obligated to any of them as an underling, preferring to be with the people of Tobali out of gratitude for their taking us into their fold after saving us. In less than a year, Sam had taught me a lot of things: how to repair boat engines, make things of wood, become a farmer, cast a fishing net, and above all, be self-reliant. In terms of survival and coping with hardships, I learned more in these long and trying months than I had in all my years at Mataram House.

Despite all the deprivations, I was beginning to be fond of Tobali and the people. Happiness seemed to come my way as I learned to embrace the same contentment of my old friend Buyong whom I had so envied in his little house down in the valley below Mataram House.

Nothing could go wrong now, I thought, until one night when Tok Rejab came to pay us a visit. It wasn't an ordinary visit. This incredibly kindly and generous-of-heart man had been more than just our saviour; he had become a friend. Diminutive in physique but a giant in moral stature and influence, Tok Rejab was the chief of Tobali. His standing extended from Pangkal Pinang, the capital of Bangka on the east coast of the island, to Muntok, the port at the north-western tip. He was a man in his fifties with a long, narrow face, a crown of wispy silver hair, and a greying handlebar moustache to match, making him look older than his age. He seemed pretty comfortable with this, as it gave him a certain reverential air. To match his amiable disposition, Tok Rejab was endowed with a soft voice, which the uninitiated often mistook for a sign weakness. That was far from the truth. Tok Rejab could be incredibly resolute when it mattered.

"Captain Sam! Captain Sam!" he called out one evening from the porch of our little house. Rarely did we have visitors after sundown, as we were quite isolated from the rest of the villagers and the path was dark and lonely.

I rushed to the verandah and saw Tok Rejab in a state of breathlessness.

"I need to speak to Captain Sam, urgently." He appeared tense and nervous.

Sam appeared, and we all sat on the verandah. The sea breeze had died down, making the air muggy. Tok Rejab, sweating from the long strenuous walk from his house, wiped himself with the long cotton scarf he had wrapped around his head. He was never without that scarf.

"Captain Sam, I have just received news that the Japanese forces have landed in Java and are about to capture Batavia. I fear you are in grave danger. I can protect Hamzah, but you, you are a white man. The Japanese will surely come after you. If there is anything I can do to help, I will." Tok Rejab looked straight at Sam with genuine concern.

"Tok Rejab, I knew about this for some time. It is not a surprise, this news you brought, but I didn't expect it to be so soon. Thank you for your concern, but don't put yourself in danger on my account. You have done enough for me and for Hamzah. I can't expect more of you. Thank you for warning me," Sam said in Malay. The deliberateness of his tone betrayed his emotion. "One thing, if I may ask of you. Should anything happen to me, would you take care of Hamzah and send him to his aunty in Malaya?"

"That is without question, Captain Sam. He will stay with me until I can arrange a passage for him to Malaya. But I doubt that such a thing will be possible. You see, Malaya has been overrun too," Tok Rejab replied without hesitation. "As for you, Captain, what are you going to do? Please tell me how I can help. I heard that the Dutch, English, and French tin miners are already rushing to evacuate their wives and children. If you wish to return to your homeland, this is the time."

"Don't you worry about me, Tok. I can take care of myself. I have faced calamities before."

"May Allah protect you both."

Tok Rejab took his leave, but not before reciting a little prayer for us.

Sam had already known about the looming war in Europe, of Churchill's declaration of war on Nazi Germany, and of the Japanese advancement in South East Asia after their attack on Pearl Harbor. It had been the subject of conversation among the European community in Banka. The captain had felt quite ill at ease about these events. He took me into his confidence, acquainting me with the looming war, knowing that it would have repercussions for me. He said to me that since I had come this far with him, our fate was now intertwined.

Sam appeared visibly distraught after Tok Rejab left.

"Are you worried, Sam?" I asked.

"Worried for myself? No, if that's what you mean. I am concerned about you, my boy. I am not afraid to be captured and made a prisoner of war. But what's going to happen to you? I had a task. I had been entrusted by your father to deliver you to your aunty Maimunah in Penang, but I botched it up by sinking the very ship that carried us. And now I have put you on this strange island halfway to your destination. It might just as well be the North Pole, because we are stuck. I will likely be captured by the Japs. What will become of you? I just can't willy-nilly dump my responsibility onto Tok Rejab, no matter how forthcoming and sincere he is." He dropped his eyes to the floor, a cloud of despair shadowing his face.

"Sam." He didn't hear me. "Sam," I repeated.

"What?"

"Return to England."

"What did you say?"

"If you return to England, I shall follow you. That is, if you would take me with you."

"Do you know what you are saying, Hamzah?"

"Yes, Sam, and I have thought about it since we arrived here."

Bafflement clouded the captain's face. "What about your family? Your father, mother, and your grandma? What will they say, Hamzah? What spurred you to make this silly decision? There's a war going on, my boy. Don't you forget that."

"I don't really know, Sam. Within a very short time, my life has changed so dramatically that it sort of changed me too. For the first time since I was born, I seem to have found myself, who I really am – not what others say I am. You are the first person who has not told me what my life should be. Instead, you allow me to decide that myself."

Sam broke into an approving smile. "You seem quite sure of yourself, my boy. I should stop calling you that. From today, it's 'young man'. Good Lord, you really have become a man." He bent his head and scrutinised me as if in disbelief. "Am I hearing you correctly? Don't mistake me. I just want to be sure."

"I am serious, Sam. I'm not a child anymore. After what has happened to me recently, I think I can now stand on my own two feet without the aid of others."

"Righto, my young friend, it's to merry England then! Not so merry lately though, with the war coming and whatnot, eh? All hands on deck, yes? First heading, the British consul general in Pangkal Pinang." Sam gave me a hearty slap on my back.

Chapter 6

S am and I went to the port of Muntok to meet with the Dutch district administrator to get some official news about the evacuation plan. Muntok is the harbour serving the Sumatran mainland to the east, the Riau Archipelago and Singapore to the north, and Java to the south. The Dutch administrator said to Sam that a ship was due to arrive from Singapore the following week.

A feeling of nervousness and fear was already spreading across Banka among the Europeans and Chinese, just as Tok Rejab had predicted. Japanese forces were advancing towards Banka and its sister island, Biletung, where the tin mining industry of the Dutch East Indies was concentrated. On Monday morning when we arrived in Muntok, there was already a big crowd of Europeans, mostly women and children. During the registration, we had to deal with a weirdly blond young Dutch officer named Vernon who was incredibly bumptious and haughty. He was the colonial type, presumably upset that his beloved colonial enclave was being overrun. He sat at his desk without looking up while rows of people waited to see him. When addressing each one, he did not lift his head once. When it came time for our turn, he said with superior air, "Mr Samuel O'Keeffe." Keeping his eyes on our documents, he said, "There are hundreds of would-be evacuees here, and the number is rising with arrivals from Palembang and Riau. It all depends on getting space on the SS *Empire*. I have orders to put on my list children first, then women, and men last." He raised his head only to speak the final three words: "and Europeans only."

"This is my son; I have to take him with me," Sam pleaded.

"But he doesn't look European to me."

"That was an uncalled-for remark, young man. He is my son. Can't you see the documents?" the captain shouted, banging the table. "Say that again and you'll never get back to Holland yourself."

"There's no point losing your temper, Mr O'Keeffe. It will get you nowhere. There's a war here, sir, I must remind you." Vernon retracted his head when the captain lowered his six-foot frame close enough to bite his head off.

"Say that again?" the captain bellowed.

Suddenly, Vernon's already pallid face turned whiter. His voice changed to a low squeak.

"I tell you what, Mr O'Keeffe, let's wait till the ship arrives. How big the SS *Empire* is, I have no idea. If she could fit everybody here," he said, panning his eyes over the myriad of faces around him, "well and good. Otherwise, we just pray to God." He gave a sardonic smile.

"Damn it, can't they handle an evacuation?" the captain mumbled. "Come, let's not lose our spirit," he said to me. "We'll wait."

We decided to stay in Muntok to wait. The flood of evacuees had taken all the hotels and lodgings available in the busy port town. We found shelter under a tree by the bank of the muddy shore, in a spot where a broken wooden junk had made its resting place. We cleaned out the boat and made it a relatively comfortable abode under the shade. The port town, used to the likes of Chinese, Bugis, Sumatrans, Malays, Javanese, and an assortment of sailors, merchants, and traders, was now swarmed with uppity white men and white women in hats, and children in frocks and pantaloons. Grand automobiles cut across the paths made by buggies and man-drawn carts, and took away places and space meant for crates, cargo, sacks, and goods. The still-fresh perfumed air brought by the ladies fought for dominance against the fetid odour of the harbour.

Two days and a night had passed. Elegant ladies and gentlemen had been seen urinating under trees, their pride soaked up by the searing heat and dwindling hope. The perfume had died; hats and hair wilted like flowers that have had their day; and children cried, their once hopeful faces now pulled down to the ground. I saw the young Dutch officer walking past us. His haughtiness had melted. He kept his eyes towards the ground, looking for his lost pride.

On the morning after that, the bow of the SS *Empire* was visible in the distance. People with faces full of hope strained their necks to catch a glimpse. The ship appeared to be laden with a black patch of unusually animated moving shadows. As the ship came closer, the images became more visible. Then, gradually, the white faces of hope turned whiter. The SS *Empire* was packed with people like sardines. People were on the bow, at the stern, and filling the deck so it appeared black. The eyes of those waiting melted; their hearts stopped beating. Despondency rose and hung in the air, ready to spread over its victims like a plague.

My spirit was crushed. Sam's despair was written on his face. There were crying faces, sombre faces, blank faces, and then nothing. I heard a child ask, "Mommy, are we going home?" The mother just broke down and wept.

"Let's go home, Hamzah," Sam said to me, his voice sombre. He kept his head down, as he was devoid of his usual effervescence.

* * *

The villagers of Tobali met at the mosque soon after they had heard what happened in Muntok. The captain's predicament had moved them. Also, they feared what would happen to him when the Japanese arrived.

Captain Sam and I settled into that little house on the beach with the nipa roof, built by the cooperative efforts of the villagers – someone donating planks, others bamboo, another utensils, and so on, all of them chipping in with their hearts. Thanks to their combined efforts, the little palace, as I called it, now became our home. In return, the captain applied his skills to build boats for the villagers, a skill he had acquired by being a master mariner for so long that he could not remember, he had told me. The villagers were as beholden to him as he was to them.

Gradually Sam and I developed the habit of sitting on the small verandah when the light of day began to fade into the horizon. In the flocculent light of sunset and amid the receding tide, the land breeze set in, the spices from the village scented the air, and Sam's eyes misted as he gazed far into the sea, saying nothing. I surmised that he must have been thinking of the *Shanghai Star* weighing anchor, putting full sails, catching the tide and wind, and heading into the ocean to travel on to England. I wished I could share his thoughts as I sat there beside him on the steps thinking about my own world.

When he broke the silence, he talked of our anxieties, the coming war, and the hardships that we would surely face. We talked of the SS *Empire*, which we heard had been attacked by Japanese torpedo planes just as she entered the Indian Ocean. The fate of the passengers was not known – how unlucky they were, and how lucky we were.

Lucky? Not necessarily so for Sam. Europeans were being rounded up, humiliated, and driven into makeshift camps. These were the lucky ones. The not so lucky were executed. The fate of the Chinese was not far from that of the Europeans. Tin mines were scotched and the equipment destroyed as the Dutch left. Some clever Chinese people buried their money and jewellery in the ground, hoping to retrieve it one day; the not so lucky had their shops looted, their food and items of value confiscated, their daughters raped. Like marauding thieves, the invading Japanese troops stole fruits, coconuts, and rice from the villagers, destroyed their simple things, and molested their women. Somehow their eyes and noses had missed Tobali, but not for very long. We already could smell their hot breath and hear the thumping of their boots.

Sam's concern was not for himself but for me. He repeatedly asked me what would happen to me in the event of his being taken away. He appeared to ask himself this question many times. Just by looking at his eyes, I could hear those questions. One night he refused to eat and didn't sleep. I had a nightmare. It was real, actually – my fears making images in the darkness.

One evening after the *Ishak*, the last prayer of the night at the mosque, the congregation marched across the palm-fringed beach towards our house. We seldom had visitors in the night. As usual, we were alone in the ghostly serenity, the lashing waves and the whistling wind keeping us company. A voice was heard above the coppery glow of torches. "Assalamualaikum." It was Tok Rejab.

"Wa'alaikumusalam," I replied.

He was accompanied by a group of village elders, many of whom I had met during Friday prayers. I noticed a sharp strain in Sam's face. He must have been thinking what I was thinking: the villagers' concern about the presence of a white man in the village had come to the fore.

We felt at ease upon seeing Tok Rejab's smile. Lebai Amir, the fair-complexioned portly imam of the mosque who wore a goatee, was also smiling. Amir was an impressive yet humble Arabic scholar who habitually donned a white robe and a chequered turban, the marks of his calling. The other three villagers in the group were members of the village committee, prominent persons in the village. There was no telltale anxiety in their faces. That brought us added relief. But their purpose seemed urgent. Our little house could not accommodate more than a few people, so we had to squeeze ourselves onto the floor of the verandah, spilling into the inner house. The captain was asked to sit facing Tok Rejab and Lebai Amir, which made him a tad nervous, not knowing what was to come. I sat behind Sam.

After the customary greetings and pleasantries, Tok Rejab opened his speech with the usual Malay formality that accompanies an occasion of import. "We came to express our grave concern for your safety and that of Hamzah, and we are unanimous in our decision to take appropriate steps to do all that is necessary to protect both of you." He turned his head around towards the assemblage. "Isn't that so, gentlemen?"

"That is correct," the group affirmed in one voice.

Sam and I sighed with relief.

"We have devised a foolproof plan. It will not fail, God willing. It is the brainchild of our learned Lebai Amir. And we hope you will agree to it, for your own sake. Captain Sam, you have become a member of our community and have helped us in many ways, not the least of which is the upgrading of our mosque. This is our way of expressing our gratitude. We would like to take things one step further and embrace you into our community. We would like to invite you to embrace our religion as a way of saving you from the Japanese."

Sam was jolted from his seat as if a bolt of lightning had struck him.

"Don't be alarmed, Captain Sam. We are not actually asking you to convert, although it is our hope that the glorious day will come when you would truly believe in the greatness of our religion. We want you to look like a Muslim. Your skin colour, your nose, your eyes, your height, and that redness in your hair and beard are not unlike that of an Arab. Tobali is a Muslim community, and to have an Arab preacher in our midst is entirely believable. With the right attire, with your beard trimmed in the Arab fashion, and with your hair cropped short, you will certainly look like an Arab preacher. We think it will work. The Japanese so far have not harmed Muslims and have stayed clear of Malay villages and mosques."

The captain was speechless. "What if I were discovered? All of you would be considered collaborators and the entire village would be severely punished."

"Captain Sam, before we came to our decision, we prayed for guidance from Allah. He has given us His answer," Lebai Amir said. He lifted his head to the crowd. "Isn't that so, gentlemen?"

"Yes, yes, indeed that is so," they exclaimed in unison.

"Captain Sam, you and Hamzah have become one of us now. Since you arrived on our shores, you have taught us how to repair and build our boats, fish in deeper waters, and increase our catch. Hamzah has beautified our mosque by painting it and planting trees and flowers. No Japanese soldier is going to harm you or Hamzah. Not without the will of Allah. We entrust our lives to the will of Allah – no harm shall come to you or Hamzah or anyone else without His will," Lebai Amir said.

"Not without the will of Allah," the group of villagers all echoed.

"And you are one of us now," someone said.

"Yes, yes!" they echoed.

"What do I have to do?" the captain asked.

Tok Rejab handed Sam a long white cotton robe, a linen turban, a necklace of prayer beads, a prayer mat, and a Koran. Then Lebai Amir took Sam's hand in his and held it firmly. In a clear voice, he pronounced, "Please recite after me: There is no God but Allah, and Mohammed is His messenger"

Sam was calm. He observed the solemnity that the simple event required. In a low tone, the captain repeated the words in good Malay. I was astonished at the clarity of his pronouncement. I even thought he really meant every word he pronounced.

"You are now, in principle, a Muslim. The rest is up to you. Our religion is simple; it is in the heart and in the intention. Allah knows all," Lebai Amir said, smiling broadly.

The crowd resoundingly shouted, "Alhamdullilah" – God be praised.

In the time that I had known the captain, I had never seen him to be godly. Never had I seen the cross or the Bible with him or heard him mention Jesus, not even in the face of calamity. I had even thought of him to be atheistic or agnostic. I did not think he knew anything about Islam – or any other religion, for that matter, outside his own. But when he recited the Article of Faith before Tok Rejab, his solemnity perplexed me. What went on in his heart, I didn't really know.

"Your name from now on is Sheikh Omar," Tok Rejab said.

The captain moved himself back, obviously taken by surprise. His mouth twitched into a smile. There was a roar of laughter. I joined in. Tok Rejab and Lebai Amir embraced Sam, and then everyone else followed suit.

"Sheikh Omar! Sounds good. I like it," Sam said.

Chapter 7

With so much having happened to me in such a short time, the idea that had been put to me by the good doctor Ottovenger, that I should start a diary, resurfaced. I hadn't given it any more thought after wondering what there was to write about except the weirdness of my childhood. *And what is a diary for anyway?* I had thought. That I couldn't answer. Now, however, the idea of starting a diary became more meaningful. So I started a journal and religiously entered my thoughts, the daily happenings, and every detail of my childhood as memory served me. I began to believe that my present was connected to my past in a very strange way.

I kept the journal a secret from Sam. As the days passed, writing in it became a labour of love, and a duty to no one but me. My diary became my companion in my solace and a listening post for my troubles, something to which I could express myself freely without restraint, or fear of what lay inside me. Sometimes I cried while writing, but there were times when I laughed. By and by, I felt that the past was gradually receding from me like a ship vanishing in a fog, and all the more I kept faith with my journal. I didn't want the present and the future to vanish too.

I was now past my sixteenth birthday, but I might as well have been forty, considering that others would have taken that number of years to live my experience. I had already turned old in mind, thanks to calamity and pain. My birthdays went by like any other day. Not even Sam knew about them, since I had never told him when I was born. I no longer felt the need for celebrations of any kind.

Although my past had become only a feature in my journal, this did not mean that memories did not haunt me. I had flashes sometimes of questions to myself. What would Grandma and Mother think if they were to see me now? Would they recognise me? When I stared at myself in the mirror, it was not a youth of sixteen that I saw. My hair had turned brown. My skin had been burned by the sun. Mother's whiteness, which I inherited, had all gone. A frown easily appeared in my expression. Only the sharpness of Father's features remained. I was taller than I had been when I left Mataram House, but I was thinner. The flightiness of youth had given way to the demands of survival.

Time flew. It was already 1943. More than a year had passed since the Japanese landed. The Japanese administration was centred in Pangkal Pinang, and so were the military police, the dreaded Kempetai. All the European and Chinese tin mines had been taken over by the Japanese civil administration. Tobali, whose population was entirely made up of Malays, was being left alone. Thank God for that. A lot of the Chinese mines were taken over by the Japanese when their owners had fled to the jungles. Those who had remained prayed that their new masters would not be pitiless.

The Malays in Banka showed only one side of their faces, like the puppets in the shadow plays they so loved, where real feelings are hidden behind the screen and only voices are heard, so they were spared the brutality of the Japanese. Once in a while the Kempetai felt that they must make their presence felt, as if their inhumanity needed to be constantly fed. This year, the occasion for that came to Tobali in March.

It was a moonless night. The fish were abundant, and Sam was planning to go to sea. Then Mois, Tok Rejab's son, brought the news that the Kempetai chief and a platoon of Japanese soldiers had descended on Tobali and were now in Tok Rejab's home. In a nervous state, Mois related that his father had urinated in his sarong at the sight of the podgy Kempetai chief wearing a samurai sword in his ample waistband. The chief was Major General Konichi, commander of the garrison in Pangkal Pinang overseeing Bangka Island. The Japanese had placed a high-ranking officer in Banka because of its strategic location and also because it was the biggest tin producer in the East Indies. In addition, the largest tin-smelting plant was located in Banka. Major General Konichi's reputation preceded him well before anyone in Tobali had ever set eyes on him. Reputed to tolerate no nonsense and to frequently and easily mete out corporal punishment even to his own men for the slightest infringement, Konichi left little to the imagination as to what he was capable of doing when dealing with his enemies.

He went from house to house while his soldiers went sniffing ahead of him like hound dogs. Children spread the news, running from home to home. I saw the tension in Sam's face. He quickly donned his white robe and turban, and slung the prayer mat across his shoulder. Under cover of darkness, he walked to the mosque in quick finicky steps, stumbling a few times. I kept close on tow. As he went along, he gathered with him many children. At the mosque, he asked them to sit around him on the floor, setting the scene for a class on the Koran. There were at least twenty children. I joined them. Sam sat with the turban wrapped around his face to hide it, a Koran laid before him. The tungsten lamps lent a yellowish hue to our faces.

The soldiers came and gathered around the mosque. Konichi stepped onto the apron, but he stopped short of entering the mosque. He gazed across the lamplit hall. My body shook. I closed my eyes, trying to evade the threatening glare of his presence.

For the first time, I saw fear creep up on Sam. When he held a leaf of the Koran, it fluttered as if touched by a breeze. He pretended to be in deep concentration as the children recited the Koran loudly in unison. From where Konichi stood, Sam must have looked the solemn preacher – the warm yellowish glow of the oil lamps shrouding his Caucasian face.

I opened my eyes slowly and could see the rigid figure of the major general, one foot on the step and arms akimbo. He seemed to stand there forever. After what seemed a lifetime, he grunted and walked away.

Perhaps it was the mosque that protected Sam. Konichi might be cruel, but he was not stupid. He evidently knew that disrespecting the house of worship of the Muslims would serve no purpose. He obviously did not wish to lose the support of the Malays, whom he considered not to be a threat. That thin invisible wall of protection had saved Sam.

When Konichi left, Sam, exhausted, fell into a heap. He had fought the elements and survived a shipwreck, but these few moments took all his energy away.

No arrest was made, nor blood spilled, in Tobali. But in a Chinese village near a tin mine, the scene was much different. It seemed that in Payung, at the heart of the Chinese mining area, proscribed rice was found in a household. The whole family was taken in and brought to Pangkal Pinang. A few days later, fresh heads were displayed on bamboo poles at the Kempetai's headquarters as a warning to the others.

The day after Sam had evaded the Kempetai, a special prayer was held at the mosque, during which every member of the congregation gave Sam an emotional embrace.

Sam thanked them all. He showered his gratitude especially on Tok Rejab and Lebai Amir.

"Sheikh Omar, it was Allah, not us, who protected you. We are just His agents. It is Allah you must thank," Lebai Amir exhorted.

"Without doubt, without doubt," Sam said, with a look of embarrassment for not having thought of that in the first place, for their sake. He was still unaccustomed to the habits of the Muslims, which he was only in name – as far as I knew then.

*   *   *

We were drawing into the third year of the Japanese occupation, and shortages in essentials were becoming more severe. Rice became more and more scarce, as it was also the Japanese staple food. The main bulk of the harvest went into the Japanese granary. Some was even shipped to Japan. Sam said the Japanese were losing the war. I always wondered how he knew. Once in a while he would feed me with news of the war.

The captain had weathered before my eyes. That stoop in his posture was recently acquired; it must have grown surreptitiously. I noticed it only now. I also detected the growing shades of loneliness in his ways. He talked less, and he fell into a pensive mood a bit too often, sometimes staring into the horizon for no reason. Knowing his character, I believed he must have felt like a deserter, being the only white man walking around while his kind were fighting the war or languishing in prison camps.

He indulged more frequently and heavily in his pipe smoking, perhaps to hide his guilt. He was beholden to the people of Tobali for sheltering him, so he frequented the mosque, never missing the Friday prayers. Whether he did this out of faith or gratitude, it was hard to say. But I knew he was ignorant of the rituals and just imitated the motions of praying. Initially, he had looked at the people beside him from the corner of his eye and copied what they did. Over time, his motions became habitual. Nothing came out of his lips; he just closed his eyes and listened. He looked like a Muslim child starting on religion, which I thought was quite funny, seeing a grown man doing that. He bowed, prostrated, and supplicated, making the villagers love him for that. He was no hypocrite though. I think he behaved this way out of affection for the people around him rather than out of obligation to any god.

From a master of a ship, he had become a fisherman. One day while scouring for clams in the low tide, he found a carcass of a boat, half buried in the sand under the clutter of huge roots. A good part of its hull had disappeared. He reported it to Tok Rejab, seeking its owner. The chief said to him, "Keep it, my brother; it is a gift from Allah to you. No one will claim the boat. I assure you."

The captain repeated Tok Rejab's exact words to me: "It is a gift from Allah to us, Hamzah." I never thought Providence ever figured into the captain's mind. He surprised me that day. Piece by piece, he brought the boat back to life using tools he had had the presence of mind to salvage from the *Shanghai Star*. After a month, a fifteen-foot boat emerged. The new side had a face and tone that was different from the original hull on the left.

Chapter 8

Something else occurred that changed the course of my life forever, paving the way for me for a future yet unknown – a future resembling nothing Grandma Tutik had dreamt for me. I became a tin-mine worker, starting at the lowest rung, to supplement our income when severe hardship began to set in as the Japanese occupation progressed into its fourth year.

Was this the underlying reason as to why Grandma was so obsessed about wanting me not to leave Mataram House? From a make-believe prince to a pauper I would be? Did Father have any idea of it at all? Or was he himself bent towards wanting to prove her wrong? These thoughts visited my mind, especially during moments of despair.

Tolok Mine was in the interior of the island. I had to live there, returning on the weekends, but sometimes not for a month. My accommodation was a large dormitory, a raised timber structure of palm roofing. There was only one window on each side. To be near that window was a privilege, something therefore reserved for the most senior of the workers. The rest had to content themselves with the gaps between the planks of the walls for ventilation. The opencast mine had a hole that could fill a village and gullies that were the size of canyons; when it rained, mostly in torrents, these gullies turned into rivers of mud. Flooding was frequent. It was an ugly desert landscape; not a blade of grass had a chance to take root, not to mention trees. During the hot spells, the

70

humidity in the dormitory was so dense that we had to pour water on ourselves to keep cool before sleep could come. The stench of sweat became part of the air; soon it became part of us. To top it all, I was the only Malay in the entire *kongsi*, which was made up of entirely Chinese, whom the Japanese depended upon for labour – as only they could endure the mines. The Malays preferred a more pastoral life.

As a novice without any previous experience, my duty was to carry the cut earth to the conveyor belts to be disposed of fifty feet above the pit. When the belt broke down, we had to carry the earth manually along the winding terraced path all the way to the top. By the first week, my skin had torn away from my palms, my face had turned to charcoal, and my muscles cried as if they had been bludgeoned.

In the first month, I couldn't return to Tobali, as I was too weak to make the four-hour journey. There wasn't a single night when I didn't hate everyone around me once my head hit the pillow. The men with whom I worked spoke as though they were quarrelling. Profanities seemed like a type of metaphor to them. They spat with great frequency, so I had to watch where I walked. I searched for camaraderie and found none. Perpetually, there was an air of survival, fierce and uncaring. One night I cried, calling out, "God, why?" There was anger in my cry. Then, as though God had heard me, something happened.

One day, one of the jet monitors for blasting the earth's surface in order to wash down the cassiterite broke down. No one was able to repair it. During the lunch recess, I went down to the bottom of the pit and examined the equipment. I discovered that it was not the monitor that had failed, but the generator that powered it. I drew a detailed sketch of the generator on a piece of paper and put it in my trunk. When I returned home at the end of the month, I showed the drawing to Sam. He suspected that one of the pistons had seized.

Sam asked me whether the Japanese supervisor stayed at the mine. I said that he lived a mile away, and on weekends he would make a beeline to Pangkal Pinang for the women. That very Sunday, Sam returned with me to Tolok. By dusk we were at the mine. The dormitory was empty on weekends, so we were alone in the engine shed. Under the gaslight, Sam dismantled the valves and pistons. I watched every step of the process, committing it to memory. By morning, the engine was back in working condition. Sam headed for home before daybreak. He had taken a fatal risk in coming to the mine.

The superintendent of the mine was the first Japanese person I had encountered whose face reflected that he had a heart. It almost seemed that he did not to belong to his race. His manners and speech, too, seemed out of place in the entire Japanese occupation. He wore round horn-rimmed glasses more appropriate for a person among a classroom of pupils than among hard-faced mine workers. Because of this, I had an added motivation to want the machinery to work, lest the commanders in Pangkal Pinang have this superintendent replaced by someone without a heart. The following Monday, Okada – that was what the superintendent was called – asked who had repaired the pump. I bravely came forward to claim my credit. So pleased he was that he didn't even ask how I did it. As far as he was concerned, the output was back to the expected level.

The workers were jubilant, as the repaired monitored lessened their burden considerably. All went positively well for me. I was immediately put in charge of the engine room. Under my charge were two Chinese workers. I was also assigned to sort the tin ore into bags for shipment to the smelter. This marked a huge improvement to my working conditions, the most obvious perk being that I now had shelter from the burning sun. As the months passed, I absorbed everything there was to know about the mine. I had a penchant for languages, and in no time I picked up Hokkien, the dialect of the workers. With it I also picked up the profanity, but never the spitting.

We mine workers were paid a fixed wage in occupation-printed currency. Soon, as the occupation went into its fourth year, the currency rapidly lost its value thanks to overprinting. A fish now cost a basketful of paper. We workers were given a choice: food coupons or tin ore. I consulted Sam, who advised me to opt for the tin ore. He said that once the war ended, the price of tin would rise. The captain had always harboured the hope that the Allied forces would one day prevail in this war, a hope which he dearly held. I was among the few workers who opted for tin. Over a period, bags of tin filled the space under our little house.

*   *   *

One night in the rusty air of the dormitory, I heard a conversation that instantly doused the elation I had experienced from my recent good fortune. Despondency returned. It seemed as if my good fortune had been merely fate teasing me, like placing cheese in a mousetrap. It was just a cruel play, this tiny bit of good fortune.

The dormitory was a conduit for gossip and tales from Pangkal Pinang, Muntok, Sungailiat, and even Lubuk Besar, where the Chinese were found to concentrate. Invariably, the gossip was about the Japanese "devil" and the atrocities the soldiers committed upon the local population. The locals hated the Japanese like cats hate dogs. Most of them would clandestinely work to undermine the occupation, but a few collaborated with the enemies for personal gain. One night, after the weekend leave, such a tale was told.

Old man Kim, the oldest among us, was a figure of exhausted manhood. He was scrawny, with a sewer for a mouth and with a perpetual grudge against his fellow men. Despite his age, everyone gave him a wide berth as if he were a disease. Because of that, he constantly sought for attention. The only way for him to get the attention he craved for was to tell tales. Rarely was he listened to. But that night was different.

Some regular inhabitants of the dormitory were animatedly engaged in a game of mah-jong. The subject of food entered the conversation. When one of them mentioned that the cook of the Fortune Restaurant made the best pork ribs in the whole of Pangkal Pinang, old man Kim suddenly blurted out from the back, "Beware of this man. He is an informer and a treacherous bastard. It seems that before the war, he landed on the shores of Tobali after being shipwrecked. He had a lot of money with him and later set up the Fortune Restaurant with it. To enable him to get a constant supply of rice and provisions for his restaurant, he services the Japanese officers with women from the brothel, which he also owns. To reinforce his position with the Japanese, he secretly supplies them with illicit information. He has been betraying his own race, I tell you."

Suddenly, old man Kim had an audience. A crowd gathered around him.

"How did you know, old man? The Japs told you? Maybe you are the devil who has been kissing the Japanese arses. I don't believe a word you say. F – – k you, old man. You shouldn't be talking like that and putting people in trouble," the mah-jong player, who had first spoken, said.

"You want proof? Go to his restaurant and let him hear you say you know something about the anti-Japanese movement. See what happens. I guarantee that you will have your proof. That's exactly what happened with someone. He was too careless with him. The man who told me this had seen him entering the Kempetai headquarters several times. What was he doing there? Tell me. The f – – – – g bastard is a traitor to his own people, I tell you."

"You know what, old man? You're the f – – – – g bastard. Talk like that can put us all in deep shit," Tong, the overseer, said. He left the mah-jong table and walked away to his window bunk. "The old bastard is digging his own grave," he mumbled.

All of a sudden, Hwa (nicknamed the Dragon on account of the tattoos on his forearms) erupted. He grabbed old man Kim by the scruff and shouted, "If you say one more word about this, I'll throw you into the pit this very minute." There was instant silence. Everyone withdrew to their quarters, ending the mah-jong contest in mid game. The Dragon, I was told, had been a Triad member before the war. Everyone in the mine just kept clear of his path.

The old man wanted to have the last word. "A bunch of bloody fools, you all are. I am doing you a favour. You should be very careful when you eat at the Fortune Restaurant." He whimpered.

When I returned to my bed, Tseng, my neighbour, a mild-mannered youngster about my age, was waiting for me. He seemed anxious. "What is it, Tseng?" I asked.

He motioned for me to come close. "Old man Kim is telling the truth," he whispered.

"How do you know?"

"A worker in the Fortune Restaurant told me."

"Who is this restaurant owner old man Kim was talking about?" I asked curiously.

"His name is Ah Fook. The story is that he was a cook on a ship that was shipwrecked in Tobali a few years ago – like the old man said. People are wondering how it is that he is doing so well when everyone else is suffering," Tseng whispered.

A chill ran through my spine upon hearing that name. *The cowardly bastard,* I thought to myself. I had never really trusted him, not from the day I had first met him. He came across to me as sycophantic to the point of being distasteful, given that I was close to the captain. So I wasn't a bit surprised to learn that he sucked up to the Japanese.

"What does old man Kim hope to gain by squealing on Ah Fook?" I asked.

"He wants someone here to eliminate him for being a traitor to the Chinese community. One must give him some credit for that," Tseng said.

There was silence in the dormitory after that.

In that silence, old man Kim's story struck a nervous chord in me. Sam had never liked Ah Fook. He had been the ship owner's cook. Sam had had little choice in the matter. If there was anything remarkable about Ah Fook, it was his extraordinary culinary talent. He churned out the most delicious dishes I had ever tasted, which would be the reason why the owner of the *Shanghai Star* found him to be useful. Despite the scant respect Sam had for him, Ah Fook had held the ship's purse for the provisioning and supplies, as Sam couldn't be bothered with the nitty-gritty of the galley

When the *Shanghai Star* was in dire straits, Ah Fook was in the lifeboat before anyone else was, and with him was a leather pouch, which he held close to his chest as if it were his dear heart. When we drifted for days on the lifeboat, Ah Fook never allowed anyone to touch the leather pouch, clinging to it as a eunuch would to his bottle of severed manhood. Sam made furtive glances at Ah Fook, curious about his odd behaviour. I suppose then, given that our lives were the only thing that mattered to us, he didn't question him about it.

When we beached in Tobali, Ah Fook disappeared without a trace, only to reappear a year later in Pangkal Pinang as the owner of a restaurant. The only way he could have bought the restaurant, I guessed, was by using the money from the ship's purse. Now he had become an informer. How dangerous it would be if he knew the captain was still in Tobali, I thought. What a jewel of information he would have with him to ingratiate himself with the Japanese, considering the fact that Ah Fook also had little sentiment for the captain.

* * *

A month later, old man Kim didn't return after a weekend leave. His disappearance was noted with little emotion. No one seemed to care. Some even said he deserved it for being a fool. Others were happy he was no longer part of our group, since he was always a disaster waiting to happen. The lack of feeling disturbed me. Everyone took care only of his own turf – a code of self-preservation. Those who sympathised with old man Kim kept their feelings under their pillow. One of these people was Tseng, my young neighbour.

"Poor Kim. He was just a silly old man," Tseng said to m e in a hushed tone. I grasped that opportunity to explore his thoughts.

"What exactly happened to him?" I asked.

"The Kempetai raided his house in Pangkal Pinang. Dragged him and his son to the Kempetai headquarters, and tortured them. The old man died, but the son survived."

"How do you know?" I asked.

Tseng crossed over to my bed and spoke into my ear. "Everyone in Pangkal Pinang knows."

"Who squealed on him?"

"Who else?" Tseng tossed his head in the direction of the Dragon.

That night I couldn't sleep a wink. Images of beastly Major General Konichi played on my fears, making me worry about Sam. It was a hot and grungy night. We hadn't had a drop of rain in two weeks. We sprinkled water over our beds. It was nearly dawn before my eyes finally closed. My mind had been inundated with anxieties. I counted the hours for the weekend to come.

*　　*　　*

My regard for the sea alternated between hatred and tolerance. I couldn't forgive it for what it had done to the *Shanghai Star*. I tolerated it because it was Sam's love. Today, as I approached our little house, returning home, I thought of the sea as a friend, the sight of it filling me with optimism. Happiness for me is like a woman's perfume – passing and unreliable. Some misalignment of my stars had slated me for recurrent misery. My destiny had already been written for me. It could not be altered. I could very well challenge it, but it would not budge. If an event were to come, it would come. My job was to receive it calmly.

As I got close to our house, I could hear the already familiar rasping sound above the lashing of the sea – the unmistakable sound of Sam's coughing. This time its resonant hollowness frightened me. In the faint light, I noticed Sam's supine body on the bed. I threw down my canvas bag and moved close to him. I needed no light to tell me he was sick. I placed my palm on his forehead. It was hot. "Why don't you just stop smoking, for God's sake, Sam?" I cried.

He grunted and gave a feeble laugh, which was followed by more crunching coughs. I wanted to give him a glass of water, but there was none nearby.

"I'll go and boil a kettle. Have you had your dinner, Sam?"

"I am not hungry."

"Not hungry? Why, there is not a trace of cooked food anywhere, Sam," I protested.

He must have been too tired or too sick to cook. Even a comb of bananas was left untouched. Maybe his appetite had deserted him. I prayed he wasn't slipping away. I just couldn't imagine the old sea dog fading away. He had become a real father to me, dearer than my own.

How could I announce to him now that Ah Fook, for whom he had nothing but contempt, had resurfaced in Pangkal Pinang and was now an informer. How could I? The implications would be obvious in his mind. Sam was getting old, not so much with age as with fatigue – fatigue arising from the indignity of having to live a life of deception.

The hardships of the time were taking their toll, working on the nerves of the people. The Japanese were losing in the Pacific. Given this, one would have expected them to be kinder to the people, but instead they redoubled their excesses. They felt more and more threatened by the growing anti-Japanese sentiments.

As it was a weekend, I took a stroll in town. I had asked Sam to come along, but he preferred to stay back and do some gardening. I was glad he hadn't accompanied me.

I ambled into a coffee shop. While enjoying my black Sumatran brew with half-boiled eggs and charcoal-toasted bread, famous in this particular Malay coffee shop, the name Sheikh Omar surfaced from a table behind me. What I heard broke the serenity which I had contemplated enjoying that morning. I dared not turn, lest the people on whom I was eavesdropping recognise me. They were talking about a Chinese fishing village in Tangjung Paku being raided by the Kempetai. The villagers were suspected of harbouring an agent of the anti-Japanese underground movement. Several people had been shot on the spot.

"You know, this could happen to us if the Kempetai knew we had in our midst a white fugitive," one of the men said.

"Shh! Not so loud," the other whispered. "Let's change the subject."

Then the conversation drifted into small talk.

I quickly paid for my meal and left the scene.

I took a detour to Tok Rejab's house and related to him what I heard. He frowned.

"I know. A few people had come to me and voiced similar concerns. I told them not to talk carelessly about these things, and not ever to let it get within earshot of Sheikh Omar. If he even suspected, he would leave us rather than put us in danger. I shudder to think what will happen to him." I returned home immediately after that, feeling quite disturbed.

Since Sam couldn't go to sea anymore, he kept himself physically occupied by gardening. Our little home was unlike other homes in Tobali. It had a pretty flower garden, catching the eye of passers-by who, without fail, would comment on how beautiful the garden looked. Sam would beam with pride.

*   *   *

I had now made it a habit to return home every weekend to be with Sam, as I didn't want him to be alone for too long. Age was really catching up on him. In that month of July, I was held back for over a month because a sluice gate had been damaged by heavy rain and needed repair.

When I returned home this time after a month's absence, I noticed that Sam now walked in slow, measured steps. And when I accompanied him to the mosque, people would know he was nearby by the coughs that he carried with him like a cowbell.

When prayer time was over and I intended to return home, Sam would opt to stay at the mosque for the next prayer, saving him the trouble of labouring back to the house. Muslims pray five times a day. The interval between the two evening prayers was barely sufficient time for him to return home, as the present pace of his walking was slow. He would take his rest on the mosque's floor and doze off, the cool concrete aggravating his condition.

This time when I returned home, Sam seemed to be worse. The incessant coughing had progressively weakened him. I began to be debilitated by the fear of the inevitable. If he were to die eventually, let it be with dignity, I hoped. Never should he die at the hands of the Japanese.

Ever since the episode at the mine regarding Ah Fook, his name had been clinging around my neck like an albatross. I felt that I must deal with this now for Sam's sake. There was no telling what the self-serving Ah Fook was capable of.

Burdened with this, I finally spoke to Tok Rejab, telling him that I had a matter of grave importance and was in need of his wise counsel.

"Let's go to the workshop. It's more private there." Tok Rejab, being a professional carpenter, had a large, well-equipped workshop adjacent to his house. His woodwork was in great demand for its fine quality. After he shut the large double-leafed door, we settled on the polished chairs he had made.

"What is it, Hamzah? You look stressed out. Is it about Sheikh Omar?" To everyone in Tobali, the captain was always Sheikh Omar, and Sam himself by now responded to the name instinctively.

"Yes, Tok. Do you recall that when you found us on the beach, there were four others besides me and the captain – two Bugis by the name of Slamad and Irwan, a young Malay called Mat, and a Chinese called Ah Fook? Do you remember?"

"How could I forget that day? A broken boat beached on the coral with six men lying half-dead in it. At first I thought you were fishermen, but there were no signs of any fishing gear at all, and boats do not land on that part of the coast because of the treacherous coral reefs. I only got the first inkling who you people were when the only white man began to speak. 'Help us, sir. We are survivors from the *Shanghai Star*.' I didn't know what *Shanghai Star* was, but I guessed he must be referring to a boat."

"Tok," I said, interrupting him. "What happened to them after you took us to the hospital in Muntok?"

"When you were discharged from the hospital, I took you and your captain to my home after he told me that you were not a seaman, like the others, but a boy of breeding from an illustrious family in Java – and that he was your guardian. You were on your way to Penang when the unfortunate disaster happened."

"Tok Rejab, where did Slamad, Irwan, Mat, and particularly the Chinese man go? What happened to each one of them, Tok? It's very important."

"Mat, the young man, asked me to send him to Batam in Riau. He said he had relatives there. I gave money for his passage, and he left a couple of days later. Slamad and Irwan, being seamen, found work in one of the many merchant ships that come to the port. As for the Chinese – what's his name? Yes, Ah Fook. He seemed like a man in a hurry. Do you know that he refused medical treatment? He said he preferred a Chinese medicine man and then asked me to direct him to one. After that, I couldn't find him. He just disappeared without a trace. Now, after all these years, why have these people cropped up again?"

"It's about Ah Fook, the Chinese cook for the *Shanghai Star*, who has opened a restaurant called Fortune in Pangkal Pinang with the money he stole from the ship. I have been told at the mine that he has become an informer for the Kempetai. And, Tok, you know what that means."

"I know exactly what you mean. You leave this to me, and do not say a word to anyone else." He lowered his eyes and remained silent momentarily. He seemed to be in deep thoughts. As we were about to part in quite a serious mood and noticing the worry in my face, he said, "Rest assured, Hamzah, this matter will be dealt with appropriately, and with the utmost urgency and delicacy. And do not tell Sheikh Omar about it."

"Thank you, Tok." I kissed his hand and then left, feeling a burden being lifted from me.

I was up very early the next Monday morning. The dawn mist was still hovering, and the dew hadn't had its fill. I doused myself in the coolness of the morning by the porch while Sam was getting ready for the day. It was only 5.30.

"Sam, why are you taking a cold bath? It will only worsen your condition."

"Don't you start to lecture me, young man."

"Sam," I repeated with a mixture of frustration and anger, "why do you do things like that?"

"Like what?"

"Bathing at dawn in cold water and then trudging to the mosque for *subuh* prayer and every other prayer. You don't have to do that, Sam, no matter what your reasons are."

"Don't you question my motives."

"Sorry, Sam, I didn't mean it that way. I worry about your state of health. And you smoke too much."

"Leave my pipe alone." He gave a series of chest-crunching coughs.

"Sam, we need to talk. I have given serious thought about stopping work and returning home to take care of you. We have more than enough tin to keep us going for a long time. I can sell a bag or two a month to the dealer in Muntok. You need taking care of, Sam. You're getting old, and you're sick."

"Good heavens, am I about to die? No, sir, have no fear of that. Not until this bloody war is over. Count on that." His ash-blue eyes twinkled and then melted. He rose from his chair, walked towards the sea, and stared at the horizon. Lifting his hand and touching his eyes, he said, "You go on with your work, my boy. Don't you worry your silly head about me." It had been a long time since he called me that.

Chapter 9

One evening, someone came walking briskly towards our house. It was dark, so I couldn't make out his face. He called out, "Sheikh Omar, Sheikh Omar, the thing has arrived." It was Tok Rejab, full of excitement and out of breath.

"What thing?" I asked curiously.

No one answered me, as the two men were engrossed in their triumph.

"Thank you, Tok Rejab. Thank you, sir," Sam replied.

"No, don't thank me. Thank Allah. This will ease your pains, Sheikh, God willing." Tok Rejab couldn't hide his jubilation.

"Yes, indeed. God willing," Sam replied, smiling broadly.

"Is that medicine? Where in heaven did you get that, Tok?" I was on tenterhooks with curiosity.

Tok Rejab threw a glance at Sam.

Sam shook his head. "It's best you don't know, Hamzah," he said.

"What do you mean?" I cried.

"For your own safety."

I was peeved. "For my own safety? What do you mean? Is there something that you people don't want me to know?"

"It's to protect you. Whatever we do is confined to a very few people," Sam said.

"That's preposterous. Have I not lived dangerously all this time? Why? Is it because I am just a boy? Cut that crap."

The two men were silent. They looked at each other, not knowing how to react.

"Tell him, Sheikh. He has the right to know," Tok Rejab said, finally.

"Well, Hamzah, here it is. We've been operating a radio station under the mosque for almost a year. Transmission is relayed during prayer times to delude the Japanese, knowing that they normally leave mosques alone, especially during prayers. I have been in communication with Force 136 of the British Intelligence, which is operating in Malaya. This medicine is from them. That's all I can say," Sam said.

"So that's why you have been going to the mosque five times a day, rain or shine, in sickness or in health. What a fool I have been, thinking you have become unbelievably pious." I laughed.

"Now you know," Sam remarked.

"Are we winning the war, Sam? Is it going to be over soon?"

"Now, you hold on there, young man. Don't you get excited."

"Sorry, Sheikh. Sorry, Tok. I can't help it."

Both Sam and Tok Rejab laughed.

"As Tok Rejab would say, we shall win the war, God willing. Isn't that so, Tok?" Sam said.

"Indeed so," Tok Rejab rejoined.

After Tok Rejab left, Sam examined the contents of the bottle, read the prescription, asked for a glass of water, and took the first dose. A glow of hope spread across his face.

Before I left for Tolok Mine that evening, I said to him, "Don't you grab your pipe just yet, Sam. Let the medication do its work first."

"Can't do without my pipe, I am afraid. Be on your way, I say." For the first time in months, I saw the return of the old sea dog.

*   *   *

The last evening bus to Tolok was half-empty. I slept through the four-hour journey, the night shrouding me in peace.

A week later, in the dorm of Tolok Mine, Ah Fook's name resurfaced.

"Hey, Ah Fook has disappeared," someone cried aloud.

"Good riddance to him," another said.

The stench of opium invaded the already mawkish air.

"What happened to him?"

"It seems the Kempetai were after him," the first man said.

"I thought he worked for them, so why are they after him?" someone asked.

"Being an informer is a double-edge sword. You create enemies, and others can inform on you too. The bloody Japs owe no obligation to anyone but themselves," the first man said.

"Shut up, you people! I've got to sleep," the Dragon shouted.

There were no more voices after that.

*　　*　　*

Three months later, the joyous event for which Sam had been waiting finally occurred. But for me, the glorious Japanese surrender that greeted the month of August in the year 1945 was as joyless as the loss of the *Shanghai Star*. Once again, destiny had cruelly cheated me. Sam didn't get to see the surrender. The victory he had anticipated and contributed to, no matter how tiny his role, passed him by without even a greeting. Sam had died. My heart was broken. He had become the father I'd never had, making sacrifices for me beyond the call of normal duty, for reasons I was unable to comprehend until this day. Like an angel he had come, and like an angel he had departed.

Yes, he finally found peace, but not in the way he had wished. He had been a proud seafarer unable to do his part in the war, not even as a prisoner of war, which would have been more dignified than being a keeper to a wayward boy of uncertain destiny just so he could fulfil a pledge to an old friend. How could I not feel devastated by his passing? How could I not feel so overwhelmingly indebted to him? My only repayment of my enormous debt to him now was the simple act of burying his remains. I did this in a simple grave, in a land not of his birth, and far away from his own people.

As for me, I dared not look forward, dared not plan, and worst of all dared not hope, since hope was like the silver lining in the dark clouds that peeked out and promptly disappeared.

I was alone. My nineteenth birthday was around the corner. I thought of home. But where was home? I had an appalling fear of returning home. For five years, I had shut my heart and had stored away my feelings in unreachable corners, away from my own self. Retrieving those hidden sentiments was not easy. Feelings are deceptive, not like goods that can be shelved away and then recovered. I thought of Mother, those soft eyes that gazed into me with so much tenderness. I thought of Grandma, for whom I carried a huge burden of guilt. Strange, I thought of Father least, despite the extraordinary act he had performed for me. What I had for Father at that moment was sympathy, not emotion. It wasn't for lack of love for him; rather, it was because I had been drained of emotion. For the first time in five years, I tried to search through the ruins of the past I had so abruptly left, but a mesh of vines blocked my path.

I had not gone to school. All the schooling I had received on refinement, culture, and art, I had left in that cloistered environment of illusions that was Mataram House.

I had become someone else now, taking on a shape that Sam had forged: the war my curriculum, Tolok Mine my school, Sam my teacher. I had turned brown from the sun; my hands had the coarseness brought about by hardship; my hair was unsuitable for elegance, curled like wood shavings; my body was taller and lankier; and my countenance was the painter's brush of a diluted Arab.

I had never met a girl and so had no knowledge of girls, nor had I any inkling of what they thought of me. There were girls in Tobali, but they were mere passers-by, guileless, innocent, fresh, and as raw as newly sprouted flowers.

Actually, there was one. Her name was Siti, daughter of Tok Rejab, now fifteen – four years younger than I – blooming like an early rose, with dark lustrous hair, a slender olive face, and eyes that could steal a secret gaze. She had always been "that little girl" to me, touching not my emotion but my affection. In fact, she called me Abang, or big brother, and I referred to her as little sister. She often came to me. At such times, I would engage her affectionately. Asking me to repeat the English words she had learned from me, she gazed into my face with eyes that spoke of danger. Recently, she shied away, as though aware of that danger.

Recently, as if having awakened to the call of her blooming youth, she shed the image of the little sister.

* * *

I made arrangements to leave Tobali, but not before disposing of the tin I had hoarded under the house. I sold it to a tin dealer in Muntok for a handsome price, raking in a tidy fortune. The price of tin had soared because of the rising demand for the metal in the aftermath of the war, just as Sam had predicted. Suddenly, I had become the wealthiest man in Tobali.

I said my goodbyes to my Chinese friends in Tolok Mine. Coarse as they were, they displayed a big heart for friendship, treating me to a sumptuous dinner in Pangkal Pinang. I would never forget them for showing me their view of the world; for planting in me the value of hard work, no matter what the conditions were; for giving me their language; and for allowing me to share their secrets – the secrets of survival.

I made a courtesy call on Okada San, the Japanese mine superintendent who had yet to return to Japan. My goodness, how the tables had turned. He bowed to me so low that it embarrassed me. In defeat, they seemed to be a different race, these Japanese, terribly ashamed by their failure. No wonder some chose hara-kiri rather than face the humiliation of defeat. I felt so sorry for him; it brought tears to my eyes. I saw demobbed Japanese soldiers still in their uniforms scouring the countryside asking for work – any work, such as cutting grass, cleaning toilets, or clearing trees in exchange for food. It was months before they were shipped back. I heard of Kempetai officers being lynched by Chinese mobs. I had not heard anything about Major General Konichi. He had probably been incarcerated by the Dutch for war crimes.

The Indonesian landscape was rapidly changing from an occupied country to a proud nation hungry for freedom after centuries of colonialism. Ironically, it was the occupying Japanese who engendered the Indonesian spirit for that freedom. Led by a visionary and flamboyant Javanese man called Soekarno, the people readied themselves to oust the returning Dutch and send them back to Holland.

News that I had become someone of wealth in Banka Island somehow reached Soekarno. He sent an emissary with the objective of inviting me to join his revolutionary movement. I declined. I had my own liberation to contend with.

My farewell to the people of Tobali was ceremonious: a big feast, a moving speech by Tok Rejab, and a prayer for the departed captain, whom they now dubbed Sheikh Omar the Pious. When I used the moniker Sheikh Omar the Pious, it was like I was referring to another person. I still wondered where Sam's heart was when it came to the matter of faith. In any event, the reverence the people of Tobali had for him would have pleased him, especially because it was sincere.

My last farewell was to Sam at his grave in the Muslim cemetery by the sea. On the granite tombstone was inscribed, "Sheikh Omar the Pious, alias Samuel O'Keeffe, captain of the *Shanghai Star* [the alias was included at my insistence], born in Ireland, died July 1945." There was nothing else I could have had inscribed on his tombstone, as I didn't even know his age.

The gravesite by the sea, I thought, was a kind of ironic gift: Sam had a view of the sea even in death.

MALAYA
1947

Chapter 10

When I finally boarded the steamer at Muntok, three months after the war ended, I found myself sailing north to George Town, Penang, in Malaya, instead of south to Java, my birthplace. George Town was where I believed Father would be, without a shadow of doubt. I was struck by a sudden whiff of conscience that made me think of Father. Grandma Tutik had lost me, and so had Mother, but Father had lost more than just a son. Father lost his pride, his self-worth, his dignity. I was certain of that. How could I not retrace his path?

I had kept the letter Father had written to Sam, which Sam had passed on to me. I took from my worn-out purse the piece of paper stained with neglect, and I read it again.

My dear Samuel,

Should I fail to be on the *Shanghai Star*, you are to take Hamzah to 27 Kelawei Road, George Town. It's a bungalow house I own. There you shall meet a woman named Maimunah, my sister, Hamzah's aunty. She knows what to do. I shall join you and Hamzah soon, by any means.

Thank you, Samuel, for all of this.

Yours faithfully,
Syed Norredin

After reading the letter, I found myself drifting to the moment when I had first met Sam on the *Shanghai Star*. Tears flowed from my eyes uncontrollably.

A week before my departure, I had bought a couple of new shirts, some pants, a pair of black leather shoes, and a shaving kit (one of those British goods which had resurfaced in the marketplace in Pangkal Pinang) for Father. I had gotten a little present for Aunty Maimunah, whom I had never met. I couldn't have gotten her a dress, as I hadn't any idea of her size, so I settled for an embroidered shawl for her.

With much sadness, I had made an emotional decision to take with me Sam's personal belongings. Meagre though they were, I had always regarded them as precious heirlooms: a collection of nine tobacco pipes of various makes and models and shapes; a blue skipper's cap, the fur flattened with use; and a leather-bound book by Thomas Hardy entitled *Tess of the d'Urbervilles* with the inscription "Happy Birthday, Samuel. Love, Helen" on the inside. I wondered who Helen was. Wife? Lover? Childhood sweetheart? There was no clue, not even a date or the name of a place.

And then there had been a matter of the padlocked box, the size of a shoe case, which I had difficulty in dealing with. An excruciating dilemma confronted me. You see, Sam had left no will or instructions. In spite of his failing health, it had never occurred to him to tell me anything about this box. *Shall I open it or not?* I had asked myself. My overwhelming curiosity leaned heavily on me. But my conscience said no. If Sam had wanted me to know what was inside, he had had ample opportunity to tell me – but he hadn't told me. So I had convinced myself not to intrude on his privacy, not even in death. I decided that the secret should be buried with him, and that was what I had done. I let it die with him. He had given me so much of himself; I must not take that which was not given.

* * *

Penang captivated me the moment the steamer docked at the pier. The morning sky bristled with the shrieks of swallows. Despite the scars of war, Penang obviously appeared to be in a hurry to make up for the lost years. Boats and people moved about in frenzy. I fell in love with Penang, and I had yet to see the tree-lined avenues or stately homes about which Sam had once told me. So far, I had only see what was left of the bombed-out government buildings by the harbour. The rising blue hills in the background hugged the city with the warm luxury of green, a stark contrast to the barrenness of the mines to which I had become accustomed. It lifted my spirit, abolishing the depressive feeling that had enveloped me upon leaving Tobali.

I took a trishaw driven by a Chinese man. With me in front and the pedaller in the rear, I felt awash with optimism and secretly crossed my fingers for nothing to go wrong. Maybe destiny was taking a break and had little time for me, I mused.

When the trishaw entered Kelawei Road, my heart pounded as No. 27 came into view. A large compound with an overgrown thicket fence and thick undergrowth, and a luxuriant rambutan tree in the foreground, blocked my view of the house. A dirt path took me to a large Malay-style two-storey building with long windows. The building had a timber porch and a diamond-shaped trellis resembling a birdcage. I had noticed the same type of birdcage design in the other houses along the same street, as if they were indicating a distinctive preference of a particular people.

The front door was closed, so I knocked softly. No one came up. I rapped again, this time stronger. I heard footsteps coming. A dark-looking skinny boy with a whimsical grin opened a leaf.

"Is Aunty Maimunah in?" I asked him.

"Mother! Someone is asking for you," he yelled, looking straight at me with big, curious eyes.

"Who is it?" a woman's voice asked in a loud, clear tone.

"I don't know."

"Why don't you ask?"

"Who are you, sir?"

"I am Syed Hamzah, son of Syed Norredin."

"He said he is Syed Hamzah, son of—" He paused. Lifting his head high, he asked, "Whose son, did you say?"

"Syed Norredin."

"Son of Syed Norin, Mother," the boy shouted at the top of his voice.

"Norredin," I said, correcting him.

"He said Norredin," he shouted back. A corpulent woman with a plump face came running to the door. She froze, muted by the shock of seeing me.

"Is it really you, son of Norredin?"

"Yes, I am Hamzah. It is Aunty Maimunah, right?"

"Yes, yes, I am your aunty." She burst into tears and clasped her ample arms around me. "You're alive. You're alive," she said in between sobs. She held me so tightly that I lost my breath. "We all had thought you were dead. No news of you whatsoever. Maybe you had returned to Mataram House. But they had heard nothing either. When the Japanese came, we thought the worst." She unclasped me. "Let me look at you." She scrutinised my face. "I had only pictures of you from when you were a child. Good gracious, you've grown so tall, and you look exactly like your father, so handsome." She turned around and shouted, "Ariffin! Come here." The boy came running back, now without a shirt. "Meet your cousin-brother."

"Hello," the boy said, grinning widely.

"Watch your manners. Address him as your *brother* Hamzah."

"Hello, *brother* Hamzah. You're Uncle Norredin's son?"

"Yes."

"Your father is in jail, you know that?"

"Shut your mouth, Ariffin. Now go away." The woman rapped the boy on the head. He scuttled into the hall. "I really don't know what to do with him."

"Is it true what he said, Aunty? About Father?"

"Come in first. Come in. Let me carry that case. Ariffin, come and help with this."

"I'll do that myself, Aunty."

She ushered me into the large living room, plunged her heavy-set body into the big sofa, and pulled my hand to sit next to her.

"Let me catch my breath. Your father is going to be so happy to know you are alive. He has been thinking of nothing else but you since he left you with that captain. I don't know what's his name – a white man. Thank God, thank God that you are alive. God bless you, my child."

"Aunty," I said, interrupting her before she could ramble on, "tell me about Father. What has happened to him? Why is he in jail?"

She panted. "When the war ended and the British came back, they detained a number of people, including your father. The British said he had collaborated with the Japanese. That's all I know. That's all I can tell you. Aunty doesn't really understand these things."

"Where did they put him? Is he all right?"

She put her head down and then raised her blouse sleeve to wipe her tears. "He's all right, in good health. They didn't mistreat him. But still, a prison is a prison. It has affected him emotionally. He never stopped thinking about you, still hoping for your arrival. When you see him, don't be surprised that he has aged a lot. His hair is all white. He keeps a beard, and that grey beard makes him look older. Look, rest first. I'll get your room ready."

On that first night it rained, deafening me with its pounding. I lay in the black hollowness of my room contemplating Father. Suddenly I felt like a child in an unfamiliar setting. The forms and shapes that peeped out of the lighting flares seemed strange and distant. I missed Tobali, Sam and our little house, the mine, and my old world. I thought of Siti. Her face flashed momentarily. How she had become a woman suddenly! I felt strangely ashamed of my thoughts. I had once thought of her as no more than a little sister.

Early the next morning, I took a stroll in the garden. I smelled decay. The luxuriant fruit trees were barren. Weeds had taken the place of grass. The bamboo fence sprouted wildly. The ground was unkempt. I imagined tiny denizens flourishing in the holes and bushes. I asked Aunty Maimunah the reason for this state of things.

She just said, "We have no one to do the work."

But I had a more pressing matter in my mind than this garden. It could wait.

I had breakfast at the long dinner table, which must have had a glorious past. Ariffin, my eight-year-old new-found skinny cousin, sat upright across from me. He wasn't good-looking at all. He was buck-toothed, dark, and skinny like a rake. The only redeeming features were his eyelashes – long and curved, ones that would be the envy of many women – adorning his whimsical eyes, and a mass of lustrous curls on his head. Since I had come, he had been suspicious and wary of me, watching my every move. I guessed he sensed something was about to happen with my sudden entry into his free-spirited world.

Aunty Maimunah had cooked rice steamed in coconut milk, garnishing it with chillies, anchovies, fried chicken, cucumbers, and omelette. A delightful cook she was. It had been a long time since such delicate food had touched my palate. We ate with our hands. There is a certain skill and etiquette required when eating with the hands: the rice must not invade the second joints of the fingers, and one must not use the hand one eats with to touch the serving spoons. I noticed that Ariffin's table manners were awful, to say the least. His eating hand was a mess, he gobbled his food, he spoke with his mouth full, and he picked up the serving spoon with his soiled hands.

When breakfast was over and Ariffin was about to leave, I thumped the table and shouted, "Ariffin." He bounced with fright. His heavy lashes flicked up, exposing his wide, mischievous eyes, which held a look of disbelief. I wanted to laugh but held myself back. "From today, I am going to set some house rules. Rule number one: you must clean yourself before you sit for meals at the table. Rule number two: you must observe certain etiquette at table; eat without messing your fingers; use only the clean hand for the serving spoons. Rule number three: Do not speak with your mouth full. Rule number four: You are going to help me to clean the house and garden."

He froze, straightened himself up, and looked in the direction of his mother. His mother just shook her head and lifted her hands in a manner that said, "I can't help you."

Early that morning, Aunty Maimunah had confided in me, telling me how ill-disciplined and lazy her son had become after his father died three years ago. He refused to do any house chores, not even washing his own plates. Sometimes, he neglected to take his bath. "He doesn't listen to a word I say. It's worse now since your father is not around. When I asked him to go to the sundry shop, he demanded ten cents for his labour. If I refused to pay, he would not clean the dishes, saying he was too young and would risk breaking the plates. When I asked him to sweep the compound, he would hide the broom and claim it had been stolen. When I agreed to pay him for sweeping, the broom would all of a sudden reappear. I don't know what to do with him, Hamzah."

Later that morning as I was having coffee on the apron of the house, surveying the unkempt garden and contemplating what do with it, I caught sight of Ariffin skipping merrily towards the entrance, which was in the direction of the road outside.

"Ariffin!" I hollered. "Where are you heading to?"

"A friend's house."

"Come over here. I want to talk to you."

"Yes, Abang. Is it about more rules?"

"You are absolutely right. Very smart. Is it true you asked to be paid for your work?"

"Yes."

"Why?"

"One should be paid for one's labour."

"Oh, really? Where did you get that idea?"

"Ah Bee told me."

"Who's Ah Bee?"

"He's the son of the Chinese *towkay* who owns the sundry shop. Ah Bee is my best friend."

"You are a clever boy."

He grinned and scratched his leg with his foot.

"Let's make a deal, agreed?"

He nodded his head.

"From today you shall be paid for every chore that I ask you to do."

He paused, observing me with suspicion. "Do you mean it?"

"Of course."

"Hooray!" Lifting his hands, he gave a broad grin, exposing to the full his buck teeth.

"There's a condition. From now on you will have to pay for your food and the bed you sleep on. And you must buy your own clothes."

Ariffin dropped his jaw and fell completely silent.

"Agreed?" I asked. I pursed my lips to prevent myself from smiling.

"No."

"No?"

"I don't agree. I've no money."

"What's the deal then?"

He paused and looked straight at me, his mouth open.

"Yes? I'm waiting. If you do not agree, you will have to find work and make the money to pay me."

He lowered his head and meekly said, "From today I shall not ask for payment."

"And?"

"I'll do what you say."

"Two more things," I said.

"What?" He stared at me.

"We are going shopping to buy some equipment. You and I are going to trim the fence, cut the grass, and clean up the ground. We are going to make the garden look like a garden."

"And what's the other thing?"

"You are going to be enrolled in a school." Much to my surprise, he looked very pleased. "You like school?"

"Yes," he said, displaying those rabbit's teeth again.

"Let's shake hands on that. Come along over here."

He came around to the coffee table, and I extended my hand. Once he had taken it, I gave it a good shake.

"Now go take a bath. You stink."

*   *   *

The next day I went shopping for myself. After scouring Penang Road, the shopping street, and not finding what I wanted, I was told to shop in Bishop Street. There I found a small department store replete with menswear. I was amazed to see neckties, shirts, trousers, belts, shoes, and even cotton jackets, not to mention tropical hats, which I had seen worn by the Dutch when I was a kid. *How on earth did these goods resurface so quickly after the war?* I wondered. I bought a tie, a crisp white shirt, a pair of black brogues, and even a cotton jacket, which, I'm happy to say, fit me. My purpose was to spruce myself up before going to the British Military Administration's (BMA) head office in Light Street to enquire about my father's detention.

When I went down for breakfast the following morning, Aunty Maimunah exclaimed in surprise to see me looking dapper. "Oh my God, it's like looking at your father when he was young." That burst of euphoria was instantly followed by a huge hug.

Ariffin gave me a thumbs up.

Finding the BMA headquarters was the easy part. Getting to the core of the bureaucratic labyrinth to achieve my mission of getting the information about my father took me two days of enquiry. Finally a kindly senior Malay administrative officer arranged a pass for me to visit the prison.

Chapter 11

The prison was sadder than I had thought a prison would be. Without its wartime inmates, a new kind of sombreness filled the ghostly vacuum. One could sense the breaths of tortured souls trapped in the eternal dusk within the high grey walls. The Japanese had gone, and benign jailers had taken their place. The new jailers were benign only in comparison. They were still jailers. I thought of the feeling I kept repressed inside me: my hidden shame. War is about victors and losers. On which side was Father?

The prison guard who took me in was a Sikh. He was cold and taciturn like the prison walls. My attempt to strike up some small talk was met by his disinterest. I trailed behind him through a corridor, passing several iron gates that clanged disdainfully. British officers appeared. We finally reached a room in the belly of the prison. Only a grilled opening high up on the wall ventilated the area. The musty odour reminded me of my Tolok Mine dormitory. There was nothing else in the room except for a long table and a few chairs. The room put the taste of old cement in my mouth, and the quietness felt like an oncoming threat. After the first guard left, another guard replaced him. Judging by his broad-brim hat strapped to his chin, I guessed he was a Gurkha. He ushered me into a room with a table and chairs.

A Malay officer in a warder's uniform with a pip, which led me to presume that he was of senior rank, entered and sat before me. He asked for my pass, which was in the form of a sealed letter. He peeled the envelope and read the letter inside.

"A British officer will interview you. He will decide whether you can see your father. Please wait here." He took the letter with him.

Half an hour later, after what seemed like forever, a tall British officer with a pencil-thin moustache, an army peaked cap, coloured decorations on his chest, and a stiff military bearing entered the room. Having settled in the chair opposite me across the long rectangular table, he eyed me with inconsequential interest, thinking I was just a young man – and an Asiatic at that. My years with Sam had made me familiar with whites, so I felt no intimidation. I had risen when he entered, but I deliberately refrained from addressing him *Tuan* – meaning "master" – a term the Malays used to address the whites. I gave my name and announced that I was Syed Norredin's son. I waited. My reticence obliged the officer to give me his name: Major Maynard.

"May I ask the reason for my father's detention, Major Maynard?" I asked, pulling up my best posture for confidence. My Irish accent surprised him.

"Where did you get that accent?" he asked.

"My foster father is Irish – a British Intelligence operative for Force 136," I boasted.

"Oh. Was he really? How's that?"

I told him about Sam and about our great exploit operating an intelligence network behind enemy lines in Banka – stretching the truth a wee bit. He listened, studying me with suspicion.

"An interesting story, but the name O'Keeffe does not ring a bell."

"Of course. I didn't expect you to know his name." I paused. "Unless one is in contact with Force 136. You may contact London to verify what I have said. You are familiar with that intelligence unit, I am sure, Major?"

"Of course," Maynard said.

I noticed the flush in his face.

"Now, Major, about my father. You owe me at least an explanation – the British Administration owes me that. After all, I am his son, and I have contributed my share to the war effort. Besides, I am the adoptive son of a courageous British operative behind enemy lines who died for the cause. That should have some measure of value. Doesn't it, Major?"

"I can only say to you that your father is classified as a collaborator of the enemy," he said coldly.

"I don't believe that. The word *collaborator* has an offensive ring to the ears, I must say, Major."

He put his head down and flipped through his papers. "Well, that's according to the report we have."

"I understand that a lot of people have been accused of collaboration. Well, there's a thin line between acting with the Japanese to fight against the Allied forces and working for a living, with the Japanese being the government of the day, as an act of survival. After all, my father was a civilian, not a soldier."

"You seem to know quite a bit about these matters, I must say."

"Certainly. I myself worked in a tin mine run by the Japanese, and so did many other Chinese like me. Were we collaborators? The Chinese especially, who hated the Japs like hell?"

"We know that, *Mister* Hamzah." This was the first time I was addressed as *mister*. "But in the case of your father, he was involved in political activities with a group that has a connection with a movement for the formation of Indonesia Raya, a union of Indonesia and the Malay Peninsula, headed by an Indonesian political activist. The group seeks the liberation of Indonesia from the Dutch with the tacit support of the Japanese."

"That would make my father a nationalist, not a collaborator. Isn't that so, Major?"

"Look, Mr. Hamzah, we are still sorting out the details. If your father had not been actually involved in armed conflict against the Allied forces, the matter could be reclassified as an aberration of war. I shall verify the testimony you've given me."

"Delighted to hear that, sir."

"All right, Mr Hamzah, that will be all, I suppose. The corporal will take you to your father."

I stood up and shook the major's hands. He touched his cap. A different Major Maynard left the room.

I followed the corporal to a smaller chamber. From ten feet away, a frail figure walked towards me, his clothes hanging loosely over his frame. He smiled with difficulty while trying to look straight at me through his cloudy eyes. He had aged. If the corporal had not pointed him out to me, I would have let him pass as a stranger.

"Is it you, Hamzah? Good God, my son, I had thought all these years you were dead," he said, his voice hardly audible. He pulled away to see me. "You've changed so much that I almost didn't recognise you. How I've prayed and prayed to God to take my life but to spare yours. It is I who sinned, not you. I want so much to embrace you. May I? I am not as I used to be, you know. I forget things, and I have cataracts. It's a matter of time before I go blind. But it doesn't matter now. I've seen you, so I can die tomorrow."

I clutched him in my arms and held him tightly.

"Father, don't you talk like that. I am here now, and I am going to take care of you. You'll be out of this place soon. I spoke to the major. You'll be coming home, I promise you. I shall see the high commissioner or whoever is in charge to see it is done."

"Don't you worry about me; it's you that's important. There's so much I want to ask you." He smiled. His face was so thin that it pulled his cheekbones and hollowed his cheeks.

"Let's sit, Father. There is so much I want to tell you too, and so much to ask as well." We were alone in that room with no guard for more than an hour. Major Maynard must have accorded us that privilege.

Two weeks later, news of Father's release came. He had been in the Penang Prison for a period of sixty-six days.

No. 27 Kelawei Road was given a spanking new garden. The grass was cut, the fence trimmed, the grounds swept, potted plants sprouted, and peeling walls scraped and repainted. A new pair of cotton trousers, a long-sleeved shirt, and a pair of black leather shoes were placed on the bed in Father's room as a welcome present. Aunty Maimunah was singing all day long, and Ariffin pranced about the house like a happy chimp.

JAVA
1948

Chapter 12

I stepped on the gangway of the boat bound for Jakarta with a heavy heart. I had parted ways with Father again, strange as it may seem, this time at his behest. I had always nursed a secret fear of returning to Mataram House, of meeting the eyes of those I had left, of finding that things had changed, and of being rejected. Yes, rejection was what I feared the most.

Father was not the same man I used to know. I could not decide whether the change was for the better or otherwise. He had transformed himself spiritually. Being spiritual might have been good for him, but being spirituality itself was something else. He prayed incessantly. I am not referring to the five daily prayers required of a Muslim. He added endless optional prayers to those. Once on the prayer mat, he would mediate for hours on end, oblivious to time, chanting the zikr thousands and thousands of times. He fasted every other day, which made him emaciated. He reminded himself of sins he had committed, repeating his penance as if God were deaf.

It was under these circumstances that he said to me, "Go back to your grandmother and your mother. Ask for their forgiveness, before it's too late – of your mother in particular." He sermonised to me at every opportunity when we were together – at breakfast, lunch, and dinner. I began to dread these moments, which was sad, really sad, as I had wished so much to be close to him.

When I set foot on the soil of Java again and rode the route I had left, passing each turn, each town, each village, and all the faces, I imagined their scorn for me. Soon before the sun set, I would be at the Great Gate. My heart beat nervously. The faces of Grandma and Mother traced the fierce magenta sky. A blank confusion set in as the bus trudged along in this once familiar world that now stood aloof like a stranger. I had not realised how strange Java was until now, now that I had become a visitor. I rapped on the door of the Great Gate three times and then waited. The smell of the timber struck a chord of memories. Scent is always a great reminder. I rapped again three times, and shifted my thoughts away from the stress of the moment, reflecting on why people always make three instinctive raps on a door just as I had done. My heart jerked when the smaller gate slid open and a longish-faced man whom I had never seen before appeared. He said nothing. He only grinned. There was a blank look in his eyes, like an idiot.

"I am Syed Hamzah," I announced. My name did not seem to interest him or to mean anything to him.

The next moment, he said, "Do you want to come in?"

"Yes," I said.

He closed the small gate and disappeared from my sight. The pause made me feel as if I were being snubbed. Then the wooden bolts moved and came unlatched, the great door creaked, and Mataram House came into full view.

"Come in," the man said, giving me a foolish grin.

I thought it was somewhat strange that he neither acknowledged me nor enquired who I was, so I decided to ask him. "Do you know who I am?"

"No."

"Then why do you allow me to enter?"

"Mataram is open to the public every day of the week except Friday, from eleven in the morning to six in the evening. Actually, we are about to close now, but I'll allow you in. You're a visitor, aren't you? But I can only take you around for half an hour."

Mataram House is open to the public? What the hell is going on? I asked myself.

"Thank you. Actually, I am not a visitor. I am Syed Hamzah bin Syed Norredin. I used to live here. Ibu Tutik is my grandmother," I said to him.

"It's all right. You don't have to be a visitor."

Strange, my credentials appeared to have no effect on him. He carried on with his wooden demeanour nonchalantly.

"I am the grandson of Ibu Tutik. I came to see her. Do you understand?" I said angrily.

Disregarding me, as though having been programmed, he continued, saying, "I am sorry, you can only tour the compound. Please follow me."

I ignored him and took a quick survey of the surroundings: the luxuriance of the garden had not changed much, only that the trees had grown bigger, their giant canopies spreading a pall of gloom over the scene. The flaming bougainvillea and the trimmed grass were as I remembered them. But Mataram House had aged, looking like an old lady who had fallen from grace, her glory fading like the dying light of dusk. I turned around and headed straight to the main door. Finding me missing, the idiotic guide came running after me, but I was already at the massive door and knocking on it.

"You cannot go in there," he pleaded.

"Who are you anyway?" I asked him.

"I am the gardener. Let me show you my garden."

I ignored him and kept knocking at the door. I heard footsteps. The door opened. An elderly man in classic attire and headgear greeted me.

"Yes, what can I do for you, sir?"

"I am Syed Hamzah son of Syed Norredin, grandson of Ibu Tutik."

The elderly man's face showed utter consternation, but then, in a sudden jolt of memory, he exclaimed, "Master Hamzah! Forgive me for not recognising you." He pulled the door wide open and proceeded to kiss my hand. It was Swastono, the butler. I had failed to recognise him, for the Swastono I had known was fuller and bigger. This one looked shrunken and tiny.

"Forgive me, Pak Swastono, for not recognising you either."

"I've grown old and frail, if that's what you mean." Swastono then turned towards the gardener and gestured for him to leave. "He's not quite right in the head, but he is an excellent gardener."

Swastono came from a class of Javanese butlers who had been bred for serving the aristocracy. He now must have been in his seventies. He was never close to me and we had never had any useful conversation together, as his attention was on Grandma. I had Pak Ali. I had thought little of Swastono and wasn't particularly fond of his condescending ways. I believed him to be a sycophant, carrying out orders with practised manners as if playing a part in a theatre play. He led me to the main hall, where I sat beside the pond. I could see through the foliage of ferns Grandma's favourite corner, the twin wicker chairs, the coffee table, and Raden Satyabrata in his timeless pose, still there and unmoved by my return. My eyes darted about like those of a curious visitor, from the courtyard to the pillars, to the alcove, to the statues. I surveyed the ceiling and the floor, examining every detail with blurred purpose as if these things were new to me. To think I had once run blindly across the house. There was not a niche or a corner I hadn't invaded. Why did I feel so alien now, so divorced to the point of being irrelevant to this grand dame that was once my kingdom? Swastono returned with a tray of coffee and biscuits. Foreign biscuits? The war was just over and Mataram House already had foreign biscuits in its pantry? I wondered about Pak Ali. What had happened to him?

"Ibu Tutik has been informed of your arrival, sir," Swastono announced.

"My mother?"

"Your mother? She—" Swastono hesitated, reluctant to speak the words. "Didn't you receive news of your mother?"

"What news?" My heart pounded.

"My dear sir, forgive me for having to tell you. Your mother returned to her Maker a year after you left Mataram House. May Allah shower His blessings upon her soul," Swastono said courteously, without emotion, just politeness – dry and formal.

"How did she die?"

"It is not my place to say." He dropped his eyes to the floor, sighed, and gave a long pause. "If there's anything you wish, sir, just strike this gong," he said, pointing to the brass gong on the table. Of course you know that. Beg your pardon, sir, for my carelessness. Ibu shall be with you momentarily. Make yourself comfortable. After all, this was your home." He bowed and left.

Left alone in a place that was once my home, I found that my eyes began to water while I was gazing into nothing. Mother's face at her happiest came back to me. Then, every other image of her that I could recall came flooding in. Into that single moment I wanted to pack – and behold once again – my world with her, which I now had lost forever. In that instant I made an unanswerable prayer to God to give me a few brief moments again with her so that I could say, "Mother, I love you very much." My face was drenched, but I didn't realise it. All this time, someone had been standing at the landing of the stairs watching me. I wiped my tears with my hands and saw Grandma standing impassively and looking at me, for how long I didn't know.

"Grandma!" I exclaimed, and tears again streamed down my cheeks. I rose from my seat, went up to her, searched for her hand, clasped it in my palms and kissed it, and then clasped her body as I had once habitually done. Shockingly, it was cold stone that I was embracing, cold like the stone gods of Mataram House.

"Sit," she said, pushing me away ever so deliberately. The icy tone pierced me like a knife. It was not a tone from someone I knew. I froze. I thought I had died. "Sit down," she ordered, pointing to where I had been sitting. She placed herself far away from me, turning me into an unwanted visitor.

I looked at her. In a trembling voice, I asked, "Grandma, how did Mother die?"

It took her a long while to answer me. In that interim, which seemed ages, she studied me, her eyes running the length of me from head to toe. She must have noticed the absence of the frills and furbelows of happier times that used to adorn me. Unless my mind was playing tricks on me, I saw signs neither of sympathy nor of kindness in her face. Nothing.

Then finally she spoke.

"It's too late to regret, to pine, to shed tears. She died of a broken heart – broken by you and your father. She fell into sickness when you left and never recovered. Your mother had a fragile heart and a more fragile mind. She married your father out of love. He was never my choice, but I consented because I knew what would happen to her if I didn't. But her happiness was short-lived. When you were born, you were the only link to that happiness. When you left, her happiness went with you. It was as if her whole life had gone too. Now why do you come back? To claim your inheritance?"

Grandma's icy words shocked me. I felt the roof crashing over me. How could Grandma have thought that I had come back to claim something, when the only claim I wanted to make was of her and Mother? Then, adding salt to the wound, she handed me a packet, but her eyes were not on me as if she were afraid they would cross mine. I opened it and found that it was full of money.

"This is not what I came for, Grandma." I placed the packet on the table, far away from me. Her eyes followed me. The icy coldness hadn't thawed a bit. But I sensed pain in that coldness, not anger or bitterness.

"What is it then?"

"To seek your forgiveness – and Mother's."

"Too late!"

"I was a fool."

"Indeed you were – and your father was a bigger fool."

"We both paid dearly for it, very dearly, Grandma. Believe me."

She paused and let out a deep sigh. I detected a slight thawing of the freeze. Her eyes gazed at the far end of the room, all the while averting mine. Then with deliberateness, she said, "Your father had always accused me of being mad, of suffering from delusions of grandeur. He thought I had made up all this glorification of the past. He cast doubts on my faith because of these idols of gods I have in this house. But these are the representation of the past. They are not for worshipping. He said all that, but he himself never prayed a day in his life. And his disdain was never open but was quietly suppressed in silence. But it was there. I read it all the time, especially during meals when we were all together. I sensed his disdain by his expressions, his attitude, his sarcasm, his body language, the very cold reticence of his presence when he was with me. Yet he knew everything I did was for you. He knew what it meant. It wasn't idle fantasy. He even took a serious oath on the matter – so serious that it would bring the wrath of God upon him if he broke it. But he fooled me. He had no intention whatsoever to keep faith with it. In fact, the whole thing was nonsensical to him. To think he was contemptuous of my faith! It was he who lacked faith in anything. Now you know. Oaths in the name of God shouldn't be taken lightly. Even a broken promise between two human beings has its consequences. What more an oath with the Almighty? I have said enough."

Throughout the remonstrance, my eyes were steaming with tears.

"Don't you want to know what happened to me, Grandma?"

"I don't have to. I knew the moment you left Mataram House that your destiny would take a turn and sorrow would follow you like a shadow – a shadow that even darkness could not extinguish. Why do you think I had built a fortress around you? Do you remember what I had told you that night on the eve of my departure to Mecca? You and Mataram House were like inseparable twins. One could not do without the other. Enough. Too much water has flowed under the bridge. The past shall remain in the past. The future holds no interest for me."

I rose from the chair, walked towards her, dropped to my knees, and kissed her feet. "Forgive me, Grandma," I said, my tears flowing uncontrollably like a torrential rain. She didn't touch me, keeping her eyes continually fixed to the farthest point of the room. Her gaze was devoid of vision, devoid of meaning. I rose from the floor dejectedly and then walked away in the direction of the corridor, without touching the packet she had handed to me earlier. I couldn't restrain myself from turning my head for one last gaze. She was still staring into the void, standing immobile like a statue. I couldn't determine whether I was forgiven.

What would I tell Father? Already he was inundated with guilt. Already he had only prayers left in his life, nothing else. This news would certainly precipitate his demise. He was the only one I had left.

As I stepped out of Mataram House, the listless night swallowed me. I had no more questions to ask myself.

MALAYA
1950

Chapter 13

Back in the transient tranquillity of Kelawei Road, I sought much-needed refuge from the heartbreaking departure with Grandma. My expectations hadn't been high, but the reality was far worse than I had anticipated. The last image of Grandma could never be erased from my memory. I wasn't angry. On the contrary, it was a consuming sorrow that I was now suffering, perhaps as much as she was, I believed. She was Mataram House. When I forsook it, I forsook her. The forlorn and dejected face of Mataram House that I saw was her own dejection personified.

Father had begun to have lapses of memory, so I was spared from having to recount the unhappy event, which certainly would have made him suffer more. Aunty Maimunah was so engrossed with her small world that did not venture beyond Kelawei Road.

My funds were running low, and soon I had to look for a job. My choices were limited. Except for my language skills and my experience in the tin mine industry, I had no education of an employable nature.

A month after my meeting with Grandma, someone came looking for me, a person unknown to me. He conveyed a message from a man named Mr Tan Siew Lim. Tan Siew Lim, the message said, was one of the biggest tin miners in Malaya. This was somewhat mysterious because I knew no one by that name.

Northam Road was a Chinese millionaires' row. One could find along the tree-lined avenue some of the finest and most pompous imitations of European architecture, homes with Corinthian pillars, neoclassical architraves, and majestic driveways, as though to display the owners' pinnacle of success. Into one of these driveways my humble trishaw entered.

I alighted behind a black Rolls-Royce parked under a semicircular white-pillared portico. A uniformed Chinese man received me with the utmost courtesy, a sign that I had been expected, which made me sigh in relief from my anxiety. I stepped into a cavernous hall with a black and white marble floor matching the marble statues of Venus de Milo; rosewood furniture; and a chandelier that dropped incongruously from the high ceiling, giving the room the feel of a cold, misplaced grandeur. The out-of-place twin *Venus de Milo* statues on each side of the grand staircase glanced at me with their dead white eyes.

A woman servant in a black samfu brought in a tray of Chinese tea and placed it on the centre table, quite out of reach from me. A few moments later a man in a simple black Chinese garment with a chained gold watch in the breast pocket came descending from the grand staircase. I hadn't the need to guess who he was.

The man was of medium build with a round face and high-cropped hair that ended flat like a tabletop. He was tan, a characteristic of the tin miners who grew rich under the scorching sun. In spite of the man's simple attire, the entrance he made exuded an air of self-possession that came with wealth.

"Mister Hamzah, welcome, welcome," he bellowed in English even before landing his feet on the floor, raising both his hands, one holding a cigarette with a long holder. "I am Tan. People call me Miner Tan." His voice echoed in the cavernous hall. He clasped my shoulders with both of his big palms, but he didn't offer the European handshake. "Come inside." He gestured at me to follow him. There was a distinct Chinese twang in his accent.

I walked behind him as he ambled with a gentle swaying of his stout body, not unlike a Chinese emperor depicted in a Chinese opera. He brought me to a lounging room with French windows that overlooked the outside. It was an opulent room, furnished with hard Chinese dark rosewood chairs and tables, which were embellished with mother-of-pearl. At the centre was a round table supporting a giant vase (probably a Ming Dynasty artefact). A huge painting of my host in a three-piece Western suit and a cane stood imposingly against a wall. It couldn't be missed.

Once we were settled in our chairs, he took out a silver cigarette case, and offered a stick to me Chinese style. I wasn't a smoker, but I obliged so as not to offend.

"Whisky or brandy?" he asked.

"Whisky."

"I am a whisky man too. With my mah-jong buddies, it's beer or *samsu*. He walked to the cabinet and retrieved the whisky and two glasses, and then he rang a bell.

The woman servant came. He ordered her to bring in the ice and water.

Then without a warning he said, "I want you to be my partner."

I was so taken aback by this sudden and incomprehensible offer, I became completely speechless. In a moment, after gathering my thoughts, I asked, "What do you mean, Mr Tan?"

"Partner, business partner." He looked at me and laughed, and gave me a slap on the back as if we were old friends.

I wasn't really sure, given that laugh, whether he was serious or was playing a practical joke on me. And he didn't know me from Adam, so how could he be asking me to be his partner? That casual demeanour and the slapping on the back on our first meeting seemed odd or eccentric at best. "Are you serious, Mr Tan?" I asked. "You don't even know me."

"Certainly serious. Why do you think I called you here?"

"But why me? What kind of partnership is this?"

"Tin, of course. What else? I am Miner Tan. You don't remember?" He guffawed, this time loudly. It seemed to me that his laughs had nothing to do with humour but were simply a matter of conversational style. Maybe it was his way of disarming people. *Pretty shrewd*, I thought. I was so disarmed that it made me instantly amenable to him.

"Mr Tan, I need to know something, something which puzzled me the very moment I received your message. How did you come to know me?"

The guffaws returned with a vengeance. He looked at me sideways with his narrow eyes and smiled astutely. "You don't know?"

"Don't know what?"

"I was owner of Tolok Mine in Banka under the Japanese. So, in a way, you were already working for me." He laughed. "After the war you made a lot of money from the tin the mine had been paying you. You made money from me – very clever. You can speak Hokkien, English, and Dutch, am I right? So I know a lot about you. Ha ha ha!"

"What!" I exclaimed. And it was my turn to laugh. "Now, Mr Tan, another question. Why do you want me as a partner?"

"I'll tell you why. I can't apply for any more mining leases in Kinta. They say I already have too many. Other Chinese miners are very jealous of me. But you are a Malay. You have experience. So you can easily get a mining lease. The government will surely give it to you. I have the money. So, you get the mining lease and I finance you. We both make money. And I say that's good partnership. Simple, isn't it?"

"You are very sure of this?"

"Very sure. I think you are a smart man. And you have experience in working with Chinese people."

The woman servant returned and announced that lunch was ready.

"Come. We eat."

"Excuse me, Mr Tan—"

"Don't worry, no pork. You're a Muslim, I know." He laughed.

"Not only do you know about me, but also you are able to read my mind."

"That's why we can be partners."

Over lunch my mind was reeling. The whole idea of a partnership with Miner Tan was coming to me so rapidly and forcefully that I was in a daze. I didn't know this man from Adam, but he had a rather blunt, disarming charm about him that seemed to reflect his true self. It comforted me. I could read people pretty well by now, and he did appear sincere towards me. Why shouldn't I take the offer? After all, he was the one taking all the risk.

Noticing I was momentarily distracted, he asked, "What are you thinking, Mr Hamzah?"

"About the business. What else?"

"That is why I think you are the right partner for me. Now we eat. We'll talk business later."

After lunch he laid down the plan for me – whom to contact, where to stay, and when to start. He seemed to have worked out every aspect of my assignment in quite good detail, which impressed me. When it was time for me to leave, he had me chauffeured in his black Rolls-Royce. This caused great consternation at 27 Kelawei Road when Aunty Maimunah saw me disembarking from the gleaming car.

Without Tan even telling me, I had already guessed that I would be working in Kinta Valley in the state of Perak, where the richest tin deposits in Malaya, and indeed in the world, lay. At the centre was Ipoh, its capital. It was going to be my new home.

Before I left for Ipoh, I paid Miner Tan another visit. I was received with as much warmth, delight, and guffaws as I had been previously. Lest I might get carried away with his friendly guffaws, I reminded myself that this Miner Tan was no ordinary man. Hidden underneath those affable mannerisms was a man of money and power belonging to the breed of Chinese who built their wealth from sheer grit and hard work, a man who, I believed, would expect complete loyalty in return for the trust he had put in me.

Chapter 14

Kinta Valley, where the tin was at its richest, stretched two hundred miles long, flanked by white limestone hills and dissected by a major river basin, which was scarred in the best possible way by mines of innumerable sizes and shapes. At Kinta Valley, literally no stone was left unturned when it came to extracting the wealth from the ground.

Ipoh, the capital town, was an oasis in Kinta Valley's mad rush for riches, with its fine railway station and town hall, its smart residences, and its classic school buildings all reflecting the appearance of British institutions. One couldn't miss the ubiquitous cricket field and its club – signs of British presence wherever they resided. From the major roundabout, avenues of wealthy homes radiated.

I rented a bungalow house in one of the lesser avenues and bought a Ford – my first worldly possession of any significance.

I had no friends. For company I had my workers, who had crude habits no different from those of the workers at Tolok Mine, people to whom I thought I had bade farewell in Banka. But this time I was their leader and master. And not being of the same race was going to be a challenge. The only influence I had was based on my partnership with Miner Tan. My fluency with the mine workers' native tongue and my experience in Tolok Mine were my only weapons of command.

The first few months at my job were hectic. Establishing my presence with the staff, the supervisors, the *kongsi* head, and the workers required me to communicate daily between the office in Clement Street and the mine in Gopeng, ten miles away. I had to put into their minds that I was a hands-on person, not just an office-bound manager, and I had to do so without delay. Slowly and surely, it sank into their minds that I knew every nook and corner of the mining business. Their regard for me grew over the days.

Respite from the oppressive mine and the clutter of clerks and voices in the dowdy office on Clement Street was a must. Such escapes came on weekends, in the pockets of little paradise that lay in nearby Malay villages. With my trusty Ford, a tiffin box, a flask, a hat, a book, and a mat as companions, I would find a clear stream with a shady bough and spend the day there.

Women had yet to come into my life. Aunty Maimunah had questioned me about it. Either my eyes were closed or the women were blind, she had said. The women who were brought into my view for my amusement in Ipoh, courtesy of the goodwill of my mining colleagues in the office, were miserable creatures. They were the miners' delights, not mine.

Women and alcohol were forbidden in the mine, so the workers tucked away their desires in their little closets until the end of the week. When payday came, off they went to the sleazy joints, opium dens, and gambling houses in the sleazy parts of Chinatown to let themselves loose.

As much as I wanted to stay clear from these social outings, I didn't think it right to be too aloof, as I was in the workers' enclave and thought it best to make them feel I was one of them. The fact that I was of a different race made this all the more imperative. Most importantly, I thought that I shouldn't refuse the invitations of the managers and supervisors, as they were my colleagues and I needed their support the most.

One such occasion to socialise with the people above me eventually came.

Foo was my manager for the mining operation, the most vital man upon whom the mining output depended. Directly under him were the kongsi head and his workers.

One of the biggest headaches at the mine was pilferage of the tin ore. Ingenious means were employed by workers to squirrel away small quantities of ore at a time in their pockets, pouches, and lunch boxes. Doing this over time meant that one accumulated a pretty good hoard. To the credit of Antony Foo, Miner Tan's mine had the lowest occurrence of shortages among the Chinese mines.

Foo was a man in his forties. He had worked with Tan for over twenty years. The fact that he was of medium height and a voracious eater and drinker led him to have an oversized tummy. On account of that, his shirt tails stubbornly refused to stay put in his waist, no matter how many times he tried to tuck them in. He was jovial with a crude sense of humour, and very much liked by the workers. He took to me very early on, without a trace of jealousy or reservations. Having worked with Tan a long time, he knew better than to question Tan's decision.

One day Foo said to me, "Come, Mr Hamzah, let's have some fun this Saturday. I will take you to a place where you can be in paradise."

I had absolutely no idea what he meant by paradise. When I insisted on an explanation, he replied, "If I were to tell, the fun would be lost."

I acquiesced, feeling that I needed his friendship. I hoped it wasn't a brothel he would be taking me to.

Antony took me in his car to the outskirts of the town along the road to Kuala Kangsar and across the big iron bridge. A small lane took us to a large single-storey wooden bungalow with overhanging eaves and wide, airy verandahs shaded with bamboo blinds and surrounded by trees, the type usually belonging to a rubber estate manager. A number of cars were parked outside.

"Whose house is this, Antony?"

"It's not a house. It's a club."

"Club for what?"

"You'll see."

The bungalow had a big lounge area furnished with cane sets. In the centre was a dining table. On each side of the dining area were two bedrooms. A Chinese man welcomed us in Hokkien and asked what drinks we wanted. The ceiling fans were running full blast, churning a familiar sweet and pungent odour, bringing back a memory that had lapsed. I then realised where I was.

Without much ado, the Chinese man ushered us into one of the rooms. When we entered the dim smoky room and saw the sight of men lying on their sides facing each other, their eyes unstirred in the mawkish air, I panicked. I had never been to a full-fledged opium den before, though I had seen smokers in Tolok Mine. *Surely Antony doesn't expect me to lie on those bunks and smoke one of the pesky pipes?* I said to myself.

"Hey, Antony, I don't smoke the stuff, but you go ahead. I'll wait outside."

Antony didn't say anything. He just smiled and quickly said, "I too do not smoke. I just wanted to show you where the miners go in Ipoh when they say 'paradise'. You must know what the workers and managers and miners do and where they go for recreation. It is always an advantage to know as much about people you deal with and work with. OK, let's have some beer. After that I am going to take you on a tour of Ipoh, to places not in the public eye – like this place."

"We ordered beers and stayed for half an hour. No one was at the bar since alcohol wasn't the object of the destination. I asked Foo who the regulars were. He said that the place was a kind of upscale den for a selective clientele who preferred a more exclusive and cleaner environment than the ones patronised by all kinds of addicts from labourers to rickshaw pullers. "You don't want to step into those places." I asked him whether Mr Tan smoked – a sensitive question. His answer was a categorical no. I had a suspicion that Antony had brought me here to see if I indulged in the bloody stuff. *What a sneaky fellow,* I thought.

"Tell me, Antony, why did you bring me here? You yourself don't care for this stuff."

He became reticent and began to play with his thumb.

"You are holding something back from me. Come on. Tell me."

"If I tell you, you must promise not to raise it with Mr Tan. Promise?"

"Promise."

"Mr Tan is very happy with your performance. I have been assigned by him to report on you. Although you are a Malay, you know the mine like a Chinese miner, I had told him. Truly, I am impressed with you – and so is he. One final thing he wanted me to report on was whether you smoked opium. He hates opium smokers. If any of the office staff is found to even whiff it, it's the sack for him. He wasn't sure about you, since you were in Tolok Mine for several years, mixing with those lowly workers. You passed the test. I'm sorry, Mr Hamzah, for leading you on. I had to be sure. It's my job."

"Thank you for being honest with me. And thank you for the good report card."

"All right, then, let's go for a nice big lunch. My treat." He broke into a broad smile.

Chapter 15

Time passed very quickly. It had been almost a year since I had begun partnering with Miner Tan. The mine was doing very well. Output and profits had increased twofold since I took over, thanks mainly to the greater recovery of ore and a huge drop in shortages and machinery breakdowns. My schedule became less hectic than when I had first started, which meant a more relaxed mind and body for me. I had enrolled in the town's book club.

Almost every Sunday I would be amid the quiet world of this book club on Station Road, blending with the book lovers by the long tables. Like them, I stayed glued to the books, without a word said to the others. My companions, apart from a sprinkle of locals, were mostly white women whose husbands were at the Perak Club, probably downing whisky or gin or their favourite Tiger Beer and bragging about their forays with local women – not to forget the British indulgence with rugby and cricket, of course.

One Sunday, three months after I had joined the book club, a woman whom I had not seen before caught my attention. Sitting alone away from the rest, she kept her eyes on her book without once lifting her head.

I must shamefully confess, never had a woman arrested my eyes so magnetically, and never had I seen such a beautiful woman in my life. Sitting in a corner away from the other patrons, her presence seemed seductively deliberate in a very mysterious sort of way.

In the many times I had been there, I found her in the same corner, her eyes on her book. She seemed sedate and composed. By now she must have been conscious that I was eyeing her, yet she gave me not a glance.

She was Chinese, not too young in age – nor was she old. I would describe her as being at an age when a woman is most sensual and irresistible. From where I sat, about two long tables away, I could define the pearly whiteness of her skin and the exquisite brilliance of her hair, but I could not determine the colour of her eyes, however badly I wanted to.

Like an artist I was, judging from a distance and catching every detail, every drop of light that touched her. As if aware of my secret attention, she lifted her eyes to gaze at the window before sweeping her hair with her fingers. And in one unexpected move, she turned her head wide towards the window, revealing a portrait of a classic oriental beauty.

The woman didn't seem at all displeased by my interest. Every Sunday she would be at the same place at the same time, and I would always sit two tables away from her at the same place and same time. Although an open book was on my table, my mind wasn't on it, nor, I believed, was her mind on her book, since the pages were not flipped. The inside of me repeatedly said that I should walk up to her, ask for her name, and not be a fool by just sitting there and suffering in silence. She might not be there the next time, in which case I would curse myself for my cowardice.

But my courage failed me miserably. I had never in my life approached a real woman before, let alone a goddess like her.

The following Sunday, when she was not there at her usual place, I felt like dying. All of a sudden I found myself morosely in love with someone whom I had seen only from a distance. Now she was gone. What an accursed man I was. I clamped my book shut and sauntered dejectedly to where she had once sat. Like a fool I searched deeply for the remains of her perfume, trying to recapture her presence in the scent she had left behind. I was going crazy, missing someone I had not even spoken to.

For four Sundays I came, but she was not there. I wasn't reading my book anymore, just picking the pages – my fingers, my eyes, my mind, in different places. I decided not to visit the book club anymore; the absence of her sitting opposite me was too much to bear. The elderly Indian woman librarian began to notice my odd behaviour of being there yet doing nothing, eyeing me suspiciously out of the corners of her eyes.

A month later I went shopping on High Low Street. I can't recall what day it was, but it was a weekday, of that I was sure, because the shops were open. I had taken a day off to buy something for Father at Joseph Brothers, the fashion store.

Father, whose birthday was a week away, liked to smoke with a holder. His was looking old the last time I saw it. The salesman took one out and placed it on a velvet cloth over the glass case. As I was examining it, someone came from behind me and said in English, "That's an elegant one, but it must go with a case too." I turned around and there she was, the woman who for weeks had brought my mind to near insanity, standing close by me. Her presence was so sudden that I froze, her perfume assaulting me beguilingly.

"I am Lai Peng," she said with a smile. Her directness made my knees give way. I had thought of her somewhat differently, as being modest with the prudery of a sparrow, shy to the approach. After waiting for me to respond, which took an eternity, she asked, "Am I intruding?"

"No, not at all. I am just surprised to see you. I am sorry, I am Hamzah," I said with a tremor, which I believed she detected.

"I know who you are – you're with Miner Tan, right?" She smiled composedly, displaying exquisite rosy lips.

I was beguiled and couldn't take my eyes off her. Her sudden appearance out of the blue rattled me, making me look foolish, like a besotted schoolboy before a beautiful woman.

"Yes. How did you know that?"

She smiled again but didn't reply to my question. "Buying for a sweetheart?" she asked instead.

"No, it's not for a woman. It's for my father," I said shyly.

"Get the case too. He'll love it. Well, nice meeting you. Hamzah, right?" She tilted her head in a gesture to leave, but her eyes were still on me.

I said to myself that if I failed this time, I would lose her forever. Commanding every fibre of my being, I said, "Why aren't you at the book club anymore, Miss Lai Peng?" I trembled, I truly did. She must have noticed that again.

"Why? Well—" She hesitated. "Your eyes were always on me. Isn't that true? Maybe that's why." She gave a coy smile, teasing me. "By the way, drop the 'Miss Lai Peng'. Just call me Pinky." Those words caught me like a trap.

"Did I offend you in any way, Miss Pinky?"

She paused. "You couldn't take your eyes off me, yet you didn't have the courtesy to introduce yourself."

"I – I am so sorry."

She looked at me again. Just as I was about to warm up to her, she changed the subject.

"Go and buy that cigarette holder for your father. It's a lovely choice. Don't forget the case either. They are a pair. I've to go. Cheerio." She turned away to leave.

"Wait, Miss Pinky. Would you come again to the book club?"

"It's Pinky, not Miss Pinky. Why do you ask?"

"Because – because I'd like to see you again."

"Maybe." She swayed her head and smiled. For a few seconds her eyes measured me.

"Does that mean yes?"

"You're pretty insistent, aren't you? Let's put it this way: it's not a promise. I don't want to make a promise and then break it." Noticing my despondent look, she asked, "Would you wait for me?"

"Certainly."

"In that case, maybe."

Pinky walked away, swaying like a leaf caught in a gentle wind, her scent trailing behind her. That episode was to stalk me for nights, walking into my dreams, my sleepless nights. I was falling in love. I bought the case for my father, as she had suggested, without question. Even the salesman was amused to see me grinning like a smitten schoolboy. For days I clung to every syllable Pinky had uttered, putting positive connotations to each word and giving incredulous meanings to them.

The Sunday came, and I was at the book club as early as the door opened. Pinky wasn't at her usual place. I waited until 5 p.m., closing time – she never came. I was again there the following Sunday. No sign of her. On the following, third Sunday, just before lunchtime, she came. The sight of her lifted my heart from a spiralling hole.

"Hello, Hamzah," she said in the most sumptuous tone, as if nothing had happened.

"I waited for you." There was a bit of a strain in my voice, the result of anger, perhaps.

"Did you?" She touched my hand gently. The sensation melted me. Never had I felt a woman's touch like that. "I am here now. Aren't you glad you waited? If you hadn't waited, you'd never see me today. I wanted to be sure. Never mind. I am here, and you are here. Isn't that what you wanted?" She smiled coyly.

She gave me her hand. I took it and put it gently to my lips.

"That's very gallant. Where did you learn that, from the Hollywood films?"

"From my heart." I pulled a bouquet of flowers from under the table. "For you, Pinky."

"Oh, flowers! Very nice. Is courting women a hobby of yours?"

"By the way, there were two other bouquets, but they died waiting for you."

"Poor you." She laughed. I watched her every motion.

"Let's go for lunch at the Station Hotel. My treat," she said.

"Absolutely not," I said.

"You mean you won't have lunch with me?" she said with feigned sullenness.

"I meant that no woman shall pay for my lunch. Absolutely not a woman as lovely as you are."

"You came in rather shyly when we first met, but now you are charging like a bull. Be careful, I might fall in love with you." She narrowed her gentle brown eyes and pursed her lips.

As we walked to the Station Hotel, a ten-minute walk away, she placed her hand on my arm as if we had known each other a long time. It was my first visit to this restaurant.

When we arrived at the Station Hotel Restaurant, the head waiter appeared to know Pinky and addressed her by her Chinese name. He ushered us to a table by the long window. It was lunchtime and the place was full. I noticed the overflowing white faces, some of the patrons in linen jackets, and a few in khakis, cotton shirts, tropical hats. They looked like planters. I scouted for some Asian faces and spotted two Malay men by the window.

A uniformed Chinese waiter ushered us to the far corner of the large room by a potted palm. The light was subdued in the high-ceilinged dining room, in the centre of which elegantly dropped a rod-iron chandelier. The place settings consisted of white tablecloths, linen serviettes, silverware, and centrepiece flowers, giving the place an English ambience.

"I like this place. It's quiet. The Chinese rarely come here, preferring the boisterous restaurants in town or the men-only clan clubs. Do you like it?"

"It's nice."

"Then you'd be the first tin miner in Ipoh to patronise it – the first non-white tin miner, that is."

Pinky ordered port, and I took a whisky soda. I watched her study the menu. In fact I had been observing her from the time we had left the book club: her walk, her gestures, her brown eyes, that slender nose, the elegant sassy hair that curled lusciously behind her ears just shy of the shoulders exuding a capricious air, the pearl necklace adorning her equally pearly chest, the floral skirt and silk blouse, and the European Sunday hat. The sum total of all these things made her more like one of those European wives the locals called memsahib than a Chinese woman.

I had also noticed, the first time we met, her perfect English. When I complimented her for that in the restaurant, she gave me a swipe, which I deserved. Lifting her head from the menu, she made a terse reply: "Why? Chinese girls aren't supposed to speak the English language well?"

"I am sorry, I didn't mean it like that. I couldn't help wanting to compliment you."

She smiled, tapping my hand gently. "It's all right. I am pulling your leg. Thank you. It's my mother; she insisted upon it. And what about you? You've a rather strong accent which I can't pin down."

I got it from my adoptive father – he was Irish."

"Really? That's interesting. I'd love to know more about you – a Malay tin miner in a totally Chinese world, an Irish man for a father, and accosting a Chinese woman in a public library. Very interesting. What else?"

"I want to know more about you too. You're pretty mysterious yourself."

"All right, an interesting man and a mysterious woman having an affair in the middle of the afternoon. Sounds like a scene from a novel. Now let's order.

I am famished. They do excellent roast beef on Sundays. Would you like that? Or would you prefer the curry tiffin that these English love so much?"

"Eating curry the English way? No, thank you. I'll go for the roast beef anytime."

She turned to a senior waiter who had been watching us attentively, and politely nodded her head. Hastily the waiter came.

"Yes, Miss Peng. May I take your order now?"

"Two roast beef, Mr Lim."

"Very good, Miss Peng, with the Yorkshire pudding of course. And the dessert, Miss Lai Peng? The usual?"

"Why don't you ask my gentleman friend what he would have?"

"Sir, we have the usual bread and butter pudding and Indian rice pudding. Or if you like, sir, I shall cook before you our special crêpes Suzette with orange sauce and Grand Marnier, with ice cream over it. Very nice."

"The crêpes Suzette sound good."

"Excellent choice, sir. And coffee after that?"

"Yes, please."

"Very good sir."

I wanted so much to know who this Pinky was. The question had been on the tip of my tongue since the time we were first seated at the table, but I didn't have the nerve to ask, in case like a bird she would just fly off and never return.

"You haven't told me how you came to know about me," I enquired casually while waiting for the dishes to arrive.

"It's very simple, Hamzah. A Malay running a totally Chinese tin mine in Kinta Valley? Now, how common is that? You know how the Chinese are. They do not trust anyone who isn't of their own kind. Even among themselves, they trust their own clan first. Now you stick out like a sore thumb – your appearance doesn't help at all. Everybody thought you would fail miserably. They were wrong. The Tan Mine is the best-run Chinese opencast mine in Kinta – I heard. If there's anything the Chinese look up to, it is success. You're the talk of the Chinese community. You know that?"

However pleasant that was to my ears, I was completely baffled. This lovely woman with whom I was already uncontrollably enamoured taking an interest in me was, admittedly, very uplifting to me. It dazed me.

My silence prompted her. "Don't you have anything to say? It's quite an accolade, you know."

"I just don't know what to say. If I were to say thank you, it would mean I am deserving of those compliments."

"Aren't you?"

"No."

"You're modest. I like that."

"Now, Miss Pinky—"

"Stop it! It's Pinky, I told you. You aren't talking to your teacher."

"Pinky. Now it's my turn. Tell me about yourself."

She paused, lowered her eyes pensively as if weighing her thoughts, and then asked, "Isn't it enough that we are friends, Hamzah?" She placed her palm gently on my hand. "Let's leave it that way, shall we, my dear?"

The "my dear" melted me. So insecure I was that this bird might just take flight that I quickly said, "Of course." After that, I never again broached the subject.

During lunch, she did most of the talking. I listened, mesmerised by her knowledge. She read voraciously, she said, to pass the time in this culturally staid environment – or else she would be bored to death. She appeared to hold a special fascination for Isabella Bird. "Who is Isabella Bird?" I enquired ignorantly. She went on to tell me about this extraordinary nineteenth-century English woman adventurer, writer, and photographer who had also travelled extensively in Malaya. Pinky admired her courage in cutting across a man's world at a time when women were expected to be homebound, producing children. An oriental woman doing that would surely be shunned into the corners of spinsterhood, she claimed. She threw her head back and laughed. Then she caught me off guard by asking, "Are you one of those men who think like that, Hamzah?"

"Well, not necessarily. I mean—"

"Caught you there. You male chauvinist!"

"What I wanted to say was, I prefer my woman to be by my side, not wandering around the world like Isabella Bird."

"In spite of that, she was pursued by suitors who were captivated by her extraordinary spirit, one of whom was a doctor. He eventually married her," she retorted.

Time went by without our realising it.

"Look around, Hamzah. We seem to be the only ones left in the restaurant." She consulted her watch. "Goodness me, it's past three o'clock. I have never stayed this late. What have you done to me, Hamzah? You naughty man. Let's go before they chase us out."

I walked her to her car, which was parked by the book club. Once again she clung to my hand affectionately, which pleased me enormously, beyond words. Before we parted, she said, "Thank you, my dear, for an enjoyable afternoon."

"I have never had such a pleasurable company. So the pleasure was entirely mine. Do I see you again, Pinky?"

"Do you want to?"

"What a question."

"I am a woman, Hamzah." She eyed me coquettishly with a swing of her head, and then threw a delectable smile. "Bye. See you at the book club."

I was at the book club very early the following Sunday. By eleven o'clock, she appeared. I rose excitedly from my chair. From far away, she waved and smiled.

Surreptitiously, like two children about to commit mischief, we chose a seldom-patronised corner behind two reference shelves that had a long table, away from the eye of the inquisitive matronly librarian. We took two reference books from the shelves and pretended to read. In soft tones we talked to each other about books; Ipoh and the miners; the English memsahibs' bored lives and their affairs; the British snobs and their fading empire; and the librarian who did not have a husband. Then we drifted into inconsequential things while our eyes met, our hands touched, and our feelings grew.

This sort of behaviour went on for weeks. Occasionally, our matron would spy on us. Since we learned to detect her coming, we were never caught talking. We smiled to each other mischievously. We also had our lunch at the Station Restaurant, and at the same table, which Lim, the head waiter, had now specially made our corner.

Then one day, I planted a kiss on Pinky's lips. She returned it with a passion I never imagined she would. We came out of it breathless.

"Let's go to my place, Pinky."

"Not yet, sweetheart. Don't rush these things. I am not going anywhere. We'll meet every week."

"I want it to be every day."

"Don't be silly. You have to work."

And from that day on, my life was not mine anymore. It belonged to her. I waited impatiently for the weekend to come. We kissed, but no more than that. The days went by. In the interim, I was like a man dying of thirst.

Then, in the week that followed, Pinky said, "Sweetheart, let's go to Taiping. I want to be alone with you. We'll have a picnic by the lake and spend the day. We'll go on a weekday so there'll be no people, just you and me. You'll have to take the day off, but that's not a problem, right? You are the bossman, aren't you?" She smiled, cupped my face in her palms, and kissed me.

Taiping, fifty miles north of Ipoh, is set against manicured trees with giant canopies, and lakes carved in a valley surrounded by green hills. We rested on a woven mat by the lake, where not a soul was in sight.

After lunch we engrossed ourselves in affections. We noticed the threatening black clouds hovering above us. Folding our things, we headed for the Burmese Pool by the waterfall nearby. The black clouds chased us as we hurried. The rain overtook us. We were drenched.

The Burmese Pool was deserted. Once we had changed into our bathing suits, the rain stopped. We sat by the side of the pool, kicking the water like children, our minds vague and indeterminate just like the mist that ghosted about the hills after the downpour.

I traced Pinky's thoughts, now freed for the first time from the curtain of restraint. As I feasted my eyes upon her, thinking how beautiful she was, she exclaimed, "Look, there's a rainbow." She arched her neck to the sky.

I looked up and saw nothing. Suddenly she stripped off her swimwear, jumped into the water, and pulled me down. I dove below to catch her ankles. She swam away, winding like a fish and surfacing behind the waterfall. I caught up with her. She pulled me towards her, enveloping me, kissing me wildly, quenching her own secret thirst. I responded with equal vigour. In an instant we became one, sending us to abysmal depths. We were swallowing, choking, and out of breath. Our love culminated with a gentle kiss and an embrace.

The sun slid below the hills and the water turned chilly. Our earlier inconsequential affections had finally conflagrated, the aftermath of which glowed and glowed inside us.

Taking the southbound night train back to Ipoh, we sat in the first-class lounge. We saw a few Europeans having pre-dinner drinks at the other end. Pinky rested her head on my shoulders. I kissed her forehead, thinking that soon we would part and I would have nothing but her scent. We huddled, the roaring of the rails making us drowsy. The three Europeans went on talking, topping off and then emptying their glasses, while the Malay attendant waited at the bar. Save for him, none of them took even a glance at us. We were alone in our new-found world.

We said nothing to each other. Not a word of love was spoken; not a question was asked. All that there had been to say and ask had already been spoken. I had no further need to know more about her. I was satisfied with just having her.

Chapter 16

Since my move to Ipoh more than a year ago, I hadn't returned to Penang, so occupied had I been with the mine. Now with Pinky coming into my life like a storm, suddenly rousing my long-dormant emotions to life, every moment of my leisure time was filled with her. All my weekends were now occupied by her. My plan to visit Father was quietly relegated to the background, but not without guilt, as I did miss Father.

I had been seeing Pinky for three months. If she hadn't taken leave to visit her mother in Kuala Lumpur, I would have further postponed my trip to visit Father. So with her away, I managed to return to Penang.

Aunty Maimunah, as expected, welcomed me with her huge bear hug, heaping me with praise about how good I looked and bombarding me with questions about why I had not come home for so long. And, of course, she asked the usual question: if I had found a woman to marry.

Redness had returned to Father's face. Also, he had added a great deal to his middle, thanks to Aunty Maimunah's making sure that the pantry was always full. She had been feeding him with a vengeance, in the process becoming a bigger woman herself. Father had grown a great crown of shocking white hair and badly needed a haircut.

When I drove him to the barber's, he sat beside me and fixed his gaze, looking right through the windscreen and onto the road, without saying a single word. At the barber he was like a well-behaved boy without a protest while being trimmed, shaved, and wrapped with a hot towel. He had his head massaged and his neck cracked – all the works Indian barbers were famous for. I felt sorry for him.

Father would awake early, do his toilette, shave, bathe, and put on clean clothes. All that he was able to do. But when I engaged him in conversation, he would look at my face blankly. Sometimes he would shake his head sideways as though in disagreement, or maybe in displeasure. I couldn't make it out.

When in the patio, he would stare at the trees, sometimes tracing the flight of the birds or looking out for cars passing by. While seemingly disinterested in the outside world, he would browse through the obituary section of the *Straits Gazette* with interest.

Was this just old age creeping up on him? Was it a growing dementia afflicting him? If so, then he would not have been able to take care of himself physically. Fortunately, that wasn't the case.

It really puzzled me. Was Father suffering under the curse of Mataram House? Or perhaps the mysterious oath was taking its toll on him, just as it had done on me. *What else?* I asked myself.

Father was humiliated when his plan to save me from Mataram House had failed miserably. Then, after the war, he was imprisoned on account of some innocuous charges, which humiliated him further. As if that weren't enough punishment for a very proud man, he lost his wife. He loved her more in death than when she was living. When I had brought the news to him about Mother's death following that appalling reunion I'd had with Grandma Tutik, he took it very badly. He wept profusely; his whole body trembled as if in a fit.

I had been wanting to talk to him about something I knew little about: how he and Mother had met and fallen in love, and what their wedding was like. I had hoped to allude to the origin of the oath Father had made with Grandma, which had now become the cosmic force shadowing my life and his. Now the window of opportunity was gone forever.

Aunty Maimunah might know, I thought. Yet I doubted it. Aunty Maimunah herself was quite blurry about Mataram House. And she hadn't attended the wedding. No one from Father's side had attended it, according to Pak Ali, because Father's family objected to the marriage. That much I knew. The whys and wherefores, I did not. Maybe I would never know.

Chapter 17

After a week in Penang, I looked forward to seeing Pinky.

I was at the Station Hotel Restaurant at noon sharp, sitting at our usual corner. She came in twenty minutes later wearing a floral skirt and hat, looking every bit a femme fatale.

"Did you miss me?" she asked even before I had pulled her chair out.

"Yes, very much." I expected her to say she had missed me too, but she didn't.

Every time we met, I would be clawing to get some serious commitment from her in words. I got nothing. With our encounters increasing in frequency and our intimacy accelerating in intensity, she never, ever talked of family or of children or asked my opinion about them. She never once asked me about my family, much less talked about hers. Most frustrating was that she had not yet uttered the words "I love you, Hamzah."

I also began to notice something curious. She began to fear the public eye, particularly the attention of her own kind – the Chinese people. When we walked in the streets of Ipoh, browsing through the shops and eating at the stalls, she would insist on keeping things formal with me, which meant no clasping of her waist with my arms, no holding hands, and definitely none of those gestures indicating intimacy.

Yet when we were in the vicinity of the book club, the Station Hotel, or the restaurant, places frequented mostly by Europeans, her sensuality would suddenly come alive. When I asked her about it, her reply was, "Chinese men are insanely jealous of Malays courting pretty Chinese girls like me. You should be proud of yourself. You are one of the rare ones. But I want you alive, not dead." Then she laughed.

As the months went by, I began to resent the fact that our relationship was purely sensual, although I had become addicted to our sensuality. Yes, I couldn't get enough of her. Yet our relationship's aimlessness wrought me, and I asked myself where it was leading me.

One day, unable to hold onto my frustration any longer, I decided to take us away from the noise and scurry of Ipoh and from the mindlessness of the bedroom. I took Pinky to my old haunt by the river in that little Malay village near Kuala Kangsar. To my surprise, she loved it. Her eyes on the flowing stream, she poetically commented how tranquil it was to the mind, how soothing to the soul, and asked why I had hidden it from her. She wanted to know if it was a secret place where I had wooed a special woman's heart.

Seeing her in that pensive mood, I seized the opportunity and asked her, "Do you like children, Pinky?"

"What are you getting at, Hamzah?"

"Merely asking."

"Are you asking me to marry you?"

"Tell me, where are we going in this relationship, Pinky?" Her eyes darted away from me and skirted the surroundings.

The next moment, revealing a surprise twist of her mind, she said, "You know, Hamzah, we are very alone here. There's no one around for miles. We can make love here." Her hands caught my face and toppled me over. Then, in the next moment she kissed me. "This is where the relationship is going – you and I deeply in love."

"I mean, besides all this."

"Aren't you happy, sweetheart? Haven't you got all of me already? Aren't you content with that? I am all yours, Hamzah – all yours. Let's not spoil that, sweetheart." Her eyes glazed.

I wanted to utter something, but she quickly put her finger on my lips. She undressed and began to release her passion, shutting down all the uncertainties, doubts, and questions that had bewildered me. In the serenity of the afterglow, as with previous afterglows, she blew into my ears the endearing question, "You love me?"

At every conclusion, her face would light up. But mine would be shaded by doubts like the far side of the moon.

She made me suffer too. She was transient like the mist of her Shalimar perfume: capricious, alternating between tempest and calm. I wanted permanency, but she seemed not to, and so the storm came and went. Sometimes to test our relationship, I took the bold step of withdrawing in desperation to escape my addiction to her. She would come to look for me.

In one of these attempts of mine to escape from her, she shocked me by appearing at the mine. I was taken aback when she appeared at the doorway of the little site office dressed in a plain samfu, wearing dark wide-rimmed sunglasses, a large straw hat over her head, and a scarf wrapped around her face to avoid recognition. Luckily the mine office was empty, as the two supervisors were in the pit.

I pulled her into the room, closed the door, and exclaimed, "What are you thinking in coming here, Pinky?"

"Never mind that! No one here knows who I am, and I came in a trishaw – and dressed like this. They'll think I am your girlfriend. Why have you been keeping away from me, Hamzah? I've been at the Station Hotel Restaurant for the last two weekends – some guests were eyeing me rather oddly, and even the waiters were whispering. I was like a fool sitting there alone. It's embarrassing. I am so terribly mad that I could kill you. Why are you doing this to me?"

"I, do to you? I thought I was the victim here. A relationship is not about making love only, Pinky."

"What? Hamzah!" she cried, raising her hand to strike my face. I caught it in midair. "How dare you say that to me? You know nothing about me," she yelled. I had never seen her so angry.

"Exactly!"

"What do you mean by that?" She burst into tears. "How can you say that? You know how shameful it is for me to come here, looking like an off-duty cabaret girl so I could see you." She put her hands to her face, tears streaming down through her fingers, her whole body shaking helplessly.

I felt terribly sorry for her and regretted what I had done. Pulling her close to me, I said, "I love you, Pinky. You know that."

"Yes! Yes! Yes!" she said emphatically, crying at the same time.

"Marry me then," I said.

"I can't."

"Why?"

"I just can't."

"Is it because I am a Malay?"

She raised her hand again, and this time it struck home, landing squarely on my face.

"You fool. You know I am not like that." She shook her head like a child. "Oh my God, why are you doing this to me, Hamzah?" Again her tears came streaming.

"Are you married, Pinky? Is that what's holding you?"

"No! No! No! Don't go over that again, please, I beg you. If you really love me, Hamzah, don't raise that again. Oh my God, why do you do this to me? Why can't you just love me, Hamzah? Just love me, sweetheart."

I decided not to prolong the argument. After all, it was desperation that had driven her to come to the mine.

"I am sorry, Pinky. I am sorry. This is not the place for us to discuss this. I think you shouldn't stay here too long. The supervisors will soon be back. Come, I'll take you back to town." I held her tightly. She began to compose herself.

"It's all right. You go on with your work. We'll meet me this weekend. Agreed?"

I buckled. "Yes, Pinky, I'll be there."

I'll kill myself if you don't come." Those words didn't seem empty at all. Never again did I dare to play the game of hide-and-seek with her.

Again I insisted on sending her home in my car, and again she refused. The trishaw would take her to the bus stand, she said. I watched the trishaw drift into the dust-strewn road and then disappear behind the white sandhills.

That day my mind was not on my work. I tried shuffling some files, but that didn't help. I gazed over at the window, but it was her image that stared me in the face. She had come to the mine in desperation. What more must I ask from her? *Yes, what more, Hamzah?* I asked myself. Recalling her tears, I was swamped with guilt and felt terribly sorry for her and about what I had done.

Thus, we continued with our rendezvous. I ceased to talk of marriage, which brought a lot more serenity to our relationship. She was visibly relieved. We drew closer than ever without having to chase for the light outside the tunnel. Yet I sometimes detected in those happy eyes of hers an unsettled spirit searching for that very light.

Chapter 18

Fortune paid me a surprise visit. Miner Tan entrusted me with the market operations of all the mines he owned in Kinta, besides the ones we operated in partnership, leaving the decision to buy and sell tin at my complete discretion. The trust was absolute, and it baffled Tan's staff, as he had never given that part of the business to anyone before. This came about after the advice I had given him on trading his ore with the smelters, which turned out to be very profitable. He thought my aptitude uncanny. Surely I was flattered. I was also the envy of the marketing staff. In the tin business, one can enhance one's earnings by trading the commodity smartly. The price of tin was slumping since the Americans had suspended their strategic stockpile buying at the end of the war. I had advised Tan to hold stocks and to sell only in order to cover the cost of operation. He had agreed. My instincts told me that the US government would soon resume stockpile purchasing, as tension was building up between the United States and communist China over the Korean Peninsula. Providence was on my side, however, as war actually broke out soon after. The price of tin went through the roof, rising from a low of £500 to a high of more than £2,000 per ton in a matter of weeks.

I received a call from Miner Tan. In his usual blunt, guttural style, he said, "Mr Hamzah, please come to Penang on Monday at 9 a.m."

Before I could ask the purpose of the meeting, he hung up. Neither could I figure out his mood, because I had so far seen only one, and it had always been that of jubilance, loudness, and guffaws. I couldn't detect any of those things while on the phone with him, as our call had been too brief.

This call for a meeting unsettled me a bit. Could it be about a woman storming into the mine in Gopeng to search for me a week ago?

When I arrived at the Chulia Street head office, Tan's secretary ushered me to the meeting room. The entire staff was already there; it was standing room only. Tan was at the head table presiding. As I entered, everyone stood up and gave me a resounding round of applause, Miner Tan leading the way.

"Mr Hamzah, the best tin miner in Kinta Valley. Give him another round of applause."

Everyone clapped again.

Tan invited me to sit next to him. Then, to my surprise, he stood up and began to deliver a speech in Chinese.

"I consider myself a good tin miner. I know where to find the ore and dig for it. I own the best mines – no wastage, no stealing, few accidents. But I am not that savvy a trader. That is entirely another skill. I used to sell my tin ore to the smelters at their given price. I never took a position. I would have made more if I did.

"The first time someone advised me to take a position, I trusted his instincts. As a result, we have made much more money. I want to announce to all of you here that I owe this good fortune to one man."

He walked behind the chair I was sitting in, placed his palms on my shoulders, and said, "The man is none other than Mr Hamzah, my partner." Everyone stood up and clapped.

It was July 1950 when Miner Tan heaped this accolade on me. I became the talk of the Chinese mining community after that – a Malay being praised by one of the most respected Chinese tin miners in Kinta Valley. All I had done was to advise Tan to hold back his stock when the price of the ore was slumping. I had predicted that a war would soon break out in the Korean Peninsula, just as Sam had foreseen the ending of World War II. To my good fortune, the Korean War did break out. Tin, being a strategic material, saw its price shoot through the roof. There was nothing extraordinarily brilliant about what I had done, not in the way Miner Tan had put it. It had been a matter of luck and, yes, included a bit of knowledge of market psychology.

Since the success of the marketing operations, Tan Siew Lim and I were more than just partners; we had become close friends. Every time I returned to Penang, I would receive his call without fail. He wanted my company in order to have someone with whom to share small talk, drinks, and outings to the restaurants and local stalls.

One day Tan asked me if I had ever been to a cabaret. I said I hadn't. He laughed.

"A gentleman like me must patronise the cabarets," he said. Once I confessed that I had heard of them but had never been to one, he laughed aloud, saying that I was too innocent. So one night he took me to the New World Cabaret on Swatow Lane.

When we arrived, a lively ten-piece band was playing while a female singer was belting an Ella Fitzgerald number. The ballroom was large, with a highly polished dance floor. Several couples were dancing a foxtrot with poise and grace. Around the dance floor, taxi dancers in cheongsams, kebayas, and long gowns sat in a row awaiting their customers. When the band switched to a Cole Porter number and the band leader blew his trumpet in the style of Harry James, everyone took to the floor, including Tan, who danced superbly.

When he returned, he asked me why I hadn't joined him on the floor. When I told him I knew nothing of ballroom dancing, he couldn't stop laughing. "No problem," he said. He waved to the waiter, asking him to summon the manager. When the manager arrived, Tan whispered to him. After a few minutes, the manager returned with a slender and fairly beautiful Chinese woman in a long gown. Her permed shoulder-length hair was parted at the centre like the Hollywood actress Hedy Lamarr's.

"Mr Hamzah, this is Annie. She is the best dancer here – and the prettiest too."

"How do you do, Mr Hamzah?" she said in a melodious tone, offering her hands to me before sitting down to join us at the table.

"Mr Hamzah, when the slow foxtrot comes out, Annie will take you to the floor. I promise you, she'll make you a ballroom dancer in no time."

I waited nervously. The indicator light flashed, displaying "Foxtrot". Anne pulled me to the floor before I was even ready. She held my left hand with her right and placed her left on my shoulder. Holding me close to her, she gently guided me to follow her moves. I stepped on her foot several times. "Never mind," she said reassuringly. Soon the rhythm caught me in the mood. I began to follow Annie more smoothly. "You learn fast, Mr Hamzah," she said, complimenting me.

After several foxtrots, I began to get the hang of it. Tan was so elated seeing me enjoying myself that we stayed on until the last dance was announced. I must say, I did enjoy myself quite a bit, and I found Tan to be wonderful company.

After that, it was the Great Wall Cabaret for us every time I was in Penang, and Annie would always join us. I suspected Annie was someone special to Tan at the Great World Cabaret. As I got closer to Tan, I noticed something: he didn't have that many friends – close ones, I mean – unlike the other miners I knew. I hadn't seen any of the hangers-on, the hard-drinking comrades, or the self-serving favour seekers who liked to hang around wealthy merchants. He seemed a loner. I could count myself rather privileged, given that he found me to be a valued companion.

Whenever I visited Miner Tan in Penang, either for the usual business meetings or for social outings, the latter becoming more frequent, I would invariably stay in 27 Kelawei Road, as that had been my home before I moved to Ipoh. Many a time, Tan had wanted me to stay at the Eastern and Oriental Hotel on the waterfront, where there was a band and dancing every Saturday night. But I declined, as it would certainly upset Aunty Maimunah terribly.

At 27 Kelawei Road, things didn't look so good. When I came down one morning for breakfast, I found that Father was at the dining table having his coffee. I wished him good morning. He stared at me and said, "Who are you?"

I feared he was fast losing his memory, not knowing what day it was, shuffling about the house, and going nowhere. Only the day before, he had gotten his sandals to go out when he actually had just returned. Sometimes he would fix a prolonged empty gaze on me rather sadly, as if wrenching out an old memory from his shrinking brain. And I thought to myself, *To lose one's life is finality, but to lose oneself while living is an empty eternity.*

I gave Aunty Maimunah strict instructions not to allow Father outside the house alone. He was not to go to the shops or the mosque unaccompanied. She was to place his name and address in his pocket. And if there was no one around, she must simply forbid him to go out of the house.

"I could forbid him to go to the shops, but keeping him from going to the mosque was impossible. I tried, but he turned to me and said, 'It's the house of God. You cannot stop me from visiting the house of God,' and waved his cane at me."

"Let's do this, Aunty: tell him he has just returned, and press on it. Do a little play-acting. Come, Aunty, you can do that. And with that loud voice of yours, he'll believe you."

"I don't know. I feel terrible having to lie to him like that. And how many times can I do that anyway? His memory seems rather to come and go, remembering certain things and forgetting others. This mosque is one of those things. At times, he reverts to his normal self," she replied forlornly.

Strange, I thought. His memory seemed to select what to remember. Was it a kind of retribution, remembering only God and forgetting all else? He hadn't been religious at all when he was in Mataram House.

Whenever I returned to Kelawei Road, I often thought about pouring out my burden to someone about Pinky and me. I had once thought of approaching Father for counsel, but now that would be like asking our house cat, Kelabu, for advice. I needed to pour her out of my system to someone of wisdom. Aunty Maimunah was all there was now for me. I had no friends. I couldn't be talking to Tan Siew Lim about this. I hadn't had even a glimpse of his wife. These traditional types of Chinese men of wealth preferred to tuck away their wife, or wives, in the back of the house. I had no idea of what his view was of women. And besides, it was too personal. I had just gotten to know him. Then again, his view of women might not fall within the same ambit as mine.

So it had to be Aunty Maimunah, and for that I had to wait for the opportune time, when her mind was not on the kitchen or on the housekeeping or on Ariffin and Father.

One evening, I settled myself by the garden in the dim porch light. When I heard the bells of the Indian itinerant hawker on his tricycle breaking the quiet night, I called out and ordered four plates of sumptuous Indian-style fried noodles, which these stalls on wheels were famous for.

"Aunty Maimunah, come and join me. It's your favourite: mie goreng."

"Let me finish off with the kitchen," she said.

"Leave that kitchen alone, and come now before it gets cold," I insisted.

"All right, all right, I am coming." She ambled out excitedly.

Father was in the lounge, oblivious to me. The house cat, Kelabu, brushed himself against Father's legs. Father put him on his lap and ran his fingers across his chin. Kelabu purred. It was a picture of solace – the cat and Father. Father's memory mattered not to Kelabu. They loved each other, Kelabu and Father, and sought each other when both were lonely. Perfect companions those two.

"Ask your father to join us," Aunty Maimunah said.

"Certainly Aunty. I was about to do that."

Then I noticed that Father was peacefully dozing with his furry companion, neither of them in need of others' company. "And where's Ariffin, Aunty? I bought one for him too."

"In his room, doing his homework."

"That's good."

"He is a good boy now, thanks to you, Hamzah. School is good for him, and he's enjoying it too. He has many friends."

As we settled on our plates, I thought it was a good time to touch on the subject that was in my mind. All of a sudden, Aunty Maimunah, in a burst of motherly inspiration, blurted out, "When are you getting married, Hamzah? You have beautiful cousins in Bukit Tinggi. Do you know that? After your father married your mother, he was completely cut off from his family and relatives. I am the only tie you have to your roots. You are a Minang. Let me take you back there. Marry a Minang woman, Hamzah. They make good wives, these women, unlike the Javanese. Javanese women are not for you. Believe me. See what happened to your father."

In one fell swoop, my plan crashed to the ground.

"Thank you, Aunty. I am not ready yet."

"But you are a successful man now. All the mothers in Bukit Tinggi would welcome you with open arms if you were to ask for any of their daughters, and you'd be doing a favour to people of your blood. A Minang man should marry a Minang woman. We are unique in that our lineage is perpetuated through the womenfolk. You marry a non-Minang and that's the end of your blood. Do you realise that, Hamzah?"

I looked at her incredulously. How in heaven could I now say, "By the way, Aunty, I am already in love with a woman – a Chinese woman"? Good God, I could just imagine her dismay!

While I was still processing what to say, she continued speaking. "Three weeks ago, I wrote to my second cousin, your aunty Halimah who has a very pretty daughter named Zaiton. She must be sixteen or maybe seventeen by now. I enquired of her and was told she was available. I didn't say anything about you, but I told Halimah to keep me posted if a suitor came Zaiton's way. I told her I had someone in mind for her. She was pleased beyond words. Wait here. I have a photo of her." She hurried excitedly into the house.

I thought to myself, *Hamzah, you are in a great deal of trouble. How are you going to get out of this?*

Just after Aunty Maimunah went upstairs, Father suddenly appeared at the patio. "Who's getting married?" he exclaimed, looking surprisingly normal and alert. He must have overheard our conversation without our realising it.

I stood up and pulled out a chair for him.

"Come, Father, join us." I was very relieved by his sudden appearance. At least there was now a buffer between Aunty Maimunah and me.

"Who's getting married?" he asked again.

"No one, Father."

Just as I thought I could engage him, his attention drifted away again.

Aunty Maimunah returned with a photo album. "Oh, you are here, Norredin. Come join us," she said.

Father looked blankly at her and said nothing.

She peeled the pages of the album until she spotted the photograph she had been looking for. "There," she said, placing her finger on an old sepia-coloured photograph of a family standing in a row against the background of a house with a high-pitched roof resembling a buffalo horn. Though the photograph was old, the resolution was remarkably clear. "There." She pointed to a little girl of, perhaps, eight years old holding a woman's hand (presumably her mother's). "That's Zaiton. Even as a child she was very pretty. Don't you think so? Imagine how she is now as a young woman. As we say, she is a flower in bloom waiting to be plucked," she said, nudging me with her elbow. "Ask your father if you don't believe me." Turning her head to Father, she said, "Don't you agree, Norredin?"

Father lifted his head, peered at the photo, and said nothing.

No doubt, the girl was pretty in the photograph. "Aunty, I totally agree with you: she is pretty. But, Aunty, I can't choose my future wife from a photo. Besides, it's not fair to her. She may not like me at all. People don't do this anymore. In your time maybe."

"Of course, you'll never listen to an old-fashioned woman like me. You know, Hamzah, marriages arranged by parents are happier and last a lifetime. Just look at your father. That was a love marriage. What happened?"

Aunty Maimunah was about to shed her tears, being habitually emotional as she was. So I pulled her towards me and clasped her ample body in my arms. I said, "How could I not listen to you? You are my mother now. Who else should I turn to when I need help – you, Aunty! But choosing a wife is not an easy thing, especially for me. When the time comes, I shall surely seek your advice. That's a promise."

I managed to compose her as the night drew to a close.

Chapter 19

My partnership with Tan Siew Lim had entered its third year. We enjoyed remarkable success in terms of profits and the number of new leases I was able to acquire. It was getting more difficult to get new leases, as competition from the dredge-operated mines of the big European companies became stiffer. The government tended to favour dredge-operated mines because of their higher royalties payout. Still, I managed to get the leases for Tan, for which he was very much indebted to me, as he himself said.

I too was very much beholden to him, for having me as partner. There were many who would give and an arm and a leg to be his partner, yet by some quirk of fate, he had chosen me.

Our profits soared. But I couldn't claim all the credit for this, since the profits had resulted from the unprecedented rise in tin prices. Tan, being superstitious, attributed this success to his lucky partnership with me. Superstition or not, I was baffled. Luck never had been my forte. Luck is impetuous and deceptive, and I dared put my reliance on it only with caution.

Although not equipped with the finest of mannerisms, Tan exuded a conviviality that was charming and at the same time disarming. With his guffaws and animation, I found him amusingly awkward. His appreciation was accompanied by a big slap on my shoulders. Making sudden, abrupt calls on the phone without salutation or explanation was his way of expressing camaraderie; offering a business deal without asking if I would accept it meant that I had his trust. These oddities must have come from a hard and rough beginning, I surmised.

In one of the social encounters I had with him, he had said to me, "You know, Mr Hamzah, I came from Fujian, and life there was difficult then. I was only fifteen when I left my family behind in China to come to Malaya to find work as an indentured labourer – meaning that a clan association would pay my passage in return for work at one of the mines. It took me five years to pay the clan back and be freed from the contract.

"When freed, I decided to set up my own business with the little savings I had. The clan association that had recruited me agreed to provide a loan. At that time, these associations also acted as banks for the Chinese immigrants. I formed a small company to do the kongsi business, that is to say, to provide a team of workers for the mines on contract. From there, my business grew. It was bloody hard work."

"You are an extraordinary man, Mr Tan," I said.

"Do you know why I picked you as my partner?"

I shook my head.

"You reminded me of how I was when working as a labourer in a Chinese mine – and then you made money for yourself." He guffawed. "I haven't seen any Malays doing what you did. You are an extraordinary man yourself, you know. Ha ha ha!"

*　　*　　*

As the days passed, Pinky became more loving, more affectionate, and more possessive. Yet one day my insecurity returned, and I succumbed to the gnawing need of wanting to know about our future. She receded into melancholy, causing the both of us to be miserable. I felt terribly remorseful for having broken my promise. So, no matter how wonderful it was, I continued to feel like a ship drifting in the ocean without a rudder, which made me deeply unhappy.

One evening, after dinner, as we were strolling around the garden of my house on Race Course Road, she said the unthinkable to me: "Sweetheart,

I love you so terribly I'd die if you ever left me. Wouldn't it be wonderful if we were to go on like this forever and ever without having to get married? Marriage spoils everything. After marriage, life becomes mundane and routine, and frictions develop as sure as the sun rises."

"What do you mean, Pinky? That is a dream, and dreams don't last. It doesn't make sense. If we love each other, isn't it natural that we end up marrying?"

"It does make sense to me. Look around at the married couples – what dowdy lives they lead," she retorted.

"You are dreaming, Pinky."

"Maybe I am. If so, I hope I don't ever wake up."

Before I could say another word, she pressed her finger to my lips. "Say no more! Just promise you will never leave me. Say it, my darling. Please say it."

"I love you very much, and I shall never leave you."

She clasped her arms around me. I felt the tremor of emotion flowing through her body as she wet my shirt with her tears.

"Why are you crying?"

"Happy, that's all."

Chapter 20

I t was my twenty-seventh birthday. Never had I felt older, happier, or more settled. Pinky, too, had an air of equanimity about her. Though she did not move in with me to my house on Race Course Road, she would stay for a night or two – but no more than that – and sometimes insisted on cooking for me. Although her cooking wasn't that superb, her boundless enthusiasm made me value her dishes. Perhaps it was her way of making up to me for her strange elusiveness about the idea of marriage. Sometimes I saw in her a woman trapped between her inner desire and her inability to fulfil it, which made me feel sorry for her.

To celebrate my birthday, Pinky suggested we drive to Lumut, a town on the west coast. We took the ferry to Pangkor Island and then booked ourselves into a chalet on Pasir Bogak beach overlooking the emerald waters of the bay.

Pinky had baked a chocolate cake. We swam. I watched her gliding through the water like a dolphin. In contrast, I splashed wildly like a fish out of water. When I caught up with her, she pulled me down below the water. She giggled and tried to repeat the performance, but I managed to escape to the shore.

"Where did you learn to swim like that, Pinky?"

"I was the swimming champion in my school," she proudly exclaimed. "And where did you learn how to swim, splashing about like a man drowning?" She laughed.

"In the river in my home town in Jogjakarta when I was a kid, with an old friend," I replied truthfully.

"Do you miss it?"

"Not the swimming, but him. His name was Buyong. We had different lives then, but fate changed all that for me. I have often wondered what became of him. Maybe fate had a better deal for him than it had for me."

"Fate? You believe in these things?"

"Yes."

"You, believing in fate? It's depressing. I never knew you to be like that. You don't look it at all. Only failures think like that. And you are definitely not a failure, not in my eyes. You have everything going for you – and you have me." She giggled, placing her hands on her bosom.

"You'll never understand. My life is complicated. Let's not talk about it. It's depressing, as you said."

"I don't understand. I really don't. Are you the type to frequent fortune tellers?"

"Nothing of the sort."

Pinky, looking puzzled, lifted her head to the sky, dropped her head, and levelled her eyes straight at me. "So, your meeting me was fated?"

"Look, let's not talk about it. Forget what I had said."

She gazed at me and held my hand in hers. "Take life as it comes, my dear. It's happier that way. Poor Hamzah, let me give you a hug. By the way, I shan't be seeing you next week, you know. You will miss me, I hope?"

"Where are you going?"

"To visit my mother in Kuala Lumpur. Now don't be naughty when I am away, like chasing girls."

"The only girl I have been chasing is you – the hard-to-get Pinky."

*   *   *

Without Pinky with me that following week, I decided I would visit Father. I called Aunty Maimunah. It was a Wednesday. The moment she got on the phone, she exclaimed, "Your father has been losing weight, Hamzah, getting skinnier by the day."

"Don't panic, Aunty. I am coming."

"You better come quickly, Hamzah. He's old, you know. I don't want something to happen to him. You know what I mean. God forbid, of course. Are you coming now?"

"Yes, yes. This weekend."

Half an hour later, the phone rang. I thought it was Aunty Maimunah, but it was Miner Tan, with his usual abrupt and gruff tone.

"Mr Hamzah, I want you to come to Kuala Lumpur this Saturday, OK?"

Tan could never drop the "Mister" when addressing me, however often I had asked him not to use it.

"To Kuala Lumpur?" That caught me by surprise. He had never before asked me to meet him in Kuala Lumpur. Our meetings and social rendezvous had always been in Penang.

"Yes, yes, Kuala Lumpur."

"Is it business, Mr Tan?"

"No, not business. Dinner, with some friends. So I want you to come and join us. OK?"

"It is a pleasure, Mr Tan."

"So you come, right?"

"Yes, definitely."

"Good. See you at Lee Wong Kee Restaurant at 7 p.m."

I waited until the next day before telling Aunty Maimunah I had to postpone my visit to Penang, fearing she might just exaggerate Father's state of health.

The following day, I called her. "How is Father, Aunty?"

"He's all right. But hasn't got much appetite."

"Is he sick?"

"No."

"Then there's nothing to worry about."

"I tell you what, Aunty, when I return to Penang I shall arrange for a doctor to come to the house and examine him. I will ask him why Father is not eating as much as he should. All right?"

"Oh, Hamzah, that is a very good idea. You are a good son. I'm proud of you."

Before she could heap more praises on me, I said, "Now listen, Aunty. I have to make a trip to Kuala Lumpur on business this weekend. After that I will immediately return to see Father, and then I'll get the doctor. All right, Aunty?"

"Yes Hamzah."

I felt relieved. An awkward situation with a highly excitable aunty was averted.

When I arrived at the Lee Wong Kee Restaurant in Kuala Lumpur, next to the Odeon Cinema on the main shopping street in Batu Road, a man was already waiting for me at the entrance. The place was full. I trailed behind my guide, winding through tables until we reached a private room at the far end. He ushered me in. Tan was sitting at the big round table with his back to the door when the usher announced my arrival. The moment Tan saw me, he rose from his chair and opened his arms wide to greet me.

"Ah Mr Hamzah, good of you to come. Please, sit," he said, pointing to the empty chair beside him. Then, addressing his guests around the table, he said, "This is Mr Hamzah, my good friend and partner." Everyone stood up, except the three ladies, one of whom had already sent my heart beating fast.

Then, one by one, he introduced his guests to me. "This gentleman," he said, pointing to the man on his right, "is Mr Robert Tang, the comprador of Chartered Bank. And that is Mrs Tang, his wife, next to her is Richard, their son. Beside him is Mr Tseng, from Hong Kong, who works with Jardin Matheson. That is his wife, May," he said, referring to the lady next to Tseng. Pointing directly to the old man at the far end of the table, he said, "That old man is my *sifu*." Finally he came to the woman sitting next to him, who had been very quiet, sitting still like a stone since the moment I had arrived. "And this is my wife, Lai Peng." I bowed politely to her. She just nodded without even a glance.

No words – I mean, no words – could describe how I felt at that moment. The room was circling. My heart was beating. The names of the people Tan had announced just went past and were left unregistered, their faces blurred. Pinky was quiet, immovable, gazing at the table. I dared not look at her. Neither did she dare to look at me. I wrestled to regain my composure. *Do not spoil the evening, Hamzah,* my mind warned me. Miner Tan, I sensed, had no idea what was going on. He couldn't be pretending – why in the world would he do that? If he had known about his wife's affair with me, I wouldn't be there at all. I would be dead. He had Triad connections – no miners could prosper without them. The old man to whom he had introduced me just now as his sifu was a Triad boss. I was sure of that, judging by the tattoos on both his arms.

Tan, turning to Pinky, said, "Mr Hamzah is a very handsome man. Don't you think so, darling? And very clever too." He nudged her with his elbow in mirth. She just ignored his remarks. Turning to the waiter, who was waiting to take his order, he said, "Johnnie Walker Black Label for this gentleman." Then he whispered into my ear: "My wife is like you. She's got class. She likes English things. Not like me. I am a Chinaman." He guffawed.

When the drinks arrived, Tan stood up with his glass in hand and announced, "Let us drink to Mr Robert Tang, our host. He has kindly organised this dinner in my honour to thank me for being a long customer of Chartered Bank."

Everyone stood up and gave a loud "Yam seng", except Pinky – she had no glass in her hand.

When they resumed their seats, Tan whispered to me, "I want to introduce Robert Tang to you. He is comprador for Charted Bank and can help you with business finance." Then he turned to Robert and said, "Robert, this is the Mr Hamzah I told you about, a very good tin miner, the only Malay miner in Perak. You must get to know him."

Robert turned to me and said, "I understand you speak Chinese, and fluently too, Mr Hamzah." Robert addressed me in British-boarding-school-accented English. His demeanour was as elegant as his English.

"Yes. Spoken Chinese, but I can't read or write it, and I am not sure about the fluency bit."

"Where did you learn it?"

"From the school of hard knocks."

"Same school as Mr Tan attended, I suppose. I mean that it as a compliment. Small wonder you two are partners. Drop in anytime, Mr, Hamzah, if you need anything."

"Thank you, Mr Robert. You are very kind."

The first dish of starters came. Everyone partook of it, except Pinky.

"You are not eating, darling? Anything the matter? You have been very quiet the whole evening," Tan said to Pinky in Hokkien.

"I have been feeling a bit unwell," Pinky said.

Tan was in a jubilant mood. Pinky was like a frozen fish. And I was suffering from my pretence. The food was flowing, the gobbling running its course, the conversation buzzing with cheers and yam sengs. I couldn't wait for the dinner to end.

Chapter 21

The drive back to Ipoh the next day was as excruciating as the night before at the Lee Wong Kee Restaurant in Kuala Lumpur had been. The grim shadow of Mataram, which I thought had retreated in the mist of memory, had reappeared, and not without vengeance. Pinky, who had appeared like an angel without even being courted, and the friendship and fortune thrusted upon me by an unknown benefactor, which I unguardedly swallowed hook, line, and sinker, was a vicious ruse to lull me into bliss and happiness only to make me pay a heavy price. These thoughts and trailing dilemmas filled my battered brain as I drove past villages and towns, lumbering slowly on the road in the heat of the late afternoon sun without any wish of arriving at my destination. Deep inside me, I knew that Ipoh could no longer be my sanctuary. It had become my nightmare in waiting.

I arrived when the sun was already down. Even before I had time to shower, the telephone rang. *It must be Pinky,* I thought. It rang again. I decided not to answer it. The more I ignored it, the more it rang. I was wrought and figured that she must be too. Must I prolong these sufferings – mine and hers? Finally I picked up the handset. The first sound I heard was a wailing and trembling voice.

"Calm down, Pinky."

She relaxed some. "I'm sorry, Hamzah, so sorry. Forgive me, my dear. I must come and see you now to explain everything. I never meant it to be like this. Please believe me." She sobbed in between her words.

"No need to explain. No amount of explanation would help us, Pinky. Can't you see that? It's a curse."

"What do you mean by that? I'm a curse to you?"

"No. No. I'm the curse. Not you. You're the victim. Fate has dealt me a terrible blow. I wanted you more than anything in the world. Now, we can never be together, Pinky. Don't you understand?"

"No, I don't. Don't give me this crap about fate, Hamzah."

"What else? You came into my life out of the blue, we fell in love, and now suddenly I discover that you are married to someone – someone who has been kind to me, trusted me completely – and I have the gall to sleep with his wife behind his back, make a complete fool of him. If I still have a shred of decency in me I should leave this place immediately and disappear. Now what must I do, Pinky? Tell me?"

"I'm not married to him, Hamzah."

"What? He said, I quote, 'Meet my wife.'"

"It's a Chinese thing. Look, I'm not married to him, not in a formal sense."

"So, does that make this horribly illicit conduct acceptable? No matter how we look at it, we have hurt this good man terribly – I have hurt him in the most unforgivable way. I feel like burying my head in the sand just thinking about it."

"Oh, you terrible man. Why do you choose to hurt me when I love you so much? Forget about everything. Let's be together. Let's run away from this place, Hamzah. You talk as if you're going to leave me. I'll die if you do."

"In this dreadful predicament we're in, it doesn't matter where we go, as it wouldn't change a thing about how I feel. Don't you understand?"

"You are only thinking about your feelings. What about mine, Hamzah? I feel like dying, do you know that, Hamzah? All right then, let's continue to meet in secret. He'll never know. Since you joined the mine, how many times has he come to Ipoh? Never. Right? So what's the problem in us continuing? Nobody would know. No one cares."

"What? Pinky, you are not talking sense. Prolong this charade? For how long? Where does it lead to? Look, Pinky, let's call it a night. Go and get some sleep. I am sorry if you are hurt, Pinky. So am I. I am fated to hurt those who love me. Weird, isn't it? But that is a fact. It has happened every time. Have I not tried to tell you about how fate plays a strong part in my life?"

"You are scaring me, Hamzah."

"I am scared also. I didn't expect this to happen, but it has. I seem to have no control over it. It is not entirely your fault. It is mine just as much. That is why you must get away from me – leave me before I hurt you more than you already are. I say this because I love you very much. Believe me, Pinky."

"Oh my God, Hamzah, what are you saying? Is it all over between us?"

"Yes, Pinky."

"Let's think this over, Hamzah. Please. Can I come to your place tomorrow?" She was sobbing, her voice trembling.

"No, Pinky, you shouldn't immediately. Let's cool off for a while, all right? I love you, remember that." There was a trace of finality in my tone. She must have noticed that. She was silent. I spoke to her gently so as not to hurt her further. At that moment, putting down the phone while she was in that state of mind broke my heart into pieces, as hers was falling apart too. I knew we were not going to see each other anymore. I felt the sky crumbling upon me.

Back in the Ipoh office, I put all my accounts, books, contracts, and files in order and passed them over to Antony, telling him I was going on a vacation. I released my housemaid and paid her generously, which pleased her very much. I told her not to tell anyone about it.

Without telling Pinky, I left Ipoh for good. My heart bled just thinking about how she would take it. I had thought about meeting her for the last time, but I changed my mind. I knew a face-to-face parting would only deepen our grief, not soothe it.

Upon my return to Penang, I sought an urgent meeting with Tan Siew Lim. I broke my partnership with him, and gave him a hollow excuse, saying I was wanted by the people of Tobali. He was completely perplexed, asking me repeatedly if he had in any way offended me or treated me more poorly than I deserved. Poor man, I couldn't look him in the eye. I handed back my share to him and then thanked him profusely for his goodness of heart. To my surprise and shame, he paid me the full monetary value of my share in return, though I had never paid a cent for it in the first place. He said I had earned it. At that moment I felt like a creep and really wanted to bury my head in the sand as I had said to Pinky. I thanked God for giving me the courage to leave Pinky. *It would be most despicable of you if you continued to betray such a man, Hamzah,* my guilt-ridden heart reproached me.

Relieved beyond words that I had succeeded in performing one painful task, I went home to 27 Kelawei Road to face yet another.

Aunty Maimunah was a wall of emotion, more difficult to contend with than I had first thought she'd be. I assembled everyone on the Sunday morning after my meeting with Tan, which had been the day before. Aunty Maimunah was seated on the long sofa with Father to her right, Ariffin on her left, and I facing her. She waited expectantly for some kind of announcement I was about to make. My heart sank and a cloud of sadness shrouded me as my eyes fell on her plump motherly face, Ariffin's juvenile cheerfulness, and Father's empty gaze.

The moment I announced I would be returning to Tobali, Aunty broke into tears. Out came a barrage of questions.

"Why, Hamzah? Isn't this your home now? This is not Ipoh or Kuala Lumpur you are talking about, but some place far away. I don't even know where this Tobali is. Are you getting married to someone over there?"

"No, Aunty, If I were getting married, you would be the first person to know. I've been called by the people there to help them open a tin mine. They saved me when I was shipwrecked. And I was just a boy then. They took care of me during the war. How could I refuse when they now need my help?"

"I have always dreamed you would marry a Minang girl, set up a home here, and have children. Your father is getting old. He needs you too. Oh, I don't know what to say. We are going to miss you terribly. Can't you say no to these people? Oh, I shouldn't be saying that." She pulled her scarf to wipe her tears. "When are you leaving?"

"Soon."

"Soon?" Out poured another flood of tears.

Father just stared at the floor.

Ariffin, who had been listening with interest, asked, "Where is this Tobali, brother?"

"Go and look it up on the map in school."

"I'll do that. Will you take me there someday?"

"Sure."

He rose from his seat and came forward to hug me. "I'm going to miss you, brother."

Aunty Maimunah was still sobbing. I went up to her and embraced her. "Aunty, you are my mother now, and I love you very much. Wherever I am, you are always in my heart. I'll come back as often as I can. That is a promise."

"I'm going to miss you, but I know I shouldn't stop you from doing what you think is right. You have so much compassion in your heart, and God will bless you for that."

I felt very relieved for having assuaged her. "Thank you, Aunty."

"Now don't you get married without telling me. And don't you marry a Javanese woman."

I told her that as soon as I was settled, I would fetch them all for a holiday in Banka. Again she wept. To my surprise, Ariffin, who had been gingerly composed throughout the episode, suddenly wept too. Father could only gaze at me. What was behind those wintery eyes, I couldn't read. It seemed he wanted to say something, but his mind couldn't form the words.

With a heavy heart, I said goodbye to Penang. That heavy heart felt heavier when I thought of Pinky.

BANKA,
EAST SUMATRA
1955

Chapter 22

I t was a cheery morning with hope in the wind as I stood by the railing of the steamer. I breathed in the promising air. The sea below was becalmed. As the dolphins chased the ship, they reminded me of Pinky. How graceful she swam. Banka could be seen as grey freckles along the still-sleepy horizon. The seabirds soared and screeched over the morning sky in merriment. How I wished I could fly like them and be merry. Passengers began to swell by the railings, some carrying their little ones over their shoulders, their faces expectant and happy. I envied them. I recalled Sam saying, "Returning to harbour is hope; leaving it is sadness. And the sailing is happiness." If only the ship could sail endlessly to nowhere.

My eyes rested on the happy faces, searching the reasons for their journey. I saw none resembling mine. I felt alone. I wanted to forget, but pain didn't want to forget me. Not a day passed without the happy moments I'd had with Pinky coming to haunt me. My mind had battled the impulse to hold her in my arms, shake the life out of her, and demand to know why she had led me on and hadn't told me who she was. I never got to ask her that. I don't know why. Perhaps deep in my heart I had known but refused to admit it, in case it was indeed true. I had allowed myself to fall into the abysmal depth of false bliss. I was as much to blame as she was. I had left her so abruptly. Was I cruel? An excruciating guilt ran through my battered mind. She must be suffering.

169

How could she not be? During the last phone call we had, she made a hopeless plea for love, and I rejected

While these thoughts were feeding my melancholy, the approaching Muntok Harbour came into full view. It was as I remembered it. The old jetty, the junks, the harbour smell and its unending bustlings, the medley of tanned faces, the ubiquitous Chinese, and the heaps of fish all welcomed me like an old friend.

By the bus terminal, amid the cacophony, a voice rang out, saying, "Hamzah! Hamzah!" A little man in a white turban popped out from the ruck of wares, heads, vehicles, and people. A more heart-warming sight I couldn't wish for. He rushed for me. His small frame, pinned by the tide of people, nearly keeled over from his excitement. "Son of Tobali, you finally returned," Tok Rejab exclaimed with great jubilation. His slender arms stretched out impatiently to clasp me. "Son of Tobali, welcome home," he said again, his eyes plumb upon my face and in disbelief about my return. After all the embracing and pleasantries, he stepped back and said, "You were a mere fledgling when you left Tobali, and look at you now – a full-grown man. And you are getting more handsome too. Have you already set a home?" Asking about setting a home was the Malay way of asking whether I had gotten married.

"Not yet, Tok. Not thinking of marriage just yet."

"Such an eligible young man still single." He cocked his head, eyed me, and smiled. "Let's go. The whole of Tobali is waiting for you – your aunty Rahimah and Siti too."

This "son of Tobali" moniker bothered me. "Tok, pardon me for asking, but what's this about son of Tobali?"

"You'll see, you'll see," he said, smiling to himself.

With my luggage loaded into his Morris Oxford, Tok Rejab took the wheel. We rode over the circuitous road, passing villagers and cultivated fields. As we reached the interior, the familiar jagged landscape of mines dug into my memory of Gopeng. The similarity was remarkable. I could never get used to the idea of its stark barrenness, not a blade of grass in sight. A pang of guilt struck me; I felt bad about my own part in causing this situation. The car turned east and hugged the coast. When we reached Koba, we were enveloped by the amber glow of late evening. By dusk, Tobali came into sight and a feeling of home touched my heart.

I heard the alternating troughs and crescendos of the *kompangs* drums and the loud singing that reminded me of a wedding.

"Is there a wedding on, Tok?" I asked.

He laughed. "Not a wedding, but a homecoming – your homecoming."

"What!" I exclaimed.

He turned his head to me and smiled broadly.

On arriving at Tok Rejab's big house, I found that it was shimmering with festival lights. A very large crowd filled its ample ground. As soon as I alighted from the car, I was greeted by the familiar faces of Lebai Amir, the imam, and the group of elders who once converted the late sea dog into the memorable Sheikh Omar.

They eagerly stepped forward to welcome me, each one taking my hand and bowing with deference. These were elderly people, so their actions embarrassed me. They might accord such respect to a young person only if he were an Islamic scholar or an ulema. I was neither of those things, not even remotely. So what was going on? In the car from Muntok, Tok Rejab had given not a hint to me, except for using the odd "son of Tobali" expression. I recalled, however, the perpetual smile that had been plastered on his face, which I had thought was about my coming home to Tobali.

While the loud drumming filled the air, the eager faces of men, women, children, and babies came forth to catch a glimpse of me or to shake my hand. I was dazzled by this unusual display of welcome, as all I had done was to inform Tok Rejab of my returning home.

When the drumming ceased, a troupe of young men in black Malay ceremonial dress entered the scene and performed the Silat martial arts dance with artistic grace and deadly aplomb, which reminded me of my own martial arts teacher, the avuncular Pak Ali, during my halcyon days in Mataram House.

When the act ended, a beautiful young woman who was exotically dressed in a manner befitting a bride and carrying a silver phial emerged like a winsome angel. She instantly arrested my hitherto dazed attention. With a smile, she sprinkled scented water from the phial upon me as though I were an arriving groom, and then she withdrew as mysteriously as she had appeared, without saying a word.

"Who is that young maiden, Tok?" I asked with great curiosity.

"Didn't you recognise her?"

"No."

"That's Siti."

"Siti? Your daughter Siti? My goodness, how she has grown," I exclaimed so loudly that it embarrassed Tok Rejab. I was about to say how beautiful she had become, but I hesitated, reminding myself that this wasn't the world of Pinky. It was Tobali.

Rahimah, Tok Rejab's wife, peeling away from the crowd hugged me affectionately, and said in a teasing manner, "Why have you taken so long to come back, Hamzah? Some pretty damsel in Malaya has stolen your heart?"

"No, Aunty, only work had taken my heart."

"Let me look at you." Her eyes surveyed my face. "I don't believe you." She cocked her head and smiled mischievously.

I was overwhelmed by this extraordinary reception, asking myself, *To what do I owe this unexplained honour? What have I done to earn this?*

The drums and singing trailed behind me as Tok Rejab ushered me into his house. Being a guest in his house was another honour he insisted on giving me. I had written to him to ask him to look for a house for me to rent. He wrote back to say that under no circumstances would he and Rahimah allow me to stay in a rented premise. He had a big house with more rooms than his family of four needed. The house had been built with having guests in mind, being as Tok was the chief of Tobali. Until such time as I had a house of my own, I would be his guest. This was not negotiable, he had categorically said. Surely it would be ungracious, or even insulting, on my part to refuse such an invitation. It was the Malay way. At a time when I most needed friends and solace, Tok's offer certainly came as an unsolicited gift from heaven.

The drums and singing were now silent, the ferry lights extinguished, and the honour bestowed. Reality set in. I was again alone. Through the window of my room, I could see the dark, featureless, moonless sky that seemed to reflect my inner feelings. Tobali peacefully slept. But my subconscious world stirred with unease, inundated with gloom, guilt, and fear. In a dark corner of that unsettling world, Pinky too was alone. Of that I was sure.

The next morning, Tok Rejab, with the eagerness of a beaver, took me to the mosque. "No more praying in the open on Fridays. The mosque can now accommodate all and sundry," he said, showing me the large spanking new brick building. His eyes brightened.

A man walked up and greeted me. "Welcome home, Mr Hamzah." Another followed. A man with a companion, who was entering the mosque, also stopped, turned, and greeted me.

I didn't at first recognise this new building. Where it stood now had once been a raised half-mortar, half-timber structure. I couldn't figure out why Tok Rejab made it a point to show me this spanking new mosque very early in the morning of my first day in Tobali.

"Why do you show me this new mosque, Tok?"

"Because it's you who built it."

"I built it? I can't remember doing that."

"Now you know why we call you son of Tobali." He smiled.

I was still puzzled.

Tok Rejab's eyes caught the figure of a man in the mosque. He gesticulated for the man to approach. The young man strutted towards us. "Yes, Tok?" he said.

"This is the man who built this mosque," Tok Rejab said to him.

The young man looked at me with scepticism, seeing we were about the same age. "This is Hamzah, I mean, the Mr Hamzah whom everyone talked about?"

"He is the mosque caretaker," Tok Rejab explained to me. "His name is Tajol."

Tajol took my hand. "It's an honour to kiss the hand that built the house of God." Then, staring at me, he added, "I had imagined that this man they called Hamzah was someone older."

"I don't understand, Tok, all this fuss about me, and son of Tobali and this mosque. What's going on?"

"Wasn't it you who gave us the money?"

"You mean the money I donated to Tobali before I left?"

"Yes that money." His eyes searched my face. He had his brow raised, wondering why I was perplexed. "Aren't you pleased?"

173

"Ah yes, of course. But what about the school?"

"What school?"

"I thought I gave the money for a new school."

"Oh! Yes, of course. The village committee had thought that the existing school, though a bit old, could still function adequately. But we were very much in need of a bigger mosque, as our congregation had increased threefold on Fridays, requiring many to pray outside in the open. Hamzah, there is no greater deed than to build the house of God, and no greater benefit in the hereafter to the donor – and that means you."

"I see," I said.

"You seem disappointed?"

"Fine, Tok. If it makes the people of Tobali happy, I am happy."

I had given a generous sum of money to Tok Rejab before I left, to be used for improving the old school and expanding it. He had nodded, completely shocked by my generosity. My wish list could have passed his attention in that moment of excitement. Or maybe I had completely failed to understand the village elders' priorities. I couldn't help being disappointed. Too much of this world had happened to me, and the hereafter seemed far remote.

I said to Tok Rejab, "I want to visit Sam's grave, Tok."

"You mean the grave of Sheikh Omar?"

"I forgot, yes, Sheikh Omar."

"I meant to take you there, and to your old house too," he said. He then led me to the west side of the mosque. Walking briskly, he kept his eyes to the ground, as always. Sam's gravesite seemed to be newly spruced up, with the weeds freshly uprooted. The flower petals strewn over it still had their blush. The headstone and inscription seemed to have been recently scrubbed of grime.

Sadly, my little house by the sea was a picture of a forgotten past – tattered and falling apart. Tok Rejab gave a deep sigh. "We didn't have the money to repair this one. Every cent went to the mosque. But I have decreed that no one should trespass upon it, let alone destroy it." He was profusely apologetic.

While deeply disappointed with how my donation had been used, and what with the state of my old house, I felt that it wasn't the time and place for reprobation. Tok Rejab wasn't an unprincipled man, nor was he dishonest. Far from it. It was I, maybe, who was out of sync with the villager elders' thinking, rather than they with mine. I should forgive them for that. They had done so much for me, and this was to be my home. *Be as generous with them, Hamzah, as they have been with you,* I said to myself.

"Tok Rejab, you and the people of Tobali have done more than I deserve. What more do I want? I never imagined that I would be so honoured like this. I am glad to have come back. It seems as though Providence has brought me back. This is my home now."

Tok Rejab lifted his head, looked into my face, and placed his hand upon my arm. "I wish indeed you were my son. My own have deserted me." He paused, keeping his eyes on the ground. Just then, a stray ball swung into the little house. A troop of screaming boys came running. They scrambled after it. "Didn't I tell you not to play by this house? Do you know who this man is?" he asked, pointing at me. The leader of the pack stood at attention in bewilderment.

"No."

"He is Mr Hamzah, an important person of our village. He used to live in this house." The leader looked at me and then at the house. His pack followed suit. "But it's small and very old," he said.

"Never mind that. Now what do you say when you meet an important person? I am waiting."

"Assalamualaikum, sir," he said.

"And then?" Tok Rejab put on a serious tone and held his palm out. The leader came forward, drew my hand into both his palms, and kissed it. The rest did the same, one by one.

I held myself from laughing. Pretending to be stern, I said, "Now go and play elsewhere, and don't you step into this house." I raised my finger. "It's sacred." I laughed as they scrambled away like chickens.

"Kids nowadays have little respect for elders," Tok Rejab rejoined. He turned to me. "Not you, though. You have always been polite, ever since I first set eyes on you."

Chapter 23

From the first day of my stay in the Rejab household, I was treated like a hotel guest. The house was big. It was raised four feet off the ground and had a large verandah. Architecturally, it was Malay in design, with a high sloping roof and decorative gables. My ample room looked over the grounds and upon an old rain tree – older than anyone still living there – spreading its sprawling canopy like a giant umbrella. Tobali was a great respite from the bustling Ipoh and Penang. Memories of my years with Sam returned, uplifting my fallen spirit.

The sea was only half a mile away from Tok Rejab's house, an area interspersed with village houses with attap roofs and coconut trees that flourished right to the beach. The sea breeze would begin to set in as the sun reached its zenith at noon, when it would be felt at the large verandah of the house. Neighbours were far apart, as houses in Tobali were adequately spaced from one another and only began to cluster towards the commercial centre, where the Chinese liked to be.

I implored Tok Rejab and Rahimah to treat me as family, not as a guest, and insisted on taking care of myself, washing and ironing my own clothes. I also helped in the kitchen. After all, I had grown up in Tobali as an ordinary man without maids or servants in the difficult years of the war with Sam. Rahimah nodded and smiled.

As the days passed, I couldn't even enter the kitchen without being told to clear out, as it was not the place for men, Rahimah said. And when I was out of the house until late in the evening, I found my shirts and pants washed and well ironed. When I asked Rahimah who had done it, she smiled and asked me to ask Siti about it. So I did.

Siti, in her girly and gingerly demeanour, replied, "You're no longer in the war, Abang, and I can surely do a better job than you. Aren't you happy with the result?"

"Indeed I am. Why did you do it? You shouldn't have."

"You are my brother, and I am a girl. I should take care of you. Don't say no. It's unbecoming of an abang like you."

I turned to Rahimah for help.

"Don't look at me. I can't tell her what to do. She's a grown-up girl now."

I swung my head to Siti. She looked straight at me, put her finger on her lips, and said, "Don't say another word."

Rahimah laughed. "She's not your little girl anymore, Hamzah."

I had noticed that on the day of my arrival, when Siti sprinkled scented water on me during the welcoming ceremony. It was a woman I saw who took my breath away, not the little girl I used to place on my lap as my little sister.

"Well, Siti, I shan't be calling you my little sister anymore. That's not you. You're a woman now, and a pretty one too."

Suddenly she disappeared into the back of the house.

"Why did she go away, Aunty?"

"You made her self-conscious."

I had brought with me a lot of books which I had accumulated while I was in Penang and Ipoh through mail order from England and Holland. They usually took a couple of months to arrive by sea mail. It was worth the wait. They were all leather-bound classics. Tok Rejab, who was a village chief by calling, was also an excellent wood craftsman in his leisure. From his collection, he had kindly furnished my room with a beautiful cupboard with framed glass doors, a writing table of polished timber, and a cushioned chair.

So pleased I was that my books had a temporary home, I began to spend my leisure time by reading in my room. I always kept my room door open during the day so as not to be seen shut inside my room like a hermit. In the first couple of weeks of my stay, Siti would pass by and, without fail, take a curious glance at what I was doing. I invited her in, but she shyly declined. Maybe she thought it wasn't proper for her to be in my room. I understood the decorum expected of her in this conservative village.

One day she stood by the door and looked at the cupboard filled with the leather-bound books. "When you were out, I had a peek at those beautiful books. I hope you don't mind, Abang."

"Of course not. Do you like to read?"

"Yes. I hope to become a teacher. I am learning Dutch now. Maybe one day I will become a Dutch teacher. I saw some Dutch books in the cupboard. I suppose you speak Dutch too?"

"Yes."

"You are such a learned man, Abang."

"No, I'm not. You know, I never went to a proper school." Watching her standing at the door and fearing to cross the threshold as if it were taboo, I said, "Look, Siti, don't just stand there. Come in and sit down with me. It's all right. The door is wide open. I've already asked your mother's permission."

"You did?"

"Yes. So come in." I had lied. Still, I knew that neither Rahimah nor Tok Rejab would be bothered about it.

When Siti beamed winsomely, I knew that she wanted very much to enter. In her characteristically high-spirited way, she said, "Right, then." Then straightaway she went to the book cupboard. "May I look at them?"

"Go ahead."

While she was glancing through the shelves, I took, for the first time since my arrival, a good look at her at close range. She had certainly bloomed from that little sister I used to know. I saw a woman, a beautiful one. She was slender, as a woman should be, with an attractive tender face framed by cascading waist-length hair. Her most engaging feature was her intriguing, melting eyes that said many things. She exuded not the seductive charm of a thorny rose, but rather the winsomeness of a soft pink petal. She was just the opposite of what I had seen in Pinky when my eyes beheld her for the first time at the book club. Yet Siti drew me just as much.

As she was about to peel a book from the shelves, she turned her head slowly and caught me scrutinising her. I guessed she must have sensed my staring. "Were you looking at me, Abang?"

"Yes. You've grown to be very beautiful, Siti."

"Really, Abang? I must have been ugly when I was young then." She laughed. "Let's talk about the books, not me."

She seemed pleased. The tension of the first few minutes dissipated.

"These leather-bound books are really exquisite. Look at this one. I love its feel." It was *Don Quixote*, one of the thickest books in the shelves. "I was told about this story by my Dutch teacher. How I wish I could read it. I know no English." She turned her eyes to me.

"I can teach you."

"Will you, Abang?"

"Anything for my Siti."

She blushed and put her head down. "I must go now. Mother must be looking for me."

"She isn't. Come on, stay on. I love talking to you. You're very inquisitive. I like that."

Her face reddened again. "I better go now, before she calls."

"Come again anytime. As you can see, the door is always open."

Siti visited me quite often after that. We talked of many things. Mostly it was she who introduced the topics, which arose from her own keen curiosity about the world I had lived in – Java, Penang, Ipoh, and Kuala Lumpur; the *Shanghai Star* and how it had been shipwrecked; and the difficult war years. No matter how I wanted to skirt it, Mataram House had to come into the picture. The simplicity and candidness of Siti's questioning, I found engaging. It wasn't a kind of prying, but more of a genuine interest in me, and it flattered me.

I couldn't help comparing, as Pinky had never had that kind of inquisitiveness about me. But why was I making this judgement? Was I taking a keen interest in Siti, one beyond that of that little girl I used to know?

A week later, when I was looking for Siti to invite her for a walk to the sea, as it was a sunny Saturday and people were heading to the beach, the young maid told me she had gone marketing with her mother at the monthly Saturday fair in the town.

Then with a naughty smile, the young maid said, "Sir, Siti had never done that before. I know she hates marketing. Maybe she is going to cook something for her favourite abang."

"Don't you joke like that, Joyah. She won't like it," I said, telling the maid off.

"But it's true, sir," she replied with a giggle.

"Go and finish your chores. You're supposed to clean the plates and sweep the floor. Go on."

"I bet you're going to have a sumptuous meal tonight, sir." She wagged her fingers mischievously. "She's really an excellent cook." She continued with a teasing, singsong voice, and then she ran inside with her giggles after I feigningly chased after at her.

When the table had been laid for the evening dinner, I could smell the inviting aroma of spice. Rahimah brought in the dishes. There was a huge whole lobster cooked to perfection and garnished with curry. This was followed by crabs, squid, fish, and an assortment of other culinary delights. I was staggered, and so was Tok Rejab.

"What is this, Rahimah, a feast? Have you bought the entire market?" Tok Rejab exclaimed.

"Don't ask me. Ask your daughter. She bought all this stuff and did the cooking too. She said it's for her brother Hamzah. I wasn't even allowed to touch a ladle. The meal is entirely hers." Rahimah chuckled.

"Mother! Don't embarrass me," Siti cried out from the kitchen. "Nothing to be shy about, Siti," Rahimah cried back. "I am just telling the truth."

"Don't embarrass your daughter, Rahimah," Tok Rejab said, chastising his wife.

"Oh, come on, Tok, you know of late she has been talking about nothing but Abang Hamzah, how clever he is and all that. Even the maids know about it."

"Stop it, Mother!" Siti bellowed.

"That's enough, Rahimah," Tok Rejab said.

"Why don't you ask Siti to join us, Aunty?" I said.

"Do you hear that, Siti? Your abang wants you to join him," Rahimah hollered.

"I am not coming, not after what you have just said," Siti cried back.

"It's me who is inviting you, Siti. Please, do come," I said loudly.

"Thank you, Abang. Since you asked me, I'll come," she hollered back. "But stop teasing me, Mama."

Tok Rejab turned to me and gave a suppressed smile. Siti ambled in. I smiled at her and put my thumb up in appreciation. She beamed radiantly back. We partook in the generous spread of food, enough for ten people. Tok Rejab enquired about my future enterprise. He remembered I had earlier broached the subject to him, but my mind was on Siti. She took furtive glances at me, and I glanced back. Rahimah, in her silently observant nature, lifted her eyes in our direction approvingly.

The next morning, Tok Rejab invited me to walk with him along the beach, which was a five-minute drive from the house. The early sun was rising, the sea breeze had yet to blow, and it hadn't rained since I arrived, making the air quite balmy.

As if something struck his mind, Tok Rejab fell into deep thought. He paced the ground with his head down. Then suddenly he said, "You know, Hamzah, you have seen more of life, in all its ups and downs, than anyone of your age that I know. From a castaway, you became a rich man. And you donated a large sum of money to the people of Tobali before you left us. Now you have returned. When you wrote to me about it, I was truly intrigued. Is it about Tobali? We are a modest community. What can we offer you? Only our welcome. You talked of venturing into mining in Banka. Why? Why not in Malaya?" His head, which had been bowed towards the ground while talking, suddenly lifted. He surveyed my face for a few seconds, as if trying to read something. "I am an old man, Hamzah. I can somehow sense these things. Tell me, is there something more personal?"

"Tok, I am a man with enormous faults. I have made a lot of mistakes in my life, only you don't know about them. And I returned to Tobali to find peace. Yes, you're right, it's something personal. You're very perceptive."

"All right, then. I shall ask no more."

As we strolled leisurely by the palm-fringed coast, I asked him a personal question. "Tell me, Tok, were you born and bred here in Banka?"

"Yes, I was born here, but my ancestors were from Minangkabau in West Sumatra. I am a Minang, and so is your aunty. My great-grandfather came to settle here because men then did not have property rights in Minangkabau under the matrilineal custom, where property and land were passed down from mother to daughter. Over here, he was free from the shackles of that female-centric custom that makes the Minang women overly assertive."

"I'm half Minang, from my father's side. My father moved to Java for that same reason."

"I know. You had told me that once."

"What about this term 'Tok'? Is it a kind of title?"

"Well, 'Tok' is the short form of 'Datok', which is a title accorded to leaders and chiefs. A common practice in Sumatra. Sometimes it's hereditary, as in my case. I got it from my father, and he from his father. We have been chiefs for four generations."

We came to a wooden shelter. Several fishing boats were moored in the water. Some smaller ones had been beached for repairs. Men were working on them. Fishing articles and boat equipment were found scattered about the wooden hut. A long bench lay empty. Tok Rejab appeared a little tired.

"Tok, why don't we take a rest over there?" I suggested.

"Good idea."

As we settled on the bench, he stretched his legs and massaged his thighs. I noticed how frail and tiny he was. It was hard to imagine this small man with a goatee, a simple white turban, a baggy cotton dress, and sandals could wield so much influence and command such respect throughout the island.

"Tell me, Hamzah, what made you suddenly want to ask about me being called Tok?"

"I'm sorry if I sounded silly. A few days ago I asked Siti about Mois. She said he had run away to Singapore. Run away? I was stunned. Then she laughed. Then she said Mois was actually afraid you would one day pass the role of chief of Tobali to him, as he is your only son, and then he would inherit the title Tok. What is wrong with that? I asked her. She refused to tell me and said I should ask you about it."

"I see. It's true. As I have told you, my forebears held the role of being chief of Tobali for four generations. I am getting old. It's time for Mois, as my son, to start thinking of taking over from me. When I spoke to him about it, he flatly refused, saying he had no interest in dealing with husbands' and wives' problems, land disputes, inter-family feuds, village politics, and whatnot. Everyone calling him Tok wasn't good for his persona either. It sounded archaic, he said. And you know what? He even chided the title. He said he would hate the idea of everyone calling him a grandfather before he even got old and grey. As you know, Hamzah, 'Tok' also means 'grandfather' in our language. It's stupid of him to joke like that. But that's my son Mois."

"Mois, as far as I remember, has a restless and adventuresome spirit, and he is somewhat playful too. Remember when he was fifteen and he caught a rare wild cock with a long flowing tail like the train of a king's ceremonial robe? It was a very rare species of fowl, and he was proud of it. And you scolded him for wasting his time on inconsequential exploits like that. But that's Mois. He wants excitement. I think that being chief isn't up his alley. That remark about the title Tok? He was just being naughty."

"You seem to know him. Both of you are of the same age, right?"

"He is a year older, as I remember."

"Yet you are much more mature than he is."

"Maybe his potential is yet to be discovered."

"See, you're younger, yet he can learn a lot from you. No better person to talk to him. Bring him home, Hamzah. I don't want the hereditary line of chiefs to just disappear after me. Do you understand my concern?"

"I do, Tok. I shall definitely try. I promise. But, please, Tok, don't praise me too much. I might not be able to live up to it."

*   *   *

In the past three months since my return, I had been busy travelling the length and breadth of the island looking for areas for a new mine. I found that most of the best deposits had already been taken, first by the Europeans and then by the Chinese. I was planning to build a house of my own. Before doing that, I needed to restore my former little palace on the beach.

Restoring this little house was a sentimental journey. With my heart in the job, the house was on its way to regaining its former self. Every detail of the house seemed to come back to life. It brought me to tears to see the finished work. I could picture Sam on the verandah smoking his pipe. Behind this little house, a bigger building was being constructed for my future home. This bigger house was being built out of necessity. Neither pride nor sentiment played a part.

In the meantime, I had been absorbed into the Rejab household. Rahimah, with her gentle and sensible ways, became my surrogate mother in place of Aunty Maimunah, but she didn't display Aunty's overabundant demonstrative affection. And Siti? She had completely discarded her earlier shyness, becoming more engaging and spending a lot of time with me, either in my room, albeit with the door always open, or in the patio. Whenever I was free, she and I would take long walks or cycle in the village. Neighbours would wave at us and greet us as we cycled to the beach or went to the market. Whenever I returned home from my business trips, Siti would be the first to ask me how things had gone, so much so that she came to know more and more about tin and how it was mined. Her mind was as sharp and agile as she was bubbly. Already she began to speak to me with a smattering of English, a skill she was bent on acquiring. I asked her why. Her reply was that English was the language of the future. How she came to that conclusion, I wondered.

I realised how involved Tok Rejab was in the lives of the people. It was no wonder Mois shunned the prospect of being chief. Maybe he was terrified of the responsibility and had used every excuse to sidestep it.

As a chief, Tok Rejab didn't have much of a private life. All manner of problems of the people, down to their most intimate lives, were his concern. The people appeared to look upon him as their father figure, asking him for guidance and for resolution of all their problems. And Tok Rejab revelled in this as he would a hobby.

During the three months I had been in his house, there wasn't a day when someone hadn't suddenly appeared without notice to seek his assistance, intervention, support, mediation, or counsel. And I unexpectedly became involved in one of these discussions just as I was about to leave the house one day to collect my new car, which had just arrived from Singapore, at Port of Muntok. Noticing the arrival of a peculiar woman, Tok Rejab asked me to delay my departure for a bit. "Hamzah, you should see this," he said to me with amusement.

The woman was accompanied by Lebai Amir, the imam, and his wife, Latifah. The woman was indeed peculiar, judging by her appearance. She had the sultriness of a demi-mondaine: bosomy with an hourglass waist and an ample bottom to match, while her face was made up like that of a taxi dancer in a Penang cabaret. Her make-up was odd enough for anywhere, but in Tobali, in the middle of the afternoon, it was preposterous. Not to appear too eager, I asked, "Do you really want me to stay, Tok?"

"Of course." There was mischief in his tone. "I want you to witness this. Sometimes things can be quite funny, and I have a feeling this one will be," Tok Rejab said good-humouredly. His eyes twinkled. *This old man actually loves his job. And he has a sense of humour to go with it too,* I thought.

Latifah went into the kitchen to meet Rahimah, leaving the woman with us.

"And why have you brought Kalsom with you, Lebai?" Rejab asked the imam.

"Kalsom has begged my wife to bring her to you, and here we are. Let her tell you her story herself."

"Is this one of your husband's gambling problem, Som?" Tok Rejab asked the woman with sternness.

"Yes, Tok, and worse," Kalsom replied hesitatingly.

"Worse? How? He beats you, sells the house, marries another woman?"

"More serious than that, Tok." She began to sob, covering her face with her handkerchief. "It's too shameful for me to tell." Som swung her gaze in my direction.

"It's all right. Mr Hamzah here is a very respectable citizen of Tobali. Go on, tell me what your problem is."

Som glanced sideways and smiled at me coyly.

"My husband said that in Islam it's a sin to disobey a husband. Is that true, Tok?"

"It's true, yes. Go on."

"He threatened to divorce me if I refused."

"Good for you. Your husband, Abu, is a scoundrel, and you would be a lot better without him. Don't you agree, Lebai?"

"Yes, Tok, I agree wholeheartedly."

"I don't want to lose him, Tok. With all his bad habits, he is still my husband."

"Those are not bad habits. Those are vices – sins."

"I love him."

"All right, all right. So what's the problem then, since you love him so much?"

"My husband, Abu, owes this Indian man a lot of money. He invited him to the house for dinner. When I was serving the dinner, this Indian man took glances at me, very naughty glances. I was terribly upset. When the Indian man left, my husband suggested I could help to wipe out his debt completely." Som paused and looked up at everyone. "I am too ashamed to say it."

"Well, you've come all the way here, so you might as well accomplish your purpose."

"He wanted me to sleep with the Indian man. Oh, I am so ashamed, Tok." She began to cry. Lebai Amir shrunk with embarrassment. Most likely he hadn't had prior knowledge of Som's story.

"Good God! The imbecile. Is he mad? What devil has got into him! Of all the preposterous things I have had to encounter, this tops them all."

"So what do you want me to do? Tell him not to divorce me."

"You mean you have come to me to plead so you can stay married to this imbecile?"

"Yes, that's why I come to you." She threw her pathetic eyes upon Tok Rejab, looked at me, and then looked at Lebai Amir. She seemed truly desperate.

"Som, Som, your husband is a scoundrel, and you are an idiot. The two of you deserve each other. Look at you, in broad daylight and in that dress, and with that paint on your face. No wonder the Indian man thought you were on offer."

Som put her head down. "Forgive me, Tok. I just wanted to look presentable," she said coyly.

"You go home now. I'll deal with your husband. And don't you do anything stupid, no matter what your husband says. Good heavens, Som. Where do you put your brain, on your bottom?"

"Yes, Tok, and thank you."

I really wanted to laugh.

After Som wiped her tears, the light returned to her face and she gave a tiny smile. The next moment, she turned her attention to me.

"Who is this young man, Tok?"

"This is Hamzah, the late Sheikh Omar's adopted son," Tok Rejab answered.

"Who's Sheikh Omar, Tok?"

Tok Rejab raised his tone. "Never mind that. Now be on your way, Kalsom. You've a mountain of trouble of your own."

She thanked Tok Rejab and said goodbye, wiggling and swaying her hips as she walked away. Tok Rejab shook his head. I let out a much needed laugh. *No wonder Mois doesn't fancy the idea of this legacy being passed down to him,* I thought.

Chapter 24

When I visited the government mining office in Pangkal Pinang, the departmental officer looked surprised that I had requested to inspect the geological maps of Banka.

"What's your purpose?" he asked with the characteristic impassiveness of a bureaucrat.

"To open a mine," I said.

He looked at me derisively. "What's your background? Any experience in mining?"

"Plenty," I said. "Why? Do I have to present my credentials to study a map?" I was beginning to be annoyed by his officiousness.

"You need to prove your experience and financial backing to apply for a concession, you know," he said.

"Do you ask the same question of others, say, Europeans or Chinese?" He did not reply, and dropped his head. "What made you presume I wanted a concession? Mister, I know these maps are available for public viewing. Could you please offer me that service, or do I have to call Jakarta for them?"

"Of course, sir, I'll bring them out to you. It's just that you are the first Malay in Banka to ask for them in the ten years I have been here. I thought you were an agent acting for some Chinese. My apologies, sir. I didn't mean—"

"Apologies accepted." I smiled.

"I shall put all the maps at your disposal, sir."

"My name is Hamzah, and as to my experience, I have owned mines in Kinta Valley, Malaya. Do you know where that is?"

"Of course, sir. It's richer than Banka. I am Herman, the administrative officer. I have not heard of you before. Are you from here, sir?"

"Yes, Tobali."

"You know Tok Rejab?"

"Of course. Like a father."

"He is a highly respected man in Banka." He smiled. The earlier pompous air had fizzled out.

"That is very nice to hear. I shall mention this to him."

The earlier officious Herman suddenly turned into a friendly and accommodative Herman.

"Mr Hamzah, let me indicate to you the location of one of the richest deposits in Banka. It is so rich there it is practically overburdened with ore. And neither European nor Chinese could get at it."

"Really?"

"Really, Mr Hamzah."

"Why is that so?"

"Let me first show you, and you'll be amazed."

He spread the maps out across the big table.

"You see here," he said, pointing to an area north of Tobali, "more than a thousand acres of the richest tin lies here and is waiting to be mined."

"Why is it not mined?" I asked, puzzled by his revelation.

"Because it is owned by the indigenous rubber smallholders of Banka, that's why. Now if you could get the smallholders to give up their land to you, you'll have one of the largest mines in Banka."

My goodness, I thought, *no wonder the vultures could not get at it.* I was sure that they had been aware of the presence of the rich deposit. They could smell tin as ants could detect sugar. If what Hermann said were true, then this deposit was a bonanza.

Herman noticed my momentary silence and said, "Aren't you interested, Mr Hamzah?"

"Certainly I am. I was just stunned by your revelation. I thank you for showing me this location. You don't know how happy you have made me today. Can I have a copy of this map?"

"It is yours. And, Mr Hamzah, I am sorry if I was a little rude when you came in. Again, I thought you were an agent of some Chinese. Good luck, Mr Hamzah. If you need any assistance, do not hesitate to call me. If you succeeded in your venture, you would be the first Malay tin miner in Banka's history."

So elated was I that I shook his hand with such vigour that it surprised him. "Thank you, Mr Herman. I shall not forget your good deed."

A few days later, I gathered a number of men, including a land surveyor, to reconnoitre the area that lay amid Koba, Airgegas, Bedinggong, and Maleh. What I discovered lifted my spirit. Some of the rubber trees had a girth as large as a hundred-year-old tree, the bark heavily scarred from overtapping. Others were similarly quite old. The trees were on average fifty years old and should have been replanted to extract an economic yield. I didn't need to be an expert in rubber to know that these trees were practically empty of latex.

I discovered that there were three hundred to four hundred smallholders owning two to ten acres each. I didn't know any of the owners, and neither could I fathom their thinking. But like any normal people, they knew, I believed, the value of money. Still, I cautioned myself to tread the ground very carefully. These were simple rural folks; I shouldn't be seen as a rich, land-grabbing businessman out to cheat them. I certainly needed to lean on Tok Rejab for counsel and support.

A few days later, after pondering on this bonanza which had been placed in my lap by a good Samaritan, I prayed to God that this wasn't one of those tricks of Mataram House. But the whole thing was as real as the sunrise. There were two things in my life that were beyond my comprehension and control: good fortune and bad fortunes. And I had to take them as they came. *No one needs to know,* I reminded myself.

In the quiet study of Tok Rejab's home, I sought counsel from him and threw about the idea of making these landowners to be stakeholders of my mine. This way, they could share the profits from the operation, with steady earnings for as long as the deposits lasted – and that could be about thirty years. At the end of the period, the land could be rehabilitated. By then, each one of them would be rich — something they could never achieve otherwise. This, I said to Tok Rejab, would be a better option than buying their land outright. A sudden cash windfall would blow over in no time and would soon impoverish them.

After intently listening to my ideas, he said he needed to reflect on the prospect for a couple of days. This concerned the livelihood of his flock, he emphasised. At the end of the meeting, which was practically a monologue delivered by me, he said with a serious countenance, "Let's see what God has to say."

In the following days, Tok Rejab was uncommunicative except for engaging in small talk at meals. If he wasn't in his room, he could be found in his study. I became terribly worried. It began to cross my mind that he wasn't in favour of this outlandish enterprise, the likes of which were unheard of in the history of Banka. I felt somewhat guilty for placing upon him such a heavy responsibility concerning the future of his people.

In this hour of need, I thought it was fitting for me to ask Rahimah what she had to say. Gazing at my curling brow and unsmiling face, she said with a smile, "He is meditating and is asking guidance from Allah. Invariably, he will receive a sign. Trust me. It is his way when faced with a heavy responsibility."

"Thank you, Aunty."

Discerning my lack of spirit and guessing that I was not totally appeased, she said, "I know what's in your mind: 'What if the answer is no?' Well, Hamzah, if it were written in your destiny, it would be yours."

That didn't appease me either. My destiny had a double face.

In the early morning of the fourth day, when we were having breakfast, Tok Rejab greeted me with a broad smile. "We will have a gathering of the smallholders in the compound of my house as soon as you are ready to meet them. I'm very happy for you, Hamzah. You're indeed blessed."

Rahimah smiled at me.

Siti jumped out of her seat, ran up to me, and gave me a hug. Both her parents were astonished. So was I. "I'm sorry, I couldn't help myself. I was so happy for Abang Hamzah," she exclaimed.

Tok Rejab lowered his head and smiled.

Rahimah seemed pleased as pie.

* * *

It took three months to research, gather, and collate all the data on the smallholders who would be participating in the scheme. Since relying on records alone was insufficient, the landowners had to be individually approached. A team of personnel and ground workers had been employed for the task.

Finally the historic day arrived – historic because never before had there been an assembly of people from Tobali and the surrounding regions, right up to Muntok and Pangkal Pinang, in such great numbers at the house of Tok Rejab.

They came, these smallholders, bringing their families and relatives with them because of Tok Rejab. There wasn't a hope in the world that I could have achieved that on my own. The word had gone around that the meeting was something to do with improving their livelihood, with the prospect of better earnings. Wisely, Tok Rejab had instructed his men to mention nothing of any scheme, as that would only lead to unwanted speculation.

Tok Rejab had advised me to leave the speaking to him. Should there be any mistrust or suspicion towards me, he could deal with that better than I could. He also advised me not to be too opportunistic or too eager, as that might appear exploitative. He warned me not to take the people for fools. "They might be simple, yet beneath their exterior they are complex, evasive, and difficult to read. They will never say no to you in your face, nor is their yes unequivocal," he reminded me.

At close to noon, the crowd in the compound had swelled to five hundred, most of them sitting crossed-legged on the mats, a few standing against the trees. Tok Rejab had laid down a feast for the occasion, as it was a village custom to do so no matter what was the purpose of the meeting.

When Tok Rejab rose to speak, children were running around, a baby cried, and some people were still at the food stalls. Few were paying attention. He lost his cool. He asked all of the women with babies and children to retreat to the back, and advised all the men to move forward. He told them all that they could resume their eating after the meeting.

Once order was installed, he addressed them in a soft and languid manner. Yet his timbre was clear and persuasive, and could be heard right at the back. "Tobali's special son has returned," he said. Then a lone voice from the assembly threw a loud remark, interrupting him. Tok Rejab paused, rearing his head to look for the source. He resumed. "At the time when we most needed a proper place of worship, he built us one. Now it is one of the finest mosques in Banka. He has now made Tobali his home." Again a rude bellow sprang from the audience to unsettle him. His face reddened, and I noticed a tremor in his arm. He paused and again scoured the heads of the audience. He spotted a figure that he recognised. "Is that you, Hitam?" he hollered. "If you wish to say something, wait until I have finished. Otherwise, leave. It's neither the place nor the time for thuggery." Curious heads swung in the direction of Hitam, who was seated against a big tree trunk right in the midst of the crowd. He had a cigarette in his mouth and was smoking it with undisguised insolence. He was a man of bulky build, his face dark and full.

"All of you here own rubber lands. Now tell me, how much latex do you get from them?" Tok Rejab asked.

They looked at each other, puzzled by the question. Then someone shouted, "Why do you ask, Tok? You know the answer. The trees are as dry as the desert."

"Of course I know. But I want you to hear it from you. And what are you doing about it?"

A low, rumbling murmur spread among the crowd.

"What are you getting at, Tok?" the insolent Hitam shouted.

Another round of murmurs, these ones louder, ensued from the crowd.

Encouraged by the murmuring, Hitam taunted Tok Rejab. "Yes, what are you getting at, Tok? Is this some wild scheme by the man next to you? Is that why he is back in Tobali?"

They all turned their heads to him. I became nervous. Things seemed to be moving in the wrong direction. It was not what I had anticipated. Even Tok Rejab, I noticed, began to lose his cool.

"Look here, Hitam. If you are bent on disrupting this meeting, you are not welcome. So please leave. I want to ask you, are you the spokesman for these people? Let me ask them. Have you all appointed that man as your spokesman? Speak up. Your interest is at stake. Do not allow him to pour sand in your rice bowl," Tok Rejab exclaimed in a voice trembling with anger.

"No!" they shouted resoundingly.

"Did you hear that, Hitam? So you can stay or leave. If you decide to stay, do not interrupt me. Otherwise, I shall ask my people to remove you forcibly."

Hitam raised his head towards the sky like a child who wasn't listening. Not a squeak came from his mouth though. Satisfied that he had regained control of the meeting, Tok Rejab continued speaking. "What Mr Hamzah is about to propose to you today will change your future. He has discussed this matter with me, and I have given my approval and blessing. I shall give him the floor in a moment. So please listen to what he has to say."

"Yes, Tok," the crowd responded in unison.

I addressed the crowd, saying, "First of all, let me thank Tok Rejab for organising this gathering, and for the sumptuous food he has laid before us. And to all of you, thank you for your kind attendance. Now let me ask you a simple question: are you satisfied with the income you receive from your rubber trees?"

"No," they all shouted.

"Why?"

"No latex," was the loud, resounding answer.

"Why?" I cried.

"Trees too old – need replanting."

"Why don't you replant?" I asked.

"No money."

"Even if we replant, it takes seven or eight years before the trees can produce latex. What do we live on in the meantime?" said a middle- man who was sitting right in the front. Then he added, "Do you have a solution for us, Mr Hamzah? Is this your plan?"

"Yes, I have a better alternative to replanting, one that will provide you with not only with an immediate income, but also a much better return than you have ever earned, or will ever earn, in your life. I promise you. Do you want to hear about it?"

"*Yes!*" they responded loudly, with exuberance.

"You all know Banka Island is rich in tin deposits, among the richest in the world. Tin has brought prosperity to Indonesia and Malaya, enriching the Dutch, the British, the French, and the Chinese. Why can't we too benefit from this tin? Do you understand what I am getting at? Don't you all want to benefit from this tin too?"

They just stared at me in silence.

Then, the middle-aged man who had made the pertinent point earlier said, "Indeed we do. So tell us, Mr Hamzah, how do we do it? We know nothing about tin or mining. We have been rubber tappers all our lives."

"May I know your name, sir?" I asked.

He stood up to speak. He was, I guessed, about Tok Rejab's age, around sixty – tall, neatly attired, with salt- and-pepper hair, and carrying the air of a man who had seen better times. "I am Haji Budiman. I own sixty-six acres of untappable trees. So I am interested to hear your idea about this tin." Turning around to face the audience behind him, he added, "This is the first time I have heard anyone telling us to exploit the rich resource of our land, instead of being just bystanders while foreigners squander our wealth. So let's hear what he has for us."

"Thank you, Haji Budiman, for your support and for appreciating the purpose behind this project. I hope others will do the same. I have a surprise for you. Do you know that your land is sitting on the richest tin ore in the whole of Banka?"

Again, silence fell upon the audience, their faces blanketed with perplexity. Even Haji Budiman was speechless.

"Why the silence?" I exclaimed. "Don't you have anything to say?"

"We don't know what to say. What does that mean?" Again it was Haji Budiman who spoke.

"All of you are sitting on riches, but you didn't even know about it – until now," I said.

"But we are not tin miners, and we know nothing about the business," someone said. They echoed in agreement.

"I shall help you to mine it, and collectively we shall form a company. The combined total of your plots will constitute the mine. We shall have one of the biggest mines in Banka, and all of you will see money you never imagined you could earn. I promise you that. I am an experienced miner. I have operated and owned tin mines in Malaya."

"But what about money? We need money to do this," a voice from the floor cried out.

"I shall take care of that. You do not need to spend a cent. I shall finance the entire operation. All you need to do is to contribute your plots in exchange for shares in the mine, in proportion to the size of land you own. It is as simple as that. And I repeat, you shall earn money you never dreamt of earning in your lives."

"This is all too complicated. I know nothing about mines or about business. It's giving me a headache. I need to think," said a man with a family sitting in the centre. He had until this point been listening quietly.

A low, throbbing murmur resonated through the crowd. They seemed lost in a sea of incomprehension and bewilderment. Some looked at the floor; others, at each other. The shadow of blankness that had descended upon the scene worried me. *This promise of wealth seems more of a spectre than a reality to them,* I thought.

Then Hitam, who had been quiet so far, suddenly reared his head again. He rose and set himself against a tree, holding a cigarette in his hand like a gangster. From afar, he said, "What is the catch in this crazy idea of yours, Hamzah? These are all simple rubber smallholders, and they have been rubber smallholders all their lives. Land is their resource, their legacy from their forefathers. Without land they are nothing. This idea about opening a tin mine to emulate the Chinese and the Europeans and to chase money is not their culture. What if the business fails? What then? No money, and worse, no land."

Before I could reply, Tok Rejab brought his small frame up to its full height and, in a tone filled with anger, said, "Who are you to sermonise us, Hitam? Chasing money, you say? You talk about chasing money? What have you been doing all your life? Chasing money, isn't that so? You are perhaps the greediest man I have ever met in my life. You grabbed every piece of land you could get from people who were in debt or in need of money. And now you are telling these people they have no business to make money. Besides, who are you to speak on their behalf? You are just being vindictive to get at me. Do not spoil their future just to get at me. I want you to leave this place now."

Tok Rejab was shaking. I tried to calm him down, but he pushed my hand away. Hitam stood stoically, unmoved.

Tok Rejab continued his barrage. "I've not finished, Hitam. Tell these people here where your piece of smallholding is."

Hitam was silent; not a syllable squeaked from his mouth. "You have none, right? Why? Because these rubber trees are of no value to you. They do not give any income. You want land near the towns. You even have a share in a mining concession, which you got for a particular Chinese, who in turn made you his silent partner. Don't you lecture us. Leave!" Tok Rejab was panting.

Haji Budiman clapped his hands. Others followed. Suddenly the entire crowd began to join in, resulting in a resounding applause. Some even stood up in support and shouted, "Well said, Tok! Well said!"

Feeling defeated, Hitam lifted his arm upwards and punched the air with his fist. Not satisfied, he threw a final stare at Tok Rejab and yelled, "Go sell yourself, Rejab, but don't sell these people." Then he moved out. A group of men followed in train. *Judging by the disgust painted on their faces, they must be his lackeys,* I thought.

Tok Rejab returned to his composed self. "I am glad the devil in our midst has left. Now let us resume our business. Does anyone wish to speak?"

Haji Budiman again rose. "All of us assembled here today have grey matter in our heads. Surely we can think what's good for ourselves. I can only speak for myself. I find this mining idea to be good and beneficial, better than what we have presently. So, I agree to put my sixty-six acres into it." Turning to me, he said, "I trust you are a good man. Otherwise Tok Rejab would not have spoken in support of you. And that is good enough for me. I wish you every success in your endeavour. May God bless you, and all of us. Thank you."

Another old man stood up and spoke. "Some of us here are already nearing our graves. Our children don't want to tap rubber. Some have left to seek the big cities; some have crossed the oceans and God knows where. What can we get from these useless trees? I have only a small piece – three acres. I agree to put in mine too."

All of a sudden there followed a flood of interest. The men began to approach the table where Tok Rejab and I were sitting, throwing questions at me. Tok Rejab had to push them back and call for order.

"Take your seats. Let us do this in an orderly manner. Those who wish to participate, give your name to Mr Hamzah. You don't have to rush and make your decision today. You can come later. While I am happy to note the positive response, I don't want you to be impetuous. I want you to be sure so that you shouldn't complain later that you have been duped," Tok Rejab said. I fully endorsed his stand, in the light of Hitam's very probable mischief. Hitam's dark face hung like a dark cloud in my mind.

At the end of the meeting, nearly eighty landowners had registered their names. While the numbers of participants was encouraging and beyond my earlier expectation, the tally of the total amount of acreage was three hundred and forty-seven, including Haji Budiman's chunk of sixty-six. It was much below my target for a sizeable mine. After Budiman's portion, the rest were of the size of two to three acres, some being as small as one. Still, the outcome wasn't bad for an introductory session.

Chapter 25

The next day, I decided to have a discussion with Tok Rejab about the previous day's proceedings. He was jubilant, and so was I. Rahimah's trepidation about Hitam's trespass had not been quelled, as she warned me to be wary of him. He had a vengeful streak, she had cautioned. Siti was on cloud nine. I had to douse her excitement, telling her that things were still in the early stage. Besides the mining venture, I wanted to talk to Tok Rejab about his son Mois. That morning, he asked me to meet him at his carpentry workshop, which was located at the annex of the house next to the garage.

Tok Rejab was polishing a tabletop with a plane when I entered the workshop. He seemed glued to his work. This was a part of his life that I had not really seen. I knew he was a carpenter, but I had never taken a keen interest. Not wanting to break his concentration, I decided to watch him work. After every stroke, he examined the surface and then repeated the task. Already to me the hardwood was as polished as a marble, but not to him, since he continued planing it, ignoring my presence.

I strolled around the workshop. A completed tall wardrobe caught my attention. I had seen this design before, in Grandma's room. It had an exquisite European design with a single door that had a full-length oval mirror embellished with a rope motif at its border. It was topped with a decorative crown. While Grandma's cabinet had come from Paris, this one was an imitation by Tok Rejab. I was amazed by its similarity to the original. Taken by the workmanship, I hollered, "Tok, this is unbelievable, an exact replica of the original. You're one great artisan."

He paused and turned to me. "Thank you." He dropped his tool and moved over to a small lounging area at the side. "Come over here. Sorry. I had to finish that table just now."

"Do you make business out of this extraordinary skill of yours?"

"No. It's my leisure activity, to take my mind off my work. But I do take orders on special request, like that cabinet you just saw. It was a request from someone in Medan, a wealthy man. He gave me photos of the original and its measurement. I accepted the assignment because he practically pleaded with me. Now, let's talk about your business. Were you satisfied with yesterday's meeting?"

"Yes, indeed. Eighty-two. On my last count. Not bad for an initial response. And it is all thanks to you. It wouldn't have been possible without you, Tok. Tok, I have good news for you."

"More will come. Just wait," he said. Lifting his eyes, he surveyed my face. "So, what's the news?"

"Mois will be back in a week's time."

His whole face lit up. "For what reason?"

"To work with me. I need an able assistant. I believe he fits the bill."

"How did you manage that?"

"I said to him that if he was looking for something exciting, he should come and join me, as I would be opening a new tin mine, the first by a Malay. He was excited. Then he asked whether you approved. Certainly, I replied. That was all."

Tok Rejab looked squarely at me and paused. "I'm no doubt very happy he is coming home. But are you sure of this, Hamzah? He is impetuous and flighty, unlike you."

"Very sure, Tok."

"All right, then." His eyes studied my face as if searching for something. "You are a fine young man. You don't know how happy you have made me." He rose from his seat, extended his hand across the table, and said with a soft voice, "Thank you."

I detected a shadow of mist in his eyes.

At that moment, Rahimah appeared. "Here, I fried some banana fritters for you. I overheard Mois being mentioned. What about Mois?"

"Mois will be back in a week's time, Aunty," I announced.

"Really? What for, a visit?"

"For good," I said.

"Yes, Rahimah. He is coming home. This young man made him do that." Tok Rejab pointed to me.

"God be praised. I have never stopped praying for this," she said. Raising her hands up to the ceiling in supplication and turning her gaze towards me, she said, "You are an angel, Hamzah." She lifted the corner of her garment and used it to wipe her tears.

"Thank you for the banana fritters, Aunty," I said.

"I'll leave you two men. I have some sewing to do," Rahimah said.

"Now, let's resume our discussion," Tok Rejab said.

We were sitting on ornately carved teak chairs, very much favoured by the Javanese, the kind found in Mataram House. I had been curious about their presence here since I entered the workshop. "Did you make these, Tok?" My hand caressed the woodwork.

"No."

I looked at him, puzzled. "Who then?"

He laughed. "I am not the only carpenter in this house. Mois is a carpenter too."

"Mois, a carpenter? That is a surprise."

"Indeed he is. Better than I am, actually, although I was his teacher. He liked to carve figures of animals out of wood when he was a kid. Wait here."

Tok Rejab went over to a cupboard and retrieved something from a drawer. When he returned, he had an object wrapped in cloth in his hand. He removed the cloth and showed to me a fine sculpture of a falcon. "He made this when he was twelve."

"It's beautiful, Tok."

"Yes, it is. That's when I started to train him in carpentry. He could make a profession of it, I thought. But, alas, he wasn't interested. His mind was always wandering. It has been like that since he was small."

"I believe if he found his interest, he would be very productive. I hope this mining business will stop that wandering."

"I hope so too. By the way, thinking about that, I should caution you. He has a short fuse and gets into scraps when provoked. If he had been present when Hitam created that nuisance, he would have beaten the hell out of him."

"Really? I have not seen that part of him yet. Well, he could also act as my bodyguard." I laughed.

"That's not a bad idea. Come, let's go back into the house. I'm sure Siti has something cooked up for lunch – and something special for you, I'm sure."

*   *   *

Two weeks later, Haji Budiman brought with him a large group of landowners. The combined tally of their holdings alone, not including those of the people who had already signed up, was close to four hundred acres. Some, like Budiman, had large plots. As a result of this extraordinary show of commitment, my name and the scheme took on a contagious effect, with owners catching up to those who had already joined, not wanting to lose out. Soon, news of this venture spread across the island, and landowners from as far away as Muntok and Bukit came to my doorstep. When I had to reject those whose plots were too far away from the site, they pleaded to be included. It was heartbreaking to see their crestfallen faces when they were told that their holdings were not contiguous to the scheme.

The final count was one thousand one hundred acres, making this the biggest opencast mine in Banka, with about three hundred stakeholders. Haji Budiman – the man who owned the biggest plot and the first man to believe in my scheme – became my staunchest supporter. He told me that a Chinese coffee-shop owner in Pangkal Pinang had asked him, "Who is this Hamzah, Haji? My customers are talking about him."

*   *   *

Luck was really on my side, as the cassiterite ore was found close to the surface, which precluded the need to remove the usual non-productive overburden covering the ground – a cost-saving advantage in mining terms.

The mine was named Nusantara Mine – *Nusantara* being the Malay name for the Malay Archipelago. At the first shareholders' meeting, the landowners unanimously proposed to name the mine after me. I rejected their proposal, knowing full well it could be the very fodder Hitam – Tok Rejab's nemesis – was looking for in order to blast me.

In Pangkal Pinang, my reputation preceded me. The Chinese raised their hands at me in recognition. Some came forward to shake my hands. Others offered cigarettes and invited me to their tables.

On the first Monday of every month, I would be in Pangkal Pinang at the Mines Department to pay the monthly tribute to the government. It was purely business – tidy – with neither distraction nor recreation in my mind. I would spend the night at the Ankasa on Jalan Depati Amir, a three-storey hotel that overlooked the busy main street. A restaurant serving Padang food – a West Sumatran cuisine – was across the street. I loved its food, as it reminded me of Pak Ali's cooking, which was served when Grandma wasn't around.

During one of these nights, something strange happened in the hotel. I was exhausted after spending a long day in the lobby bar of the hotel interviewing several candidates for the job of supervisors.

I took a shower and dressed for an early dinner at the Padang restaurant across the street. As I came out of my room and walked along the narrow corridor, I thought I saw a figure of a woman walking ahead of me and towards the long window facing the main road. As it was late evening, the figure was backlit by the retreating sun, forming a silhouette. My blood drained from my face as my mind registered the image of Pinky from her back. The shape, the back of the head, and the sway were unmistakably Pinky's. She hurried across the aisle towards the stairs. I pursued her, only to see her vanish into the pale light of the evening. Was it her, or was that my tired mind playing tricks on me? Nusantara Mine was draining me. Sleep had become a luxury.

That night, it took a longer time for sleep to come to me. Tossing to the right and to the left, pacing the ceiling, I kept my eyes closed – but my mind was wide open. And all the time it was Pinky that I saw. When sleep finally came, I saw her again. She was sitting under a big tree beside the Taiping lake, her face radiant in the glow of the sun. She picked up a pebble, threw it out across the lake, and watched it skip away. "Remember this lake, sweetheart?" she said, turning her head to me.

I awoke, calling out, "Pinky." It was still dark. I found myself in tears.

* * *

My new big house had been completed. It dwarfed my old little palace, which had become an annex and now seemed like a poor cousin. No matter how charming and quaint the little palace was to me, to passers-by it was an odd combination of architecture and sight. The two residences were different from each other in every way. One had everything; the other, none. Many people had commented to Tok Rejab how strange I was to have kept the littler house after having built a big one.

Even after the new big house had been completed and was ready for occupation, I was drawn to the little palace. And I became ever the more attached to it, spending more time there than in my new house. This prompted Tok Rejab to chastise me by saying, "God has blessed you, my son. Be thankful for His bounty."

I was lounging on the long rattan chaise longue in the terrace of the little palace one Saturday morning after eating a big breakfast that had been prepared by my maid, whose portions were as consistently large as she was. I felt drowsy as a strong breeze blew in from the sea. It was rather early for the monsoon season to begin, as it was only October. I fell into day dreaming. Pinky had faded into the mist of memory. She hadn't come back to me in spirit or in my thoughts. It had been a month since she had appeared in the corridor of the Ankasa Hotel in Pangkal Pinang, the veracity of which appearance remained a puzzle to me. Stranger things had happened to me, so what was another mysterious vision I couldn't account for? Suddenly, she now returned as though the wind had brought her back. "Go back, Pinky. I'm with Siti now," I said to her. I was suddenly wakened from my doze by a noise. *My God, it was a daydream,* I said to myself.

From the garden path, a loud voice rang out, saying, "Mr Hamzah! Mr Hamzah!" It was Sujak, the mine overseer, running up breathlessly, as if he had seen a ghost.

"What is it, Sujak?" I asked.

"There has been a terrible accident, Mr Hamzah. A *palong* has collapsed, and two workers were buried under the heap of scaffolds. They were killed instantly."

I jumped out of my siesta. My first thought was the bloody monsoon, the bane of miners. I had seen before how the heavy rains could ravage a pit when I was working in Tolok Mine during the war. Banka, unfortunately, was in the path of the monsoon. "Wait here. Let me change. I'll go down with you."

We hurried over to fetch Mois from his house. An hour later, we were in Koba. From there, we headed to the mine, which was five miles away.

What I saw on arrival brought back unpleasant memories of the war: mayhem and death. The bunds that supported the palongs and the sluices had collapsed into a mountain of mud, piling atop the jet monitors and other equipment. The palong superstructure was a huge pile of twisted poles, planks, timber, wires, and steel – like a nightmare coming alive. Underneath were two dead bodies. There would have been more death if the stop-work-order siren had not been activated in time.

Mine disasters were not an uncommon occurrence, but a disaster at the Nusantara Mine, which was barely six months into its operation, that caused deaths – and on my watch at that – was a tragedy made for me. I was deeply concerned.

Soon enough my concerns ballooned into a nightmare. Rumours of the disaster spread rapidly across Tobali. As is the nature of rumours, this one began to roll downhill, getting bigger with every turn like a snowball. The two workers who died became four, and then eight – and – soon after that, "so many". Before this, people in Tobali had never talked about mine disasters. In fact, nobody in Tobali had ever talked about mines at all, as if that particular corner of Banka was of no concern to their existence. Suddenly, mining was on the lips of everyone, and for the wrong reason.

Mois was by my side in those moments when I most needed friends and allies. I had faced hardships and calamities and had survived, but those calamities had been of the physical kind. Emotions were another matter, as they were like shadows. One sees them but can never grasp them. Whereas I already knew that emotions were ungraspable, they were also often unseen to me.

A week after the calamity, Mois came to my house in a state of agitation and anger. He opened up. "Before I relate this story, I want you to know I am with you all the way. What happened was that Hitam came to meet my father. I wasn't present. It was Siti who told me about it. She eavesdropped on the whole conversation. Siti said that Hitam was respectful and polite, hoping to get my father's sympathy. He claimed that Kusomo, who died at the mine, was his distant cousin. He brought the late Kusomo's widow with him. He claimed he had warned Kusomo about the dangers of the mining pits and had advised him against working in the mine. But you, Hitam said, had convinced Kusomo that your mine was very safe." Mois looked into me. "Did you say that, Hamzah?"

"Never. You know I wouldn't make such a claim."

"I know. I just want you to say it. Anyway, Hitam had the audacity to ask my father who had been proven right after all, you or him? He told a sob story about Kusomo's wife becoming a widow with two children who no longer had a father. In concluding, he said he had come so my father could understand his earlier objections to the mine. Mining, he told my father, was unsuitable for Malays. It was a matter of time before more deaths would come."

"How did your father react?"

"Don't you already know my father? He was definitely moved by the woman's grief. Then he said to Hitam that what had happened was the will of God. Hitam cleverly replied, 'Indeed it was, but as human beings we are responsible for our actions.' My father looked down, nodded his head, and promised to speak to you. You know what?" Pausing, Mois again gazed at me.

"What is it, Mois? I'm already flabbergasted as it is, so cut out the suspense."

"You are not supposed to know about the meeting. Hitam wanted to keep it personal between him and my father. Clever, isn't it? He asked that so my father would not question you and you would not have the opportunity to refute his claim. And you should hear this. It sufficed for my father to know that you – yes, you – were not as experienced as you had claimed to be. And that's not all. Before departing, Hitam kissed my father's hand and asked for forgiveness for his recent behaviour. He truly played on Father's sentiment and soft-hearted nature – the creep."

After that encounter he had with Hitam, Tok Rejab became somewhat cold towards me. I noticed this immediately when I went to his house for lunch the following Sunday on Rahimah's invitation, probably to placate the old man. At the doorway, I greeted him, "Assalamualaikum, Tok."

He obligatorily replied, "Wa'alaikumusalam," with his head down and his eyes averting mine. I felt the utter lack of the usual warmth. It upset me terribly. During meal, he was uncharacteristically quiet and distracted, causing Siti to throw glances at me upon detecting my discomfort. Rahimah compensated for this by being additionally attentive to me. Mois engaged me in futile conversation, pretending as if nothing had happened, and once in a while shook his head. After lunch, Tok Rejab left the table and headed straight to his study. Usually, he would sit at the patio with me enjoying a pot of coffee and passing the time by talking about various topics close to his heart. He was always ebullient and talkative. So this act of suddenly giving me a wide berth was certainly a sign of displeasure towards me on his part.

This cold wind blew in my direction for almost two weeks before I thought it was time for me to talk to Rahimah. So one day when I found out that Tok Rejab was not in the house, I took the opportunity to talk to Rahimah. She, it appeared to me, was also eager to talk to me.

It was late morning when I arrived at the house. Rahimah invited me to sit at the dining table. She immediately opened up.

"Siti told me about Hitam's meeting with Tok. I had wanted to talk to you earlier but waited for the right moment, when Tok wasn't in the house. First of all, I want you to understand that Tok Rejab has high regard for you and loves you as his own son. If he reacts the way he does, it is because he feels responsible for the tragedy that has occurred. The mine is as much his venture as it is yours. After all, he has been backing you all the way. He hasn't changed his mind about Hitam. But the death of one of Hitam's relatives weighs heavily on him. It was an unfortunate turn of events that the deceased Kusomo was related to Hitam, and it somehow vindicated Hitam for his earlier negative attitude towards the mining scheme. Apart from that, Tok has a soft heart and is easily moved by a tragic story."

"Aunty, Kusomo is no relation of Hitam. Before this disaster happened, Hitam didn't know who in heavens Kusomo was. This was all a ruse by Hitam to get at me," I said.

"Not to worry anymore. Tok just came to know about it last night. I told him. I had a gnawing suspicion something wasn't right when Hitam was overly polite – the hand kissing, the apologetic conduct, the outpouring of concern for others. It wasn't Hitam at all. So I did my own investigation."

"You did?"

"Yes, through a friend who knows Hitam's wife."

"You are great, Aunty. So, he is no longer angry with me?"

"No. He wasn't really angry with you. As I said, he has much respect for you. So while he loves you like his own son, he couldn't question you as he would Mois. This dilemma wrought him terribly. That accounts for his odd behaviour. Do you understand, Hamzah?"

"I didn't know that. I had thought otherwise. After what Hitam said to him, I thought he had lost respect for me. What should I do, Aunty?"

She looked consolingly into my eyes. "You know, Hamzah, the trouble with you is that you try so hard to be good, and your goodness is your very undoing. Be a little like Hitam for heaven's sake. Tok Rejab's weakest spot is his heart. Go for it."

"Thank you, Aunty. I'm so relieved to hear what you have just said. I love Tok, and I love you. I don't want anything to come between us." I kissed her hand in gratitude.

She paused and gazed at me but said nothing.

"Anything the matter, Aunty?"

"I have been wanting to tell you something concerning Siti. Maybe this is as good a time as any to talk about it."

My heart pounded. "Concerning Siti?" I asked nervously.

"Yes, and why Hitam resents you so much."

"Is it about Siti and me? I don't understand. I thought Hitam was jealous of me because of the mine." I was rattled.

"No, it is not about the mine. It has something to do with Siti. Let me tell you a bit of history. Hitam is known as a fairly wealthy man in Banka. He has a son called Razak, who is the same age as Siti. They were in school together. Somehow Razak mistakenly believed that Siti's friendship with him was love. He is a spoilt kid – immature and stupid too. He told his father about it and asked him to seek Siti's hand in marriage.

Naturally we had to decline the offer. No matter how polite our conduct was, rejecting an offer of marriage is often regarded as an insult in Malay society. But what choice had we then? Indeed that was how Hitam took it. He said we had brought shame to his family. After that, he had nothing but hatred for us. It all happened when you were in Malaya."

"I have wondered who this man was since the gathering of the smallholders, when he came out so vehemently against the mining project. I had never seen him before. I had honestly thought he was genuinely speaking for the landowners. But why is he picking on me?"

Rahimah smiled. "For a man who has seen life and who is smart, you can be pretty dumb. Hitam is jealous of you. Can't you see that? It's your sudden reappearance in Tobali, and staying with us."

Rahimah gazed at my puzzled face. "Can't you figure that out? You have always been very close with our family, and you've always had a special bond with Siti. He must have perceived that we had you in mind for Siti, thinking that that was why we rejected his son."

I felt quite embarrassed being told that I was a contributing factor to the Rejab family's unwarranted trouble. "I'm so sorry for being the cause of all these troubles with Hitam, Aunty. I don't know what to say."

She bent her head slightly sideways to view me, as if I were a child she was coaxing. With a soft look in her eyes, she said, "Say nothing. Who is this Hitam – or, for that matter, who is anyone – to judge whom Siti should marry? You've done nothing wrong. To hell with this Hitam." She patted my hand affectionately.

"Who is he, this Hitam, Aunty?" I asked, the only thing that popped into my mind at that moment.

"Hitam was originally from Singapore – a cloth merchant, married to a local woman. He used to have a big textile store in Muntok. He is now a big land broker. He is involved with all kinds of deals, some of which I would rather not talk about."

We heard the sound of a car engine. Soon after, Tok Rejab was outside the doorway. After alighting the doorsteps and dropping some bundles on the doorway, he sat on the ledge to remove his shoes.

"Oh, it's you, Hamzah. Been here long?" he said.

"Long enough, Tok, chatting with Aunty."

"Good for you. Your aunty is a chatterbox when I am not around. Make coffee, Rahimah. I bought some cakes. You're not to go yet Hamzah. Where's Siti?" Not only was there a cheer in his voice when he addressed me, but also he smiled – the first smile I had seen from him in two weeks.

The return of old spirit, which I had been missing for a while, gave me so much relief. I quickly replied with a broad smile, "I'm not going anywhere, Tok."

"Rahimah! Where's Siti? Where's Mois? Where's everyone?"

"They are both out, Tok. It's not even five o'clock yet. They'll be back soon for dinner. It's Saturday, remember? Family day," Rahimah hollered.

"Yes, I forgot. I am going to take my bath. Get the dinner ready. I'm famished."

Turning to me, he gestured convivially with his hand "Come, Hamzah, you are staying for dinner. I've something to tell you. We will talk later."

"Of course," I replied cheerfully.

He sauntered into his room. "Where's my towel, Rahimah?"

"On the rack, by the window."

"Oh, it must've dropped down. Could you get it?"

"I'll get it, Tok," I said.

I caught Siti returning and putting her bicycle by the workshop. The sun was receding, scattering shafts of light through the trees. Moments later I heard a car engine roar into the garage. Mois emerged from the vehicle with a gunnysack in his hand, and a hunting rifle slung across his back. I saw him disappear towards the back of the house. I guessed that whatever was in the gunnysack was something he didn't want his father to see.

"Your father has been asking for you, young lady," I said, tilting my head down, keeping my eyes on Siti.

"Was he cross?" Siti asked.

"I think so."

"I didn't count on him being home so early."

"I was kidding. He only asked for you. He appeared very cheerful."

"Don't tease me like that. You know how he is about me going out even though very soon I will be eighteen."

"Especially when you're coming to eighteen, young lady!" I said with a smile.

"Don't you be like him too, brother Hamzah. You are my mentor. You're supposed to be on my side."

I laughed. How much she had changed, I noticed, from that impish little girl to this attractive young woman. With her waist-length hair tied neatly in a ponytail, she glittered in the light. Each time I set my eyes on her, there was something new about her that attracted me. It wasn't like the whirlwind that had caught me when I first met Pinky. With Siti, it was more the touch of the breeze.

"Why do you look at me like that, brother Hamzah?" She pursed her lips and smiled mischievously, quite aware of my gaze.

"Thinking of what your father is going to say."

Just then, Mois appeared from the back, looking tanned with his outdoor ruggedness.

"Been here long?"

"Long enough. Had a chat with your mother."

"Did she tell you?"

"Yes."

"Very good." He gave me the thumb's up. "Well, see you at dinner. I better clean up. I don't want the old man to ask me too many questions."

No wonder he and his father can't relate, I thought. *They seem to live in separate worlds.* Even in looks, Mois did not take after Tok Rejab. He looked more like his grandfather, judging from the photos I had seen hanging on the wall. Mois was tall and athletic, and a tad darker than his father. I couldn't imagine him as chief of Tobali prying into the closet affairs of the people. Being the manager of a tin mine was more like it.

"Wait, what did you have there in the sack just now?" I enquired.

"A small deer."

"Shot that alone?"

"Yep. Not a word about the deer, you hear?"

"My lips are sealed."

Family dining with Tok Rejab was at the back section of the house nearest the kitchen. The proper dining room was seldom used, except on special occasions for festivities, like celebrating the end of Ramadan or entertaining government guests. The silverware, glasses, and plates were kept in pristine condition in a glass cupboard inside the dining hall.

Tok Rejab's house was the most conspicuous in Tobali, with its high sloping roofs and giant gables, an expression of Sumatran heritage. It had a large raised patio that opened to the chatter of passers-by, the antics of garrulous children, and the rustling of trees. The ampleness of the house seemed too commodious for the small family. Having stayed there, I realised that the large patio and ample space were meant to accommodate the life of Tobali that flowed into the house continually. Seldom was there loneliness, as visitors would come without notice. It would be uncalled for to turn anyone away.

At dinner that evening, Tok Rejab was more animated than usual. He commended the cooking, every now and then picked a dish for me to partake of, and ate voraciously. I wondered what had made him so jubilant.

When the dinner ended, he cleaned his hand, took a sip of coffee, and patted his tummy. "That was a good meal. Now listen, everyone. I have an important announcement."

All heads turned towards him. We all ceased what we had been doing.

"When Mecca beckons you, you'll feel it in your heart. It came to me a few nights ago. The Prophet – peace be upon him – said that when you have the means and your health permits, do not delay in performing the fifth tenet of Islam." Looking at his children, he said, "I must tell you about my father. I have never told anyone before except your mother. My father was a pious man, but somehow he was afraid of long sea journeys. He would get seasick, even on a fishing boat. So he repeatedly postponed his haj, until one day he found himself unable to raise his body from the floor. His legs had weakened and he could not walk. He died at the age of sixty, his obligation unfulfilled. On his deathbed, he whispered to me, 'Rejab, don't be like me. Perform your haj at the earliest opportunity.' I had completely forgotten about this episode until I dreamt of him three nights ago. So, God willing, your mother and I are performing the haj this season."

"That's wonderful," I exclaimed.

Mois was quiet.

Siti was close to tears. "How long will you be away?" she asked.

"Two months," Tok Rejab replied. "The haj season begins in December. We'll depart in early November and be back in January."

"But that's a month's time," Siti sadly said.

Noticing Siti's unhappiness, Rejab said, "My child, you should receive this news with jubilation, not grief. You're a big girl now."

"We've never left home since she was born, Tok. It's understandable." Rahimah intervened.

"Exactly. I am going to be alone in this big house."

"Your brother is here, and Hamzah too, to look after you," Rejab said.

"But Brother Mois is seldom at home with his work and his hunting and fishing. He has no time for me," she replied.

"What about Hamzah? He's always been like a big brother to you," Rejab added.

"But he has his tin mine, which is his life."

"I'll take care of you, Siti," I said.

"There you are," Rejab exclaimed.

Siti turned towards me and, with a cheeky smile, asked, "Promise?"

"I promise."

"Say it aloud to my father."

"Tok, I promise to take good care of Siti. I'll make sure she stays at home and behaves."

"Not that last part."

Rahimah nodded and gave a wide smile of approbation.

"Now listen, all three of you. The Kaaba is the most efficacious spot for your prayers to be answered. So I am going to ask each one of you your wishes, beginning with you, Hamzah. What is your wish?" Tok Rejab said in a serious tone, taking me completely off guard.

I struggled for an answer. "Honestly, Tok, I have never thought of it."

"I know you have the type of worldly success that any man could wish for, but surely you do have something you've dreamt about."

Pinky flashed in my mind. I wished I could turn the clock back and listen to Grandma. I wished I hadn't met Pinky. I wished I hadn't been born.

"Hamzah, I am waiting." Tok Rejab shook me from my thoughts.

"Happiness, Tok," I said.

"What? Aren't you happy? Aren't you satisfied with how life has treated you?"

Again I was caught without an answer. God help me! I had never thought someone would one day ask me these questions. "I don't really know what to wish for, Tok. Honestly, I don't."

He raised his eyebrows. "You really are one peculiar man, Hamzah. I've never met a man who couldn't determine a wish for himself."

Rahimah turned towards her husband. "That's enough, Tok. It is not right for us to ask Hamzah a very personal question like that. Perhaps it is not for us to know. It is between him and his heart," she said with a serious face.

"I fully agree," Mois said, joining in to support his mother.

"Whatever it is, Hamzah, I shall pray for your happiness. May God lighten all your burdens."

Before I could say anything, Mois butted in. "Always the chief," he quipped.

"Thank you, Tok," I said.

Tok Rejab turned to his son. "What about you, Mois?"

"Please do not pray for me to be chief of Tobali," he replied.

"Just for that, I shall indeed pray that you shall be."

"Please, Father, please don't," Moss said, pretending to cry and to bow down to kiss his father's feet.

"That's enough foolery, Mois," Rahimah said, chastising her son. "It's a serious matter. Be respectful. It's the Holy Kaaba we're talking about."

"I'm sorry, Mother and Father."

"It's enough that you never pray. You shouldn't also make short shrift of the pilgrimage to Mecca," Rejab said, scolding him.

Turning to Siti, who had been amused by her brother's foolery, Tok Rejab asked, "And you, my child?"

"I want you to pray for your and Mother's long and healthy life, and for both of you to return home safely to me," Siti said, her eyes reddening.

Rejab gazed affectionately into his daughter's eyes. He saw a film of water swelling therein.

"That is a wonderful thought, Siti. What about for yourself?"

"That *is* for me," Siti replied.

I noticed Rahimah's emotion welling up as she tried to control her tears.

Chapter 26

On weekends, Mois and I took Siti out for picnics on the wide sandy beaches south of Muntok, to cheer her up. Otherwise, on her free days, she occupied herself with reading books and with crunching the English that I had been teaching her. After acquiring some fundamentals of grammar, she conscientiously referred to the dictionary to increase her word power – with me by her side to help her. She reminded me of myself during my own childhood in her propensity to learn. Already she had a good command of Dutch. Her motivation was amazing. I often wondered what it was that was driving her.

And if she wasn't reading, learning, or correcting her students' homework, or attending to the garden she had created by the house, she would seek my company and engage me intellectually, discussing the books she had read, questioning me about Javanese culture and its Buddhist, Hindu, and Islamic antecedents. She was fascinated with the Ramayana epic and was impressed when I told her I could perform it. Once in a while the subject of Mataram House came to her mind, and I would talk about Grandma Tutik. Grandma Tutik fascinated her in no small way. She said, "What an extraordinary woman."

On one such occasion, sitting at the dining table of my house, Siti paused, supported her chin with both hands, gazed into my eyes, and with a smile said, "You are one mysterious man, brother Hamzah, just like your grandma Tutik."

Siti was not only intelligent but also an extraordinarily inquisitive and uncannily perceptive, and I felt that my past intrigued her in a very curious sort of way. She suspected that there was more about me than I wished her to know. At that very moment, Pinky popped into my mind. *That isn't the kind of mystery I ever want Siti to know about me,* I said to myself. A silent fear rose in me.

I would be lying to myself if I didn't admit that Siti, now a woman, was engendering feelings within me that went beyond the brotherly type of affection with which I used to regard her.

It was early December. Four weeks had passed since Tok Rejab and Rahimah had left for Mecca. I had been faithful to my promise to take care of Siti, and she had taken it to heart that I was truly her guardian. And as she herself had predicted, Mois had little time for her, except when I was around. Unbeknown to her and to me, this "guardianship" had begun to bloom into something more endearing, fostering feelings that touched the heart. Her playfulness and affection drew me closer to her and she to me. I had to remind myself: *Be careful, Hamzah. Tok Rejab trusts you.*

I was by the terrace of the little palace, with the lapping sea, a pot of hot coffee, and a few books as my companions. With a Thomas Hardy book on my lap, I noticed the dark, hovering clouds hanging threateningly over the horizon. It was still late afternoon, but the day was dying early, turning into dusk. So lost I was with my reading that I didn't realise Siti had tiptoed by the side path to spring on me. Stealthily, she tapped my back hard and startled me. The next moment she was standing beside me. "Did you think it was a ghost?" she said, laughing.

"No, I thought it was an angel – and an angel it is."

She pushed my shoulder and replied, "Don't call me that. It's not proper. Angels are holy creatures. I am neither holy nor a creature. I brought you something special." She lifted the tiffin carrier to my nose so I could savour the fragrance of the spiced stew. "You shouldn't be eating your maid's cooking all the time. She's an awful cook. You'll get skinnier by the day and become sick." She laughed.

"Don't say that of her cooking. Mois likes it," I quipped.

"My brother will eat anything you eat, even your own cooking. Besides, he'd eat stones if *you* asked him to. I have never seen him looking up to anyone before."

In spite of my protests, and despite the fact that I had my own cook, Siti insisted on cooking my meals when she was at my house. "What was her last job? Feeding cats?" she asked of my cook. "I'm kidding. I shouldn't say things like that. She's a good cook – I'm merely jealous of her cooking for you." She laughed.

Siti would set the table formally, European style – tablecloth, linen napkins, silverware, and china in their proper order, just as I had taught her. She had so often asked me about this European style of dining that I'd finally acquiesced.

Of late she had acquired a certain keen interest in things urbane. Perhaps this was to show me she could be more than just a village girl, or perhaps she had imagined that such was the way I preferred things to be. Any resistance on my part might only fuel the very thing she was insecure about, and so I let her whims have their way.

There was a certain oddity about her I found amusing. For instance, at dinner, she always refused to join me, preferring to watch me eat alone, except when we were in the outdoors or at her house with her parents. Serving was one thing, but eating together as a couple, and in my own house, seemed to touch a chord with her. When I asked her why she wouldn't eat with me, she said it would be too much like being husband and wife. When I insisted and said to her with a smile that I liked the idea of being perceived as husband and wife, she blushed and shyly assented.

This vacillation of playfulness and shyness, confidence and hesitation, boldness and demurring, was at once amusing and fascinating. I had to remember though, as she was highly perceptive and would instantly notice any patronising signs on my part.

"What are you reading?" she asked me, leafing through the book.

"It's a novel by Thomas Hardy."

"I have seen that book in your shelves. What's it about?"

"Tragedy."

"I love reading novels. What kind of writer was he? I mean, what kind of novels did he write?"

"Tragedies mainly."

"You like his books?"

"Yes, very much."

"Why? Because of the tragic stories?"

"You are one inquisitive girl!"

"Correction – woman."

"Sorry, inquisitive woman."

"You haven't answered. Why do you like tragedies, brother Hamzah?" She narrowed her pretty eyes and dipped them into mine, and suddenly I felt conscious of her closeness.

"Because tragedies are part of human experience. Life is never all happiness."

"And for that you love his novels? I don't get it. I don't consider you a person who likes to wallow in melancholy. Do you?" She eyed me seriously.

Catching me admiring her more than had been my custom, she lowered her eyes.

"Sometimes I do feel melancholic," I said defensively.

"You're a strange man, brother Hamzah. You always look happy to me. Is there a secret behind that melancholy? A woman perhaps?" She threw a mischievous smile. "Have you been in love before?" she asked me all of a sudden.

"No, Siti. My melancholy has nothing to do with a woman. My life has been full of tragedies. It's complicated."

"Liar!" She landed a slap on my hand. Suddenly she put on a serious expression. "Brother Hamzah, speed up my English lessons so I can read Thomas Hardy. Then I will join you in your melancholic reverie." She laughed.

"But first I want you to drop the 'brother' bit. It's old-fashioned. Just call me Hamzah."

"You mean that?"

"Of course."

"Does that mean I am no longer 'that little girl' of yours?"

"Exactly."

"Hamzah! Nice, I like it. Now about my reading Thomas Hardy?"

"Certainly. We start immediately."

"Don't make fun of me."

"I am not. I am serious."

Outside the rain suddenly began to pour in a deluge, turning the sunny sky into night.

"It's raining cats and dogs outside. You're trapped here, and it's already dark. People will talk," I said, quite anxious about her being detained.

"To hell with people. We're not doing anything wrong. Besides, Mois knows I am here. Just look outside. I'd catch the death, or a bolt of lightning could strike me. Do you want that to happen to me? Remember that you've promised my parents to take good care of me."

"You always have an answer for everything, don't you?"

"Yes, I have. Now tell me the story. Better still, read to me. When I don't understand some words, I'll stop you."

"A mayor is, like your father, the chief of a town, and Casterbridge is the name of a place. It's the story of a man called Henchard, who in a drinking binge sold his wife, only to realise later he had made a horrible mistake."

I went into a good pace reading the story. She listened with genuine interest. When I stopped, she said, "Go on, tell me more. Rain gives the right mood for storytelling. Mother used to read stories of Malay folklore to me when I was a child, so I have a treasure trove of Malay tales. Are you familiar with Malay folklore?"

"I am not. The epic of Ramayana, yes."

"Let me clear the table and wash the plates first," I said, testing her eagerness.

"Can't the maid do that?"

"She has gone back to her village this weekend. Her mother is not well."

"The washing can wait. I'll do that later for you. This story first." She folded her legs over the sofa and fell back against the cushion. The rain continued to pound. She was right: the rain did give the right mood for storytelling.

When I reached the twentieth page, her head fell onto the cushion. She succumbed to sleep thanks to the lulling patter of the rain and my slow and deliberate reading. I looked at the clock and saw that it was midnight. We had been taken by the passing of time without realising it. The rain persisted. I had to decide whether to wake her or to let her sleep. The reposed image was not that of the little girl I used to know a long time ago. This was a woman that my eyes beheld. I took a blanket, covered her up, and let her sleep the night.

Chapter 27

I received a letter from Aunty Maimunah. Even in her letter I could hear the sound of excitement about the happenings in No. 27 Kelawei Road, which in the normal course of everyday life weren't out of the ordinary. Yet in her accounting, such happenings could be mistaken for catastrophes. Father had all of a sudden asked about me and where I had been, and she had seen him engaging Ariffin in a conversation, telling about his childhood days in vivid detail, remembering people, places, and times with remarkable accuracy. With excitement, she declared to me that Father had regained his memory. It was a miracle, she wrote. Then the following day, Father forgot who Ariffin was.

In the next sentence, Aunty Maimunah asked me whether I had gotten quietly married without telling her. In the same paragraph, she wrote about Ariffin's being fifth in a class of forty, mentioning that he was well behaved, took his bath twice daily, and performed his chores without being told. She ended with hugs and kisses and reminded me again to tell her if I had gotten married. Her script was huge and its construction simple; her spelling was phonetic but readable. Not bad for someone who had only three years of education. Folding her letter, I laughed to myself, thinking how funny and lovable she was, and how incorrigibly maternal.

Rejab and Rahimah had been gone for over a month. Nusantara Mine was doing well, and the shareholders were happy. Right before my eyes a young girl had suddenly become a woman, and day by day she drew closer to me and I to her. Yet alone, in the dead of night, my pains remained when the memory of Pinky resurfaced in my inner being, visiting me before sleep, re-emerging in my dreams. The more I began to be aware of my feelings for Siti, the greater was my pain for Pinky.

Soon Siti would be eighteen, marriageable, and sought after by any man who set eyes on her. She was, by any measure of a woman, a mother's choice for her son's bride. She took care of the house single-handedly, with culinary skills far exceeding those of her mother, feeding Mois and me like we were some potentates on a visit to Tobali.

The idea that we were supposed to look after her seemed like a poor joke, since she had instead become our guardian. To say no to her would only invite a melting stare from her eyes, reducing us to acquiescence. As she stepped into womanhood, I could already discern the feisty character of her matriarchal Minang blood emerging, not unlike Aunty Maimunah. To Aunty Maimunah, Siti would be the perfect candidate for my spouse.

One night, a week after Siti's unplanned sleepover in my house, trapped by the weather and by the tragedies of Thomas Hardy, I fell back into the past just when she was gradually entering my heart in the present. Pinky came back, haunting me with all the unbridled passion and sensuality we once shared. I was like an addict being revisited by his temptation. The world I had had with her swirled about my mind tempestuously. I shut my eyes, but my heart refused to close.

Forget her, Hamzah, my conscience spoke to me. *What you had with her was a sensual fantasy made for her needs, certainly not yours. It was beautiful while it lasted. And as beautiful as the morning mist is, it was transient, disappearing with the sunrise. Look, before your very eyes now is a girl in the early glow of womanhood, untouched, unblemished. She awaits you.*

I was buried in my thoughts when suddenly someone came from the rear and startled me.

"Who's that?" I yelled.

"Sorry, brother, to creep up on you like that. I could smell the Sumatran coffee from afar and knew you'd be by the terrace." Mois must have walked the dark garden path that weaved through the garden that straddled the big house and the little palace in order to surprise me. This was Mois's idea of camaraderie. He plonked down onto the wicker chair and then moved it closer to me.

"So what's up?" I asked.

"Plenty. Hey, could I have a cup?" He rose up to the serving table and removed the lid of the coffee pot. "Ah, smells good. Where do you get your coffee anyway?"

I yelled out to the maid to bring an extra cup.

"So, what's this about 'plenty'?"

"In a moment." He looked at me. "What were you doing gazing at the dark ocean like there was something there? Hey, you're the loneliest person I've ever met in my life. If you're not with us, or with Siti, or at the mine, or away on business somewhere, you are here with your book or else are lost in thought. You've no friends that I know of, and no pastimes of any sort, except when I ask you to come fishing with me. Even then, I see neither glitter nor excitement in your eyes. You're like a ghost, alone and mysterious."

"Mysterious? That's unflattering, really. A mysterious person is someone you shouldn't trust."

"I don't mean that."

"What do you mean, really?"

"Never mind that. I can't explain it. But you're strange, really." He stood up, walked to the edge of the apron, and faced the sea. I heard him sigh. Turning to face me, with arms akimbo, he said, "You attract the good and the bad with the same intensity. Many love you, and yet there are some who hate you just as much. And you bring nothing but good to Tobali. You disappeared and came back without telling anyone why. Now tell me if that's not strange?"

"You're not making sense, Mois. What's this all about? Why suddenly this third degree?"

"You're in a bit of trouble, brother. We all are."

"What trouble?"

"You and Siti have been accused of improper conduct – the two of you, unmarried, in close proximity behind closed doors, and at night. In this bloody place, this is a damn serious accusation, brother. I will say that."

I felt like a thunderbolt had hit me. The blood drained from my face. Momentarily lost for words, I peeled away from my lounge chair and began to stand up.

"Are you all right, brother?" Mois quickly caught both my arms as I was swaying sideways, about to fall. "Come. Sit back on the chair."

"That's a damn lie, Mois," I said softly.

"That is why I hate this bloody place – and my father wants me to be chief. They love gossip and rumours. They luxuriate in such things. No proof is needed when condemning a person. As far as these people are concerned, it doesn't matter what you did or didn't do. A man and a woman unmarried and in a house throughout the night is fodder for an accusation of immoral conduct. And don't forget, brother, that there's an enemy watching for an opportunity like this."

"So, who is making this accusation?" I asked, still dazed.

"Someone has written an anonymous letter to my father about Siti spending a night in your house. I know you're innocent, and so is my sister. I assure you of that. I am 100 per cent on your side. But the people in Tobali delight in this kind of story. It will take root no matter how unfounded it is. We've had a history of anonymous poison-pen letters as far back as I can remember. Innocent people have suffered from them."

"Was the letter signed?"

"Oh, it was signed all right, but not with names, only with 'Concerned elders of Tobali'."

"Who do you think is behind this?"

"Come on, brother, you don't have to be a genius to figure that out."

"Hitam?"

"Who else?"

"May I see it?"

"Of course. Here."

"It's in Jawi!" I remarked.

"Yes, certainly. What do you expect, Hitam writing Dutch to Father?"

"In Romanised Malay, I would've thought."

"Father writes only Jawi script. Don't you know that? And Hitam knows that. Charming scoundrel, isn't he? He knows Father is from the old school, not like you and I. Using the Jawi script makes the origin of the letter more credible."

"I don't read Jawi," I said, with much embarrassment.

"What?" He laughed. "That is a surprise. You know English, Dutch, Javanese, Chinese, and I wonder what else, yet you can't read Jawi. How come?"

"My grandmother, for some personal reason, was loath to anything Sumatran. And, according to her, since Jawi is of Acehnese origin, I should have nothing to do with it."

"Why?"

"Because my father is Sumatran. Enough of my history. Now read the letter to me."

With a good-natured laugh, Mois said, "For once I am one up."

"You've never been lesser than me, Mois. What makes you think that? You're smart, a go-getter, restless, unsatisfied with the world, hard to manage —and a pain in the arse to your father. Who can beat that? So just read the letter."

Mois read it, as follows:

Dear Tok Rejab, whom we dearly love, honour and respect as our chief. May you and Rahimah complete your haj with the full blessing and acceptance from Allah the Almighty, and may you return home in good health.

Since you are our elder and leader, we are duty-bound to protect your name and that of your illustrious family. While you were away in holy Mecca in the performance of your obligations to Allah, something untoward has happened here at home which is, we are sure, not to your liking. Hamzah, in whom you have placed your trust, has enticed your daughter, Siti, to stay overnight in his house, and there was no one else in the house at that time. Now we are not making any assumption of what they actually did, for only God knows that. But an unmarried man and an unmarried woman in close proximity behind closed doors and in the dead of night – what will people say? You are the chief of Tobali. Hamzah's reckless behaviour is putting a smear on your good reputation, and on that of this village. Above all, it is a gross betrayal of your trust. We write with the good intention of protecting your daughter, and also to forewarn you of the shock that you will receive on your return.

Our motive is pure and noble. May God forgive us for conveying this news to you.

Signed,
Concerned elders of Tobali

I was taken by the ingenuity of the letter. "My goodness, I myself find it believable. If I did not know the author, I would reckon it to be sincere," I said with disgust. "How did your father react?"

"Not good at all. He fell ill, according to my mother, who wrote to me when relating this letter," Mois replied solemnly.

"Was he angry with me?"

"Naturally."

"I thought so. Stupid of me to even ask. What exactly did he say?"

"A short letter. I'll read it to you."

My dear son Mois,

Your mother cried when she read the letter, and I don't have to tell you how I felt. It is indeed a trial from God that this tragic event has happened at the time we are performing our pilgrimage, and we can only pray for deliverance from Him. In our absence, it falls upon you to protect your sister and to regain the family honour and dignity. Convey our love to your sister.

Your loving father,
Rejab

"Is that all? Is there no mention of me, no castigation or censure? My God, he must be quite pissed off with me." I felt utterly dejected. I wasn't even worth a bother, and that deeply hurt me. I sat in silence.

Mois came up to me, held both my shoulders, a thing he had never done before, and looked straight into my eyes. "Hey, brother, don't take it too badly. We'll get to the bottom of this. I'm your friend, and you're like a brother to me. I'll fight the bastard who did this to you. I promise you," he said. I could feel his genuine concern.

"Should I write to your father?" I asked in desperation.

"No, absolutely not. That would only make you appear guilty. I shall write."

"Thank you, Mois."

"Hey, let's go to town and have some satay at Majeed's. I'm famished."

"I'm not hungry," I said. Food wasn't in my mind at that moment.

"Oh, you'll whip up an appetite when he starts burning his satay. Come on, brother, keep me company at least. I'll drive. Go change. You don't want to be seen in those shorts and T-shirt." Mois looked at me pleadingly. I believed he was trying to cheer me up, and so I felt I should oblige.

"All right, I'll go and have a shower." I rose and walked over to my room in the big house.

"Could I have another cup of coffee?"

"Go ahead. Ask the maid," I hollered from the corridor.

In the car, he pulled out a cigarette and offered me one. I took it, to oblige, although I didn't care much for cigarettes. We drove into the night towards the town, which was a mere ten minutes away by car.

"How is Siti taking all this, Mois?"

"Now, this is going to cheer you up. She was livid, and at once suspected it was Hitam's handiwork. And she was angry with my parents for believing this stupid crap. Yes, 'stupid crap', that is what she said. And guess what?" He turned his heard towards me, smiled, and paused.

"What, Mois?"

"She will not stop going to your house. No one in Tobali is going to tell her what to do or not to do. Those were her own words."

"Really?" That piece of news uplifted my spirit.

"Really. That's my sister for you." He laughed.

The town lights came into view. As we approached the alfresco food bazaar on Alamanda Street, Majeed's stall was conspicuous by the billows of smoke that were spewing from his barbecue pit.

As we pulled over, my appetite returned, whipped up by the aroma of spice and simmering meat. At the table under an open sky, it was Mois who monopolised the conversation. I ate in silence and listened. Not once did he touch on the subject of his father's letter, hoping, I believed, not to spoil the evening.

With that he succeeded in assuaging a little my unsettled heart – but not for long. My night was yet to come. In these unhappy moments, I feared the night more than I feared the day. Once the curtain finally fell and everyone else slumbered in peace, I would be wide awake and alone.

Chapter 28

The people of Tobali began to take an awkwardly detached and distant attitude towards Mois, Siti, and me. Our everyday encounters with them, reduced to brevity, were met with nothing but coldness. This occurred at the shops, in the restaurants, at the mosque, or when our paths met, as though the villagers were secretly contriving to punish us.

Not a squeak of my alleged affair with Siti ever came close to our ears, as though nothing unusual had ever occurred. At the Nusantara Mine it was the same. Indeed, the ingredients of trouble seemed already in the cauldron. It was a matter of time before things simmered to a boil. Hitam had certainly done a remarkable job. Heeding my advice, Mois held back from confronting him. We had no clear evidence that he had written the letter. It was best to wait for matters to unfold – and unfold they did, at quite a rapid rate. What manner of action the people had in mind, we had no idea, as we had become strangers in our own place.

In the meantime, there was no further news from Tok Rejab. It could be that he and Rahimah were totally immersed in worship and were blocking their hearts from all worldly things, as pilgrims normally do.

I soon realised how deleterious rumours are. Even nice people without a sliver of malice in their hearts would be drawn in and caught up in them as though the rumour were a celebration of sorts. Like a contagious disease that had no vaccine, the rumour continued its path. As it moved from mouth to mouth, it gained in extravagance. Siti hadn't been in my house only that once, they said. She had been coming every night prior to that. Siti had been keeping away from the public, on Mois's advice, to which she demurred with great reluctance. Soon her absence became part of the rumour. She was pregnant, it was said. That was why she stayed at home.

How was Siti coping with these tribulations? Remarkably well. Fortified by anger, she resorted to defiance right in the face of the people of Tobali. She also held a simmering anger towards her parents for their not even asking her to answer for whatever she had been accused of. She persisted in coming to my house, staying back to eat formally with me at the table.

"Now let them see me eating with you like we are husband and wife though we are not married," she said defiantly.

I protested, to no avail. I had said to her that doing thus would only make those who were on our side turn against us.

She laughed and replied, "Who is on our side, Hamzah? Not a single person made even a squeak in our defence. Look, even my father believed the rumour without question."

To that I replied, "Look again, Siti. We're not entirely blameless. I am particularly not. It was stupid and utterly careless of me. I forgot that I was in Tobali. I should've known better. Where did I put my brain? Don't blame your parents, Siti. To them we were found together, and that's all that matters. People can draw unimaginable conclusions from that. Even if we had locked ourselves in separate rooms, no one would believe our story. In such a situation, the worst-case scenario is the most accepted and popular."

She drew back in disbelief. Looking askance, she said, "You're giving up already and abandoning me?" I noticed her eyes reddening. She struggled to keep herself from bursting into tears. The next moment she said, "It's getting late. I'd better go now. I don't want to put you into more trouble."

"Siti, what's wrong? Did I say something wrong?" I panicked, knowing the kind of person she was.

"Not at all. The honourable Hamzah has said all that is to be said."

The sarcasm struck deep into me. "Please, Siti, don't leave. I am really sorry." I took her hand. She pulled it away. I knew there was no way I could change her mind. "All right, but at least let me take you back in the car."

"I've my bicycle. I'll cycle back."

"I'll send it back tomorrow."

"No." She walked briskly to her cycle and disappeared.

That same night, I drove to her house and found Mois standing on the verandah. Even in the faint light of the moonless night, I could discern the concern in his face. He tried to smile when greeting me, but it was forced.

"Where's Siti?" I asked.

"In her room. What happened? Her dress was drenched in tears when she climbed up the stairs. She must've been crying all the way from your house. I've not seen her cry like that before."

"Can I see her?"

"Not even an earthquake could move her out of her room. She locked herself up and refused even to eat."

"Can we talk, Mois?"

"Sure."

"Let's drive somewhere," I said.

Mois, obliging me, suggested that we go to the bay area where there was a café that served good coffee.

When we arrived, the sea was deadly calm and the beach almost empty in the dying day. We sat by the spine of an old, heavily bent coconut tree in front of the café and ordered some coffee. The sky was dull; the air was still with a feeling of quietude. Some children and adults were seen picking clams on the wide sand amid the receding low tide. Someone shouted at the children to return. At the inner cove of the bay, several boats lay lazily on their sides.

Mois asked me, "What did you tell Siti that upset her so much?"

"I told her we weren't altogether blameless and that I should take the brunt of the blame for my stupidity. That was the gist of it."

Mois glanced sideways and said, "Don't you see what you have done? Of all the people, it was you whom she wanted to lean on for support. Even I don't matter, and I am her brother. If you yourself found her blameworthy – no matter your taking the brunt of it – she took it as betrayal. For heaven's sake, my sister adores you. Can't you see that? Are you blind or something?"

"She said I had forsaken her."

"She is absolutely right. You are clever in every damn thing but women."

"How stupid I have been. You know what, Mois? I *am* pretty dumb about women. I shouldn't have said to her that we were blameworthy when she had poured her heart out to me about how she had been unjustly wronged, even by her own parents. I grossly misread her."

"Bravo! Now you know."

"What should I do, Mois?"

Mois threw a long gaze at the sea and paused. Then, turning to me, he said, "I can't help you there, brother. She is my sister. Shall we go now? The café is closing up."

"Wait a moment, Mois," I pleaded. "I want to tell you something. Would you give me an ear?"

"Sure. When my captain commands, it is for me to obey." He chuckled.

"Stop this nonsense, Mois."

"Sorry."

"I hurt people, Mois," I confided in a grave tone.

"What?" He swung his head in shock. "What do you mean, you hurt people?"

"All the people who were close to me or who had loved me ended up being hurt one way or another. It happened in the past. I can't explain why. I am afraid, Mois, very afraid. I don't want it to happen to your father and mother, and to Siti and you. Look, it's happening now. It's like a curse."

He took another cigarette – his fourth – lit it, and took a deep breath, his eyes searching the ocean. Without looking at me, he finally said, "You believe in curses? Come on. A worldly guy like you? You could be imagining this. Things do happen to people. I am no thinker. I don't look at life deeply. I am a simple person. I take life as it comes. I don't even look at the future. I don't know what really happened between you and those people you said you have hurt. Maybe they were just coincidences." His eyes led him far into the horizon. He threw his cigarette away and turned towards me. "Look, brother, don't let this problem spook you and make you talk about curses. I think that's nonsense."

"Anyway, I'm glad I was able to talk to you about it."

"Let's go. It's getting dark."

As we walked to the car, he came close to me and, in a subdued tone, said, "Don't you worry about my sister. Tell her what you've just told me. She will surprise you. I promise you that."

* * *

A month after the poison-letter incident, Lebai Amir (the mosque imam), accompanied by some of Tobali's elders, came trooping to Tok Rejab's house. They had specifically requested my presence. These elders, unfailing mosque-goers and members of the mosque committee, had now turned into morality judges.

Siti was spared the ignominy of the inquisition, though she feared it not. Mois had earlier advised her to be circumspect and polite if asked to face Lebai Amir and his men. With Siti being of young age and being a woman in a society where she was expected to stay in the back of the house, it would be unwise and foolish of her to be confrontational. That was Mois's advice to her.

Mois himself was on his best behaviour and acted with great equanimity, receiving the group of men with courtesy.

After the customary affected greetings and hollow politeness, Lebai Amir addressed us. "We came here today with the most honourable of intention. We wish neither to accuse nor to judge. We merely wish to put forward the facts before us and to offer our carefully considered counsel. The matter before us concerns our duty to uphold the religious principles by which we live, as well as to protect the good name of the community and, by the same token, the good name of Tok Rejab's family. The whole of Tobali has been talking, and it is unhealthy and damaging. Unless this rumour-mongering is stopped, it will surely get out of hand, to the detriment of everyone. We have a solution that we wish to present to you, one which we believe will end this unwarranted situation."

Mois, who he had been at pains to preserve his cool, suddenly burst out: "Lebai Amir, with all due respect, may I ask what are you getting at? Please say what you actually want to say. Don't beat around the bush."

I quickly calmed him down and whispered, "Hold your temper, Mois. Let Lebai finish his speech."

Lebai Amir overheard me. He said, "Hamzah is right. Let me finish. We owe a debt of gratitude to Mr Hamzah for what he has contributed to our community, and certainly we have the highest respect for him. That is why we are here, to restore his good name. But things have happened, either through carelessness or oversight. It does not matter. All that is now water under the bridge, as they say. The fact is, it has happened."

"Lebai," Mois again interrupted, his much constrained composure about to come loose.

"Please, Mr Mois, allow me to proceed, I beg of you. On the night of Tuesday, 10 December, Hamzah and Siti were found together in close proximity in Hamzah's house right till morning. They were alone. No one else was in the house. We have four witnesses to confirm this. Now, Mr Hamzah and Mr Mois, it does not matter what transpired behind the closed doors. In Islam, an unmarried man and an unmarried woman found together alone are committing what is termed *khalwat*, a punishable offence under strict sharia law. But sharia is not practised here. Still, a tenet of Islam has been transgressed. To remedy the situation and restore the moral standing of Hamzah and Siti, and to uphold the good name of the Rejab family, Hamzah and Siti should solemnise their relationship without delay. And you, Mr Mois, as a brother to Siti, can, in the absence of your father, act as wali to give consent to the marriage."

Mois was incensed. Wagging his finger, looking like a teacher, he cried out, "Lebai Amir, I do not want to disrespect you, but the matter of the marriage between my sister Siti and Hamzah cannot be determined based upon a rumour, and neither is it, pardon me for saying, the affair of anyone except my family. Not to be accused of lacking in manners, I would ask with respect that this discussion be ended. I shall await my father's return and let him decide the matter. And before we depart, I wish to reiterate here and now that Hamzah has been exemplary in his conduct with my sister, and that Siti is a girl with impeccable morals. The culprits are not us, but Hitam and his cohorts. Why are you against us when you should go after the culprits who have spun this preposterous tale? Where is the justice, I ask you?" Mois was unflinching, bringing down all the guard rails of polite conduct. The crimson in his face didn't escape the eyes of his audience.

Lebai Amir was not a man disposed to open confrontation. With admirable patience, he turned towards his colleagues and said, "We have offered our counsel, and that is the best we can do under the circumstances. We shall await the return of Tok Rejab." Addressing Mois, he said, "We thank you for your kind hospitality. We shall take our leave." After the normal courtesies, they departed. Judging by the expressions on their faces, they were incensed.

The following morning before the break of dawn, I was shaken from my sleep by a loud shattering of broken glass. On the floor among the shards was a stone wrapped with paper. I untied it and found a note which read, Repent Hamzah. It was the time of morning when mosque-goers were returning from the dawn prayer. Someone among them must have hurled the rock through my window, I suspected.

Later in the day, Mois came over to my house. He was calm and composed, bearing a somewhat serious deportment judging by the lack of cheer in his greeting to me.

"Hi, brother. Let's go to your patio and chat." Once we had seated ourselves, he said, "I'm furious at this bunch of pious hypocrites sermonising to us about morality without even the decency to seek the truth. So, brother, I don't want you to give them any face. Don't be afraid of these bastards. I'm still simmering with anger. You've given so much to them, and yet there isn't an iota of gratitude. Their sense of moral behaviour is so medieval that it's unbelievable. That's why I bloody hate it here. And my father wants me to be their chief." He turned his head and looked at me straight in the eye. "Aren't you angry, brother?"

"Of course."

"Why didn't you show it then?"

I had no answer.

"Do not play the do-gooder with these people. Don't you see? The devious Hitam wins while you, the do-gooder, loses."

I put my head down, chewing what he had just said, feeling utterly despondent. Noticing that I was momentarily lost for words, he said, "I'm sorry for being blunt. I didn't mean to hurt your feelings."

"I wasn't hurt. I think you are absolutely right. The truth is, I'm quite awkward when dealing with my own kind, more so than I am with other races. I tend to be overpolite with my own kind, not because I respect others less, but because of my own kind's overindulgence in feelings and sensitivity." Mois, seeming puzzled by my confession, became silent.

To break the silence, I asked, "By the way, how is Siti after yesterday's episode?"

"My sister is a strong-minded girl. Once the bunch of moralists had left, she said to me, 'Who, how, when, why, I marry is none of Tobali's business. They can go to hell.' If you're ever to be my brother-in-law, I truly wish you the best of luck." He laughed and then gave me a slap on the shoulder.

The maid came in with a tray of hot coffee and fried banana fritters.

In the conversation that followed, I made no mention at all to Mois about the rock-throwing incident that occurred earlier in the morning so as not to infuriate him further. There was already enough anger from him to last me for the day.

*   *   *

One late afternoon a week later, as the sun was dipping, I saw Siti approaching my house on her bicycle with a tiffin carrier at the back. She was merrily ringing her cycle bell to greet me. As I was standing at the porch entrance of the big house, I noticed two middle-aged women walking languorously by and overheard them remarking loudly, "Have you no shame, Siti?"

I clearly heard Siti retorting with bravado, "Hello, ladies. Actually I am coming over to stay for the night. Do spread the word around."

They lifted their heads and briskly walked away.

As she was climbing up the stairs, I said, "You really are one hell of a girl," and clapped my hands.

"The way to deal with these people is to do as I please. Thanks for the cheer. I brought something for you. I have been told you have employed an additional maid, a white-haired matronly woman, to act as chaperone, so to speak. Does that mean I can stay over tonight?"

"What?" I exclaimed.

"I was kidding. Just look at the fright in your face." She giggled, pointing her finger at me. Gingerly, as though the whole episode with the elders had been a big farce, she prepared the table and laid out the food as usual, with my new maid looking on with amusement. Siti sat by my side and began to serve me, pretending to be my wife. I smiled to myself.

"Why the smile?" she asked.

"Nothing," I replied.

After dinner, I did some English reading for Siti at the dining table and found her English much improved and her pronunciation more polished. Her conscientiousness to learn was unfazed by the problems she was facing. In fact, I sensed a renewed vigour in her. I found her forbearance utterly incredible for a woman her age. She easily put me to shame.

After the dismal failure of the mosque elders' preposterous intervention to have Siti and me married off, the rumour mill seemed to have lost steam. The elders appeared to be in retreat. Except for the few heads turning in the marketplace, the hostility seemed to have subsided. Of Hitam, there wasn't much news. In hindsight, I thought that Mois and Siti had been right after all. Fight fire with fire, as it were.

However, when all seemed calm, a dark cloud appeared on the horizon. We received news that the pilgrims' ship was arriving at Muntok Port. My heart sank.

Chapter 29

Never before had I experienced such unease. Thoughts of Rejab and Rahimah had been churning as the day came nearer. Their faces had hung in the ceiling when I lay down to sleep, bedevilled I was by dire expectation.

A day before the ship was expected to dock in Muntok Harbour, Siti paid me a quick visit just to give me a message. She looked stressed but presented me with her bravest face. When I invited her in, she declined.

She glanced around her and, seeing that no one was passing by, said, "Let's just sit at the porch, I'm in a bit of a hurry to get ready for tomorrow. Here's what I want to say. Whatever is the outcome of this unfortunate episode, you do not have to marry me because my parents want you to, or because the morality-givers of Tobali ordain that you do so. That decision is entirely yours and mine, no one else's. I am not some kind of chattel to be exchanged at the whim and fancy of others. I may be a woman from a little village, but that does not mean I don't have a brain. I want you to know that." Her eyes misted as they looked straight into mine without flinching.

For the first time, I pulled her against me. She didn't recoil. Without a second thought, she allowed herself to fall over my shoulder, reposing there for a long comforting moment. A feeling that was more than affection struck deep into my heart – a feeling that I had been fearing to admit to myself existed. I replied to her, "No one can force me to do anything I don't want to. Marriage is about the heart, Siti. No one knows what's in my heart. Only I do." She lifted her head up and gazed at me with questioning eyes. I smiled. I didn't let her go until some moments later.

Later in the night, Mois dropped in. It was to prepare me for the heavily apprehensive event that was to come. "Hamzah, I want you to say nothing to my parents. I shall do all the talking. I know my parents better than you do." The uncertainty in his eyes disturbed me.

"I'll go along with you, Mois. You're my one and only ally."

It was early January. The weather was cool with a south-westerly breeze. Muntok was filled with an assortment of Muslim men and women from all over Banka and Belitung Island. They had come to receive the pilgrims who had answered the call of Allah. The mood was sombre.

Mois, Siti, and I were at Muntok early the next morning. We spent the time waiting at a restaurant. Siti didn't touch her food. We sat in silence as the minutes ticked away. None of the village's elders were there, nor were there any familiar faces from Tobali. Yet the pilgrims' departure more than two months ago at the same place had been filled with emotions, tears, prayers, and the call to azan performed by Lebai Amir himself. Obviously, the elders had deserted their chief and pronounced their verdict. Only the punishment was waiting. Our hearts pounded as the ship docked.

The long pilgrimage seemed to have taken its toll on the pilgrims. They trooped down the gangway looking worn out and exhausted while carrying their trunks, bundles, and paraphernalia – not unlike an arriving caravan. Some of them looked really sick. There was none of the elation, anticipation, or hope that I had seen during their departure. The air was muted and somnolent; the pilgrims' minds must be stuffed with tales of the bizarre, of the sublime, and of the miracles they had encountered, all ready to be told to awaiting relatives.

We affixed our eyes upon the stream of people. Our hearts thrashed anxiously as our eyes searched for Tok Rejab and Rahimah. There was no sign of them, and the flow of pilgrims was beginning to thin. Our anxiety turned into fear. Then, at the tail of the exodus, the figure of Rahimah emerged, but there was no Tok Rejab. A wooden box in her wake did not look like a luggage trunk. Rahimah placed her feet on the ground. The box rested by her side. She spotted us and broke down. Her first words were, "Your father is gone." Siti was stupefied; Mois was stunned; and I sank into a hole.

Suddenly, Siti began to sway unsteadily. I quickly caught her before she hit the ground. Holding her in my arms, I laid her down against the pile of baggage. Someone in the crowd came forward and put smelling salts to her nose. She came to and gazed into her mother's face. Rahimah poured some water from a bottle onto her hand and wiped Siti's temple. She sat down and held her daughter on her lap.

Recovering from her shock, Siti immediately freed herself from her mother's clasp and went straight to the casket. "I must see him, Mother," she exclaimed as she clawed at the coffin to uncouple it, but without success, as it was tightly sealed. Rahimah rushed towards her. So did Mois.

"You can't, my dear. It's sealed. Wait until we get home," Rahimah exclaimed.

Siti turned to her mother. "He died because of me? O why must he die?" She pleaded, her tears raining down her face. Rahimah clasped her in her arms, stroked her hair, and tried to console her.

"It's the will of Allah, my dear. We must accept it," Rahimah gently said, her expression stoically serene.

Siti placed her head against the casket and cried out, "Forgive me, dear Father. Forgive me."

"He has forgiven you, Siti."

"He died because of what I did. Isn't that so, Mother?"

"No, he didn't die because of you."

"Tell me how he died, Mother?" Siti implored in between her sobbing.

"When we get home," Rahimah calmly said.

Rahimah had had no words for me since she set foot on the pier, but she did give a momentary polite nod to acknowledge my presence.

A stream of pilgrims came by to offer their condolences, some embracing Rahimah, a few shedding tears.

The agent for the pilgrims arrived with the van to transport the casket. Mois and I opted to ride in the van. Siti and Rahimah went in my car. The prospect of the two-hour journey to Tobali was a horrifying one for me, as I didn't know what to expect of Mois.

I was like an island away from everything that was going on, ignored and abandoned. Even my ally Mois seemed distant.

He had been unduly quiet at the pier. It was uncharacteristic of him not to have an expression during such a calamitous event. He seemed to be in turmoil, devoid of expression.

I surmised. Could it be he was disgusted with me? I wouldn't be surprised if he were. *He is paying the price for his unflinching loyalty to me,* I thought.

In the van, we sat on either side of the casket. With a bent head and a blank mind, Mois placed his hands on it. I hadn't noticed him shedding a drop of tear, not even at the harbour. He wasn't in the mood for conversation. I hadn't offered a word in the way of condolence. I had been at a loss as to how to mitigate the family's bereavement, as things had happened so suddenly, so confusingly. I was losing an ally and a friend.

Finally, I called out, "Mois."

"Yes?" he asked, lifting his head.

"I ask from the bottom of my heart for your forgiveness. Please, do not shut yourself off from me," I pleaded.

"Brother Hamzah, my silence has nothing to do with you. I place no blame on you for Father's death, as I put none on my sister. As my mother said, it's Providence. But Providence aside, I am certainly holding Hitam responsible, and I shall not rest until I make him pay. I promise you that." He resumed his silence and returned his hands to the coffin, hunching his body over it.

"Would you care to share your grief with me, Mois?"

He straightened himself and said, "I had taken my father for granted all my life and was never really close to him. I couldn't live up to his expectations, so I avoided him. We disagreed all the time, seeing things differently. Sometimes, I thought he didn't love me. Now that he's gone so suddenly, I miss him terribly. Now I think I ought to have been kinder to him." Then he trembled and broke down, covering his face with his palms. "I love him, Hamzah," he cried.

I moved to the other side to be beside him. Putting my hand across his shoulders, I said, "He loved you too. Very much."

The funeral took place the following day. People as far away as Pangkal Pinang, Membalong, and Muntok came to pay their respects. The procession was long, solemn, and sedate.

Every member of the mosque committee was there. Lebai Amir, among the earliest to arrive, was the one to lead the procession and to perform the last rites at the burial site.

Siti's eyes were swollen, but at the burial, as she poured holy water and sprinkled flowers over the grave, she was a picture of composure in a white scarf beside her mother. Mois and I were covered in soil as we and some other young men of Tobali placed the body into the ground and filled in the grave.

That evening, after the burial ceremony, a prayer was conducted at the house, with the recital of the *Yassin* performed by Lebai Amir. There were a hundred people in attendance. Food was laid out. When all was done, it was time for reckoning, as Rahimah had yet to tell us how Tok Rejab had died.

The next day, the empty feeling that comes in the aftermath of a funeral hung over the Rejabs' house. Rahimah, in her usual unruffled way, looked settled, the burden of expectancy and pessimism having now receded. She now had to cope with the sudden absence of half of her existence.

Being a woman of great fortitude, she didn't show her pain. I sensed her lack of enthusiasm to discuss the cause of her husband's death. But since Rejab's demise was so intertwined with events that had rocked the equanimity of Tobali, Siti, Mois, and I were dying to know. After the sombre atmosphere subsided and we were left to our quiet selves, Rahimah finally unhinged her silence after being pressed to do so by her daughter.

"Your father had been unwell even at the start of the haj. At the Plain of Arafat, the heat during the day was intense. Many people were coughing. Because he was already weak, he got infected. He began to cough, and a fever developed. It was sheer determination and faith that gave him the strength to plod on.

"Fortunately, the irresponsible letter came days after we had completed the haj. All the same, he was devastated. What affected him was not what you, Hamzah and Siti, were accused of. He had complete trust in both of you. It was the callousness of the writer or writers, their total disregard towards him who was in the midst of performing the haj. And if indeed the letter had come from the elders, which he doubted, he was all the more appalled.

"That very night, he complained of having chest pain. The long sea voyage home didn't do him any good, I believe, the anxiety of arrival and the anger that had been simmering in him pressed heavily upon him.

"Two nights before we docked, he told me he had dreamt of his father, who said to him, 'Rejab, come. I am waiting for you.' I told him that, it was just a dream. He chastised me. Then, the following night he breathed his last. Now, when I think of it, he was actually telling me he was ready to go, and very much at peace."

We were sitting on the floor mat at the back hall of the house, where Tok Rejab had habitually dined with his family. Siti, who was beside her mother, put her head down and began stroking the palm-leaf floor mat with her left hand. "Oh, I miss him so much that I can feel his presence here," she said softly. Then her eyes began to stream with tears. In the next moment, I saw her rising up. All of a sudden, she cried out, "I can't sit here." Then she ran out of the hall.

Instinctively, I gazed at Rahimah and then in the direction of Siti. Rahimah nodded her head to me and said, "Go ahead, Hamzah. Go and console her."

I found that Siti was in her room with the door closed. I could hear her sobbing. "Siti, may I come in?"

She opened the door and let me in. I sat by the chair and she on the edge of the bed. Her sobbing had subsided.

"We lose those we love at one time or another. We just have to be strong," I said.

"He was the gentlest father anyone could ever have."

"I know."

* * *

Two weeks later, when I thought Siti was slowly recovering from her grief, I took her for an outing without telling her the destination. It was an hour's drive away. She was quiet all the way as we passed through settlements and scenery with which she wasn't familiar. "Where are you taking me, Hamzah?" she asked repeatedly. I kept a solemn face and didn't reply.

When we finally arrived at the coastline of the vast blue ocean, she said, "What is this place? It's deserted. Why are you bringing me here?"

I replied, "This very beach was where your father found me as a castaway. I wish to relive that propitious moment, and to show his daughter where my destiny began. Look over there," I said, pointing to the black rock across the bay. "That rock, which I called the Black Ghost, had haunted me for years, and it was because of her that the *Shanghai Star* went asunder. Yet, in an ironic way, it was the Black Ghost that put me on the path of my present destiny."

"But why are you showing me all this?" She grimaced with curiosity.

"From today, that Black Ghost shall never haunt me again. Today is a new beginning. To grace the occasion, I have an important announcement to make."

"Stop it, Hamzah. This drama of yours is spooking me. Is this some kind of ceremonial goodbye?" she asked with a sad, puzzled look. The wind ruffled her flowing hair, and her eyes twinkled as they searched mine. I pulled out a little red box from my pocket and opened it. A sparkling stone dazzled her eyes.

I said, "Will you marry me?"

She turned her face up in utter surprise and exclaimed, "What?"

"Will you marry me, Siti?" I repeated.

She stared at me. Not a word came out of her lips. She was motionless. Then she placed her palms to her face and cried.

"What's the matter, Siti? Aren't you happy?"

"Indeed, I should be very happy, but I am not," she said in a trembling voice through her tears. "Did my mother set you up to this? Tell me!"

""Absolutely not. Why do you say that?"

"Because of what has happened. The whole of Tobali wants you to marry me, and now with Father gone and Mother grieving, you bring me to this place. And suddenly you want to marry me. It's all like a sudden flood, and I am drowning." She wiped her tears with her hands like a child and then raised her watery eyes to me. "You know, I've always been in love with you, ever since I was a girl, like you were a sort of Prince Charming. I should be walking on clouds now. But I am not. I am confused. I think you are marrying me out of guilt, or maybe you were pressured into it. I don't know. Oh God, help me! Hamzah, help me. Assure me, please. I don't even know whether you love me." She took my hands into her palms and held them tightly.

"I want to marry you because I love you. Your mother did not put me up to this. In fact, before I brought you here, I had formally asked her for your hand in the presence of your brother. And they both gave me their blessings, for which I am most grateful."

"Is that true, that you love me?"

"Yes! Yes! Yes! As God is my witness."

"No need to bring God into this. Your declaration is what I want most." She gave me a broad smile.

"Thank you for that smile. Since we left home, you have been like a dark cloud. Your smile has opened up the sky. The sun is shining brightly upon me now." I kissed her forehead and embraced her tightly, to which she responded delicately.

On the journey back, her insecurity apparently revisited her, as she posed another question. "I had often wondered why a man like you didn't have a woman. You've told me a lot about yourself, yet I still don't know you."

"No. There has been no woman in my life, and that's the truth," I feebly replied.

"Should I believe you?"

"Why not? There are men who have remained celibate all their lives."

"True. But that doesn't mean they didn't have women in their lives."

"You know, Siti, there's no getting away from you. When you bite, not even thunder can release it."

"That means you had a woman before, but you're not telling." She chuckled.

"Do I have to swear?"

"If you lie, not even God can help you. … I am kidding." She burst into laughter. "Oh, it doesn't matter. I don't really care."

"You are a very tricky girl."

She was quiet for a while. Dusk was approaching, throwing a shroud of grey in our path. All of a sudden, in the middle of nowhere, she exclaimed, "Stop the car."

I pulled the car to a stop. "Anything the matter, Siti?"

"Yes. Why haven't you kissed me if you love me?" she asked, looking not at me but into the dusky night.

"Because I didn't want to violate—"

"Don't give me that old-fashioned crap. Just kiss me."

It wasn't about being old-fashioned with her. I had wanted so much to kiss her, but I was afraid to cross the threshold of brotherly love and become her lover. I took her face in my hands and kissed her for a long time, endearingly.

After that threshold was crossed, the curtain lifted. I wanted to love her now as the true woman I had longed for her to be.

I held her close and felt a wetness on my shirt. She recomposed herself and gently wiped her silent tears. Avoiding my eyes, she gazed into the night and said, "Let's go."

It was getting dark. We didn't talk very much. Siti rested her hand on the seat and closed her eyes. As the car's lights tunnelled through the darkness, Pinky reappeared in my mind. Suddenly, I recalled that not once had Pinky ever talked of love. I suppose that to her, it sufficed for passion to do the talking. I turned and looked at Siti, who was reposed in the seat with her eyes closed, and warned myself never to hurt her.

Chapter 30

I decided to give Siti the biggest wedding Banka had ever seen. Underneath that gesture of love for Siti was also a motive: to spite Hitam. The news spread far and wide. The scandal, along with the dark clouds that had shrouded Tok Rejab's family, was now just another leaf blown away in the wind. Lebai Amir, in a gesture of forgiveness, offered to act as my emissary in all the ceremonies since I had no relatives in Tobali. All was forgotten. It was as if nothing had ever happened. *How short people's memory is,* I thought.

I wrote to Aunty Maimunah and broke the news to her. I made special mention that my future wife had the Minang blood flowing in her veins, knowing very well that any Minang woman would meet with Aunty's full approval. She wrote back in her characteristic voluble way, expressing her utter happiness, with loads of blessings from Allah thrown in.

Rahimah went to town on the guest list, which turned out to include almost everyone who was somebody in Banka. She planned the ceremonies to last three nights, culminating in a great feast.

Cooks were selected from among the best in Banka; waiters and helpers were drawn from Banka's young men. Siti was kept out of everything, as such was the custom. Her life was not hers anymore. It now belonged to the maid-in-waiting, an old woman with a doughnut bun and a high-pitched voice that could drown a cacophony. She knew all there was to know about weddings, this rustic maid-in-waiting, and that included what to do on the wedding night.

One evening, in the heat of these preparations, a sullen Siti shut herself up in her room. Rahimah, deeply anxious, sent someone to look for me. When I hurried to the house, I found a depressed Siti in her room, sitting stone-like by her window, her eyes glazed and staring into the outside. It was pre-wedding jitters, I thought. But no, it was something more unsettling than that.

When she saw me, she began to weep.

"What is the matter, Siti?" I asked anxiously.

She didn't answer me. Instead she asked, "Do you have any doubts in your mind? Any doubts at all, even a wee bit deep, in your heart?"

"Doubts? What doubts, Siti?" My heart started to race.

"Yes, doubts. I am serious. Doubts about my being your wife."

"Do *you* have doubts, Siti?" I asked.

"It's not doubts but fears," she said, looking straight at me with despondency.

"Fear of what, Siti?"

"Fear that you will not love me. Fear that I might not live up to you and that I would only be an item of familiarity – just like a piece of furniture in the house that loses its novelty."

"Was your mother a piece of furniture to your father?"

"No. But Father was a simple man who knew no other world but Tobali. You're different. You're like the migrating bird, having been to faraway places, seen many women, experienced many things. Compared to you, I am like the frog under a coconut shell, like the Malays say."

"Do you know what you are to me, Siti?"

"What am I to you, Hamzah?"

"An uncut diamond whose true value is yet to be revealed."

"What a beautiful thing to say. Still, I am unpolished like the uncut diamond. Isn't that so?"

"Siti, why is there always a negative side to what I say?"

"Because you frightened me with those words. They seem far away, like a speck on the horizon where I don't belong."

"Your feelings will change once we are together. I promise you."

"Do you love me?"

"Yes, with all my heart."

She smiled and seemed assured. But that was on the surface. What truly was churning inside her, I found hard to predict. Beneath that outward acceptance, I feared, she hid a complex emotional insecurity. There was, I suspected, a dark shadow of mistrust of the truth that I had been declaring to her. I prayed to the heavens that my past would remain buried in the past.

*   *   *

Three weeks before the wedding, I made a trip to Pangkal Pinang to do some shopping, accompanied by Mois. We dropped into a popular restaurant on Jalan Permata for lunch. It served Sundanese cuisine, which was popular in West Java – famous for its raw vegetables and salad. As the place was full, we took a table near the entrance.

While I was about to order the food, Mois rose from his chair and turned his head towards the far end of the restaurant nearest to the wall. "I think it's Hitam over there," he said. Pulling me up, he pointed to a dark, heavy man sitting alone at a corner, his back facing us. "That is definitely Hitam. I can recognise that ugly huge head a mile away."

"Bless our lucky souls, it is him," I said.

"Now you go to the police headquarters and ask to speak to Colonel Buyong, the new chief of police. He has a full report on Hitam, and he's my friend. I'll wait here and keep an eye on him," Mois said.

"Be careful, Mois. He may not be alone."

"Don't you worry! I can take care of myself. You go ahead." Whereas Hitam was heavy-set, Mois was younger and sinewy. Getting into a fight would be, for Mois, a walk in the park.

A long-forgotten person was suddenly jolted from my memory when Mois mentioned the name Buyong. My childhood friend Buyong came to mind, the boy with the limp who lived in the village below the Great Gate, the very first friend I had had in those heady days at Mataram House. Could that be him? No. I couldn't imagine him being a colonel. *Buyong is a very common name in Sumatra anyway,* I thought to myself.

At the police headquarters, I was taken to Colonel Buyong. A dapper man in uniform, with army-style high-cropped hair, greeted me with an affable smile. As he strutted smartly forward to take my hand, I was immediately struck by the limp in his gait. If this was the same Buyong, it was a remarkably transformed one from that dishevelled, poor-looking barefoot boy I used to know. This man was a portrait of military poise and resplendence.

"Aren't you Buyong, my old friend from Jogjakarta?"

"Indeed I am. And you're, of course, the famous Hamzah. Am I right?" Without hesitation he warmly clasped me in his arms. "Wow, you look good and prosperous. How long ago was it, fifteen or sixteen years?"

"To be exact, seventeen years. And look at you, too, so dapper and distinguished in uniform. And a colonel at that," I said.

"What happened, Hamzah? You suddenly disappeared into thin air. You're a legend in Jogjakarta. You know that? Yes, they talked much about you. Ibu Tutik, your grandmother, particularly, tells amazing stories about you."

"You know my grandmother? I mean, are you in touch with her?" I asked in surprise.

"Yes. I've a lot to tell you." Buyong's broad jaw broke into an engaging smile. "I've been here for three months already, but I waited for the right time to call on you. You're a big man and all. You might be very busy, and may not remember me," Buyong said quite genuinely.

I took no offence. "Not remember you? You were the first and only friend I ever had. The first chicken I ever caught was with you. And I recall the meals we had, the swimming, the fishing in the stream. How could I forget? They were the best moments of my childhood!" I stepped back to admire him. "Look at you, a colonel of the elite Indonesian army. Now who's the big man, really?" I asked.

"Aw, don't say that. Come have a seat." In spite of his limp, Buyong's extremely fit, elegant figure, and a certain magnetic masculinity in his swagger that came along with it, would be the envy of many a perfect man.

"Now to what do I owe the honour of your visit?" Buyong asked with a commandingly polite manner that rather impressed me, as I was still adjusting to this most unexpected new image of his.

"You know Mois, right?"

"Yes. What about him?"

"Mois and I were entering the Sundanese restaurant in Jalan Permata, and we saw a man whom we believed to be Hitam. According to Mois, the police have been looking for him. So he wanted me to tell you that."

Buyong thrust himself forward from his chair, placed his arms on the table, and exclaimed, "Indeed, we've been looking for him. He has a record with us for assault, criminal intimidation, and whatnot. Somehow he managed to slip away. I was told by Mois that he was the author of a poison-pen letter involving you and Siti. Now that too is a serious offence in my book. Come on, what are we waiting for? Let's get him."

As we were leaving, Buyong's men cracked to attention and saluted. We left, accompanied by four armed men.

I sat in his car. As we sped off to the Jalan Permata, he said, "I heard your name when I first arrived, but I wasn't sure if you'd be the same Hamzah I used to know. The stories were such that this Hamzah seemed shrouded in mystery. He was shipwrecked, was brought up by a white man, became rich after the war, and built a fine mosque for the people – and so on. Yet, when I enquired, no one knew anything of his origin, not until I met Mois and put everything together."

I put my right hand on his shoulder and said, "You know, Buyong, I never thought I would ever see you again. Now, by some twist of fate, we meet again – and of all places, here in Banka. Now, that's really something – things turning full circle. I'm so happy to meet you again, my friend. Really happy." I gazed at him affectionately. Me too, Hamzah. Me too. We have so much to catch up on."

Suddenly, he put his hand out and said, "Hey, you are getting married to Siti. Congratulations."

"Thanks, and you must come."

"Certainly, I shall. I would be terribly hurt if you didn't invite me."

When we arrived at the restaurant, there was a commotion. We walked through the mélange of patrons to the back of the restaurant. Behind a screen divider, we found Mois assisted by another man firmly holding down Hitam by his shoulders. Immediately, Buyong's men strutted in and handcuffed Hitam.

While he was walking past, being sequestered to the awaiting van, Hitam lowered his head, avoiding eye contact with me. He was docile and appeared defeated.

That night, when I sat by the terrace drinking my usual nightcap of black Sumatran coffee in the dim glow of the moonlight, my thoughts flashed back to Mataram House. For so long Grandma Tutik's name had remained secretly cloistered in my mind. Now, in the strangest of coincidences, it had come out of the mouth of the most unlikely person – Buyong, the village boy from the labyrinth of hovels below the Great Gate whom Grandma least wanted me to befriend. That very same boy now spoke of Grandma with improbable familiarity and closeness. I wouldn't have believed it if the tale had been told by a person other than Buyong himself. I was dying to know how that had come to be, but I had to wait until after my wedding.

*   *   *

A week before my wedding, I received a letter with a Malayan postmark. The familiar handwriting on the envelope caused my heart to jump. My hands trembled as I tore the cover. My eyes fell upon a feminine script that once had charmed me. Nervously I unfolded the letter and read it.

My dearest Hamzah,

I know I do not exist in your life anymore, but you will never, ever leave my heart as long as I have life in me. Have no fear; that is not what this letter is about. I write for Tan Siew Lim – my husband, your good friend. He is dying of a serious illness. Isn't it ironic? Love seldom falls into the right places, and is often mismatched. Tragic, isn't it? He has wondered why you haven't contacted him since the time the two of you parted company. With all his cleverness in other areas, he has failed to see the connection with me in your flight from his life. Now he has asked of his old friend. Do not deny a dying man his wish. I don't know how much time he has left in this

251

world. You are one of the most trusted friends he has ever had. I should know. He talked of you to others with glowing praises. Please come, for his sake.

Yours truly,
Pinky

The feeling which I had felt when I forsook Pinky returned to me in a flood. My wedding was a week away. My bride-to-be was battling with doubts. The past was now beckoning to me like a heartbroken spirit. A man whom I once betrayed asked for me in his final days. *Is fate playing with me again?* I asked myself. I cried. I drew the letter up to my nose; its perfume burnt into my heart. For the love of God, why the perfume? I never knew until then how dangerous a lie was. I'd lied to Siti to save her the pain, and now a greater pain awaited her. What must I do now? What else, except to continue to lie?

Early the following morning, I sought Rahimah, Mois, and Siti to deliver my lie. A sombre meeting it was in a glorious morning awash with the upcoming celebration. On the occasion of a wedding, when the groom absconds or changes his mind at the last minute, a dark cloud of shame and misery is cast upon all concerned. That fear shrouded the three of them when I implored them to allow me a short leave of absence so that I may travel to Penang on an urgent matter.

"My father is very sick. I must go. I'll be back by Thursday, maybe earlier," I shamefully lied.

"But that's barely two days before the wedding," Siti exclaimed with a tearfully gloomy look.

Rahimah quickly came to my rescue and replied, "It's about his father, Siti. You can't expect him not to go."

Mois said nothing. A distraught Siti was about to cry. I fully understood her feelings, especially after her outpouring of doubts a few days ago. How could she not feel even more miserable and depressed? I embraced her tightly in front of her mother to comfort her, reassuring her as much as I could. She forced a smile without saying another word. Her silence, I feared, amounted to more than all the words she could have spoken. I felt similarly about with Rahimah and Mois, who also had nothing much to say.

This time, I thought, even the loyal Mois was not with me. My lie delivered, I felt utterly miserable. At that moment, I envied those without scruples.

*   *   *

When I arrived in Penang, it was Tan Siew Lim's funeral that I was attending. I had come too late.

A river of people meandered across the sprawling ground of Tan Siew Lim's mansion on the tree-lined Northam Road. I waded through the jungle of mourners, wreaths, chanting priests, fuming joss sticks. A giant photograph of Tan Siew Lim greeted me from across the hall. It had been placed beside the huge casket in which he was lying in state, dressed in a black mandarin-collar suit. He looked peaceful, but no amount of embalming fluid could hide the grief that his illness had caused on the one-time wholesome face.

Pinky sat in the clan's row by the casket. To her right was a thin middle-aged woman whom, I guessed, had been Lim's first wife. Pinky had a child with her, whom she held between her knees. She must have been crying, for her eyes were red and swollen. I circled the casket once. When I finished, I found Pinky beside me. She whispered, "Thank you for coming. Could we meet after the funeral?"

The next day, we met at the Wing Look Café in Penang Road. Pinky wore her hair neatly tucked at the sides with silver pins. She donned a black ankle-length samfu. Not even that subdued image or the sombreness of mourning could prevent my heart from swaying at the sight of her. Her apparent sorrow for Tan brought out a tinge of jealousy in me.

She brought the little boy who had been with her at the funeral. A Chinese amah minded him. The two sat separate from us, at another cubicle. I asked Pinky to have the boy join us, but she said no. I took a curious glance at him. Who was this boy? He bore no resemblance at all to Lim. But he certainly looked like Pinky, particularly in the extraordinary whiteness of his skin. *That rich, billowy hair looks odd for a Chinese boy,* I thought.

"Are you all right?" Pinky asked me after noticing my puzzled look.

"Yes, I am," I said.

Then, touching my hand, she said, "You don't have to feel guilty for not being able to meet Siew Lim before he died. He did ask of you. That's true. But he didn't ask for you to come to see him. I did."

"You did?"

"Yes."

"But why?"

"To make you come. I was afraid you wouldn't."

"Why? Whatever for? Do you know, Pinky, I am about to get married? In fact in a few days. I rushed here in the middle of the preparations because a dying man had asked for me. Yes, I wouldn't have come otherwise," I said, raising my voice.

"Please, Hamzah, don't raise your voice with me. I've enough grief as it is."

"You don't seem surprised that I am about to get married."

"No."

"You knew?"

"*My love,* you left me, but I never left you. Doesn't that mean anything to you?"

I took those words with pain and anger.

"Why did you use this ploy to get me here? Whatever for, Pinky?"

"Because I am now free – and I love you."

"Free because he is dead?"

"Yes, free, Hamzah. Don't you understand free?" She broke down. Tears came streaming down her cheeks. I had never seen her cry like that before. It shook me. I drew out my handkerchief and gave it to her. She shook her head, and used her own. I controlled myself from taking her in my arms.

"How could you cry for him and now cry for me? How could you, Pinky?"

"I'm not crying for him, you fool. I am crying for you. When I learned you were getting married, I cried and cried. I was torn, Hamzah, between loving you and being grateful to Lim. Siew Lim provided for me well. He was kind, gentle, generous, and a wonderful husband. It would be any woman's dream to be his wife. But I didn't love him. How could I tell him that? Then you came to fill my emptiness. Can you blame me for that, Hamzah? If you blame me, blame yourself too," she said, sobbing while choking on her words.

254

"Why didn't you tell me you were married?"

"What! When someone says hello to me, should I say, 'Please don't come near me. I am married'? Come on, Hamzah, we fell in love without knowing it was happening. We share this blame together. Don't you just pin it on me alone. It takes two hands to clap, remember?"

"What do you want me to do, Pinky?"

"Marry me, Hamzah."

"What are you saying, Pinky? I am getting married in a couple of days."

"Do you love this village girl who has been like a sister to you?"

"How do you know that?"

She gave a sly smile.

"Yes, I love this *village* girl. Very much."

"I don't believe you. You are so driven by guilt that you refuse to admit it's me you love. Don't hurt her, Hamzah, as you have hurt me. If she comes to realise one day you don't really love her, she will suffer. Call it off before you make a huge mistake. It's kinder to do it now instead of later. Don't wait until it's too late. You will end up hurting two women. Do you really want that?"

I closed my eyes, put my head down, and said nothing, as I had no words to say.

Pinky clasped my hand in a comforting manner and said, "Hamzah, look at me. I want to show you something."

She walked to the other cubicle and fetched the little boy. Holding his hand, she said to him, "Li, say hello to Uncle Hamzah."

The boy raised his head and stared at me. "Hello," he said shyly.

"Look very closely at him, Hamzah. Now, what do you see?"

I turned away and swung my eyes elsewhere. She pulled my chin towards the boy.

"You can't run away from it, Hamzah. Li is my son, but do you see a trace of Siew Lim in him?"

I stared in amazement at the boy.

"Oh my God! What are you doing to me, Pinky?" I cried.

"What have I done to *you*? What have you done to us?"

Now at a closer range, I stared at the boy, and was stricken with panic. True, there was not a trace of Siew Lim in him. There was more me than even of his mother in him, except for that extraordinary whiteness of his skin.

"Why didn't you tell me you were pregnant?"

"How? After the episode at the Chinese restaurant, you practically wiped me out of your life. Remember?"

"Did Siew Lim know?"

"No, he didn't. You see, with all his huge success, he was at heart a simple man, naïve to a pitiful point when it came to women. When he saw that Li had no resemblance to him, he thanked God for making the boy look like me, not like him."

She summoned the maid to take the boy aside. When we were alone in the cubicle again, she took my hands and held them in hers. Pearls of tears danced in her eyes. She pulled me towards her and spoke in a low tone. "You still love me, Hamzah. I saw it in your eyes when you looked at me at the funeral. I wrote so many letters to you, but they were returned back to me without being read. You should at least have read them, but you refused to do so. Why, Hamzah? Tell me now, to my face."

I covered my face with my hands and looked down, saying nothing.

"Look at me, Hamzah, and tell me that you hate me – and that was why."

"I don't hate you, Pinky."

"So that's not the reason? What is it then?"

"Look, Pinky, it's over between us. That is why." I kept my eyes down as I spoke.

"Look at me, Hamzah. I'll tell you why. You were afraid to read my letters. That was why you returned them. It was a coward's way of avoiding the truth that you still love me."

I was on the verge of bursting into tears with frustration, but I controlled myself for fear of appearing defeated. Then I looked straight into her eyes and said, "Why are you doing this, Pinky? A lot of water has passed under the bridge. I'm getting married in a couple of days. What we had is now in the past."

"You are dreaming, Hamzah. I and your son, Li, will not just disappear into thin air. The memory of us will haunt you if you marry this girl. Should I die one day, your son will be alone and will surely ask who his father is. You will have to live with that."

I put my palms to my face, lost my control, and cried. She didn't console me. She went over to the other cubicle, picked up the little boy, and came back. I quickly wiped my face.

"Say goodbye to Uncle."

"Goodbye," the boy said shyly.

"When he grows up, I wonder how he would feel if he were told that he was abandoned by his father," Pinky said. After a few moments of silence, she spoke again. "Well, Hamzah, I have said all I wanted to say. It's all up to you now. Whatever decision you make, you will have to live with it for the rest of your life. Remember that you are my life. Without you I have nothing. Goodbye, Hamzah. Give me one final hug, at least."

I embraced her. She held me very tightly, her tears streaming all over my shoulder. Then she left, without looking back. My heart sank into the lowest pit. If Pinky had wanted to throw me into a cesspool of guilt and sorrow, she certainly succeeded. I was completely drowned, with no one to save me.

*   *   *

The journey home to Tobali was shadowed by the old demons and ghosts of Mataram House. I could feel them eyeing me with their warped design for my life. *There has not been a single moment in my life when happiness was given to me without condition,* I sadly thought.

Tobali was already festive when I returned. Marquees, decorations, bunting, lights, and merry children enlivened the atmosphere. Siti ran down the stairs, her face lit up. With jubilation she cried out, "Mother! Mois! Hamzah is back!"

When I saw Mois coming out of the house, I shouted, "I am back." His broad grin and a wave of his hand told me how relieved he was.

He must have bet on my returning. He confirmed my suspicion when he yelled back, "I never doubted it."

Siti and I were married in the most colourful wedding Banka Island had ever seen. People thronged in from all over the island. The fires of the cauldrons and pots kept on burning. Guests came and went until late evening. For three nights, Siti and I sat on the dais while friends and relatives sprinkled scented water in blessing, and fast-witted old ladies with a penchant for theatrics cracked humour and clowned uproariously before us while the music played non-stop. On the dais, we were not to move, or even to smile, or to react in any way. Such was the custom. Once in a while, Siti's hand stole a gentle touch of mine. That alone showed how happy she was. When I glanced sideways to catch a glimpse of her, I saw the radiance in her eyes. In the midst of all the gaiety, bliss, and delight, only I was alone, an island, far from everything around me, while the noise, the music, the joy, and the people floated by, regardless of my turmoil.

Chapter 31

At the start of our new life, as if driven by guilt, I drew up a generous trust fund in Siti's name with an international bank. Siti was an incredibly insightful woman with uncanny intuition. Instead of reinforcing her confidence, this act fed on her insecurity. "I don't need this, do I, my dear? Your love is worth more than all the money in the world."

It was only after I had assured her that it was for our future baby that she accepted it with a clear heart. She didn't question it again after that.

My house on the beach was upgraded to depict the style of homes found in my father's homeland of Bukit Tinggi in West Sumatra. I named it the big house. Sam's old little old house was something I retained as a piece of memory. And this I called the little palace. It was at the little palace where I whiled away the time when I needed to calm my unsettled soul, with the spirit of Sam as company.

Siti took great pride in the big house. It was her own new world in which she was mistress, with her new-found passion for homemaking, husbandry, and cooking. A copious library was added for her intellectual pursuit. After much persuasion on my part, she agreed to engage helpers and maids, but only if the kitchen would be her domain and hers alone. As it was for her mother, Rahimah, cooking for Siti was more love than duty. Like her mother, she excelled at it splendidly.

In the evenings, she would put her mind to advancing her English skills. I continued to be her tutor and interlocutor. What a keen pupil she had become, advancing remarkably, even developing a proper English accent.

When the table was laid for dinner, it was with full service: forks, knives, spoons, and serviettes. My preference to eat with my hands was refused. *Why is she so keen on things European?* I asked myself, but never did I dare question her. She seemed intent on discarding her image as the unsophisticated village girl. Poor girl, she was still unsure that I wasn't looking for that in her – not at all.

In the calmer days of married life, I had time to retrace my friendship with Buyong. I found that each of us shared an eagerness to know how the other had spent the missing years. I was as much a mystery to him as he was to me. Each of our lives had metamorphosed beyond each other's expectations and recognition. Buyong became a frequent guest to our house. In one of the cooler seasons, when the south-west wind blew, Buyong came to spend the weekend.

One night at the little palace after dinner, he and I took to reminiscing. Siti brought in the coffee and pastries. I took out the cigars and offered one to Buyong. Adroitly he lit it, like a man used to the good life. Turning his face towards the sky, he let out a roll of smoke. I recalled those broad craggy feet I had seen on him when we first met, the underprivileged face, and the challenging gait. *He certainly has come a long way,* I thought.

At my behest, Buyong related to me the story of how he became close to Grandma. He and his parents had been taken by Grandma Tutik into the Mataram House household a year after I left. He was baffled by this unusual act of generosity on her part. As the years went by, he began to believe it was all done in my memory, because he was the first friend I had made. There was no other reason he could think of, he said. They were poor, and there were many others like them. Why had she chosen them particularly?

His mother worked in the kitchen; his father, in the housekeeping. He himself was tutored to take care of the collections of paintings and artefacts and the array of krises. He and his siblings were enrolled in good schools in Jogjakarta. That was how he later joined the military, he said. They were lodged, fed, clothed, and generously recompensed as members of the household, not having to spend a cent on anything. To them it was a gift from heaven.

Then one day, Buyong said, Grandma Tutik asked him not to call her *Ibu* anymore, but *Grandma*. "I think it was all about you, Hamzah. She must have missed you a great deal," Buyong reiterated.

I was baffled by Buyong's story, and was all the more struck by his account of Grandma Tutik. These were sides of her which I had failed to see. Maybe the opportunity had not come, or maybe that part of her had not yet surfaced when I lived in Mataram House. Maybe Grandma Tutik was just wearing armour to protect her soft side. It was that armour Father had noticed, not what it was protecting. I failed in that too.

Buyong saw me drifting away. "I am sorry if my story affected you," he said.

"Yes, but not in a bad way. It's just how wrong one could be about a person, even the one closest to you. I must have hurt her a great deal. Tell me, Buyong, what did she say about me?"

The chilly breeze of the night and the lashing sea caught Buyong's attention. He paused.

"Go on, Buyong," I said impatiently.

"Oh yes. Ibu Tutik didn't have to talk about you. Her actions spoke more than words. She preserved your room, your clothes, your playthings, and every memory of you like they were all invaluable works of art. Your room was out of bounds to everyone except her, and she took pleasure in taking care of it herself. One day Grandma Tutik caught me browsing in your room. She burst out in anger and told me never to step foot in there again. I was surprised by the ferocity of her outburst. When she calmed down, she said the room was sacrosanct, that the spirit there must not be disturbed. Mind you, she used the word *spirit*. You are somewhat godlike to her. Ah yes, she said you were the last descendent of Sultan Agung, a message she got from a dream. A legend you are, aren't you?"

"Were there still theatres and performances after I left?" I asked.

"No. Not a single one since you left. Neither were there any feasts or guests. In fact, she shunned society and abhorred socialising of any kind. And I mean abhorred, discarding invitations into the wastebasket. She became sort of a hermit. Mataram House became her lonely and only world. Yet in that loneliness she took pains to groom herself, being always attired in fine clothes throughout the day. In fact, I have never seen her in any other state. Her presence about the house was always regal, always proper, not a strand displaced, not a manner out of turn."

"Did she allude to my leaving her?" I asked.

"She did." Buyong paused for a moment. Moving his gaze away from me, he peered at the horizon outside.

"What did she say?"

"She blamed your father. He was the cause of all that had happened to you, she said."

"Did she say how?"

No, she didn't elaborate. And I didn't ask."

"Does she hate me for what I've done?"

"Hate you? God, no. She loves you, Hamzah, more than her life." Buyong paused, wanting to say something.

"What is it, Buyong?" I asked.

"I don't know whether I should mention this to you."

"Come on, what is it? We've come this far."

"Your grandmother feared for you. She said your father had made a kind of vow, the breaking of which would have terrible consequences for your father and for you. Were you aware of this?"

"Hazily."

"I am sorry."

"Nothing to be sorry about. Fate is my guardian angel, for better or for worse."

"Let's not talk about it anymore. It's not a happy subject. Let's go fishing tomorrow? Ask Mois to join us," Buyong said, seeing that my mood was drifting away.

"Damn good idea. Let's call it a night."

Buyong rose from his chair. As an afterthought, he turned towards me. "Would you return again to Mataram House, Hamzah?"

"I can't say really. I don't know. I did once, after the war. I'm sure you knew. She didn't want to have me."

"Go back, Hamzah, before she dies," he said. I was silent, my thoughts mingling with the wind.

That night I dreamt of Grandma Tutik. She was standing on the balcony and facing me. Behind her was the dark night sky. She said to me, "Remember that night when we talked at this balcony, Hamzah? You asked me if I heard the dog crying. I said no. I did hear the dog. I didn't want you to know I heard, because he was calling for you."

*   *   *

My fortune from the Nusantara Mine increased. I now had more time at my disposal to spend with Siti, which she valued more than all the comfort I could shower upon her. And she had come to trust me now absolutely – well, almost.

One day while vacationing in the rhapsodic air of Hakok Beach on the east coast of Banka, the shadow of doubt, like a dark memory, found her again.

"My dear, do you mind if I ask you a personal question? There is this thing that has been nagging my mind. I want to bury it once and for all," she said with a guilty smile.

"Shoot. What is it?"

"I think it is not possible for a man like you to have never met any woman."

"Siti, my dear, you've asked the same question before, many times, and I have given the same answer every time. What more can I say?"

"I know. It's not fair on my part to nag you like this, but I love you very much, and it's gnawing me. I have tried to ignore it, believe me, but it keeps coming back. It's spooking me, Hamzah. Believe me."

"Cut my heart. I had no other woman in my life."

"So does that mean I am your first love?"

"It's obvious, isn't it?" I said.

"It really doesn't matter. After all, you're a man, and it happened before my time. But you wouldn't hide it from me, would you, if there had been one?"

"Of course. Why should I lie?" I replied feebly with a feeling of terrible guilt, hoping against hope that she would end this interrogation.

"You see, it's not that I am jealous, but knowing is better than not knowing, and the truth is better than guessing. It makes our bond stronger, our trust in each other beyond question. Who knows, someday, somewhere, a woman might cross our path and say hello to you. I would look like a fool if she happened to be someone from the past. Do you understand what I am saying, dear?"

"No such woman would pass our way, Siti, I assure you – because such a woman doesn't exist," I said. Then I gave her a loving hug and prayed that the conversation would end.

Just then, a waiter came. I seized the opportunity to ask Siti whether she wanted anything. "Later," she said.

To my great relief, she didn't pursue her questioning. Whether it was still lingering in her mind, I hadn't a clue. The issue never surfaced again. Even then, I failed to understand the true nature of her feelings, or more accurately the true meaning of that question. Its simplicity belied the complexity of the emotion it was hiding.

Chapter 32

Siti was pregnant. Not too soon after, Rahimah consulted a midwife, the one who had delivered Siti when she was born. Now in her sixties, this big woman was aptly known to everyone as Big Mother. She installed herself in our home and, without much ado, began to set the ground rules as to Siti's well-being and my conduct, right down to my conjugal duties, without sparing any details. In no way must I upset my wife emotionally, especially during the first three months, Big Mother cautioned me. As for Siti's cravings, I must go to the world's end to meet her request. Siti wasn't concerned about knowing the baby's gender until the fourth month. Then one day she raised the issue.

"What's your wish, my dear, a boy or a girl?" she asked.

"It doesn't matter to me either way," I replied.

"Don't you want a boy? Husbands prefer boys, don't they, to preserve their male line?"

"I don't really think in that way, Siti," I said. Deep in my heart I had wished for a girl.

"Since you have no preference, I shall make the wish for you. A boy it shall be, for your sake, so that he shall carry down your name. Don't you agree, my dear? Oh, I pray it shall be a boy."

"Yes, my dear." It would hurt me very much to see her unhappy, so I made a silent prayer for her wish to come true.

Siti shopped for baby boys' clothes, toys, and other things as if her prayers had already been answered. When the baby arrived, her first words were, "Is it a boy?" She asked this of Big Mother.

"No, it's a girl, my dear, a lovely, healthy girl," Big Mother said.

Siti frowned for a moment. But when the baby was placed in her arms and the new mother's eyes fell upon her daughter, then the cloud of disappointment vanished as suddenly as it had come, and joy came flooding in. "Oh, my beautiful angel!" she cried.

"God loves you, Siti, He gave you a girl. Nothing like a girl for your old age," I said, comforting her.

Rahimah was overjoyed – her own wish had come true. To her, a girl was preferred in order to assure the continuity of the ancient matrilineal lineage of her Minang clan.

When it came to naming the baby, no ceremony was performed, no almanac referred to, and no astrologers consulted, as would have been the case if Grandma Tutik had witnessed this birth. Instead, a lively bandying about of names took place between mother and daughter. I watched the polemic between two iron-willed matriarchal women, hoping that something preposterous did not come of it. As it turned out, Siti prevailed. By a quirk of divine irony, she cried out, "It's Tutik Indriani," thereafter lifting her gaze to me for approbation.

"But that's Javanese," I exclaimed in surprise.

"Why not? After all, you're half Javanese," Siti said to me.

"And it's my grandmother's name too," I said, puzzled.

"After what all that you have told me of her, there couldn't be a more fitting name." Then, with her eyes upon the baby, she said, "You'll be as great as Grandma Tutik when you grow up, won't you, my sweet?" The baby closed her eyes as if she had heard the message.

I said to myself, *If Grandma Tutik were here to witness this, that injured heart of hers would surely heal and all my past sins would be forever erased.*

Chapter 33

When Indriani was three months old, an unexpected visitor came to our house. This happened when I was away in Penang. The nature of the visit was strange and puzzling. When I returned home two days later, I was surprised to find that Siti didn't rush to the door to greet me, as was customary. When I entered the house, I found her already seated, holding steadfastly to a grim expression while the receding daylight turned the house into a pall of gloom. So sombre was the air that it troubled me. The sign that something was amiss was palpable. My first thought was of Indriani.

"Is anything the matter, Siti? Is Indriani all right?" I enquired with extreme anxiety.

Without turning to me, Siti said, "We had a visitor – a woman."

"Who?" I asked, blood rushing to my head.

"A Chinese woman. She said she was Lai Peng."

"Who's Lai Peng?" I asked, instantly realising how stupid I sounded.

"'Who's Lai Peng?' Say that again!" she exclaimed, twisting her mouth with sarcasm.

"I am sorry, Siti. I've had a long trip and I'm tired. Let me take off my shoes and settle first before we talk about this." If Siti had been close enough to me, she would have sensed my furiously beating heart and the fear that ran through my veins.

"You said this Lai Peng was here?" I endeavoured to act as natural as I could. "Now tell me about it."

"This Lai Peng was looking for you."

"Looking for me?"

"Why don't you just spill out the truth, Hamzah, and stop acting like you don't know? Don't make a fool of me. Unschooled as I am about the modern world, I am no fool. This woman spoke in a tone and with familiarity that could only come from someone who knew you beyond the ordinary."

I sat down and took a deep breath. "Beyond the ordinary? How? What do you mean by that? Why don't you tell me what exactly happened? I know when a woman comes calling, a wife's imagination starts to run wild."

She stood before me with folded arms, and raised her voice. "Excuse me. I certainly am not that kind of woman. I am not your sick, jealous woman. I certainly am not. But I do not like to be lied to or to be made a fool of. I had always harboured a sneaking suspicion that you were hiding something, so come clean, Hamzah." Siti's voice was laced with such strength and purpose, I felt utterly rotten and ashamed.

"Tell me what actually happened yesterday, and I'll tell you all there is to know."

Settling myself in the lounge chair, I took off my socks deliberately while mustering my strength to gather my thoughts that were scattering in all directions. Pinky being here in person was something I never imagined would happen. I suppose that I had miscalculated women just as I had done with everything else in my life. Even under an obviously deep strain, Siti admirably held her composure and kept her good sense, but her tone was unbending. With her arms still folded, she sank into her chair and placed me under siege, allowing her eyes to speak what she felt inside.

Then, in a voice filled with pain, she recounted the episode. "At noon yesterday a black car rolled in and an attractive woman alighted. She was clad in a long white dress, black scarf and dark glasses. I was by the window, with Indriani in my arms. The woman, accompanied by her driver, walked up the steps to the door and, once I opened it, greeted me in Malay. Then she asked whether this was Mr Hamzah's residence. When I replied in the affirmative, she introduced herself. 'I am Lai Peng. May I come in?' I naturally invited her in. She looked curiously at Indriani and asked, 'Your baby? Looks like you. You must be Hamzah's wife, I am sure.' When I nodded my head, she added with a smile, 'You're very beautiful.' She referred to you as Hamzah, not Mr Hamzah – did you get that? We sat, drinks were served, and she removed her scarf and glasses, revealing soft but tired eyes that scrutinised me with the utmost curiosity, tracing my face, my body, right down to my feet, as if she was painting me on her mind. Silent moments passed as her eyes held me with a deep questioning air that made me feel uncomfortable in my own house. She looked rather sad and troubled. 'Why have you come here?' I asked politely. She said she was visiting Pangkal Pinang to attend to some family affairs and thought it fit to look up an old friend – you, an *old friend*. But she quickly qualified this by saying that you were actually her late husband's dear friend. She talked of Ipoh and of how she had met you through her husband. 'I have a son, four years old,' she suddenly said. After her husband died, she led a quiet and sedentary life in Ipoh, spending her time at the Ipoh Book Club. Sometimes on Sundays, she and her son would lunch at the Station Hotel Restaurant. This unfolding of her private life to me – a total stranger – seemed odd, I thought. She spoke gently. Every now and then her eyes flirted with the room before turning back t o me. I noticed she seemed shrouded in gloom, and that gloom affected me too. I listened in silence, becoming more and more puzzled as to what was really in her mind and why she was pouring out her life to me.

"After sipping the coffee, she rose from her chair and started to walk about the room without being invited, touching a piece of furniture, the silver vase, and the lampshade, and feeling the drapes, without purpose. When she came to the stack of albums labelled 'Wedding', she passed them over hurriedly. All the while, ever since she had arrived, the hard-to-miss large portrait of yours was looming over us, yet not once did she even take a glance at it.

"After close to an hour, she suddenly seemed exhausted. The small talk ended abruptly. She plunged into her chair and stared at the outside world, unaware of her own silence. But it made me uneasy, a stranger sitting with me in my house without saying a word, behaving in a way that gave me the impression that something was wrong with her. When I asked if she was unwell, she broke her silence. Of late, she said, she had been having bouts of this mindless reverie, her mind emptying itself all of a sudden. It was embarrassing, she said, when in the presence of others. I shouldn't be offended, she said, apologising. Then she admitted that this had begun to happen after her husband's death.

"Finally, before taking her leave, she asked whether she could hold Indriani in her arms. When holding her, she locked her eyes on her, touched her cheek, and said, 'You're very pretty, like your mother.' Then her eyes reddened. She quickly gave Indriani back to me and said, 'Please forgive me if I have intruded into your home unannounced, and thank you for your kind hospitality.' Before parting, she said, 'Please say hello for me to Hamzah.'"

Throughout Siti's narration, her words just buzzed about in my mind, which was drained of all consciousness.

"Hamzah," Siti called out. I then realised she had ended her story.

"Well, there isn't much to say. She was the wife of a late friend coming to pay me a visit," I said with false innocence.

Siti pulled herself against the sofa and folded her arms again, her eyes looking straight into mine, her face painted with disgust. I felt utterly miserable. Then, without saying another word, she lifted herself in a huff and walked towards the corridor. After that, I heard the loud slamming of a room door.

That night was the most silent night we spent together since we had gotten married. She was quiet. We were like two strangers lying side by side. After that stunning narrative she had given, no more questions were asked. The bed suddenly shook and trembled. In an effort to console her, I gently touched her shoulder, but she pulled away from me. At that moment, I realised, a thousand words from me would not suffice to console her.

"What do you want me to do?" I asked. It was not the most appropriate thing to say, but I was under such pressure I could think of nothing else to do.

"Go to sleep. Leave me alone," she said. Her silent rumbling disturbed me. Images of what was to come crawled out from the darkness. Time seemed to stand still; the minutes turned into hours, and the hours an eternity. It was the longest night of my life.

Dawn came in the shape of white streaks of light across my eyes. When I awoke, I found that Siti was not beside me. Panic struck me. I jumped out of bed to look for her.

She was up and about, busy in the kitchen preparing breakfast. No greeting was expressed, and our eyes did not meet. The gloom of the previous night hung heavily in the air. With remarkable pretence, as good as a breakfast scene in a play could possibly be, was played out. She set the table and meal, served me, and ate with me - as if nothing unusual had ever occurred, but she uttered not a single syllable to me.

As the days passed, the episode of Pinky's visit seemed to gradually fade from our lives. But that was on the surface of things. What was rumbling, what was creeping in hidden corners, and what secret pains gnawing at Siti's heart, I couldn't tell. Pride could hide many things, and no one I had ever known had pride the size of a mountain like Siti's. I would have welcomed a violent outburst, a tirade of interrogation, or a severe cold shoulder, but not this nonchalant, there-is-nothing-amiss charade. Siti was too smart for me. I just had to take her as she came, and to take life as it came, hoping against hope that things would revert to normal. If she was punishing me, she had certainly succeeded. I was suffering.

Chapter 34

Pinky's intrusion into Siti's heartland and into her marital home had a severe effect on me. I should have been furious with her for wanting to hurt Siti, but it didn't appear that she had come with that purpose. If she had, she would have poured out to Siti the details of our tumultuous life together, throwing in for good measure the sufferings she had endured as the unwed mother of a four-year-old son. It wasn't a woman scorned who had come but a woman deeply injured and wronged, and she had wanted that part of her to be etched in my memory.

Seven months had passed since Pinky's visit. That was quite enough time for the memory to fade, but it hadn't. Once in a while I would ponder, *How is Pinky coping with her injured heart?* I wished the wind or a breeze would send me a message about her to ease my turmoil. All I got was her image.

Alone in the amorphous night when these images came to me, I shuddered in fear that I would succumb to my secret longing to hold Pinky in my arms. At these moments, I asked myself which woman I truly loved. The answer had always been Siti. Yet, why had Pinky surfaced and again and again in my mind like a bad dream? Either the images of her refused to go away or else I wasn't prepared to let them go. If I were to consult the village shaman, he would say I had been charmed and would instruct me to get a strand of her hair, some of her nail clippings, or a piece of her intimate wear to bury in the earth in order to cure me. But no silly charms were making me feel as I did. It was just me, destined for misery.

In one of these vicarious journeys in the night, while I was making love to Siti, it was Pinky I embraced in secret. When it was all over, a terrible shame came over me. In the morning after, I was doubly affectionate with Siti to atone for my sin of the previous night.

That sinful episode, I discovered later, was a premonition of things to come.

Soon after that, I was visited at the Nusantara Mine by a well-attired Chinese man in a crisp white shirt, starched pants, and a Panama hat. As he was brought into my office, I instantly recognised him as the fifty-year-old Francis, the fastidious English-educated accountant of the late Tan Siew Lim. He had flat straight hair that glistened with pomade, and he wore round horn-rimmed glasses. I remembered him as Lim's trusted aid, the man with impeccable manners more suited to an English establishment than to Lim's mine.

The cheerless demeanour with which Francis presented himself could only mean bad news, I surmised. Cocking his head to one side, he looked at me with sympathetic eyes and then softly announced, "I came to convey the sad news of Lai Peng's passing."

The words stabbed me like a knife. I stared at him like he was the angel of death himself. Francis touched my hand gently and said, "I am sorry, Mr Hamzah, to be the one to bring you this sad news."

"Yes, Francis." That was all I said to him, as my mind was a total blank.

"May I sit?" he asked. I had forgotten he was still standing. Francis was the most proper Chinese man I had ever met – so proper that he made everyone around him seemed coarse.

"Excuse my manners, Francis. Please take a seat." I sauntered back and then sank into my chair. "Pinky is dead, you said?" I asked foolishly. "When? What did she die of? Had she been sick?"

"Two weeks ago. I am sorry, my friend. I wanted to come earlier, but no one could tell me where to find you. So I had to look for your father's house in Kelawei Road. I decided not to send you a telegram – you understand? I had to be very discreet, and here I am. It would be best, I thought, if I saw you in person – and at this mine office. You understand, I am sure, given the circumstances. She spoke of no one but you in her final days. She confided in me, discreetly of course. She trusted me, and you can too, Mr Hamzah."

"And her son?"

"Li is in good hands for now. Mr Hamzah, we need to talk – very discreetly of course. Yes?"

"This place is as private as we could wish for, Francis."

"All right then. What I am going to tell you is—" Francis paused, bent forward, exhaled, wet his lips, and whispered, "Lai Peng took her own life."

"What!"

"Yes, very sad. Very sad indeed. She hadn't been well for quite some time. I am sorry, Mr Hamzah. Very tragic ending, really, to end one's life in such a way and for a beautiful woman at that. She had everything going for her – well, at least that's what I had thought." He lowered his head, removed his glasses, pulled out a handkerchief, and wiped his eyes. "I deeply regret my failure to see Lai Peng's suicidal tendencies."

"You were close to her?" I enquired.

"Yes. Very close. Since Mr Tan passed away, she shunned public life and went into seclusion. I became her only friend and her confidant."

My mind drifted away.

"Do you want to be alone, Mr Hamzah?"

"I'm sorry. Please stay. I want you to tell me everything."

"Yes, certainly, Mr Hamzah." Hesitantly, Francis asked, "May I use your washroom?"

I rang the bell. A staff member entered the room and then took Francis to the restroom. His brief absence made me want to cry out for Pinky.

When Francis returned, I asked him, "Had she been depressed?"

He regarded me with concern. "Mr Hamzah, it's not my place to pry into your private life, but as I said, I was close to her and sort of became her sympathetic ear. If I may say that. She told me about you. When she heard you had gotten married, she was totally devastated. She had hoped when her husband died, you would take her with you. I could understand her hopelessness. She loved you terribly, she confessed to me, and your rejection became very painful and terribly unbearable. She met your wife and your daughter. That was the end of the line for her, as it were. I am sorry to be brazen." Francis pulled out a white envelope from his leather case. "Here, Mr Hamzah, this is for you." I was about to open it, but Francis stopped me. "Please, Mr Hamzah, do not read the contents in my presence. It's very personal." I detected a trace of supressed anger in Francis's voice; after all, his sympathy seemed to be totally with Pinky. In his eyes, I was the villain.

"Yes, of course," I said, placing the envelope in my desk drawer. "Pardon me for asking, Francis. You said to me just now that you had failed to see her suicidal tendencies. But just before she was about to take her life, weren't there any signs at all that she would do it, like words or odd behaviour?"

He shook his head. "Mr Hamzah, you see, a week before she took her own life, she invited me for lunch at the Station Hotel. Over lunch she told me she was making preparations to go somewhere far from this world. The grim irony totally escaped me. Naturally I didn't ask her where she was going. It wasn't my place to ask."

"It wasn't your place, obviously," I said, feeling irritated.

"Yes, indeed."

"One more thing, Francis. Where's Li now?"

"He is in Kuala Lumpur with his grandmother. I believe you'll have all that you need to know in the document I just handed you."

"You know the contents?" I started to get annoyed by his tight manners, as he seemed to know more than he had earlier admitted.

"I know of it, not the actual contents. I've no reason to be privy to them."

"I thought the two of you were close."

"In certain specific matters." Suddenly, he smacked his forehead. "Oh dear, I almost forgot – so engrossed we were." He dug his hand into his briefcase and retrieved a stack of envelopes bundled with a red ribbon. "She wanted me to hand this to you too."

As Francis placed the bundle of envelopes gently on my table, my heart instantly raced up, suspecting what they were.

Francis said nothing about what they were. It was not his place, as it were. But I guessed he knew.

He quickly said, "I must take my leave now, Mr Hamzah. My duty is done. If there's anything I can do to assist you during this period of bereavement, please don't hesitate to ask. I am totally at your disposal. Remember, I am more than just an acquaintance of the late Lai Peng, of the late Tan Siew Lim, and, I trust, of you as well. Your secrets will die with me. I can assure you of that."

"I would like to invite you to lunch, Francis. That's the least I could offer you in the circumstances."

"In the circumstances, Mr Hamzah, lunch for me is the least of your burden. The offer of your hospitality is much appreciated, but I must decline. I should be returning home as soon as possible. A mountain of tasks awaits me in Ipoh. You are at liberty to call me at any time."

"Thank you, Francis. I shall consider your offer." I shook his hand.

All of a sudden, and much to my surprise, he embraced me in a gesture of genuine sympathy. *I might have misjudged him,* I thought.

"I am deeply sorry, Mr Hamzah," he said, and then he politely took his leave with a slight bow of his head.

I couldn't wait for Francis to leave so I could read Pinky's letter. I sent him to his car. Again he said, "I am at your disposal twenty-four hours a day. Call me. Neither rain nor storm could prevent me from being at your service. Before bidding farewell, may I say once again how deeply sorry I am for this very tragic event."

My heart pulsated as I returned to the office and headed straight for the drawer. With feverish hands, I unclasped the ice-blue envelope and opened it.

My dearest Hamzah,

I write neither in tears nor in sadness, for I have none of those things left anymore. I write so that the memory of me will be given the truth it deserves when I am gone. My biggest mistake is my having fallen in love with you. You know, Hamzah, you were my first, and only, love. I have never been with another man before, besides my husband. Believe me. I was brought up in a school run by nuns. A more cloistered, clean, or proper school one couldn't find. If there had been a man in my life then, it was merely in my dreams. And I know that I am your first love too. Isn't that true, Hamzah?

I felt that in my heart when we were together. We are meant for each other, and we were made for each other. Only you, with your baggage and silly conscience, refused to admit and accept it. I was willing to give my all and to lose everything for you. Yet you were not prepared to give up anything. Instead, you fled to your safe haven. That, my dearest, is my greatest tragedy. After seeing your wife and child in that safe haven of yours, I finally knew I had nothing left in this world. For months I tried to cope with it, but I failed. Please do remember me in a good light. That's the least you should do for me. And take good care of our son, Li. He is the living memory of me.

P.S. Herewith is a stack of letters I wrote to you and which you returned to me unread, with the cruel label "Return to sender." Please read them in my memory.

Goodbye, my love.

Your true love,
Pinky

I drew the letter to my lips and inhaled her scent for the last time. Then I carefully put the letter back in the envelope and placed it in my desk drawer.

After locking the door, I sat at my desk and unclasped the stack of envelopes. I opened each letter and read every one of them. Tears streamed down my face until I was blinded.

Time just went by. I got hold of myself and consulted my watch. It was past 6 p.m. and getting dark. I had spent two hours with myself. I opened the door and peered out to find only darkness except for the mining lights. It would be late by the time I reached home. Home? At the thought of that, my stomach churned. *How do I face Siti? How do I answer for myself?* I felt hungry, but dinner was far from my mind. I walked to my car and was not even aware that the guard had wished me good night. I didn't even realise he had opened the car door for me.

Chapter 35

These days I made a habit of travelling to Penang once a month to visit Father, so there was usually no problem with my taking leave of Siti to go to Penang. This time, however, posed a slight problem. It had been barely a week since my last trip.

Father had become ill all of a sudden, I said to Siti. With her usual sharp intuition, she cocked her head and gave a frown while wishing me a safe journey and conveying her well wishes to my father and Aunty Maimunah. If she held any suspicion, she didn't show it.

My journey to Kuala Lumpur was that of a man stepping into the unknown. *How do I, a stranger, tell a boy of hardly five that I am now his father – not the one who died – coming as I am from nowhere, and from a world he knows not?* Part of my charge was to tell Li that his mother was now to be replaced by Aunty Maimunah, who would tell him that there would be no more of the chopsticks and no more of the idols. Instead, there was now a God he could not see. The mosque would now be his place of worship; the Koran, his life's guide. From a Chinese boy, he was going to become a Malay overnight. Aunty Maimunah would make sure of this. What if he refused me? What then? The future of my own blood would then lie in the wilderness. My past would never leave me alone. It would trail me wherever I went. Even after closing my eyes I would see it.

It was the most unhappy sea journey I had ever experienced. The night sky, the black sea, the endless void, the slow drifting of time, all became a misery. I had lied to Siti and would continue to lie. I saw no other choice. Lying would now become me. I would be playing the same old tune about visiting my father, about his being unwell. What if Siti asked to come along? No, that wouldn't be Siti. If she had a whiff of suspicion, she would just keep it under her skin and let me live with it. Her pride wouldn't allow her to confront and expose me.

Aunty Maimunah, Father, and Ariffin tossed about in my head while the ship swayed. Father wouldn't raise a question about the sudden appearance of Li, as it would not make any difference to him who the boy was. Ariffin would gladly welcome a new friend. What about Aunty Maimunah? Well, she would certainly shriek in hysteria to learn that I had had a son out of wedlock. A bastard in the family would be unimaginable to her. How in the world could I have committed this sin, and then caused the mother of this child to die in suicide? To Aunty, such a world existed only in folklore or in old wives' tales.

The sea sloshed, my world rocked uneasily, the ceiling moved in the swinging light, and the cabin finally closed in upon me. When I awoke, it was late morning, with the sun slicing my eyes. There was the crunching sound of anchors. In a sudden jolt, reality came back to me.

It was getting dark when I finally arrived in Kuala Lumpur. My car took me into a narrow lane off Petaling Street. I had to alight because the driver could go no farther amid the crowded tables, chairs, kiosks, carts, sacks, and baskets that the hawkers and traders were preparing for the night. I had never been into the belly of Kuala Lumpur's Chinatown before. I trekked through the clutter amid the confused sound of voices that bellowed like a discordant opera. I seemed to be an oddity in the sea of Chinese. Their faces seemed unwelcoming until I greeted them in their mother tongue. Noticing an old man smoking a cigarette, a vendor of Chinese comic books, sitting alone on a bamboo stool, I approached him to ask for Ah Meng's sundry shop. He raised his head and pointed disinterestedly to the two-storey shophouse across the lane. A loud-coloured board with large Chinese characters led me to my destination.

Apparently, my arrival was expected. A slim woman in her sixties, dressed in an embroidered Malay kebaya and sarong typical of the Straits-born Chinese, her hair in a bun with a gold pin, welcomed me in English with the demeanour of a schoolteacher. "Call me Aunty Meng. Everyone here calls me that," she said warmly. Her smile revealed a composed, self-assured woman with a privileged past. "Is everything all right with you?" she asked me, as if she had already taken into her heart all my thoughts and fears. There was empathy in her eyes, not anger or indictment. At once I was comforted.

"You're a baba?" I asked of her Straits-born appearance.

"Yes, indeed. For four generations. Didn't Lai Peng tell you that? Originally from Malacca, I moved over here to Kuala Lumpur when my late husband took a job in Harrisons and Crosfield.

"You called her Lai Peng?"

She broke into a smile. "I guess she was Pinky to you. I never liked the nickname, but all her friends in school called her that on account of her pinkish cheeks. But she loved it, and it stayed. Poor girl, bless her soul." She became a bit teary. After pulling a small handkerchief from her kebaya lapel, she dabbed her eyes.

"It suited her very well. And it was charming, I must say." I concurred.

"Pinky had always been an enigma. All that was occidental was to her very agreeable, and yet she married a Chinaman, one who was as Chinese as a Chinaman could be. And then she fell in love with you. I never for one moment ever imagined her falling for a Malay – no offence, Mr Hamzah – since she hardly had any Malay friends. But seeing you in person, I can understand why. That's Pinky for you. You said it. Even her name was a charm."

Meng then took my hand in a motherly way. "Come inside," she said. I felt the softness of her palm; it seemed never to have touched labour. She ushered me into the airy open courtyard potted plants and ferns that gave the feeling of calmness and serenity, which was in stark contrast to the noise and clutter of the street outside. Under the low eaves, I was brought to one of the sandalwood chairs in the seating area. It was a modest house but rich with the owner's love of her origin and heritage, with its Chinese old vases, Chinese furniture, and ancestral photographs on the wall. A wooden staircase led to the second floor, which I presumed was where the bedrooms were.

The maid brought in Chinese tea in a Chinese set. Ah Meng settled herself by the marble-top round table, opposite me. She made a survey of my face and looked straight into my eyes with keen curiosity. Then, to my surprise, she gently reached out to me with her hand and said, "I see much sadness in your eyes. Don't carry this burden with you. It's not entirely your fault. Thinking about what you should or shouldn't have done is not going to change anything. You may think you knew Lai Peng, but I think not. When she was young, she envied her schoolmates who came to school in chauffeur-driven cars, who lived in mansions, and whose parents could send them to English boarding schools overseas. Almost all her friends were rich kids. She said to me one day, 'I want to be rich one day, Mama. I don't know how, but I shall.' She was fifteen. I was concerned because there wasn't a hope in the world that a woman could become rich on her own. A woman's place was in the home. At best she could be a doctor, or a teacher like me. She was the prettiest among my four daughters – and was absolutely aware of it. I was afraid to admit to myself that her pretty face would one day bring her unhappiness." She lowered her brows and waited for me to answer, looking like she was conducting a class. I had been listening intently, as if she had been describing to me a person I hadn't met.

"Then on her twentieth birthday, one of her rich friends threw her a birthday party. That's where she met Tan Siew Lim, who was known to that family. Actually, it was Tan Siew Lim who had arranged the party. How and why, I wasn't supposed to know. She was smart in school but foolish in many other ways. I had warned her to be careful. That's all I could do. I knew her too well; she would pursue her goal no matter what I said. Her dream to be rich came true. That's Pinky for you." She gave a weak smile, but a cloud of sadness shadowed her face momentarily. She tried to hide it by lowering her eyes to her tea. She picked up her cup and invited me to join her. After a pause, she continued. "She was happy for a while, as Siew Lim treated her like a diamond. And it was exactly that way – she was a trophy to be shown to the public like a collectors' item. Don't forget, Siew Lim already had a wife. It's not unusual for these traditional Chinese when they become rich to take many wives. In the old days in China, it would be concubines. I said to Lai Peng exactly that. She began to grow bored, feeling that something was missing in her life. Mind you, she had become a full-grown woman who needed more out of life than just being regarded as a possession. She needed love, romance, and passion

281

on top of the money – like in the novels she loved to read. You see, Hamzah, when she met you, it was like a dream come true. I've said enough. Now let's talk about you. What are you going to do, Hamzah?"

"I've come for Li, Aunty."

"I don't mean that. You have a wife and a daughter. Does your wife know about Lai Peng and you?" Again she eyed me with her schoolteacher's gaze.

"I am afraid not, Aunty."

"I shan't ask you for your reason. Maybe it's for the better. Unfortunately, telling the whole truth is a kind of finality, leaving no room for hope for the aggrieved party. How do you plan to hide Li? Pardon me for using the word *hide*. That's what it really boils down to. Isn't that so?"

"I'll take him to my aunt in Penang."

Meng broke into a wry smile. "And what are you going to tell her about the sudden appearance of a five-year-old boy in your life?"

"I'll think of something."

From the schoolteacher, she turned maternal. "Though Lai Peng was my daughter, and I deeply grieved for her, my sympathy is with you. Throughout her life she never looked at consequences, only at the benefits of the moment, believing matters would sort themselves out somehow."

"Don't you think you're being hard on her? Didn't you love her?"

"Of course I did. Why do you ask? Is it because I spoke of her frankly and without reservation? Actually I loved her the most. It's ironic, really. She was the most flawed, yet I loved her dearly. Perhaps it's because I had always felt in my bones that she wouldn't be able to get the happiness she so much craved for." Suddenly the hitherto subdued emotion welled up and her eyes reddened. "Excuse me." Retrieving her handkerchief, she wiped her eyes.

Just then, the maid appeared and interrupted her to say lunch was ready.

"I've prepared lunch. We'll get Li to join us so that you can get to know him."

"One moment, Aunty," I interjected.

"Yes?"

"With everything that has happened, something still lingers in my mind. I have wondered if things could've come out differently."

"What do you mean?"

"I had wanted to marry Pinky, but she avoided the issue all the time. Why didn't she want to marry me?"

"There you are. That's Pinky for you. She wanted the best of both worlds and foolishly believed it could work. Or there might have been the fear of what Siew Lim might do to her, and to you. Maybe, I say maybe, that was her true reason. Who can say?"

"Thank you, Aunty Meng, for being totally honest with me."

Li came down the staircase with the maid. He was dressed in a starched cotton shirt and shorts. On his feet were black leather shoes complete with white socks. His hair was neatly combed, looking like a pageboy.

"I haven't told him who you really are. I just said to him that a very close friend of his mother would be coming to take care of him. He hasn't yet recovered from the loss of his mother. Ah, I forgot to tell you that Li has been living with me for the last three years. That is from the day Siew Lim died – to be exact, from the day you and Lai Peng met for the last time at Siew Lim's funeral. Lai Peng wanted to be alone, so she left Li in my care. You'll find him to be proficient in Malay, since we babas speak Malay. I have also taught him English."

"Did Lai Peng visit him often?"

"Oh yes. Once a month, and they would spend a few days together. She loved him, but she wasn't much of a maternal person."

Bending down to address the boy, Meng said in Malay, "Li, this is Uncle Hamzah, a very close friend of your mother. *Salam* him."

He perked up his head and stared at me, offering both his palms to take mine in the traditional Malay fashion. He appeared nervous and unsure.

At the dinner table he was prim and proper, used his chopsticks adroitly, picked the centre plates only after asking, and drinking from his glass without spilling, all the while not paying any attention to what else was going on. He didn't look at me, not even once, pretending I wasn't there. I felt sort of sorry for him. I wished he would be bouncy, excitable, or even mischievous, because then I could console myself with the thought that he was happy. But that was just a flash of nonsensical expectation. He had just lost his mother, whom he saw only occasionally, and now he was about to lose his grandmother. And suddenly a stranger whom he had seen only briefly at his father's funeral has come to claim him – all that piling up in his five-year-old head in a single day.

"He is very quiet?" I asked Meng.

"Yes. Reticent by nature. He hasn't got a friend, as I don't want him to mix in this neighbourhood. I am glad he is already due for school."

"Is there anything I should know about him – his habits, likes and dislikes, hobbies?"

"Nothing out of the ordinary for a child. He is well behaved. But I think he needs friends of his age. That will cure his reticence. If you win his confidence, you'll win his heart. You'll be surprised how a child can deal with calamity – better than adults can."

When lunch was over, I asked Meng if we could sit near the courtyard, away from the boy.

"Is there something you wish to ask?" Meng asked.

"Yes, Aunty Meng, one final word. You don't have to answer me if you don't want to. Why did she have to take her own life? Why?"

Meng breathed out a heavy sigh. "People take their own lives to punish the living, particularly those closest to them. Perhaps in her case, she wanted to punish you, to make you remember her for always. What better way to ensure such an outcome than to die because of you? The ultimate self-sacrifice, since she couldn't have you." Meng grasped my hand. "Let it go, Hamzah. Don't blame yourself."

"Thank you, Aunty."

"Let me talk to Li to comfort him before he leaves." She called up the boy, who was sitting quietly with the maid, his luggage by his side. Li rose from his chair and obediently walked towards his grandma, his face clouded with the inevitable.

Meng lowered herself to the boy's level so she could look straight into his eyes. "This kind man is going to be your father now. Promise Grandma you will be a good boy and listen to him."

"Yes Grandma. Aren't you coming with us?"

"I have told you that I can't. I am old, and I have to stay here to take care of this shop. But I promise to visit you as often as I can, and you will visit me as often as you are able to. Grandma loves you. Remember that."

"All right, Grandma." The next moment, Li gave his grandmother a tight embrace.

Before we departed, I noticed that Meng's eyes had melted, but there were no tears. She said to me, "I could shed all the tears in me, but they would never wash away the sorrow I feel for him. God knows what is in his mind. I wanted to bring him up, but Lai Peng made me promise to give him to you should anything happen to her. I had no idea then that she was preparing to take her own life." She paused for a few moments to nurse her sorrow. Then, with a trace of tremor in her voice, she said, "Take good care of him or he will be no different from just another orphan in the street."

I said goodbye to Meng with a promise. I took Li by the hand. He followed me obediently. Gazing at his grandmother, he mumbled a soft goodbye. As we passed the threshold, he again turned his head to give her a long goodbye glance. The lament in his face brought me back to the time when I had taken a last glance at Mother at the balcony as I was leaving Mataram House. I wondered what was going in Li's mind at this moment.

*   *   *

Since leaving his grandmother, Li had said almost nothing except to answer me with a yes or a no. It wouldn't have been so hard for me if he were much older. But this was a child who was about to build a new life with me. I felt inept. To be the guardian to a five-year-old was a totally new challenge, a task of immense proportion.

To enliven his spirit for the long journey to Penang, I asked him whether he had ever travelled in a train. He said, "No." Would he like to travel in one? He said, "Yes." I had also noticed something: he had refused to look at me in the eye from the moment we first met at his grandmother's house until now.

And another thing: he had yet to call me Uncle as he had been instructed by his grandmother to do. So I decided to ask him. "Li, you must start calling me Uncle from now on." Without raising his head, he said quite indifferently, "All right."

When we arrived at the Kuala Lumpur Railway Station, Li's face sparkled as he watched the steam locomotive come thundering next to the platform with steam spewing from its giant wheels. Fascinated by the machine, he exclaimed,

"I like trains." It was the first sound of excitement I had heard from him since we met.

"You like trains, do you?" I asked, to capture that enthusiasm.

"Yes, very much." He looked at me and nodded his head.

"Well, you'll travel in one now."

When the train came to a complete stop and the coaches lined up along the platform, Li was already surging forward ahead of me to climb aboard the nearest car. "Our car is right at the back," I said, pointing to the first-class sleeping coaches to the rear. There was a look of disappointment in his face as he noticed that our car was far away from the majestic engine.

After we had settled ourselves into the wood-panelled cabin, the train pulled out of the station. Li sat by the window, enthralled as he watched the buildings give way to tracks and then to trees, until finally it was dark and only his reflection was left in the glass. Drowsiness then overtook him. He turned around, lifted his head up to me, and said, "I am sleepy." That was the first time he'd looked straight into my eyes. I carried him to the upper bunk. Before closing his eyes, he said. "Good night, Uncle." A warm feeling rose in me with a promise of hope.

We arrived at the Kelawei house in Penang under a cloudy sky. My heart was lifted upon seeing the garden that I had resuscitated. It had come to life with exuberance. Father was sitting in his usual chair on the terrace, like an old car in a garage. The odour of Sumatran coffee, which had now become a part of him, made me remember happier times. Perhaps he was thinking of that too. Poor old man, his eyes rising to meet mine and yet seeing nothing. His mind could no longer speak for him.

"Father," I said, "I am Hamzah, your son, and this is Li." I kissed his hand. He looked at me and then at Li with empty eyes, yet I sensed an emotion struggling to break from the invisible wall that separated him from the world. I welled up with pity for his impotence. Li looked at him with the utmost curiosity, tracing his face with innocence, seemingly probing that invisible wall. Suddenly, Li moved closer to the old man to touch his hand as if he had found a new friend – a silent, uncomplicated friend like himself.

Excitement and the clatter of running feet surged across the corridor. In the next moment, Aunty Maimunah loomed large in the doorway, crying with joy upon seeing us. Merriment always preceded her in the first encounter after a long absence. After the initial hugging and kissing, like I had never really grown up, her eyes fell on Li. She said, "This must be the boy." She bent down to embrace the stunned child, showering him with her kisses. "Call me Grandma!" she exclaimed excitedly.

All that crying, excitement, and spontaneity shook the boy at first, but, as if the case with all children, warmth instinctively won him over and he was quickly assuaged.

"Ariffin is at school. He has been looking forward to meeting his new brother." Turning to me, Aunty said, "I've made a big breakfast for you all. Come, come, don't just stand there. Let me carry that." Her eyes were on the biggest of the suitcases. I stopped her.

"Haven't I told you not to carry heavy stuff, Aunty? One of these days you're going to hurt your back." Actually, I was amazed to see her energy, which hadn't seemed to diminish with age.

Once all the excitement had abated, we sat for breakfast. Aunty Maimunah's sambal and steamed rice were like no other when it came to sharpening the appetite. Li, like the rest of us, ate with relish. Suddenly Aunty Maimunah's mood changed. I braced myself for an assault.

"Who is this boy actually, Hamzah, that you've adopted? Your letter didn't say much."

"Can we talk about this later, not in his presence?"

"I am speaking Malay," she said.

"He speaks Malay perfectly."

"What?"

"Yes."

The interrogation ended there for the time being, but I knew that sooner or later I had to face her and tell the truth. When I came to the brink, fear like a demon gripped me. I receded to a corner in a cold sweat. I had never thought that truth could be such an awesome enemy, so I chose the easy way out and let truth remain concealed in some corner somewhere, hoping no one would ever find it.

I told Aunty Maimunah a tale of an unfortunate boy who had been recently orphaned. His father, who was an old friend of mine from my days in Banka, had died three years ago. Then the boy's mother, never having recovered from her extreme grief, finally took her own life, leaving Li in the care of an only grandmother, who was old and infirm. The grandmother had given him to me for adoption, I said. It was all very pragmatic – the way of the Chinese, which is very admirable really, I said. I could only feel honoured by the gesture. How could I refuse such a trust bestowed on me? I also said it was in the Malay heart not to refuse to adopt a child, particularly if the child was given amid circumstances of goodwill. I told Aunty Maimunah, never did it cross my mind that adopting the boy would be a burden. On the contrary, I quickly thought of it as a gift from Allah proffered to me on a silver platter.

It was so poignant, my tale, that Aunty Maimunah blessed me for my act of benevolence and then poured her sympathy on Li. I fell back in relief, but I felt full of shame.

*　　*　　*

I had been away from Tobali – and Siti – for over three weeks. Unexpectedly, a telegram came. It was curt and disturbing, as is the nature of most telegrams.

I said to Li, "Uncle is going away on a short journey across the sea for a while and will be back in a week or two. Grandma Maimunah will take care of you." He just nodded, keeping his head low. "Will you be all right?" I enquired, feeling utterly foolish. What could he say? Again he nodded, not lifting his head. I had expected of him to be unhappy or to ask if he could come as well. There was none of that at all. I had wished he would ask me to take him along, although I knew that my doing so would be impossible at the moment. I would have been overjoyed by the idea that he wanted to be with me. In the few days that had passed since I took him, our relationship had been no more than perfunctory, like I was an avuncular guardian to an orphan. Meng's last words to me had been precisely about that: win his confidence to win his heart. Why was he so indifferent towards me? He couldn't possibly have the knowledge that I was the cause of his mother's death. Or could he? Nurturing his trust as Meng had suggested was more daunting than I had thought. Yet he was at ease with Aunty Maimunah. And with Ariffin, there seemed to be no barrier.

Seeing them playing together made me envious. Even with Father there was a strange kind of bonding.

At the door of the house, with the car waiting for me, it was not Li who cried but Aunty Maimunah, who considered my departure too premature for Li, just when the boy was about to settle down in his new home. "That poor boy is just beginning to build up his hope," she said through her tears. "Why don't you take him with you?"

"He has found as great a grandmother as a child could," I said, sidestepping her query.

"But he needs a father," she said, pressing on.

"Don't I know that, Aunty?" I said.

How lucky I was to have Aunty Maimunah, I thought. She was not one who did things in little morsels. With her, everything had to be magnified, and not least her love. Li could not be in better hands. It was as if God had proffered the gift of guardianship of this child to her, not to me.

Chapter 36

Even from a distance I could discern the grave expression on Mois's face when he came to fetch me at the Muntok jetty. I waved, but he didn't wave back. I thought he didn't see me. I waved again, but still he didn't return it. As I came closer, it was indeed a grave Mois that I noticed. I offered my hand, but he deliberately ignored it. "What's wrong, Mois?" I asked. He didn't reply or even look at me. Obviously something was upsetting him. That something was me. Since patience wasn't one of his endearing qualities, he couldn't wait to let his anger out, which fact accounted for his fetching me at the port himself. While we were walking towards his car, I asked again. "Tell me Mois, what is going on?" Still he said nothing. But his face was tight and reddening, as if about to burst. As we entered the car, I persisted. "You seem very angry with me. Are you, Mois?" I asked, puzzled.

"If I didn't care that I owe you a debt of gratitude for giving me a job at your mine, I—" The words got stuck in his throat. "I would kill you."

"Mois! What are you saying?"

Several seconds of excruciating silence passed, leaving me befuddled.

Then, almost inaudibly, Mois said, "Siti is gone."

"What do you mean, gone?" I exclaimed.

"Gone, don't you understand? Gone! She and Indriani are gone – disappeared. We don't know where."

"What? What the hell are you talking about?" I howled as fear gripped me and blood rushed out of my head.

Rearing his head up like a cobra, he hissed at me. "Who are you really, Hamzah? You landed on our shores from nowhere with a strange Englishman, and then you disappeared only to return and lavish us with your charity. Then you caused the death of my father, and now this with my sister and her child. Your offspring has fled. Who are you really, Hamzah? If I were to believe in spirits and demons, I would say you are Satan."

The fabric of our friendship and trust, which had been woven throughout the years, was now torn to bits by his venomous words. So stunned I was, I felt instantly sick. But I felt no anger, because all that he had said was true. Still, I was hurt. The words were all the more painful since they had come from Mois, who not only stabbed me but also twisted the knife.

"What can I say? I cannot deny what you have said. I have left a trail of tragedies wherever I've been, for whomever I came close to. I *am* cursed, Mois. Yes, it is true. Now tell me, what has happened to Siti and Indriani?"

Mois continued with his silence, his eyes on the car windscreen. He was driving rather slower than his usual speed, as if in no hurry to arrive.

"Where have Siti and Indriani gone to? No matter what I have done, we are talking about my wife and my child, Mois," I pleaded.

Mois didn't respond to me. He was all desolation, distant and icy. There was no relenting of his anger.

We continued to ride in silence for what seemed forever until I couldn't take it any longer. I cried out in desperation, "For God's sake, Mois, please say something. Do anything you wish to me, kill me, but don't blackball me like this. Tell me what happened? Please, Mois, I beg you," I implored, to the point of breaking into tears.

Seeing me in that state, he burst out, "A week after you left, Siti began to act in an odd manner, refusing to eat with us, sitting in prayer and supplication for long hours, and erupting in tears. She began to dote on Indriani beyond the normal pampering, whispering words and singing into her ears. Most worrying was her melancholy and the loss of all desire for everything. When we asked her what was wrong, she just shook her head and said, 'Nothing.' I thought your absence was the cause of this strange behaviour. But Mother, thinking that such inexplicable behaviour could only be the work of people who wished Siti harm, so Mother had wanted to consult the village shaman. I stopped her. I don't care for such nonsense." Mois dug into his duffel bag and retrieved a white envelope, passing it to me without a glance. "Read it, and tell me what it means." His voice was just a shade away from rancour.

To my surprise, the letter was addressed not to me but to Rahimah.

Dearest Mother,

Forgive me, dearest Mother, if I act out of the norm for a filial daughter. I am doing this for my own peace of mind. I have always suspected that my husband could never love me, but I was a fool not to have heeded my own instincts. His heart has always been somewhere else. But don't be mistaken – he has not cheated on me. It's just that he can't free himself from his past. Please do not blame him. It happened before he married me. I cannot live in this town anymore. I cannot take the shame and humiliation – not after the biggest wedding Banka had ever seen. I am taking Indriani with me – my only hope and salvation. Hamzah has been kind to create a trust fund for her – for that I thank him – so Indriani's future is secured. So is mine, as he has taken care of that too. So don't worry. I know what I am doing. We are safe. Give me your blessings, Mother. I shall write to you from time to time. Convey my love to Abang Mois. Please forgive me.

Never doubt my love for you and for Abang Mois.

Your loving daughter,
Siti

I folded the letter and placed it carefully back inside the envelope – with delicateness, as if it had a soul. My mind whirled and twirled, sorting out the many possibilities that could happen to me in this latest ordeal of mine. I was silent, and so was Mois. The quietude was a respite, the calm before the storm. I thought Mois felt it too. And for the first time since we had gotten into the car, he turned towards me. I was crying.

Maybe he had turned to me because I had broken down, or maybe he thought he had been too harsh on me. Or perhaps he had been nudged by his soft side. He called my name. "Brother Hamzah."

"Yes?"

"We shall talk later."

"All right," I said softly.

Again came a long, unbearable silence as the car plunged into the night. Then, when I felt the moment was right, I said to Mois, "I would appreciate it if you would make a slight detour to the mine before we go home. Will you, Mois? Please?" In my hopeless state, I stooped to begging in order to make myself heard.

"All right," he replied, slight warmth returning to his voice.

When we arrived at the mine, I asked Mois to run the engine, as I would not take long. I doubted whether he knew what I was up to. I unlocked my office and went straight to my desk. As I had suspected, the drawer was unlocked and empty. Pinky's last letter, and the stack of envelopes containing all the unread letters she had written to me earlier, were all gone.

I cursed myself for being careless. I recalled that I had left Pinky's letter and the envelopes in the desk drawer, but in that moment of distress I had forgotten to lock it. It wasn't in the nature of Siti to pry into my private things. She was too dignified for that. She must have found the damaging letters by way of an odd chance during one of her occasional visits to my office. This fateful visit might have been prompted by her missing me. And as my rotten fate would want it, my desk drawer could have been slightly ajar, revealing its content.

Chapter 37

That Thursday of November 1961 was the loneliest day of my life. I awoke to an empty house and greeted by an empty morning of an empty future. The dent in the bed beside me, the stray fluffs of Siti's hair, her leftover scent, the remains of little things, and their ghosts, I grasped them all in desperation, as if they were her. When I heard the sound of footsteps and the clinking of plates outside, I quickly rose and opened the bedroom door, thinking she had returned. My heart sank like a stone when I beheld the face of Piah, the old maid – the only living thing left in the house.

It was a dark day that Thursday, the day when my incomplete life in Tobali ended. If there were a place on earth that was like paradise for me, I had always imagined it to be Tobali, a place of my winter days, a place where when the inevitable came I would like to be buried. It was sad, I thought, when one was unable to choose one's place to die, sadder than not having a choice of a place to live. In a few moments, it would be decided if I would still be welcome in Tobali, and welcome to die here too. If not, then I would have to live a life alone without friends. Already I had no family. I would be consigned to die in a place where I would be buried with indignity and irreverence. I felt it already in my veins, that feeling of not being wanted anymore, as I walked the familiar path to Rahimah's house, a path I had so often walked hand in hand with Siti. Our footsteps had carved the stones into time like relics, revered by the little denizens of the soil.

Rahimah's house was now like a stranger to me. An air of unfriendliness bore upon me as I stepped across its threshold. All was quiet. No greetings. No calling of my name. None of that usual familiar cry of joy upon seeing me. Everything seemed to withdraw into the dark, shunning me. It was quiet repulsion that awaited me.

Rahimah was already sitting on the mat. Her eyes were unwilling, so they never met mine. Her face was drawn away as if I were an object of distaste. She was evidently overwhelmed with sadness, undeniable sadness, and maybe disgust too. She gave me no greeting. Mois stood up to offer his hand, a touch of regard for me still remaining.

"Please sit down, brother," he said, offering a place on the mat. Light refreshments and coffee were laid out. Mois poured a cup for me and invited me to eat.

"Did you have a good rest last night after such a long journey?" he asked. I assumed there was no joy in those words, that they were just a courtesy.

"A bit," I said politely. The forced politeness was beginning to feel embarrassing. After all, I thought, I was still family.

Nothing came out of Rahimah's mouth, her eyes still refusing to indulge me, her face tight under the strain of repressed emotion. What that emotion was, I could only guess: anger.

How much do Rahimah and Mois know beyond what was revealed in Siti's letter? I wondered. *Should I spill out my guts or let them reveal what they know?* I opted not to be the first to open up, so Mois was forced to do so.

"Brother Hamzah, if what I am going to say ends up hurting you, please forgive me. I love you as I love my own brother, and I will always be indebted to you for what you have done for me. The people of Tobali, too, are indebted to you for what you have done for them. But in your own interest, after what has happened, it is no longer wise for you to live in Tobali. The elders have conveyed this to us. I shall say nothing here of the reasons behind this decision, as you already know them. I am sorry, brother, but that is the purpose of this meeting. It is most regrettable that I am the one to convey this to you." He breathed deeply to pause. As if offering a concession, he added, "But you are free to live elsewhere in Banka. As for the mine, we have no right whatsoever to tell you what to do with it. As for me, I shall no longer want to work there. I cannot, not after this pronouncement made upon you, of which I am a party."

Rahimah sat frozen while her son delivered this black verdict. Now her hand moved to draw her scarf to her wet eyes. Were the tears for me? No. They could only be for her daughter.

No matter how cold that indictment was of me, I had absolutely no defence. I had driven my innocent young wife and child away.

I turned my gaze to Rahimah. "Mother," I said softly. Still she did not turn her face towards me. "Mother," I said again. I tried to hold her hand, but she pulled it away. Her eyes cast about the floor lifelessly. "When I married Siti, you became my mother – and you, Mois, my brother. That makes the pain I have caused to you both all the more profound, all the more unforgivable. I cannot begin to imagine how hurt you are to lose your daughter and granddaughter, all on account of me. No amount of punishment meted out to me could heal the wounds. So my apologies, regrets, and sadness have little value. I've told Mois, and I tell you too, Mother, that my life is not my own, my destiny is not for me to decide, and my future is one big empty pit of darkness I am unable to see. So this is what I have decided." I rose from the floor, went to the cupboard, picked up the Koran, and regained my seat on the floor. Rahimah and Mois watched in puzzlement. Placing my right hand on the Holy Book, I said, "On this Holy Koran I swear in the name of Allah the Almighty that I shall, from today on, dedicate my entire life in search of Siti and Indriani. I shall not rest until they are found or until there is no more life in me."

I gazed straight into Rahimah's eyes and continued. "My father swore upon the Holy Book, but he betrayed his own vow, for which transgression he is now paying dearly. So I know the gravity of this solemn vow, and I know that I shall pay for it if I too fail to honour it. Should I fail to find them because they don't wish to be found, then that would be my just punishment, and I shall die with it."

I took Rahimah's hand, which she finally released as the emotions she had suppressed found their way out. She broke into tears and finally allowed me to embrace her. But still no words could come out of her mouth. "Forgive me, Mother," I said. She nodded. That tiny gesture produced in me an enormous comfort. I couldn't ask for more.

Then I turned to Mois. "To you, Mois, my brother, I bequeath the entire amount of stock I own in Nusantara Mine. I have no need for the mine anymore. My wish is for the shares to be divided equally among you, Mother, Siti, and Indriani. The Nusantara Mine must continue to operate. It's the promise I made to the landowners. I know the mine will be in good hands under you, Mois. You're capable, you're honest, and you have the trust of the landowners. Your father wanted you to be the chief of Tobali. This is your way of honouring that wish."

Rahimah received this offer of mine with virtually no expression, perhaps unable to absorb or comprehend what it really meant. Or perhaps worldly things had little significance to her, particularly at this moment, when grief took precedence over everything else.

"Where will you go, brother?" Mois asked.

"I don't really know."

"And where do you start to look for them?"

"For that, too, I really have no idea."

"Please continue to come to the house and see us."

"Do you want me to?"

"Yes, we do. And thank you, brother Hamzah."

"For what?"

"For the mine. I accept your offer, not for the money but because I want to carry out your wish for the sake of the landowners."

"You owe me nothing, Mois, while I owe you all a mountain of debts. The mine is but a tiny drop in the ocean of repayment."

"You're a good man, brother. I truly am sorry."

"Thank you. Goodbye, Mois. Goodbye, Mother."

Chapter 38

Dear Journal,

I returned to my little palace on the beach, which is where it all began. As I sat at the little verandah, the late evening sky blanketed my sadness. I threw a long, pleading gaze into the darkening sea. I cried out for Siti. There was no answer, only the incessant splashing of the waves. The silence was depressing. I was alone in a hollow world of my own. Tobali was now neither my home nor my grave. I looked back into the past, and it was Mataram House that came to me. By taking away Siti and Indriani from me, fate had finally succeeded in her quest for revenge. And what a fitting revenge it was in the end, wrenching from me my last precious possessions after having taken everything else along the path of my ill-omened life. The road ahead of me now is so dark that I can't even see my toes. My own free will no longer has any role in this journey. Let my accursed fate lead me to my destination.

I am only thirty-three, too young to die, yet too old to live.

I neither have the desire nor the will to write anymore. This journal is closed.

Hamzah
20 December 1961
Tobali

Part 2

The Journal and Sophia

MALAYSIA, 1987

Chapter 39

The city lights of Kuala Lumpur were gazing upon me in the starless night. I was wondering why I was talking to myself on the twelfth-floor balcony of my apartment in a wooded area just outside the city limits. I lived alone in one of the Impian apartments that overlooked a golf course, a kind of little forest enclave away from the city traffic, noise, and mugginess; the steam of hot air from the emerging skyscrapers; and the ubiquitous building cranes of progress that now defined modern Kuala Lumpur. I had been besieged by this inscrutable journal, which I had recently discovered. It was as if a bug had gotten under my skin and was creeping into my bloodstream. For the life of me, I couldn't get rid of it. If I weren't a scientist, I would begin to believe that a spirit had possessed me.

I have been an anthropologist since I had earned my doctorate degree more than two years ago. Driven by my love for out-of-the-ordinary cultures, I had visited odd worlds to study customs, faiths, and practices that time had forgotten – places where strange happenings needed no explanations. I wallowed in these fields with ease. I was by nature not superstitious. In my encounter with strange cultures, I reminded myself always of my role as an observer, not as a believer.

Yet, oddly enough, in this particular instance my resolve had failed me when I accidentally found this journal in the Malay faculty archives of the university where I was a lecturer. I couldn't stop myself from thinking that this journal had travelled an intricate journey for a considerable amount of time in order to reach me. I hadn't been looking for it. It had come to me like we had a rendezvous. Buried among old texts, it seemed to be waiting for me to release it from its solitude. When my eye caught it, I felt that it caught me too. Its blood-coloured velvet coat and hand-scripted title appeared strangely out of place amid the shelves of decrepit papers and documents. When I drew it out of the shelf, a tiny storm of dust flared from it, obviously having been in a state of neglect for years. I unravelled the four side ribbons securing it. When I unclasped the hard cover trimmed in velvet, I was amazed to discover a beautiful work of art, a handwritten script on old manuscript paper, a product of an old felt pen of a lost time.

Though the leaves were, in places, discoloured with age, the script remained immaculate, as though written by an expert scribe. There was not a single mistake in the calligraphy. I thought, *How can such be the case with a handwritten manuscript?* There were bound to be mistakes, unless, of course, the calligrapher had performed the incredible task of rewriting each page whereupon a mistake had occurred. The length to which the author had gone in this regard was evidenced by the complete absence of even a tiny blob of ink – an ever-present risk when writing with a felt-tip pen. Why anyone would go to such a distance for this inconsequential task baffled me, unless the author had meant to create a work of art. But even that did not fully explain the immaculate script.

Another question I had was, how did this journal happen to be stored in the archives of the Malay-language faculty of the University of Malaya?

I took the journal with me. Suddenly I realised it was already dark outside. At the entrance to the faculty building, a guard was waiting for me to leave.

"Working late, Miss Sophia?" the old Malay guard asked, his baton swinging in his hand. He was rather old and wiry. Even in his uniform and with his baton, I wondered whether he could really protect the university.

"Late?" I quipped, giving him a smile.

"Very late, and it's not smart for a young lady to be about alone at this late hour in this lonely spot."

I looked at my watch. "Goodness me, it *is* late. Thank you, Pak Mat, for waiting."

The kind old guard walked me to my car. The Malay faculty area was located in an isolated building in the tree-covered part of the sprawling campus, away from the main library, the Union House, and the hostels, so in the evenings the building was quiet and deserted.

At eight o'clock the next morning, I was at the office of Professor Zain, the dean of the Malay faculty. His secretary informed me that he had a lecture at eight thirty and couldn't say whether he would come into the office at all. I decided to wait, the manuscript in my briefcase. Minutes later, the dean strutted in wearing the trademark bow tie. Like a rhetorical pedant he was. His white curly hair dropped to his neck to prop up his intellectualness. A short man he was. *He must blow a pompous air to make up for his lack of height,* I thought. He wasn't that unpleasant, though, but I did wish he would trim his hair and eyebrows. If he did so, then there would still be hope that I would like him.

He entered the room, his hair flapping like a French legionnaire's cap. I quickly jumped out of my chair.

"May I see you, Dr Zain?"

"Can't remember we have an appointment." He didn't even drop an eye on me.

"We don't. Just a few minutes, Dr Zain. Something important," I insisted.

"I've a lecture in a few minutes." He looked at his watch. "What's so important that it can't wait?"

I followed him into his office, which looked like a part of a book godown. His secretary, I was told, was not to touch anything, as that would make him lose his sense of direction through the rubble.

"Ten minutes," I said.

"Five," he replied.

"Five it is." While still standing, I pulled the manuscript from my case and placed it on his table. "Have you seen this, Professor?"

"No. Can't remember that I have. What is it?" His eyes narrowed down to inspect the blood-red document.

"I found this in the archives. It is handwritten in the most exquisite form – a journal of sorts."

"Oh, that. So what about it?" He gave me a cursory glance.

"How did it come to be here?"

"Some eccentric Englishman donated it."

"Donated by an Englishman? When?"

"Don't know. Not during my time." He consulted his watch and crimped his brow. "Look, why don't you ask my secretary? I've got to go."

"Can I see you later?"

"Ask my secretary." Briskly he walked away, leaving me in the room hanging by my nerves.

I got to see Professor Zain again two weeks later. The cocky little man had refused to see me prior to that on account of the manuscript's being too mundane for him to give it his time. Only when I threatened to resign did he relent to my request.

Our second meeting about the manuscript took place very late in the afternoon. In fairness to him, he did seem to be a pretty busy man, judging by the size of his disarray. Books were piled up on his floor, and papers and files lay about in a mad rush for attention, presenting the image that Dr Zain was about to move office. He himself was a mirror image of his room, seemingly having just awakened, with his ill-fitting shirt carelessly tucked into his equally ill-tailored trousers. The old-fashioned bow tie was his only saving grace, giving him a semblance of order.

"What's so important about this thing that you're prepared to throw away your job?" His gaze was sharp under his bushy eyebrows.

"Tell me, Dr Zain, who's this Englishman who donated it, and why did he donate it?"

"Let me see. … Now what's his name? Ah yes, Dilby. That's it, Dilby, an old Englishman left behind by the British who had a penchant for Malay culture. Why are you so worked up about this anyway?"

"I want to find out more about it, to study it."

"Study it?" He laughed. "Whatever for? Don't you have better things to do? There's not a thread of academic value to that, whatever it is." He sneered.

"Have you read it, Dr Zain?"

"Glanced through it some time ago. Some balderdash about a curse."

"Exactly. It's that balderdash curse, as you put it, that has fired my curiosity. I am going to look into it. I am thinking of applying for sabbatical leave." I looked straight into his eyes.

"You're not serious? What academic benefit could the university get from this?" He retracted in his seat, his finger stabbing derisively at the document.

"Curses are a load of rubbish to you, Dr Zain? Being the head of the Malay faculty, you shouldn't be saying that. The concept of curses is very much in the Malay psyche, in the Malay social dynamics and belief system. Plus, this phenomenon exists not only among the Malays but also in other, older cultures," I affirmed, feeling quite peeved.

"Sophia, I wouldn't waste my time on *superstitions* if I were you. There are many books on this already. What more could you add? The subject has been thrashed to death."

Professor Zain's face tightened. I reminded myself that I was talking to the dean of the faculty and that I was just an assistant lecturer, barely two years at that. But since I had come this far, I might as well plod on. "I beg your pardon, Professor. I am an anthropologist, and I *do* feel passionately about superstitions, as much as a doctor feels about diseases."

He raised his eyes. "I'll have to consider the merit of your request. But for the moment, I think that this thing has no merit."

I let that comment pass. My sabbatical leave depended on it. As I walked out of his office, I wondered how I would react if he ended up denying my leave. I had an uneasy feeling that my career might suffer an early demise. With or without my sabbatical leave, I was going to pursue this document. My mind was made up.

The next day, I dug into the department's records and found no trace of the whereabouts of Dilby. I made enquiries among the faculty members, but no one had even heard of him. He was quite a hard man to find, this Englishman, a member of a lost tribe of the former British Empire. There were not many of his kind still living in Malaysia. Their reasons for staying were rather simple: an enduring love affair with the Malay culture, or a love affair with one of its women.

My best bet to locate the members of this lost tribe would be to delve into the records of the British High Commission, the British Council, and the clubs – the Selangor Club, the Lake Club, and the Selangor Golf Club, the once favourite haunts of the British. Once I did so, I turned up with nothing. Their records were either skimpy or entirely absent. A week after I'd finished perusing those records, I received a call from the British High Commission's cultural attaché, who suggested that I try the former Malayan Civil Service records – Dilby could have been a member of the former colonial civil service.

There his name was in the National Archives of Malaysia. His last known address was in the Cameron Highlands. There was also a cross reference on him: he was a member of the Kuala Lumpur Theatre Club. A thespian of sorts, he directed and acted in plays, including *A Midsummer Night's Dream*, which were performed at the Lake Gardens in the 1950s. He had also written a book on Malay architecture. It was entitled *A House without Nails*. Unfortunately, there wasn't a copy available anywhere.

When I got to Cameron Highlands, I found that the old Briton called Dilby was as odd as a coconut tree among tea groves. At the end of a winding path, atop a hillock, was Dilby's house, at the fringe of a tea plantation, as pointed out by my guide.

It had been many years, when I was a child, since I had seen a scarecrow. And before me was one now – in a T-shirt and a sarong, looking as tall as a nut tree with the forward bend of age. Its high, bony nose was crowned by an elongated bald head. Its discernibly Caucasian shadow cut into the sun. I guessed at once that it must be Dilby.

"Mr Dilby?" I hailed.

"Who's calling?" he replied without turning around, his attention glued to his task.

"My name is Sophia." I said loudly. He gave no response.

As I came closer, he swung his head and said, "You came just in time." He plucked a strawberry and offered it to me. "Try one. Tell me what you think."

"It's good," I complimented. I had never really gotten used to strawberries, no matter how delectable they were. But it would be ungracious of me not to humour him, considering that I was about to solicit a favour.

"Pick up a basket and help me harvest. I always have to do this all alone. *She* wouldn't help me." I wondered who the she was. He addressed me with the familiarity of an old friend.

"You grow them all?"

"Oh yes. Where we stand, we're four thousand feet above sea level, you know. Look over there," he said, pointing to the horizon. "That's the Straits of Malacca."

I couldn't see the point in his mentioning the Straits of Malacca, but I nodded in agreement anyway.

I endured a good thirty minutes of plucking the strawberries. Dilby jauntily conversed with me about strawberries, the destruction of the rainforest, and strawberries again. He did most of the talking. I couldn't get a word through to introduce myself. And not once did he ask me why I had come. His age could account for this oddity, I thought. I guessed he must be quite old. *How old?* I wondered. I concluded that he must be in his late eighties, or nineties even. His hollow cheeks, hairless head, and skeletal structure easily confirmed that. I played along, allowing his talking to lead me where he wanted me to be. Hopefully, I prayed, the non-stop talking would exhaust itself.

Just as I was about to bravely venture to put a stop to his rambling and announce my purpose in coming, he said, "What's your name again?"

"Sophia, Mr Dilby."

"Ah yes, Sophia. How do you spell that, with a *ph* or an *f*?"

"With a *ph*."

"That's Greek, you know that? It means 'wisdom'."

"I didn't know that, Mr Dilby. Sophia is quite a common Malay name."

"Well, common to the English, Germans too, and particularly popular with the French. It's a beautiful name. There's also a Saint Sophia – you know that, I am sure. Now that our work is done, do you care for tea? You must have tea when you're here, but my tea is not from here, you know."

Somehow, I felt that the old goat had used me as free labour.

"Come over here." He took my hand like I was a child and brought me to a spot under a big tree with a garden table and some chairs, the tea plantation sprawling carpet-like in the undulating valley below.

"The view is magnificent, don't you agree? Remind me. Oh, never mind. You wait here. Feast yourself on what's left of what was once primeval jungle. That was a long time ago. The British came and removed the forests to make way for tea. Merdeka came, and things got bigger and bigger. Ah well, at least you're master of your own destiny. Better you mess it up than we do it for you. Now where were we? Ah yes, tea."

"Tea after the forest isn't so bad," I said, bantering with him. "In some countries it's utter baldness and desolation."

"What?" He sauntered into the house, ignoring what I had said.

I looked around and took stock of the surroundings. The house was quite large, its architecture Malay. The wood seemed aged and weathered. I presumed, judging by the period structure, that the house must have been put together from pieces of old Malay houses to become what it was now – a piece of remarkable antiquity. *How I wish that we Malaysians had the same passion for our own heritage,* I lamented to myself. But the garden with its flower beds was rather English. *A little England for a stranded Englishman like him,* I thought. The weather was pleasantly cool, but the breeze was temperamental, once in a while blowing my hair into my face.

Dilby came out carrying a tray. I quickly jumped to his aid, only to be brushed aside. There was no sign yet of his wife, whom I believe was the *she* he referred to several times in our conversation. Nor was there anyone else. He poured the tea into the cups with deliberate care, and graciously picked up one for me.

"Darjeeling, special reserve – very hard to get," he said with pride.

"A bit of the old empire, I suppose, Mr Dilby?" I quipped.

"What? The empire, you say? Don't care for it, really. Darjeeling tea is not Indian, you know. The leaves originated in China, which gives them the dark colour of oolong. Sugar?"

"That's something new I learned today. ... Ah yes, three please."

"Can't have that luxury anymore, you know." He did not take any sugar for himself.

"Still enjoying the old times, Mr Dilby?"

"Yes, yes. Tea in the afternoon, port in the evening, and a good book by the fireplace. There's no fireplace here though. I wish I had made one. It can be quite chilly at night, you know, for an old man like me, especially around December. When you're old like me, weather is the enemy."

Dilby sat back elegantly cross-legged, tea in hand. I couldn't help but admire his face. Though his cheeks had hallowed to the bones, the dominating feature, his cheekbones, remained quietly refined. The indelible Englishness in him, despite the sarong, evoked in me a kind sympathy. I thought that he must still miss his old country. Alone, with scarcely any friends of his kind left, it was too late for him to look back. I was about to ask him whether he missed England, but then I changed my mind, lest I rekindle in him long-lost sentiments which he might prefer not to discuss.

"Now, Sophia, why do you come looking for me? Rarely do I have visitors nowadays. In a year I hardly get one. All my contemporaries except one have died. Fletcher is in Kelantan and doesn't travel. Neither do I. Occasionally I get a letter from him, telling me about the flood. We're in the war—"

"Mr Dilby," I said, cutting him short before he could amble towards the war, "I am an assistant lecturer at the University of Malaya, a graduate in anthropology."

"Anthropology, eh? That's impressive." He studied me with liquid grey eyes and then turned away from me, carrying his mind with him.

There was a pause.

"Go on, I am listening," he urged, his eyes looking into the valley.

"I found this beautifully handwritten manuscript in the archives of the University of Malaya. I was told you had knowledge of it."

Suddenly this relic of the British Empire turned his attention to me.

"Very rightly so. Acquired it at a Sotheby auction in Jakarta. It's of no antique value though. Gave it to Professor Shamsul, an old friend, who was interested in it."

"Who's Professor Shamsul?"

"He was then the head of Malay studies at the university. I believe he is now a fellow at the School of Oriental Studies in Oxford."

"Mr Dilby, do you know of the manuscript's contents and origin?"

"Not precisely. You see, the document was not a piece offered by itself in the auction. It came as part of batch of antiques that was put to the hammer."

"Do you have knowledge of its contents, Mr Dilby?" I insisted.

"My dear girl, I too am proficient in Malay – meaning that I read, write, and speak it – and that's rather rare. The Englishman has always thought it unnecessary to learn other peoples' tongues. You see, in spite of the Norman Conquest, the English have remained thoroughly English.

"My good fortune, Mr Dilby. Then you *have* read the contents?"

"Yes, indeed. You don't let go of something you have bought at a Sotheby auction without examining its value. Are you hungry?"

"Not really."

"Oh, come on, let's have some sandwiches. *She* makes nice little cucumber sandwiches, and we'll have a fresh pot of this marvellous tea. Tea is to be savoured like fine wine. Don't you agree?"

Before I could say another word, he was already up and walking away towards the house. Half an hour later, he returned.

"Sandwiches coming up. It's not often that I get company, you know." Then he hummed to himself, "Tum, tum, tum, tidum."

"I have heard that tune before. An Irish drinking song, right?" I looked at my watch. It was almost five o'clock. The sun was receding, and it was getting a bit dark. Dilby placed the tray of sandwiches and tea on the table, serving me proficiently as if he had previously been a waiter.

I was getting quite impatient by his dilly-dallying. Sandwiches were not foremost in my mind.

"Mr Dilby, about the—"

"Try this. You must."

He offered me a plate. I took a bite of the sandwich. It was delicious. I knew that it took skill to make these English thin-sliced cucumber sandwiches. The one I was eating was superb.

"Delightful, isn't it?" he said.

"Yes, Mr Dilby, indeed. Mr Dilby, what do you think of the manuscript?"

"Nothing. Nothing at all. But what came with it was priceless."

"My goodness, what was it?"

"Antiques. Another sandwich?"

I took another to please him.

"What about the curse? Do you believe it?"

"The curse? What curse?"

"The curse in the story. Don't you recall?"

"Oh yes, of course, the curse. Dastardly awful. It made Lord Carnarvon utterly sick. He was later undone by it too. Imagine, killed by a single mosquito."

"The curse of Tutankhamen," I said, interrupting him. "Do you believe it?"

"Not really. It's in the mind … or just imagination run wild."

"What about the antiques, Mr Dilby?"

"What? What antiques? In the tomb?"

"Not the tomb of Tutankhamen. The antiques you said you bought."

"Come along." He ambled stoopingly into the house.

I walked beside him, I succumbed to my earlier temptation to ask him about his mother country. "Do you ever miss England, Mr Dilby?"

He stopped short and turned towards me. "Do I miss what?"

"England."

"What about England?"

"Do you miss it?"

"Well, my dear, when you come to be my age, long-forgotten places come back to you and you glide into foolish sentimentality. Yes, I do miss England, but I have no desire at all to return. I'd be lost there. All my friends are quite dead, I am sure."

"What do you miss most?" I asked, searching his eyes for any sign of regret.

"It's the winter, that grey, stodgy London winter – though it will not do me any good now, at my age."

We walked through the living room, which opened into a larger inner chamber separated from the front of the house by a long corridor. Everything that I passed as I walked by was old. The floor creaked and squeaked. The air felt damp with age. We finally got to the heart of the house, which resembled a little museum, and Dilby ushered me to three long glass-cased tables that were suffused with the musty smell of time. The four sides of the chamber were not wooden walls but were books from floor to ceiling, giving the ambiance of a veritable library.

"My, what a great collection of books," I exclaimed with amazement.

"When you are alone away from civilisation, books are your companion." Pointing to the centre of the room, he announced, "Here you are, my dear, the answer to your curiosity."

In the glass cases was the largest collection of krises that I had ever seen, each one lying on its side and coded. A more magnificent exhibit of exquisite Malay weapons I had not seen.

"The kris is the most seductive weapon I have ever known. It is as awesome as a work of art as it is intimidating as a weapon – and it is shrouded in mystery. That is why I am enthralled by it," Dilby said, his eyes gleaming with devotion.

"You're absolutely right, Mr Dilby. I am totally seduced. It's incredible, your collection." My eyes affixed on the array of hundreds of krises – easily the biggest collection in a single display in the country.

"It cost me a fortune, you know. There was another collector – a Dutchman – at the auction. He had originally no intention of acquiring them, having viewed them in the catalogue alone. He was more into paintings until he sighted these. Instantly he fell in love with them. I won the auction only because his wife had stopped him from outbidding me, seeing how depressed I was getting."

"Do you remember, exactly, when the auction took place – the date, I mean? And who was the original owner?"

"Oh, many years ago."

"The exact date, Mr Dilby. Have you got the details?"

"My dear girl, do you need to be that precise?"

"It's important," I insisted. "Please?" I looked at him pleadingly.

"You're quite taken by it, aren't you?" I noticed a paternal glint in his eyes. "I'll have to rummage through my records."

"Thank you, Mr Dilby. Much obliged." Alone to myself, I feasted my eyes on the show of art. Dilby had uncustomarily unsheathed the collection of krises, the scabbards and blades lying side by side. I picked up one labelled "18th-Century North Sumatran kris with a Bugis pamour" and imagined its intriguing past. As I held it in my hand, the hilt falling into my palm, a strange sensation ran through me. I couldn't say what it was, but it was something silently beguiling.

Dilby returned. "Enchanted?" he asked.

"In utter awe."

"Here it is. It's 19 March 1970. That's about seventeen years ago." He showed me the deed of sale.

"But the former owner is not stated here," I said.

"Sometimes in these auctions, the seller prefers to remain anonymous. I believe they came from a place or a mansion called Mataram House. They were an heirloom belonging to the woman mentioned in the journal. I can't recall her name."

"Then the story in the journal is not a fictional account after all," I said.

"I believe so. And tell me, Sophia, what's your interest in all this?"

"I don't really know. To say it's academic wouldn't really be true. The manuscript took hold of my mind the first time I set eyes on it. I just can't let it go. It has caused a curiosity-inflicted fever that refuses to go away. In all my years of doing research, never have I been pushed to the edge like this."

"Good heavens, it really got to you. My dear young friend, I am at your service. I've still got my skill, you know – the intelligence stuff. I was doing that sort of thing during the war. Too old for combat, they said, so I had to work behind the lines—"

"Mr Dilby!" I cut him short before he started to narrate the entire history of World War II. "Is this woman still alive?"

"What woman?" he asked, startled by my abrupt interruption.

"The woman who once owned this heritage."

"She was there at the time of the auction. Did not meet her, though. She could be dead by now. It's seventeen years ago, you know."

"What about Mataram House? Is it still there?"

"I suppose so. Buildings don't die like people do. They may get old and become neglected. I think you may find it still standing in Jogja, unless someone razed it to make way for this new grotesque – what do you call it? – condo."

"Why do you think Hamzah wrote that manuscript?"

"What manuscript?"

"The journal Hamzah wrote."

"Yes, yes. Why do you call it a manuscript? A manuscript is some kind of academic work or an historical document or artefact," he said with a frown.

"It is a manuscript to me. The elaborateness of the script, the paper used – it's a work of art." I pressed on.

"I can't really recall how it looked."

"I have brought it with me."

"Have you now? May I look at it, then?"

"I've brought it with me with that purpose in mind."

I pulled out the neatly clothed bundle from my carry bag and carefully unwrapped it. Dilby's eyes lightened. He studied the manuscript, flipped the pages, and caressed the paper with his fingers. "My goodness, the script is absolutely superb. Look at the swing of each letter of the alphabet, the artistry of the capitals, the cursive of the ending letters. My word, I didn't take due notice of it before, as I had been utterly taken by the kris collection. Now we come to the questions: What is this manuscript – as you term it – for? Why should anyone go to this extent of writing out his pains? Unless this Hamzah was a bit of a nut," Dilby surmised.

"Well, Mr Dilby, poems, elegies, and songs have been written from inner pains and personal tragedy. Hamzah was doing just that, I believe," I argued.

"Did he dedicate this artfully written journal to anyone? Do you have any idea?" Dilby asked.

"You found this manuscript together with the heirloom, right?"

"Yes, that's right."

"So, I believe that Hamzah must have dedicated it to his grandma Tutik. It is one final display of extreme remorse. Since he couldn't fall to his knees in person before her, what could be more outrageous than to present an elaborate tableau of written confession done with the utmost pain and labour?" I affirmed, as I believed that such was the case.

"It's seems like a long suicide note to me," Dilby said with a sardonic smile.

"I have never thought of that."

"I was just kidding; I know that Muslims very rarely take their own life," Dilby remarked.

"But you may be right, Mr Dilby. Rarely, of course, but there have been the odd instances. And this might just be that."

"So why not just close the book? What's the point in all this? It's just a conjecture, this suicide. For all we know, he is still alive, hale, and hearty."

"It's not only about that, Mr Dilby. I am dying to know what happened to his wife and daughter. He had so many loose ends when he left Tobali. Like, for instance, whatever was the fate of Li, his bastard son – I am using the term as a matter of fact, not disparagingly – whom he dumped on Maimunah, his aunty? And how did his journal get to Mataram House and land at the auction? I am getting quite worked up, Mr Dilby, I must say."

"My dear girl, this is one hell of a huge curiosity. You are spending all your energy and time, and at quite an expense. Whatever for? You're an academician, not a common investigator searching for a client's family history." Dilby gave a burst of laughter.

"I can't answer that even for myself, Mr Dilby."

"By Jove. Utterly consumed, eh?"

"By my whims, regretfully."

"A bit of that, but driven, perhaps, by an inborn curiosity. Curiosity and creativity are two genetically based characteristics of human beings. Inventions were created and discoveries were made out of curiosity. If I may be so bold as to suggest, I believe you picked up anthropology out of an intellectual curiosity to know more about the human species. Am I right?"

"Yes, indeed. Pretty perceptive, Mr Dilby. Thank you."

"So, little lady, this little exploit of yours is just another walk in the park."

Dilby's grace touched me. In that brief encounter, already there was a glow of empathy between us. Dusk was approaching. I was afraid of driving the dark, winding road to my hotel.

Finally I got to meet Meriam, Dilby's wife, a short, fair-looking, chubby woman who was gentle and provincial in a Malay way. I reckoned she must be in her sixties, her hair short and greying. She had been a modest beauty in her younger days, I believed. The two contrasted widely in every sort of way. To begin with, one was very tall and the other short – not to mention the East and West in their orientation. But the bond between them was immediately apparent.

Speaking in English with the distinctive Malay accent, Meriam said, "He talks and talks all day long, and if it's not with me, it's with himself. He'll live to be a hundred, you'll see. People who talk a lot live long, the Malays say."

They both asked me to stay for dinner. "Meriam can whip up anything from sambal petai to Yorkshire pudding. So just name it, Sophia," Dilby said.

I had to refuse because of the late hour. I bade them farewell. I knew in my heart that I would be seeing them again, quite soon.

*   *   *

From my twelfth-floor apartment, I sat on the verandah enjoying the fluorescent glow of the city sky in the distance. I pondered on my meeting with old Dilby. Finding the collection of krises in his possession was an incredible breakthrough in my quest for answers. The manuscript was on my lap. My mind was in a quandary as to where to go from here. Research was not new to me. For my doctoral thesis, I had traversed the labyrinth of Madagascar in search of answers to the phenomenon of the Malay migration westward across the expansive Indian Ocean centuries ago, but this new project had taken away all my objectivity.

Back at the university, I was told that my request for sabbatical leave had been denied.

"There's absolutely no merit, Sophia. The university has no interest whatsoever in this 'manuscript', as you called it. While we do make exceptions, only in special cases, your case, I'm afraid, does not come anywhere near special," Professor Zain had said to me quite bluntly two days prior. I then surprised him by resigning on the spot, not giving it a second thought. "You mean you would throw away a promising academic career for that thing?" he had exclaimed.

Holding the document in both of my hands and flashing it in front of his face, I had said, "For this 'thing', yes."

To my surprise, the professor broke into a tiny smile and shook his head. "You're one crazy girl. I wish we could get along better. You're a good lecturer. I've heard good feedback about you. I tell you what, why don't you stay on as tutor. The tutorials are just weekly. You'll have to correct some papers. The stipend is not bad. What do you say?"

"Thank you, Dr Zain. That's really very kind of you."

Before we parted, he had said, "Come back full-time when you've retrieved your senses."

"All right. It's a deal," I had said. *He isn't all that bad after all,* I thought.

He gave me a conciliatory nod of the head. We shook hands. Before I left his office, he called out, "Sophia, good luck."

BANKA

Chapter 40

For a couple of days, my mind wondered about Banka, that out-of-sight, out-of-mind island which hardly any Malaysian knew about. In my enquiries with the travel agents, I learned that the only people who went to Banka were those who were directly connected with the tin-smelting plant located there.

Based on the manuscript, that island was where Hamzah's ill-omened life, as he had called it, began. Banka had made Hamzah the man he was. When he left it, he also left so much of himself there that he became almost a legend. No one had changed so dramatically the lives of the simple people there as much as he had. I thought that retracing his paths in Tobali would be a step in the right direction. Why not? He had enriched the villagers beyond even their own capacity to dream, and the success must have bred a change in their attitude towards life, which should still be in evidence now.

When I arrived in Tobali, the village wasn't what I imagined it to be. A thriving town confronted me, whipping out almost all traces of the rustic past I had read about in the manuscript. The bee-like Chinese had breathed commerce and industry into Tobali, and had infected the people there too. I gathered that such things hadn't existed there before. After putting on proper attire to cover my body and head, I headed to the mosque to ask for the chief of the village – shall I say now, the chief of the town. My guide, a young man, took me to a large brick building which was part of a sprawling compound. A couple of cars and commercial vehicles were parked in an unruly way at the entrance. *A pretty urban chief,* I said to myself. *Certainly not the likes of the rural Tok Rejab.*

The young man ushered me in. I took off my shoes and followed him into the spacious living room. Suddenly, ornately decorated teak furniture, a gleaming white marble floor, flat, inartistic Indonesian paintings, and a common tapestry of the Kaaba greeted me. The young man disappeared in the back. A few moments later, he returned with a heavy-set man. There was nothing, I noticed, about his garb to indicate that he was the village chief. I had already conjured in my mind the image of Tok Rejab, and had expected to see a somewhat similar representation. What I saw was a business person in a batik shirt, not a villager in the image of Tok Rejab, as I had mistakenly expected. He was wearing a *songkok* that sat smartly over his head, the tip of which almost covered his brow. He reminded me of the great President Sukarno.

"This is Mr Jaffar," the young man said to me. Mr Jaffar was tall and towered over me. In a polite baritone voice, he invited me to take a seat, in the same breath asking me where I was from. He appeared to me to be Sumatran. When addressing me, he exuded an air of authority. *He must be in his forties,* I presumed. At first glance, he seemed refined and well mannered. I supposed that such things came with the territory as head of a community

"Mr Jaffar, thank you for receiving me. As I said in my letter, I am a university lecturer from Kuala Lumpur. The object of my visit to Tobali is to undertake research on Tobali's famous man known as Hamzah—"

I stopped myself when I noticed his eyes suddenly narrowing and his facial expression turning into annoyance.

He interrupted me. "Yes, I read your letter, Miss Sophia, with interest. I do not know where you have obtained your information, as you did not mention it in your letter. Famous, did you say? Are we talking about the same person here, Miss Sophia? The Hamzah that we knew brought ruin to the people of Tobali." He broke into a laugh, rose from his chair, and looked over towards the window. "My father was one of those landowners who participated in his mining scheme. We lost our land when the company collapsed."

I was taken aback. "What happened to the company?" I asked in astonishment.

"Hamzah suddenly disappeared from Tobali after his wife and child left him. He then transferred all his shares to his brother-in-law, who ran the mine into the ground – literally," he said, with cold detachment.

"You mean Mois?"

"Yes, that's him."

"Where is he now?"

"I believe that after the company folded, he and his mother went to Padang. They must be living there now. I don't know what is the purpose of your research, but my advice is to forget it. Hamzah's name is no longer on people's lips. They've forgotten about him. It's best that you leave it that way. It's history. Bury it, for his sake. It is not wise to open old wounds. That's my advice to you."

I had many questions to ask, but to ask them now seemed futile. Still, I ventured to ask one last question. "Before I leave, will you tell me what happened to Hamzah's house on the beach? Is it still there?"

"Yes, it is still there, but it belongs to a big shipping businessman from Palembang. Mois sold it to him before he left Tobali. He even sold his own father's house. That was another mistake Hamzah had made, handing over the business to Mois. This Mois, people say, had neither the experience nor the business acumen that Hamzah had. Even his own late father didn't think much of him, I was told."

"Are you related by blood in any way to the Rejabs?"

"Why do you ask?"

"Because you are the chief of Tobali. I understand it is dynastic."

"No, I have no blood ties with the Rejabs. To be fair to Mois, he didn't want the job. So the council of elders elected me."

The refreshments arrived along with some cakes. Jaffar invited me to drink. I took a sip but did not touch the food.

An uncomfortable silence hung in the air. Jaffar broke it.

"Why do you want to write about him?" he asked.

"It is of personal interest." I did not elaborate, and he did not pursue. I offered my thanks and then took my leave.

Jaffar accompanied me to the door. Before we parted, he said, "I am sorry I can't be of much help in your research. I have nothing against Hamzah. Maybe it wasn't his fault entirely. Given the predicament he was in at that time, I can't blame him for leaving Tobali. I believe that his intentions were honourable, but they say he had an accursed life. It's just rumour. Maybe it was just bad luck. Who knows? It's best we leave it at that. Goodbye, Miss Sophia. Should you need any assistance while you are here, do let me know."

*   *   *

Before leaving Tobali, I decided to perform one other act of honour: to visit the grave of Captain Sam, alias Sheikh Omar, and that little palace on the beach. The taxi driver took me to the cemetery, which was by the sea. It was a little colony of small headstones. They were placed very close to each other, so it was almost impossible to find a gravesite without having prior knowledge of its exact location. I had to examine every headstone. After labouring for some time, I found no Sheikh Omar, as if he had never existed. In the end, I concluded that the old headstones must have been removed. When a grave was thus unmarked, a new body would fill it.

Not knowing the location of the little palace, I ventured to ask the driver if he knew the famous man of Tobali called Hamzah.

"Yes, of course. I was a young man then. There are so many stories about him, such as that he had a white man as his father."

Before he could ramble on, I asked, "Could you tell me where his former house is?"

"Sure. It's just a few minutes from here."

"Please take me there."

As we arrived at the coastal road, I saw that the lonely beach and swaying coconut grove that I had read about in the manuscript had given way to a sprout of houses, huts, and food stalls.

"There. The big house with the tall roof," the driver said, pointing to the biggest house in the vicinity.

"Stop here. Please wait for me."

The driver gave me a puzzled look but said nothing.

I walked over to the big house and searched for a passage that would lead me to the beach. I trod through the maze of bushes and found the beach. There was not even the ghost of the little palace. In its place was a cluster of food stalls with the unsightliness of disorder. *I have seen enough,* I said to myself with sadness. All traces of Hamzah had been obliterated, a sad testimony to a man the villagers had once dubbed "the son of Tobali".

I left Tobali with the lingering thought that this Hamzah was indeed accursed. I questioned my own objectivity as a social scientist, yet I could not resist being drawn to that conclusion. Here was a man who had been driven by his conscience, who had done everything in the way of goodness, and yet who had left a trail of disasters in his wake as though caught by some evil force from which he could not escape. *Is not that being accursed?* I asked myself.

MALAYSIA

Chapter 41

On my return to Kuala Lumpur, I took a leisurely drive to Ipoh. Maybe there the remnants of the old mines would have kinder memories of Hamzah.

Ipoh lay quiet after all the tin had almost been exhausted. In the city's outskirts, the holes were still there like lakes without a future, as they had neither beauty nor features to be of use to anyone. In the placid calmness of the aftermath of the boom, Ipoh retained traces of its former charm. It was still a town with two parallel streets, low shophouses, and avenues that radiated like sunrays from a nostalgic English-relic roundabout where colonial bungalows still stood like old ladies having long passed their prime.

The miners and workers had retired, I was sure. Their sons, I believed, had turned their faces away from an industry in its death throes. No one talked of tin anymore. Stories about tin mining had been relegated to books for students and inconsequential museums. How would I go about asking about Tan Siew Lim, Lai Peng, and Hamzah when things had changed so much?

I ambled into the Ipoh Station Hotel restaurant, which I hoped had survived the sweeping current of change. There, I guessed, Hainanese cooks and waiters in their white tunics, like moving relics, still did the dishes and laid the tables. I searched for the oldest waiter, the only one who, I hoped, could retrieve the tapestry of the social swirl during colonial times and relate to me the secret rendezvous that took place there. Maybe he could remember a beautiful Chinese woman and a good-looking young Malay gentleman huddled in their special corner every weekend.

There he was, ancient and lean, slightly bent by age, with snowy hair, and wearing a black tunic. I was optimistic, as he seemed old enough to be my great-grandfather and must have lived through times that spanned war and peace. I invited him to sit with me. He said he was Lim.

The restaurant had the smell of burnt meat. This was the latest version of steak, called sizzling steak, which was furiously grilled on a greased cast-iron plate. Without wasting a minute, I asked him, "Mr Lim, do you remember about twenty-five years ago a beautiful Chinese woman called Pinky who used to come here on Sundays with a young Malay man called Hamzah?"

He paused for a moment to switch on his memory bank, and then without hesitation he said, "Very clearly. I was the head waiter then. I made it my duty to know the names of the regular guests and their favourite drinks. A regular guest would only have to say to me, 'Lim, the usual,' and I would reply by addressing him by name. No one escaped my attention. Oh, those good old days." He sighed. "Fast-food restaurants have taken away the elegance in dining."

"You speak quite good English, Mr Lim. Were you educated in an English school?"

"When I was twelve, I was a boy in the household of the Perak British resident. All the staff had to learn to speak English – good English, that is. I was young, so I mastered the language better than the older staff."

"So you can tell me a lot of secrets about Pinky and Hamzah?"

"If you were to ask me then, I would tell you nothing. Keeping such secrets was my honour. Now, twenty-five years after, I look upon them with nostalgia. An Englishman once told me, 'Lim, nostalgia is a great liar, as it always likes to stretch the truth.'" He smiled, showing perfect prosthetic teeth. Then his parched, blotched hand touched mine. "But I shall not lie to you. What do you want to know?"

"Everything that you know," I replied.

He laughed. I ordered Chinese tea for him, opting for coffee for myself. He spoke with ease. I was amazed by the clarity of his mind and by the confidence with which he engaged me. Lim related to me what I already knew from the manuscript. But something that he added staggered me.

"Tan Siew Lim – or Miner Tan, as he was famously known – knew his wife was having an affair with Hamzah. And that was not Pinky's first affair. She was beautiful, whereas he was ugly and old. She was young and full of energy. Men couldn't take their eyes off her. How else could he have kept her? He loved her so much. How could he not know of his wife's infidelity – a man who possessed wealth and power and who had eyes and ears everywhere? But he was also a very wise man. Destroying all her lovers would only make his wife leave him. You must understand the Chinese. She was not, after all, wife number one."

He paused to take a sip of the Chinese tea. "Pinky never counted on falling in love with Hamzah. As it turned out, she gave more to Hamzah than Hamzah gave to her. Then there was the question of the child. Hamzah could have solved it by marrying her after the death of her husband. After all, Muslims can marry as many as four women. What's the problem? She died for nothing. Poor woman."

"By the way, do you know if Hamzah is still alive, and do you know where he is?"

Lim raised his eyes. Biting his lips, he said, "After Miss Lai Peng died, Hamzah never returned to Ipoh. I knew he had a house in Penang. I can't really recall where exactly in Penang. I am sorry I can't help you there."

"Mr Lim, I am sure you know that Miss Lai Peng had a son by Hamzah?"

"Sure. His name is Li. I didn't know his full name."

"Do you know where Li is now?"

"When Miner Tan died, Miss Lai Peng found herself incapable of taking care of his son. She had lost her husband, and her lover had rejected her, so her life began to spiral downwards, poor woman. So she left the boy with her mother in Kuala Lumpur."

"Did you know that Hamzah adopted him after Pinky died?"

"I know that too."

"What happened to Li after Hamzah disappeared? Do you know?"

"I don't really know, exactly. I can only guess." Lim hesitated.

"If you have something to tell me, please do not hesitate, Mr Lim. It's important."

"Li came to this restaurant a few years ago … Let me see, it was around Christmas of '82, I think. That's five years ago, right? He remembered me, he said, from when he used to come with his mother. So he chatted with me. He introduced himself as Miner Tan's son and said he was on holiday from Paris. I asked him what he was doing there. He said he was studying architecture."

"Did he make any mention about a woman name Maimunah? This was the old woman who was supposed to take care of him."

"No. Can't recall he ever mentioned that name. He did talk about his grandmother in Kuala Lumpur, whom he was visiting."

"Thank you very much, Mr Lim. You have been very kind." Just before saying goodbye, I held his hand and placed a gratuity into his palm.

"Please, Miss Sophia, no need to do this."

"I want to. It's a gift."

"Thank you." He gave me an amiable smile.

*   *   *

Having spent a night in Ipoh, I continued my journey to Penang. Fortunately, many of the road names in George Town had remained as of old, as had the architecture of the houses, mansions, and shops of a bygone era, but they were now devoid of the glitter of their time, succumbing to decay and neglect. I had little difficulty in locating 27 Kelawei Road. The old part-brick, part-timber house, as Hamzah had described it, was almost in perfect condition, except for the fruit trees and garden, which gave way to a wide-open ground with an incongruous annex. There was a gate and a guardhouse. I enquired of the Malay guard as to the owner. He said it was the residence of Mr Ariffin, the state assemblyman. *My goodness! Ariffin, a politician?* I said to myself. Deciding not to enter without an appointment, I returned to the still very colonial E&O Hotel, where I had been booked, to arrange for one.

To get an appointment with a politician was a bit tricky. Using a ruse wasn't an option, as I was no politician myself. So I leaned on the old adage of honesty being the best policy. I declared to Ariffin's secretary my desire to see him on an important matter that concerned his cousin Hamzah. To my surprise, the response was positive and prompt, but the appointment had to be very early in the morning at his office before his busy schedule started to kick in, and even then it would be for only fifteen minutes.

The next day, I was at the government office on Light Street opposite the esplanade. Ariffin wasn't what I imagined him to be. The spindle-legged, wiry, dark urchin, as described by Hamzah, had gained a great deal of weight, transforming him into a six-foot-tall, heavy-bodied man of state. The ample nose, dark face, and shining black hair made him look very Indian. His manners were abrupt and officious. He rushed his words as he spoke, giving an impression of being permanently distracted.

"Did you say you know my cousin Hamzah?" Before I could respond, he added, "What is your interest in him, Miss Sophia? You're a researcher from which university?"

"University of Malaya," I said.

The phone rang. He picked it up. "Yes. … Thursday. … Balik Pulau. … No, tell him to come. … OK." He dropped the receiver and then turned back to me. "Sorry about that. About my cousin. … Excuse me." He buzzed his secretary and growled, "No more calls, Surina." Turning back to me, he said, "Sorry, Miss Sophia. Representing the people is a twenty-four-hour-a-day job. My time is theirs; everybody wants to see me, everybody asking for this and that. Even getting someone's child into a school is my problem. Yes, about my cousin?"

"Someone I know has a collection of exquisite krises that once belonged to your cousin Hamzah's grandmother called Tutik. Is that of interest to you?"

"Miss Sophia, firstly, I am not a collector of krises. Secondly, anything connected to my cousin is of no interest to me. My cousin Hamzah, as far as I am concerned, is history best forgotten. Is that why you came to see me? I gave you an appointment thinking you had knowledge of his whereabouts. I don't want to be rude, Miss Sophia, but I am a very busy man. If it is about those krises belonging to him, I don't want to have any part of it," Ariffin said, lowering his eyes to me and slumping into his high-backed leather chair. His blatant rudeness and anger took me by surprise.

"My apologies, Mr Ariffin, if I have offended you in any way," I replied. That immediately brought a more amiable shift in his posture. "If I am not being too inquisitive, tell me, Mr Ariffin, what actually happened."

"Not at all. It's no secret. My cousin was a philanderer of the noble kind. He left his son from his Chinese lover – to whom he was never married – with my mother and then disappeared into thin air. He lied to my mother, saying that the boy was given to him for adoption by a poor Chinese family. When my mother discovered the truth and learned about the boy's mother's suicide, she suffered a stroke and never fully recovered from it."

"Where is he now, this son of his?"

"When my mother fell ill, he returned to his grandmother in Kuala Lumpur. We remained in touch until he went to Paris to study. Lucky for him, his rich Chinese 'father' – not my cousin – left him a great deal of inheritance."

"Do you have his address, Mr Ariffin?"

"Yes. Why?"

"May I have it, if you don't mind?"

"Not at all." He buzzed his secretary and asked her for Li's address. "Why? Do wish to get in touch with him?"

"Yes."

His secretary returned with a slip of paper. "Here," he said. For the first time, he gave me a smile.

"One last question. Where is Hamzah's father, Norredin, now?"

"The poor man died six years ago. There again my cousin just left him with me. He suffered from dementia. Poor man, I loved him."

"What about Hamzah's wife and daughter? Do have any idea where they are?"

"Sorry, Miss Sophia, I don't even know what they look like. We didn't attend his wedding in Banka, as my uncle – Hamzah's father, that is – wasn't well at the time. And he never brought them here."

"Thank you, Mr Ariffin, I won't take any more of your time. You've been very kind." I shook his hand before I departed.

Chapter 42

My imagination had swung into high gear. I thought a great deal about the unfairly maligned Hamzah, and I shuddered at the unfair indictment and injustice his people had inflicted on him. I had a fair idea of Li as told to me by Lim, the waiter at the Station Hotel Restaurant. But the images of Siti and Indriani remained merely silhouettes in the foliage of a dark forest. I had no idea where to begin to look for them. *How could a person disappear without a trace?* I asked myself. But Hamzah I must find. The pull was near providential. If he was dead, then he must be on to me from his grave. If he was alive, then I was hearing his voice calling me.

* * *

The search for Li took me to France. I found myself in the early spring of Paris, when the street cafés begin to come alive. The season for people-watching had just begun. From the restaurant window of La Tour d'Argent on Quai de la Tournelle, I joined in to watch people strolling in the street like birds picking up the scent of spring. My heart was pulsating with a mixture of excitement and trepidation as I was about to meet someone who was an enigma. Many questions had come to my mind. Li had said he was the son of Siew Lim, according to Lim, the waiter. But did he know who his real father was? On the other hand, if he knew the truth, how was he coping with it? It was preposterous even to imagine myself asking him that question. At best, I could only rely on my instinct and judgement upon meeting him. People with that kind of past sometimes do develop strange psychoses. I hoped Li hadn't.

I had written to him that he was the subject of my research on Malaysians living abroad. I had to lie. How else could I meet him? I was an anthropologist, I had mentioned, to add credence to my pursuit. To my surprise, he responded quickly, stating his pleasure to meet me. I must admit I was all the more curious. I hadn't sent my photo, of course. That would have been risky, as he might think I wanted a date. But one could never know with men. On the flip side, why should he bother with a Malay girl when he was in Paris?

I arrived at the restaurant fifteen minutes early. As a matter of habit, punctuality had always been my obsession. I wore a red scarf around my neck. *Look for a woman with red scarf,* I had written. I looked around me for anyone else with a red scarf. *What a cliché,* I thought after having written that, and I felt rather silly, like being on a blind date arranged by a matching agency.

Li had not appeared. I began to feel odd sitting there alone, like a woman being stood up. The restaurant was filling up. A waiter had come twice to ask for my order. It angered me that Li was making me wait. He was half an hour past the appointed time. I had been waiting for an absolute forty-five minutes. I removed my red scarf and flung it on the table. *Let him find me,* I said to myself.

So peeved I was, I had a mind to say to him, "You must be Li, the bastard."

At that very moment, someone came up from my rear.

"Mademoiselle, may I join you?" he said to me.

I turned around to see an Asian man in a dark blue sweater. Smiling, he enquired, "Sophia?"

"Yes."

Before I could pounce on him, he said, "My humblest apologies. Actually I was on the dot and waiting for you downstairs at the entrance, asking the waiter whether a young lady in a red scarf had arrived. The idiot said no. Only later, another waiter – one with a brain – said you were already upstairs. Am I forgiven? I know you're about to kill me."

"You are very right there. Since it's an honest mistake, I'll forget the killing."

"May I?" he asked, pointing to a chair.

Before even settling down, he waved his hand to summon the waiter. "Shall we begin with an aperitif? A Dubonnet maybe, or Campari?"

"Mineral water, sparkling."

"Oh, come on, *this* is Paris." He lowered his gaze at me patronisingly.

"No, mineral water will do."

"A religious thing, is it?"

"Nothing to do with religion. I just don't drink."

"So no wine later either? Not having wine in Paris? That's sinful."

"I am not about to change my life for the French. No matter it's Paris."

"All right, then, mineral water it is. Sparkling, right?" He looked at me directly and gave a smile.

"Yes," I replied, feeling a bit uneasy with this display of suavity.

He ordered a Dubonnet for himself and a San Pellegrino for me.

"This restaurant is famous for its foie gras," he said, flipping through the menu.

"You mean that stuff from geese that have been fed to death? No, thank you," I said without looking at him.

"No foie gras? In Paris?"

"Absolutely. What about Paris that is so special? Are you trying to impress me?" I replied, looking straight at him. I was beginning to get irritated by his smooth demeanour. He pulled himself back into his chair, seemingly shaken by my remark.

"Maybe I was. I am sorry. I am just excited. I never expected in my wildest dreams that such a beautiful Malay girl would come all the way from Malaysia to meet me," he replied sheepishly.

"Let's forget it," I said, feeling a bit sorry for having snapped at him.

I had caused him to retract in silence. As we browsed through the menu, I sensed I had bruised his pride.

"I am sorry. I shouldn't have said that," I said as I peeped over the menu.

He lifted his eyes and smiled. "I deserved that. You're no ordinary girl, I must say."

"Not ordinary? What do you mean?"

"Not run-of-the-mill."

"You mean that I am *off* the mill, like an off-road vehicle?"

"Exactly. Let's be friends, shall we? We hardly know each other. … People argue only after they have become friends – or lovers. Oops! There I go again," he said amusedly, and laughed.

The air settled to a more relaxed mood.

During lunch, Li was bubbling like a fizzy drink, engaging me with his very easy-going manner. I related to him about the growing Malaysian diaspora – which included Malays – that I was studying. To my relief, he wasn't the least interested, otherwise there wouldn't have been the tiniest chance that I could keep up this silly charade of mine. Who had ever heard of a Malaysian diaspora?

And that was the easy part. Unearthing from him the secret of his birth was a task I began to dread. He seemed too nice a person for me to subject him to a probe into the inner closet of his other existence. Plus, I was beginning to like him, even to feel sorry for him. If I were to ask him and then he lied, later to discover that I knew the truth, what would happen then? That likelihood crossed my mind momentarily. So I decided to set it aside for now. Let matters take their course. Hopefully he would take it upon himself to open up to me.

When my eyes were on my plate, I felt that Li was watching me. When I popped my head up, he lowered his gaze. At such times I demurred, rather than respond with my eyes on him. That, I must say, was strange. It was my habit to look people straight in the eye when I engaged them.

Li was good-looking. There was no doubt about that. The dark mane that swept gently across his temples lent an air of boyish debonair to his narrow, angular face. His eyes showed the mixture of cultures from which he had come. He had his mother's fair skin and his father's nose. That was perhaps the real reason why I couldn't make myself look at him straight in the eye.

Time passed without us knowing it. As the restaurant crowd began to thin, the waiter stood by impatiently, ready to thrust the bill on us.

"We better go before he chases us out," Li said as he dropped his credit card onto the tray. The waiter scampered away, probably so that he could make it to his joint for a beer before returning for the evening shift. I had offered to pay, but Li glared at me. "Don't you dare!" he'd exclaimed.

"I only wanted to imitate the French. Each one pays," I quipped.

He laughed.

"Let's go to one of the cafés on the street. It's such a waste to allow this great sunny day to pass," he suggested.

He pulled out the chair for me as I rose. It impressed me, as men seldom did that nowadays. *Sophia, you are here for work, not romance,* I reminded myself.

The café was filled to the edge. All the patrons faced the street, Parisian style. We managed to find a couple of seats by the corner. An aproned waiter quickly arrived. I ordered café au lait, and Li asked for a glass of white wine. Every two out of three patrons were smoking, I noticed.

"Aren't you smoking a French cigarette? Everyone seems to do so here," I said in a jocular vein.

"Are you still at it? That's not the same as liking wine."

"It's not? It's Paris, and Frenchies must smoke Gauloises. Isn't that so? You should be smoking one."

"I thought you wanted to be friends."

"I am just pulling your leg. Now tell me about yourself. So you threw away a future as an architect to be a photographer. Isn't that quite a waste of talent and study?" I enquired.

"If you take architecture as an education and photography as a calling, then you see it's not a waste at all. The two share a common goal – art."

"I still don't get it. You could do both, couldn't you?"

"The real reason is that I just hated my clients, particularly those with poor taste. And there were many of those. In this profession, your clients impose their taste on you. I could not stand that. How could I survive, unless of course I were already famous? How could I become famous when I was losing clients before I even got started? I would often dismiss myself if my client's ideas didn't fit mine. But in photography, I find freedom – freedom over my subjects. And my subjects, no matter what their taste, don't talk back to me."

"Isn't that mere ideals rather than a profession?"

"Maybe."

"You know, Li, not everyone has the luxury to pursue lofty ideals. In your case, earning a living is not of concern, I presume?"

He turned silent and pensive. I suddenly realised I might've touched a nerve. For a moment, I sensed danger. Then he changed the subject.

"Would you like a boat ride on the Seine? The booth is only across the road. It's a nice day. What say you?" He held me by my waist as we crossed the road. A warm tingle rose inside me.

We took to the open deck at the stern, away from the horde of tourists and the guide on the loudhailer. With the wind in our faces, Li fixed his gaze on me again. His eyes remained there for what seemed a long time. Suddenly appearing to realise what he was doing, he turned away as if having been caught prying.

"I am sorry if I have made you uneasy," he said apologetically.

"It's all right. I hope it wasn't something awful that caught your attention."

"On the contrary. I was actually taken up by your face."

"What's wrong with it?"

"I've never seen such intelligent eyes on such a pretty face."

"You're kidding me. You mean a pretty face should have stupid eyes?"

"And funny too. Pretty face, intelligent eyes, and funny."

"You're not flirting with me, are you, Li? We've just met – hardly hours ago."

"And I would add another thing – you're hard to get close to. Am I right?"

"I am supposed to research you, not you me. Now you're scrutinising me. It's time we reversed the role. Now you tell me about yourself, no holds barred," I remarked. I wanted to run to the restroom and congratulate myself for this breakthrough.

"What do you want to know?"

"For a start, tell me about your origin – your parents, for example."

He moved back. For the second time that day, he fell into a pause. His whole demeanour changed from one of light-heartedness to one of withdrawal. I was caught flat-footed. *Not very smart after all, Sophia,* I thought.

"Let's enjoy the cruise. It's too good a day to talk about me," he said, rather pensively.

Later on, we parted in a somewhat sombre mood.

* * *

Early the next morning, the phone in my hotel room rang. When I picked up the receiver, a chirpy voice announced, "Bonjour, Mademoiselle Sophia. Would you like to see more of Paris?" The French-accented tone was playful.

"Thank you, but no. Yesterday was quite enough."

"Paris from the Seine? That was just a boat ride. What about museums, galleries, gardens, architecture?"

"Nope. I have seen some. I don't have to see them all."

"Ah. There's something, I bet you, that you've not seen and that would certainly interest you."

"What is it?"

"Les Catacombes."

"What's that?"

"The cemetery of skulls."

"Oh no, not that."

"You're an anthropologist. Why not?"

"You've a pretty wrong idea of anthropology, my friend."

"Now, what could excite you? I tell you what: put on your comfortable shoes, dress casually, and I'll come and pick you up at ten. Please, say yes."

I held back my answer.

"Sophia, are you still there?"

"OK. Just so you don't torment me further." I smiled to myself.

"Thank you. Thank you, *ma chérie*."

"That was sweet of him. *Hold on, Sophia, do not get carried away,* I said to myself.

On the back seat of his Peugeot, there was a basket smelling of cheese in addition to a blanket and a load of photography equipment.

"What's that?" I asked.

"That's our lunch, and also my trusty companion."

"Are we going on a picnic?"

"Why, yes. Marvellous weather and good company. A perfect combination for a picnic. I am going to take you to a place I am sure you'll like."

Li's ebullient spirit had returned, much to my relief.

"Are you always like this, high-spirited?"

341

"No, not always. Only when I am with pretty company. I can get morose sometimes."

"Do not flatter me, Li. I do not like flattery."

"Don't be too stiff, Sophia. Loosen yourself. You are in the spring of your life. Enjoy yourself."

"Me, stiff? Is that your impression of me?"

"I think you're holding back on yourself. Release the bubbles in you."

"I don't remember you saying you studied psychology. I thought it was architecture."

"There we go again."

"Don't say I am stiff. I can be zany. You just don't know me. Do you want to see how zany I can be?"

"Nope, let's save that for when we get to know each other better."

I slapped his arm, and he grinned like an idiot.

"I surrender," he cried, taking his hands off the wheel.

"Don't you do that! Your driving is already atrocious, whizzing through the traffic like a madman."

The driver of the car that Li had abruptly overtaken shouted out an expletive in French. "There you are, your countryman cursing you."

"Don't bother about it. They all drive like mad in Paris, and they curse too. When I first arrived, I drove slowly, not knowing the roads. Then one day someone shouted, 'Allo, mon amie. Where are you from?'" He laughed.

A park came into view.

"Voila. Parc des Buttes-Chaumont, Paris's lesser-known garden," he said, throwing out his hands like a Frenchman would.

We skirted the park, came to a suspension bridge, and pulled up by a lake. Li spread out the blanket and set out the lunch. From the trunk of his car he retrieved a tripod and a bagful of equipment.

"What's this, a photography shoot?" I asked.

"A photographer and his camera are inseparable."

"But this is not just a camera. It is a lorryload of them."

We ate by the lake under a cottony sky. The park, I noticed, was without the symmetry and order of the garden at Tuileries that I had seen in the centre of Paris. "This place is really wonderful. It's not what I expected. I have never really liked

the regimented look of Parisian parks. This is different. It's natural and flowing."
I was savouring the scene when I overheard the rapid clicking of a camera.

"Hey, don't," I exclaimed, waving my hand towards him.

"Don't look at me. Pretend I am not here." He went on clicking away, moving from one angle and then the next. So adroit he was that I didn't realise so many close-ups of me had already been snapped.

"Enough!" I cried out, putting my palms to my face. He shot several frames of that too.

"When you said you would be taking photographs, I thought you meant of the landscape. Enough of this! I am not your model."

"Oh yes you are!" He paused, and changed to another camera.

When I was peeling an orange and putting it in my month, he took shots of that.

"Enough!" I howled. "Please let me eat in peace."

He ceased. After lunch we walked up the bluff and took in the view of Montmartre. Li ran up before me, and clicked and clicked and clicked. The breeze blew my hair into my face, and he shot that. I pointed to a building, and he shot it. I waved to desist him, and again he snapped. Finally, I gave up. When I started to dance around in the field, he went wild.

"What are you going to do with those silly photos, Li?"

"I haven't decided. Maybe they'll be part of my forthcoming exhibition in Paris."

"Don't you dare!"

He gave a loud laugh.

When we packed our stuff into the car, he said, "Bravo. And thank you, Sophia, for a lovely day. What a sport you are, and what terrific company. You changed my mind totally about you."

"I told you I could be zany. Hey, I have a great time too," I replied.

We drove to a little village with art deco buildings and parked by the side of a café.

While sipping coffee under the terrace, Li all of a sudden stretched out his hand and placed it on top of mine. His eyes fell on me. I was about to pull my hand away, but I quickly refrained, not wanting to embarrass him.

"Is there anything the matter, Li?" I asked.

"You're leaving tomorrow?"

"Yes. Why?"

"I had imagined you to be like one of those pedantic scholars. I was wrong. I find you very personable and honest. Sophia, I think I should be honest with you too. I am not an architect. I did three years in architecture school and dropped out. I am just a photographer. A common photographer. Surprised?" The glint in his eyes turned to sadness. He paused.

"Yes," I replied.

"Disappointed?" He smiled sheepishly.

"No, not really. Why should I be?"

"What are you going to write about me?"

"My paper is not so much about the individual as it is about his reason for leaving the country and the factors contributing to that. Be assured, the personal part of your life will not be touched at all. If I do enquire about it, it would be only as a matter of personal interest to me, sort of to give me the right perspective of the person." *Goodness me, what am I saying? He just said I was an honest person.*

The radiance returned to his face.

"You need not tell me anymore about yourself if you don't want to," I added, feeling utterly horrible about my deception.

"You're a good person, Sophia, honest and forthright. I'll tell you about myself. My parents died when I was just a child, and I was brought up by my maternal grandmother. My father, who was a tin miner, left me a trust, but the fund ran out, due entirely to my reckless spending on leisure. So I could not finish my studies. I worked as a waiter in a hotel. I went to Switzerland to take a course in hotel management, working part-time to pay for it. When I finished, I got a job in a hotel in Paris, a two-star hotel where I was the bellhop, the front-office man, and the waiter too. The hours were long; the pay was miserable. I was expected to live on tips. I got into this photography thing by accident after I had gone to a photography exhibition in Versailles. I bought myself a camera and discovered my hidden talent. Two years later, I had my own small exhibition. And voila, here I am – your photographer."

He made no mention of Hamzah, which I thought was curious. Surely his grandmother had told him something. Everyone seemed to know, from Lim, the waiter, to Maimunah and Ariffin, but he did not? Could that be possible? I gazed at his face and asked myself, *Shall I ask him about it? Do I dare do that? For goodness' sake, Sophia, that's a no. A big no. Don't I have any decency? I am supposed to be a good person — honest and forthright, he just said.*

"A very nice story, Li. Thank you for your trust." That's all I managed to say.

*　　*　　*

The next morning when I was checking out of the hotel, Li was already there to take me to the airport.

"You don't have to do this, Li," I implored.

"I want to," he insisted.

Turning to the bellboy, he said in French, "I'll take that."

"Come on, Li, you don't have to carry bags too."

"I was a bellboy once, remember?"

"Get off," I replied.

At the airport, he insisted on doing everything for me. He placed my bag on the conveyor, checked me in, and pushed my trolley right up to the gate.

At the departure gate, he asked me in a solicitous tone, "Will we see each other again?"

"God willing," I replied.

He kissed me three times French-like, on both cheeks. On the flight, after dinner was served and consumed, I readied myself for sleep, putting on an eye mask. But sleep would not come. *Li is falling in love with you,* my mind kept saying to me. I felt disturbed. I had never felt like that before. Quickly I shook those thoughts out of my head. Gradually my eyes closed, and I hovered between sleep and half-sleep in the droning, stuffy air.

*　　*　　*

Back in my apartment in Malaysia, I rose to a blustery morning with the onset of rain. My head was like lead from jet lag. The phone rang. At the other end was a despondent Meriam.

"Sophia, Dilby has passed away," she said, sobbing.

"Oh, my dear Meriam, I am *so* sorry. I have been thinking of coming to see you both. I'll come immediately."

I arrived in Cameron Highlands at about noon and saw that a crowd had gathered in the grounds, many wearing skullcaps and speaking in low voices. I headed straight into the house, where all the women were seated on the floor. Some were reading the *Yassin* verse from the Koran. Old Dilby lay on the bed, his body covered in batik cloth, his exposed face cold and grey. How lonely I thought he looked in death. None of his kind were there. *The last of the lost tribe,* I reminisced. I had never seen death before, not in real life. And to see the end of Dilby, whom I had just begun to like, was a very sad moment of my young life. Prior to the departure of the cortège, a prayer was said for Dilby's soul. Young men from the village came to carry the simple coffin on their shoulders. The size of the procession amazed me. The entire Cameron Highlands community seemed to have descended upon Dilby's funeral to honour him. This was a measure of his popularity. I walked with Meriam, holding her hand.

"He was very much loved," I said.

"Yes, he was," she calmly replied.

Meriam insisted I stay back after the funeral. In spite of her bereavement, she found time to tell me, "Dilby left something for you."

"For me?"

"Yes, so please stay back."

Meriam prepared a meal as though unaffected by the burden of grief. Perhaps the thought that she was now alone had not yet overtaken her. I kept her company in the kitchen and tried to make myself useful, laying the table and boiling the water.

"Are you going to stay alone in this house?" I asked.

"Yes."

"How are you going to manage it all by yourself?"

"I'll manage. I have friends here."

When dinner was over, she went into her bedroom, soon returning with a large envelope in her hand. "This is for you."

I opened the envelope, and in it I found a title deed in my name for the collection of krises.

"Oh my goodness, tell me this isn't true, Meriam. I can't accept this. This is priceless. Why bequeath them to me? These are yours, Meriam, not mine."

"I've no use for them. Dilby knew that. In fact, he had thought about it long before he met you. He wanted to pass the krises over to someone who would passionately care for them. He was glad to have found you just before his last days, as though you were destined to have them. Those were his very words."

"What about Fletcher, his dear friend, or the museum?"

"Fletcher had no interest in them. He had said so to him. Besides, he too was growing old. What would he want the krises for? As for the museum, Dilby didn't think much of it."

"But, Meriam, you could dispose of them handsomely."

"Don't you worry about me. Dilby has taken care of that. Look, Sophia, Dilby was not one given to foolishness. He knew exactly what he was doing. The krises are destined to be in your possession. Don't refuse them. It's the wish of a dead man."

"Thank you, Meriam. Thank you so much. I'll come and visit you as often as I can. Please call me if you need anything. Call me at any time. Promise?"

"Promise."

I hugged her close and long. Just as I was about to step out through the door, she cried, "Good heavens, I almost forgot. Wait here."

She shunted to her bedroom again, soon coming back with a box.

"Here, he left this too. The package came with the collection of krises."

The priceless collection was already too much for me, and now there was this sealed box, the contents of which were unknown to me. I just couldn't hold back my curiosity. I wanted to open it there and then, but Meriam stopped me.

"You don't have to open it now."

She wasn't in the mood for trivial things, so I took the box away unopened, so as not to appear too eager. I drove back to Kuala Lumpur immediately after that. While driving, the box sat temptingly on the passenger seat. My eyes darted at it every now and then. At one point my car swerved dangerously towards the precipice.

Once back in my Impian apartment, two hours later, I tore open the neatly wrapped box with the impatience of a little girl opening her birthday present. Inside was a stack of vintage black-and-white photographs.

When I spread them on the table, I saw that they represented a story waiting to be retold.

Chapter 43

Mother was coming to Kuala Lumpur. This wasn't good news for me. She had called from Brussels, speaking in a tone that sounded angry: "I am coming by Lufthansa 924, arriving in K.L. at 7.40 a.m. Pick me up." There were no pleasantries, just the message.

That was the way she normally communicated with me anyway. We did not hate each other. Far from it. In fact, Mother was my mentor, the beacon in a fog, so to speak. Always there for me, she was a mother extraordinaire, I would say, smart and full of life. She would battle people on my behalf no matter who they were, if she believed I was right. There was a lot of her in me, and that accounted for the frequent friction between us. She tried to run my life as if I had never grown up. My doctorate in anthropology, and my positions as president of the university's Cultural Society and vice president of the Malayan Historical Society, did not count towards growing up. Add to that the fact I hadn't had a boyfriend yet. She had already signalled me with an early warning: "Tell Mama when you start getting serious with someone!" But she loved me like hell and would give away her heart so I could live. I had no doubt about that.

Early the next morning, I looked at myself in the mirror and noticed a spot on my chin – a sure sign of stress.

At the arrival hall in the airport, my mother's first words to me were, "What's this about you resigning from the university?"

"Where did you get that idea, Mama?"

"From your professor – when I called the faculty to look for you, since you were nowhere to be found. Where were you, anyway?"

"I was away, Mama." Hopefully she wouldn't ask where I had been. Paris was a stone's throw from Brussels, but I hadn't visited her while I was there.

"The professor also said something about you doing research. What research might that be?"

"It's something personal." That was a slip of the tongue. What an idiotic answer. I regretted it instantly.

"What do you mean personal? You threw your job away for doing something personal? I gave you an education so you could have a future. Is there money in this research you're doing now?"

"Please, Mama. You've just arrived. Settle yourself first, and then we'll talk. How was the flight?"

"Boring – the food bland, the coffee lukewarm."

"Don't complain all the time, Mama; it'll make you older faster."

"I am old. What difference does it make?"

"You're not old. Look at you. Unlike your friends, you don't have a strand of white hair. And I don't see any wrinkles." That softened her.

"I hated that long flight."

"Come, Mama, you don't have to fight an airline over a meal."

"I paid a lot to travel first class, so I expected first-class service. This research you're doing, what's it about?"

"I'll tell you later, Mama."

I had wondered how long I would be able to keep the manuscript away from her. There was no point in telling her now, or ever. I would not be able to defend the rationale of my decision. I just could not support my decision on academic grounds. What could I say to her about doing it for personal reasons? Once Mother decided to put me in the dock, it would be hard to dislodge her. Persistence was her middle name.

In the few days before Mama's arrival, I had been wading through the maze of photographs that Meriam had handed to me from her late husband.

Photographs had the magic of transporting a person through time. The older they were, the greater their power in drawing a person into the past.

That was what happened to me. Mataram House seemed to come alive before me, and I found myself walking through it, seduced by its bizarre, dreamlike existence, sensing its aura, and feeling the presence of Ibu Tutik, the matriarch herself in her aristocratic garb. How enthralling it must have been to those who saw her in person, I imagined.

*   *   *

Mother and I were like two hot flints in close proximity; the risk of combustion was always present.

Mother was an avid painter, subscribing to the Picasso school of cubism. She had a natural talent, which she had only discovered in middle life. When she took a course in a conservatoire in Brussels, her teacher told her to go abstract, and so she chose cubism. That was a style of painting, I thought, that deformed reality. Sketching philosophy on canvas must come from a pretty brilliant or, perhaps, warped mind. Mother loved the deformities she painted. It gave her the freedom to express herself. Her works were incomprehensible with misplaced noses, eyes, and ears. I couldn't understand that, so she thought I was artless. Perhaps her paintings were really good and it was just me who did not have the mind for them.

She had brought her painting kit, which filled a suitcase. She turned the balcony of my apartment into her studio, occupying it, setting herself up permanently. I was totally ignored, which pleased me – for the time being.

My current occupation with the manuscript and the photographs was uninterrupted. Mataram House was beckoning me. I thought, *I must see it in real life. My intense curiosity must be quenched.*

I would be lying if I said I had not thought of Li at all. When I walked in the morning in the wooded grounds near my apartment building on weekends, Buttes-Chaumont came to my mind. And when I received Li's letter and the pictures he took of me, I was overjoyed beyond my every expectation.

The letter was just a page. I wished it had been longer. He said he had enlarged the pictures to exhibition size, in black-and-white. He wrote, "Sophia, you, your pose, the pictures, are superb." He was somewhat economical with his words. But his closing sentence disturbed me. "I've been thinking about you and hope to see you again soon." My heart fluttered upon reading that, and I seemed to have little control of its direction. The whole thing disturbed me.

I flew to Java without telling Mama.

I arrived in Jogjakarta, the syncretic city of several religions, a city of mosques, temples, kings, and kingdoms. In this rich tapestry lay the supposedly microcosm of it all: Mataram House, the embodiment of a woman's belief in the destiny of her beloved grandson. But where was this Mataram House? No one seemed to know. *Does it exist at all?* I wondered.

My tourist guide, fortunately, had an opinion. Mataram House, far from qualifying as a site of historical or cultural interest, was not even on the tourist map, he said. When I asked him whether there existed any myth or legend surrounding the history of Mataram House, he giggled and said he knew nothing of the place whatsoever. If myths and legends were my interests, he recommended to me Imogiri. There, I would actually find the tombs of the Mataram kings, he said. According to him, this Mataram House could possibly be found there too. If I so wished, he would me take me there and help me search for it.

Leaving busy Jogjakarta behind, we were on our way towards Imogiri. We entered a plain, and then an escarpment, and then tobacco fields, and after that a village. Suddenly the road began to narrow and twist. Out of the plethora of hills and ridges, a shady forest appeared, and then there was nothing, only a track climbing a hill.

We were lost. My heart sank.

Noticing my despondent look, my guide said to me, "We passed a small village just now. I shall go and enquire."

We made an about-turn and headed to the village. He parked his taxi and asked me to wait inside.

I watched him talking to several people at a nearby stall. There were a lot of hand movements. He and his interlocutors kept pointing to a particular direction.

When he returned, he said to me, "They know of a big haunted house on the hill at the end of a track overgrown with thick brush about two miles away. But none of them was sure if that building is the Mataram House you are looking for. The place is spooky and haunted, so do not go there, they warned."

We returned to the spot where our taxi had earlier stopped, at the foot of a thick-forested hill. My driver found a dirt track leading up to the hill. We had earlier missed it because the heavy foliage of undergrowth had hidden its entrance. Unless someone was deliberately looking for it, there was no way it could be found. Not only was the path virtually invisible from the road, but also there wasn't even a glimpse of a rooftop or a shadow of a façade to show there was a building on top of the hill. It was as if for all these years Mataram House had not wanted to be seen or found – not until now.

After a winding drive through the brush-clad dirt road, a great ornamented gate emerged at the top of the hill. A gate just like the Great Gate described by Hamzah.

Junaidi, my guide and driver, stopped his car, turned his head to me, and said hesitatingly, "This, I think, is Mataram House. Do you really want to go inside there, Miss Sophia? This place is spooky, as those villagers said."

"Yes, certainly. That's why I am here. You may stay in the car," I replied.

I stepped out of the car, eager by the prospect of discovery. Ruins, tombs, jungles, and strange sites were familiar places to me, yet this place suddenly gave me a chill.

As I walked up the path towards the Great Gate, I heard Junaidi scurrying behind me. "Wait, ma'am, I am coming along with you," he yelled. "I do not want anything to happen to you."

"Thank you, Junaidi."

We heard the barking of a dog. As we approached the massive gate, the barking became louder. Then, before I was even close enough to the house, I heard the creaking and grunting of heavy metallic handles as a door was being released. Out of a smaller door, an old man of medium height, stoutly built and with a round, short-cropped head of hair, emerged. He didn't seem surprised to see me, as if I had been expected. Was I imagining this, or was this strange house really beckoning me? Only just now I was pondering that this Mataram House had revealed to me the road to itself. A frightening thought came to me.

To the man at the door, I said my already famous lines. I addressed him as *Bapak*, an Indonesian term of respect.

"Bapak, my name is Sophia, a researcher from the University of Malaya, undertaking a study on historical buildings. This is Mataram House, isn't it?"

353

The old man smiled, showing his remaining teeth. Without hesitation, he waved his hand to welcome us. "Come in." The dog straggled by his side, barking at us a few times. "Since we haven't had any visitors for – how long I can't remember – he could smell from a mile away if a human was at the gate."

The man amiably escorted us in without a tinge of curiosity about who we were or why we had come.

The sight that appeared before me took my breath away: an extraordinary mansion emblazoned with Islamic, Hindu, and Buddhist motifs, at once flamboyant and uncomely, yet bewitching, making the onlooker wonder about the mind of its creator. In a certain way it was not unlike the Gothic architecture of Europe with its lancet arch, ribbed vaults, flying buttresses, and shroud of gloom. Even my sceptical guide and driver was stunned and wide-eyed with shock, saying, "This is no haunted house. It's a mind-boggling monument. If only it could be restored. I would certainly put it on my itinerary."

"Come into my little abode," the old man said. By this, he did not mean that august building, but a small annex by the side of the giant gate, which, I recalled from the manuscript, had been the former guardhouse.

"Wait, Bapak, let me feast my eyes on this great edifice."

I stared at the phantom from the manuscript materialising before my eyes. I wanted to walk the grounds, but a thick forest – a former garden – blocked my path. I advanced towards the main entrance of the mansion and was immediately restrained by the old man. He gestured to me not to enter.

He ushered me instead to his little house. When we sat across the table, I had a good look at his face. He reminded me of someone I had met before, although someone much older – but of course. I pulled out the set of photographs from my duffel back, sieved through them, and selected the one with him in it.

"Is this you, Bapak?" I asked, pointing to the stocky man with a cigarette in his mouth posing in the garden with the young Hamzah by his side.

He glared at the photo in surprise and exclaimed, "Where did you get this?"

"You're Pak Ali, aren't you?"

"Yes, I am. Where did you get that?" he asked, pointing to the photo.

After relating to him that I had gotten the photographs from old Dilby, I told him about the collection of krises too. He appeared deeply puzzled by my story.

"Do you have others?"

"Yes." I placed the array of photos on the table.

He feasted his eyes on them, flipping one after the other, deep in his thoughts. Then he wiped his saggy eyes with his fingers.

He sauntered to the shelf, picked up a packet of clove cigarettes, and offered one to me. I shook my head. Then he offered it to my guide, who gladly accepted it. They both lit up, making a cloud of pungent smoke. Pak Ali returned to the photographs. His eyes became watery again.

"Tell me, Pak Ali, what happened to Mataram House?" I asked.

"Let me make coffee." He went to the little kitchen, filled a kettle with water, and fired the stove. His movement, though slow, was steady. While the water was heating to a boil, he invited me to follow him outside. We walked out. Suddenly he stopped in front of the mansion.

"Let me tell you something. A few weeks ago I dreamt that Mataram House was going to have a visitor. Since then I have been waiting. So when Koning, my dog, barked just now, I knew it was the visitor. This house has a sad history and deeper secrets. One day I hope those secrets will be told."

He turned his gaze towards me.

"Look at it, Miss Sophia. Look at it. What do you see?"

"A house, neglected."

"Look at it with your heart, not with your eyes. What do you see?"

"Sadness."

"Very true. You are indeed gazing at sadness. If this house could cry, it would shed a river of tears, pining for its master and waiting for his return. I've been its guardian for so long that I have lost track of time. I am old. I hope I will outlive the master's return so I may die with my obligation fulfilled."

"Who do you mean by 'master'?" The answer to this question was obvious, but I wanted to hear it from the horse's mouth.

"Hamzah – Tutik's beloved grandson. Tutik had this strong notion that her grandson was the descendant of Sultan Agung of Mataram, believing unfailingly in her grandson's destiny. That is why Mataram House was built in the vicinity of Imogiri, where lie the tombs of the Mataram kings. When Hamzah left Mataram House, Tutik's heart shattered into pieces. Everything around her shattered too, until she completely lost her will to live. And you know what is sad, the very tragedy of it all? Hamzah did not share her belief. Instead he chose to listen to his father, who made short shrift of the whole thing. In spite of his grandmother's dire warning, Hamzah left Mataram House. I was also responsible for what happened, and now I live with that guilt. I will be here until my dying day, waiting for Hamzah's return. Tutik's dying wish for me was that I atone for my sin. Every time Koning barked, my heart was lifted, thinking it was Hamzah at the gate – or someone bringing news of him. Every time, my heart sank back into despair.

"Tell me, Pak Ali, did Tutik put a curse on Hamzah?"

"Curse? How did you know about that?"

"I do possess some knowledge of Mataram House."

I felt droplets of rain on my head.

"Let's go inside." Pak Ali looked up at the giant grey clouds moving over us. "We have entirely forgotten about the coffee."

When we returned, the kettle was spewing steam.

Pak Ali made superb coffee.

"About the curse, Pak Ali?"

"In a minute." He looked at the clock. "It's almost four. I'll miss my *zohor* prayer. Let me pray first."

Ten minutes later, Pak Ali was back with us. Then he retraced his story.

"About the curse? No, absolutely not. She didn't curse Hamzah. She loved Hamzah and would never allow anything bad to happen to him. Tutik had a beautiful daughter, Sita Dewi, who was never short of suitors. After taking one look at her, their legs crumbled under them. But Tutik's demand for her daughter's hand in marriage was too much for the suitors to accept, unless a young man was willing to lie and deceive – and that's what Norredin did. He lied, so besotted he was of Sita Dewi.

"In exchange for her daughter's hand in marriage, Tutik demanded of Norredin total allegiance to Mataram House. He had to make it his abode for life, and his first male heir had to be put under Tutik's complete tutelage from the cradle to adulthood. Neither parent would have any role to play in his upbringing. And the boy had to make Mataram House his abode for life too. A guilt-edged prison was built! Tutik demanded of Norredin an oath upon the Holy Koran to keep his side of the bargain. A week before the wedding, the swearing ceremony was performed at midnight in Mataram House, replete with candles, incense, yellow rice, yellow cloth, black rice, black cloth, the krises, and all the works, plus, of course, the Holy Koran and a holy man to perform the ceremony. Norredin swore that God Almighty should strike him with calamities if he broke the oath. But Tutik had made a terrible error of judgement. Unwittingly, she had sent her beloved grandson to the same fate as Norredin.

"Norredin, who hated Tutik and who was derisive of ulemas, oaths, and the occult, had no qualms in breaking the oath. But he did not do it immediately. He bided his time. At the right moment, when the opportunity came, he pounced upon it. Believe it or not, the curse began to unravel. It followed him like a shadow. It followed his son, Hamzah, too."

"This saga includes retribution too. The author of the oath lived her last days in loneliness, pining for her grandson like the owl pines for the moon. She died here in that garden." He paused and pointed to a patch of weeds and dead leaves. Only a simple stone marked the grave.

An unceremonious ending for someone who lived by ceremony. A very tragic ending it is, I thought, sadly.

Pak Ali lowered his head. I could hear him saying a prayer under his breath for Tutik. I was knocked off my balance, overwhelmed with sadness, and lost for words. Junaidi sat in silence, looking stunned.

Outside, the rain poured. Noticing the effect of his story on me and on the guide, Pak Ali asked, "Shall I make more coffee?"

We nodded our heads.

"Do you know where Hamzah, his wife, and their daughter are, Pak Ali?"

"I have no idea whatsoever. I am still hoping for his return. Maybe I am just hoping against hope. When I told you I had dreamt someone was coming, I thought it was Hamzah. I am afraid that I, like Ibu Tutik, will die without seeing Hamzah again."

I thought of telling him about the manuscript, but I changed my mind. That would not put him nearer to seeing Hamzah again. It might instead deepen his grief.

I left Pak Ali and Mataram House in terribly low spirits. The heavy air of tragedy weighed upon me like a stone. Junaidi, too, seemed visibly affected, saying very little on our journey back to Jogjakarta.

Chapter 44

Mama had been with me for a month. So far it had been relatively peaceful, the peace broken only by her occasional nagging about my attire. Too much of my neck and chest was showing, too hugging was my blouse, and so on. Recently it was about my coming home late. Past midnight was an unacceptable hour for an unmarried woman, she decried.

"Mama, I've been doing my own thing when you are not around, so what is the problem?" I asked.

"Not in my presence," she retorted.

"Mama, I am twenty-four years old! I can sleep with a man and you wouldn't even know about it – not that I would."

"Then you're a stupid woman, degrading your own self-worth for a moment's pleasure."

"Mama, this is the twentieth century. Virginity does not covet the moral high ground anymore. A virgin woman is a laughing stock nowadays."

"Are you telling me you're no longer a virgin? A woman mustn't lose herself to a man before marriage. It's our way. I've brought you up with good values. Remember that. A woman is not like a man. When a woman beds with a man, she comes down a notch, whereas for a man it's a conquest. He'll brag about it. Do not adopt the modern ways, Sophia."

I believed that years of living overseas had strengthened my mother's resolve to be more Asian, more conservative, and more traditional – lest, she feared, she lose her identity.

"Sexual morality is a social concept, Mama. In one African tribe, sleeping with many partners even after marriage is not a moral issue but a custom. One antiquated custom in a particular Asian country was to offer your wife to a house guest. It was seen as the ultimate in hospitality."

"Enough! Do not give me your anthropological crap."

"Don't worry, Mama, it's just an intellectual discourse. I am just playing with you. Your daughter is a virgin! All right? And at this rate I will be an old maid." I laughed and went over to hug and kiss her.

Then without warning me, she said, "I am going to paint you."

"Oh my gosh, Mama, no. I don't want to come out with my face distorted. No way."

"Don't be cheeky. It's a proper portrait."

"No, Mama, please. Find another subject."

"If you do not want me to paint you, I shall paint your professor. What's his name? Zain. Yes, Dr Zain."

"Excellent idea. Why don't you? I'd love to see him in modern art. Have a field day. I'll enjoy seeing the result."

She took a cushion and threw it at me.

* * *

Since my return from Jogjakarta, my mind had been busy ruminating over Hamzah; his wife, Siti; and their daughter, Indriani. How could anyone disappear like that, unless they didn't want to be found? But what about Hamzah? He had sworn to search the world for them. What happened to him?

It was a Saturday. Mother was out with some friends. I was alone, sitting on the balcony of my apartment. I watched a golfer hitting a ball into a pool of water and raising his hands in despair. My thoughts were on Hamzah when the phone rang. It was an overseas call. I thought it was Li, but a Frenchwoman's voice came on the line.

"Allo, may I speak to Mademoiselle Sophia?" she asked, speaking in melodic, heavily French-accented English.

"It's Sophia speaking."

"I yam sorry to trouble you. I yam speaking for Monsieur Li. He had an auto accident a few days ago and is badly 'ert."

"He is what?"

"He is badly 'ert."

"Oh, you mean *hurt*." I laughed to myself.

"Yes, and he cannot walk and cannot speak much. Ee said to tell you, so I call you for eem. He ees now in American Hospital on Avenue Victor Hugo."

"Who are you, Mademoiselle?"

"I yam Monique, une amie de Monsieur Li. You will come to Paris, oui? He asks for you."

She hung up abruptly before I could ask her more. She sounded as though she were speaking from a script, one which did not include answering questions.

That dutiful thread in me instinctively came forth. This I had gotten from my mother, who would stop traffic in the middle of the road to save a terrified cat. Without hesitation I decided to head for Paris.

I had to lie to Mama. That was imperative. There was no way could I get away with telling her I had to be by the bedside of some strange young man whom she didn't know. And in Paris at that.

Twenty-four hours later, I was at the arrival hall of Charles de Gaulle Airport, the white Parisian sky greeting me with the glow of summer.

I checked into Hotel Astrid, a small hotel, with continental breakfast thrown in, located on a side street close to Avenue Victor Hugo.

Lying on the bed in the American Hospital, Li resembled a wounded soldier who had returned from battle. His head, his entire midriff, and one of his ankles were bandaged. Seeing me, he gave a look of surprise and joy. He struggled to move. With great effort, he forced himself to speak.

"Sophia, how sweet of you. You needn't have come, but I am glad to see you," he said in voice that came from a distressed larynx. I held his hand. He responded by gently gripping my hand. He smiled from the corner of his mouth and then coughed, prompting a nurse to come in.

"He is very weak," the nurse said to me in an aside. "It is good you came. This is the first I've seen him smile since the accident. He has been quite depressed. You're his girlfriend?" she said to me in English.

"No."

"A relative?"

"Just a friend."

"Your presence will lift his spirits."

I parked myself at the hospital, staying at Li's bedside until late at night. He was like a log, alternating between sleep and consciousness. When he awoke, he showed his appreciation with his eyes, some words, the clasp of his hand, and the occasional smile, which seemed to cause him pain. The doctor told me that Li had suffered a head concussion, broken ribs, and a fractured ankle.

One day, the nurse reported to me that Li had had a bout of panic because I was missing for two days. I hadn't been well. I realised how tiring it was sitting there doing nothing for hours. It taxed my mind and body more than any physical work I had ever done.

One morning, to my surprise, Li was propped up against the pillows with the bed raised. The bandages on his head and upper body had been removed, leaving a patch of plaster on his forehead and a wrap across his chest. He smiled broadly upon seeing me.

Soberly he said, "I may need an operation on this eye," pointing to the injured eye. "There is a risk of a detached retina. Also, I'll be on crutches for a while," he said, showing the cast on his lower leg.

"At least you're not crippled or paralysed. That's the most important thing. Were you driving like a lunatic, Li?"

"For the first time, I was driving sanely, but a crazy truck came out of nowhere and crashed into me head-on from the opposite side on the single-lane country road to Clermont-Ferrand.

"There's no such thing as a vehicle coming out of nowhere, Li. You looked for this accident. I've seen your driving. It scares me to death."

"Honestly, after your lecture, I took stock of my driving. That's the irony. The moment I behave – bang! Hey, I am really glad you came – really. The nurses said you had kept vigil for me. You're a true angel. You know, Sophia, I was thinking of you just before the crash. Maybe my mind was not on the road."

"Are you putting the blame on me for your accident?" I quipped with a smile.

"No, don't take it that way. It's just that I have not stopped thinking about you. I have never felt like this with anyone before, honestly. I have had lots of girlfriends. With you, it just happened from the first day we met. Like spontaneous combustion. I think I have fallen in love with you, Sophia." He touched my hand and held it in his.

His words came like a thunderbolt. I swallowed my saliva. Slowly I pulled my hand away. I don't know why I did that. Blood rushed to my face. I wanted to say something, but the words fell just short of my throat. I panicked – yes, panicked, feeling deeply disturbed. Never had a man said that to me before. I had never been close enough to one.

"Sophia, did I upset you? I … I am so sorry."

"No, Li, you didn't, surely not. It's just that it came to me as a bit of a shock and – and I am confused."

"Have you no feelings for me? Do you already have someone?"

"No, I have no one. You're the closest I've ever gotten to with a man in my life. It's my feelings I am confused about. Li, could we not talk about this now? Let's leave it that way. Let's see where it goes. Will you? Please?"

When I returned to my hotel room that night, I cried. Why? I couldn't get my mind to explain it. But one thing I was sure of: the blame fell entirely on me. When Li wanted me to know he had gotten into a serious accident, I should have known he was after my heart, but I failed to see it. Did I respond because secretly I was in love with him? The angel on my right shoulder whispered, "You're in love, Sophia. Admit it!" The angel on my left shoulder reprimanded me: "Don't you play with love, Sophia, unless you are sure." Love at first sight. I had always thought that it was just a cliché. Now it smacked me right in the face.

The next morning I decided to leave for home. I had spent the previous night preparing in my mind what to say to Li. The fragility of it bore heavily on me like I was walking on a bed of eggs. The last thing I wanted to do was to hurt him.

When I arrived at the hospital, I noticed from afar a heavy shadow that swathed his face, as though he were anticipating what was coming.

Bad news shouldn't come in trickles, I said to myself, so I decided to get straight to the point.

"Li, what you said to me yesterday didn't go into the wash. Last night, I searched my heart, pondered deeply, and asked myself if I have feelings for you. I wouldn't have come if I didn't. So, there you are. I am terribly fond of you. But love must eventually lead to marriage. I am old-fashioned, but not in the way you might think. Marriage to me is a jump across the canyon, an undertaking not to be engaged in with closed eyes and an impetuous heart. For the sake of both of us, don't you think we should give ourselves some time? After all, we've just met. Let this 'spontaneous combustion', as you put it, be not just a flash in the pan. Let time decide where our hearts will lead us. We need to know. I need to know."

I had come to nurse a wounded body and departed leaving a wounded heart.

*　　*　　*

My life was taking an unexpected turn. Strange feelings were besieging me like ghosts in the night. Deep inside me, a voice warned, "Be careful, Sophia. You are getting too deep into this manuscript. In doing so, you risk losing your mind."

I looked across my balcony and saw a couple strolling with their three children. It painted a picture of my future on the canvas of my mind, exuding a good feeling. Then, just as suddenly, something tugged me away from that picture, something inexplicable.

Li was relentless in his pursuit of that future. He had begun to write to me. Judging by the number of letters that I was receiving, he seemed to be doing nothing else but writing to me, giving an account of his daily life, acquainting me with everything he was doing from morning to night. At times he broke into silly sentimentality.

On the other end, my letters were prosaic. Compared to his they seemed out of place, like a woman in plain dress in the midst of a glamorous costume ball. Instead of moderating him, the dowdiness of my letters provoked him to redouble his efforts in wooing me. Perhaps he feared that I was slipping away.

In fact, I was not. Actually, the lack of emotive words in my letters was the result not of an absence of emotions but of the fear of expressing them.

Whenever I found a word that reflected love, something held me back from writing it to Li.

This tumultuous affair by mail was something I kept completely outside my mother's knowledge. The deeper I got with Li, the more reluctant I was to let her know. For her, a little knowledge would not suffice. Neither would she be content to be just a bystander. But it was not she who was holding me back from plunging head first with Li. It was something else. Or was it really? I had no answer.

I decided not to tell Mama, not until I had decided to marry Li. I'd play the card of fait accompli, putting her in a corner to make her agree. Brave thoughts they were indeed. Could I really do that? I doubted it myself. I loved her too much.

*　　*　　*

It had been almost half a year since the manuscript had come into my life. I had kept it lying on my work desk, unhindered and unhidden. Since my mother's arrival, I had placed it in a drawer, meaning to keep it safely away from her inquisitive eyes. This was meant to be an act of wisdom on my part, but unfortunately that wise act had not been accompanied with due care.

Unexpectedly, something dreadful happened.

The manuscript suddenly went missing, and so did the photographs. When I asked Mama if she had seen them, coldly she said that she had put them away.

"What do you mean, you have put them away, Mama? Do you know how valuable they are?" I was shivering with anger, thinking that my mother had really gone insane.

"Is that what you've been secretly doing?"

"Doing what?"

"This research you told me about."

"Yes! What's wrong with that?"

"If that's what you've been wasting your time on, at the expense of your career, I do not approve of it."

"If you do not approve of what I am doing, do you have to take my items away? What deranged logic is that? Explain to me, Mama!"

"I do not have to explain to you anything." The cold calmness with which she uttered those words frightened me.

"Oh yes, you do! Explain to me, Mama. I am not going to move from here until I get an answer, no matter how long it takes."

She was solid stiff like a stone, gazing towards the balcony. And I was like a fool lashing out at a statue. In no time I found myself waning. Finally, I broke into tears. I ran into my room and locked the door.

In the following days, Mother and I became strangers, eating separately and passing each other without a word being exchanged. When I sat at my desk, she was at the balcony; when I watched the TV, she rested in her room. I wondered how long this stand-off was going to last. Who would falter in this tedious game of immovable hearts? I was beginning to see myself losing, as I saw in her not a sign of weakening. Not knowing the missing manuscript's whereabouts was gnawing my insides as if someone close to me had been kidnapped. Mama wouldn't have hidden it in my apartment, knowing her. That would be too obvious.

Unable to make headway amid what seemed to be a solid mass of impenetrable rock, I decided to go away, and to find solace with someone who was dying to have me. With a polite note to my mother telling her I needed a break, mentioning only my destination, I left for Paris. I made no mention of Li.

My journey was filled with uneasy thoughts and trepidation. Leaving my mother behind in a state of unresolved anger, and running away to a man who was waiting with bated breath for me, was a feeling I endured more than I enjoyed. I pictured Mama in pain, as I was in pain. This was a crisis of wills. In the past, the patching up was quick in coming. But this was lingering rather too long.

Li came to fetch me at the airport. He was recovering very well. The crutch had been replaced by a more presentable walking stick. His hair had grown over the site of the injury, and he was regaining his former ebullient self.

Upon seeing him, my heart was filled with images of a beautiful house with children prancing beneath a sapphire sky. I quickly snapped out of it, reminding myself of the danger of impetuousness. My future shouldn't be built upon my present anguish with Mama.

Li's face lit up like the passing of an eclipse. We hugged, doing no more than that. My feelings had yet to find wings to fly.

I stayed at the Hotel de l'Abbaye. We dined at Les Deux Magots, strolled the streets of Montmartre, had my portrait made, lunched at a little unknown café, munched crêpes by the pavement, scoured the Louvre, sailed on the Seine, and allowed our moods to wander under the canopies of Buttes-Chaumont, where it had all begun.

It was a week of happiness, the likes of which I had never before experienced. Yet in the far horizon, the image of Mama seemed always to be there to remind me that I should tell her whom I wished to marry before marrying him. Somehow, that simple wish for my mother's blessing was holding me back like a covenant. It stopped me short from saying yes to Li.

I left Li with my heart split in two, one half in Paris and the other half at home. Paris was holding me back, and home was beckoning me to return.

*   *   *

Back home I was filled with conflict. It was me vs. Mama. In that air of floating anxiety, I decided to break the news to her.

I waited for evening, not morning or afternoon. Morning is not good for shocking news, as the mind and body are just about to grind into life. Afternoon is bad, as the mind is sleepy and the ambience too stark. When the sun comes down, the heart softens. The night offers copious shade wherein one may seek refuge. That's the poetic logic I had applied when choosing the time to speak to Mama. That much I had prepared for. The end, I hoped, would be as I wished for.

The week Mama and I had spent after my return had lowered the fence between us. It was now more crossable. We began to talk again.

I had planned the auspicious night to be as conducive as I could. I cooked her favourite dish – fish baked with aromatic spices and lemongrass, and wrapped in leaves. It was a recipe she herself had taught me. I saw it as an appropriate olive branch. "Lift not a finger, Mama, and see how good I am at this," I announced to her. When she smiled, I felt relieved.

I made a good job of it. She enjoyed the meal and complimented me, or maybe it was perhaps her offer to make amends. I met her headlong.

When coffee was served, I opened up.

"Mama, I have something important to tell you."

She raised her head and peered at me over the top of her reading glasses. "Yes?"

"I have met someone very nice. I am sure you will approve. He has asked me to marry him. He's Malaysian. Chinese, actually. Living in Paris."

"That's why you went to Paris?"

"Yes."

"Have you accepted his proposal?"

"I shall, after I get your blessing."

"I am glad for that. Without a mother's blessing, a marriage will fail. Is he a Muslim?"

I was caught there by surprise. I cannot recall ever asking Li about his faith, a thing that had never crossed my mind.

"If … if he isn't already, I shall surely ask him. I don't think he is the type to bother about this if he loves me – and he does."

"You mean you aren't sure?"

"Don't you worry, Mother. I am not going to change my faith to his, whatever that may be."

"Listen, Daughter, marrying a man not of the same faith is a recipe for disaster. Do not go into a union with your eyes closed, believing all differences will disappear with love. In reality, differences magnify themselves after marriage. The union of man and woman is difficult enough as it is. Do not add to it problems that will surface in the future. Iron out things like religion before you make your decision. You'll thank me later for this."

"I will, Mama."

"What's his background?"

"His father was a prominent businessman from Ipoh – a tin miner, actually."

"What was his name?"

"Tan Siew Lim. He died when Li was still a child."

"What did you say his name was?"

"Tan Siew Lim, also known as Miner Tan."

"No. The boy's name."

"Li."

"Li as in LI?"

"Yes."

She rose from her chair.

"What's the matter, Mama?" I exclaimed in surprise.

"What's his mother's name?"

"I think it is Lai Peng, but she was known as Pinky."

Mother turned completely white. Her body began to sway. Before I could grab hold of her, she toppled over face down and hit the floor with a thud. I moved straight for her in utter panic. Luckily the thick carpet had cushioned her fall. I turned her over on her back and placed a cushion beneath her head.

I noticed that her breathing was shallow. She was conscious, but the greyness of her skin frightened me. She seemed drained of blood. I had no knowledge of first aid, nor could I tell what exactly had happened. I called for the ambulance and at the same time contacted a doctor in a nearby clinic.

The doctor arrived before the ambulance.

"Your mother has suffered a heart attack. We must get her to the hospital quickly," the doctor said.

Mama was admitted to the intensive care unit of the General Hospital. Her condition was stable, the doctor said.

Seeing her lying helplessly with tubes sticking out of her body, her eyes closed, and her breathing assisted by a respirator, I was overwhelmed with guilt about being the cause of her collapse. But why had she collapsed? I was as anxious for her recovery as I was for an answer. Every now and then I whispered in her ear to ask for forgiveness. I packed a few things with me and stayed by her bedside day and night until I too began to look sick. The nurse advised me to go home and get a good night's sleep. She promised to call me the moment Mama recovered.

After thirty-six hours without proper sleep, I passed out on my own bed. A bit later, the prolonged ringing of the phone woke me. It was half past nine in the morning.

"Miss Sophia, your mother asked for you," the female voice said.

I jumped out of bed, showered, and headed for the hospital, my heart thumping my chest.

Mama was now breathing without the respirator, but the tubes were still attached to her. Her eyes opened once she sensed my presence. I kissed her while holding back my emotion, tears streaming down my face. She gave me a smile. Her first words to me were, "Forgive me, Daughter," spoken in a weak voice.

"Whatever for, Mama? I should be the one who ought to seek forgiveness," I replied in tears.

"I've done wrong to you."

Beads of tears trickled down her eyes.

"What are you saying, Mama?"

"You cannot marry Li. You can't! He's your brother – half-brother. He is Hamzah's son. You're Hamzah's daughter."

"What? Oh my God!" I was thrown into a chair, my mind reeling in confusion.

"Listen, Daughter, I've much to tell you, but I am afraid I may not have much time. The years of folly and deceit have gone on too long. It's time I put a stop to it – put things right again. I've caused so much damage to you, all because of an injured pride – mine – and my selfishness to seek revenge on your father. I've dreaded this moment, and finally it has come." She paused to gather her strength.

"Not now, Mama. You're too weak to talk. Don't you worry, Mama, I'll wait until you're well."

"No, this cannot wait. God may take me any time now and you'll be deprived of the truth. Please come close to me. One thing you must not ever doubt is that I love you. You're my life, my heart."

"I know that, Mama. You're the best mother God could ever give to a daughter."

"Listen, Daughter. Listen carefully. Your father loved you too. … He had combed the globe in search of you – and of me. You are the Indriani in the manuscript, and I am the Siti your father, Hamzah, married. I changed our names so he could not trace us, and then I migrated to Belgium."

369

Mama's confession struck deep into me. I became limp from shock. "Oh my God, Mama, I am Indriani? How could you, Mama? Is this true? What do I say to Li? I'll look like a fool. ... I don't know what to do." My head fell on her chest. I cried.

"I am so, so sorry, Daughter. What can I say? It's the curse making its final call. The fault is entirely mine, not yours. Tell Li the truth. ... Neither is it his fault. Tell me: you and Li, did you ever—?"

"Thank God, no. ... Nothing of the sort, Mama; rest assured of that," I replied, weeping profusely.

"Yes, thank God for that." Mama caressed my head with tenderness. "You are a good daughter. Don't cry. It's history now."

"Where's Father now, Mama?"

"Your father was very much an aggrieved man, a deeply maligned man. After he failed to find us, his health, like everything else around him, began to take a heavy toll on him. ... He finally succumbed to his fate and died a broken man."

"Where was he buried, Mama?"

"In Penang."

"Tell me, Mama, about the manuscript. All that had been written, is it true?"

"Yes, every word of it."

"Who was it dedicated to?"

"Me." Tears suddenly streamed down her face.

"Mama, if Li is my brother, why did he say to me his father was Tan Siew Lim?"

"I don't really know, but he is your father's son. Will you forgive me, Daughter?"

"I forgive you, Mama. I forgive you. You mustn't also suffer the pains that Father had. It's fate, Mama. We are all victims of this curse."

"Yes, yes. The longer I kept this charade going, the more painful it became, until I found myself unable to undo it. Then, when you came of age, a new anxiety – a fear – came to me. What if you and Li were to meet? That would be the ultimate act of malediction. I prayed it would not happen, and it did."

Suddenly Mama's breathing became shallow. Her eyes faded as her head flopped to one side. I yelled for a nurse. Two nurses rushed into the room and immediately put her back on the respirator. The doctor was summoned. I stood there praying for Mama not to die on me.

Epilogue

THE HOMECOMING, JOGJAKARTA

Epilogue

"Is this how it was in the good old days, Pak Ali?" I asked.

"Yes, quite close. You've done a marvellous job, Sophia. Don't you want to change your name back to Indriani?"

"No. I've lived as Sophia all my life."

Pak Ali was all spruced up in his Javanese upper and batik sarong, a kris slung at his back as if he were a Javanese courtier. His new teeth sparkled in the sun as he smiled. He stood proudly next to me, waiting for the guests to arrive.

I too was in a Javanese embroidered costume of indigo batik – a colour I had deliberately chosen to match the one worn by Tutik Indriani, my great-grandmother, in her life-size portrait. After all, we shared the same name. I'd worn my hair in a style similar to hers. I looked with vanity at her portrait. The resemblance struck my senses, as if I were looking into a mirror.

Pak Ali exclaimed, "My God, you *are* Ibu Tutik! That's the only painting done of her. Even then, it was kept secluded in her private chamber. No one had ever set eyes on it till now. She was about your age when it was commissioned by her husband. The resemblance to you is uncanny, as if it was you who had been painted. Don't you agree? Perhaps her spirit is in you." He smiled.

The ambrosial air of burning incense infused the present with the past. Decorative flames reddened the night sky as ghosts from the past danced to the mellifluent gamelan music.

375

My mind drifted.

The past was no longer a fiction, no longer a figment of the imagination, and no longer distant. It had become one with the present.

My thoughts wandered to the people who had died, the ones who were part of me but whom I never met. They had all passed away because of a dream that refused to die. I hope that dream would now find peace.

A red carpet ran from the Great Gate to the entrance of Mataram House. Chairs in theatre style sat under marquees. A rostrum awaited a speaker.

The air was regal.

Thespians, historians, academics, artists, dignitaries, and royals were all there to honour the occasion.

The master of ceremonies called the guests to be seated. The event was about to begin. I was called to take up the rostrum and address the audience.

"Distinguished guests. As chairperson of the Hamzah Foundation, it is my great pleasure to welcome you to the inauguration of the Tutik Memorial in memory of the woman who created Mataram House. Mataram House was built from a dream, a dream to recapture the glory of Java's past. It was a remarkable dream, remarkable in its tenacity to fulfil it, remarkable because the past evidently is never concrete. The greater part of the past is a nebulous fugue in the people's minds. Yet Tutik dared to dream. Empires were built upon dreams – the more fantastical the dreams, the greater the empire.

"Mataram House was not an empire, only a reflection of it. It matters not if the reflection is just a figment of the imagination.

"It is now restored to its former glory after years of slumber, and it will henceforth be called the Tutik Memorial to house all her collections, including all the artefacts reflecting Mataram history that have been collected or retrieved by the Hamzah Foundation.

"It would be remiss of me if I failed to express here the debt I owe to three persons for the success of this undertaking. First, to my beloved mother, Siti, who is over there smiling at me. It was her brainchild to restore Mataram House to its former glory in honour of my great-grandmother Ibu Tutik, and to create the Hamzah Foundation in memory of my beloved father, Hamzah. Second, to Pak Ali, the remarkable old man who, during the period of Mataram House's long slumber, has been its loyal guardian. Last but not least, to Li, my beloved brother, the architect of this magnificent restoration."

When the ceremony was over and all the guests had departed, Mataram House once again basked in the era of its creator, whose tomb lay quietly in its keep. The black cloud had forever vanished. Tomorrow would be a new beginning. I turned to Pak Ali.

"The curse ends here, doesn't it, Pak Ali?"

"Yes, it ends here."

Li looked at me. We smiled at each other. Then I asked him for the answer to the question that had bugged me. "Tell me, dear brother, why didn't you say when we first met that you we're Hamzah's son?"

"To protect him."

In the shadows, someone smiled.